Relative Sins

Also by Cynthia Victor

CONSEQUENCES

Relative

Sins

CYNTHIA

VICTOR

VIKING

VIKING
Published by the Penguin Group
Viking Penguin, a division of Penguin Books USA Inc.,
375 Hudson Street, New York, New York 10014, U.S.A.
Penguin Books Ltd, 27 Wrights Lane,
London W8 5TZ, England
Penguin Books Australia Ltd, Ringwood,
Victoria, Australia
Penguin Books Canada Ltd, 10 Alcorn Avenue, Suite 300,
Toronto, Ontario, Canada M4V 3B2
Penguin Books (N.Z.) Ltd, 182–190 Wairau Road,
Auckland 10, New Zealand

Penguin Books Ltd, Registered Offices:
Harmondsworth, Middlesex, England

First published in 1992 by Viking Penguin,
a division of Penguin Books USA Inc.

1 3 5 7 9 10 8 6 4 2

LIBRARY OF CONGRESS CATALOGING IN PUBLICATION DATA
Victor, Cynthia.
Relative sins/Cynthia Victor.
p. cm.
ISBN 0-670-83884-5
I. Title.
PS3572.I263R4 1992   813'.54—dc20   91-40039

Printed in the United States of America
Set in Cochin

DESIGNED BY JESSICA SHATAN

For Jean Katz and Harriet Astor,

with love and gratitude

A heartfelt thank you to the following people for their help and encouragement: Carole Baron, Richard Baron, Carolyn Clarke, Robin Desser, Susan Ginsburg, Donald B. Louria, Susan Meredith, John Major, Constantine Menges, Susan Moldow, Diana Revson, Jane Scovell, Ellen Seely, Jacquelyn Serwer, and David Snyder.

To Meg Ruley, Jane Berkey, Pamela Dorman, and Paris Wald, special thanks for their insight and wisdom.

Warmest appreciation to Lorraine Shanley, whose cleverness made all the difference.

And for his invaluable assistance, endless support, and generosity of spirit, loving thanks to Mark Steckel.

Relative
Sins

Prologue

1 9 6 7

Kailey Hawkes bit her lip
as she stared down at the motel registration pad.
Name and address. She couldn't seem to focus.
Think. *Think,* she told herself sharply.

The man behind the desk rustled some papers, indicating that her hesitation was keeping
him from more important matters. He eyed the
woman across from him. She seemed very young
to be traveling alone. "That'll be twenty-five dollars. Cash or credit card?"

Kailey looked up, startled. "Cash." She
picked up the pen. Linda Cashman, Cleveland,
Ohio. That sounded okay. She paid and hurried
back outside to the car where her infant daughter,
Bonnie, lay sleeping in the arms of the au pair.

It was a scorching day, the temperature well
into the nineties. Kailey cursed herself yet again
for not having had the Jaguar's air-conditioning

fixed. Four days of nonstop driving, and nothing but the heat of summer from the East Coast to the West.

Parking the car at the far end of the lot, Kailey took her sleeping seven-month-old from Nina and entered the hot, musty motel room. She placed Bonnie carefully in the center of the double bed, so she wouldn't roll off. Watching her daughter sleep so peacefully, Kailey was overwhelmed by love for the little girl, with her fine baby hair and peach-soft skin. Then came a stab of fear so painful Kailey had to shut her eyes for a moment.

I've got to stay calm, she thought. It will all be fine. No one knows where we are, no one can find us. As soon as we get settled someplace, we can call the police, and everything will be all right.

Kailey turned to see the Norwegian au pair setting down her suitcase. The girl immediately headed to the room's old air conditioner and turned it on. It screeched and sputtered feebly. Nina flopped down on a chair and pinned her long dark hair into a bun to keep the damp tendrils off her neck. Seeing how uncomfortable and tired Nina was, Kailey wondered how much longer they could continue. She desperately needed Nina's help, but knew she was asking too much from her.

Kailey had offered little explanation of why they had to drive right through to California, and was relieved that Nina asked so few questions. Seeing that Kailey was in a hurry, the au pair had even helped with the driving so they wouldn't lose any time. But at any moment, Kailey knew, Nina might get fed up and leave. When Nina finally asked Kailey to stop so they could have a shower and a rest, she felt she owed it to the girl to comply. Besides, now that they had driven all the way across the country, they ought to be safe.

I'll make it up to her, Kailey thought wearily. We're almost there. Right now, I have to concentrate on keeping myself together.

It wasn't that much farther to San Francisco, only a few more hours. Still, Kailey had to admit that she, too, was exhausted, in no condition to present herself to Michael Warner. Grimy, disheveled — at the moment, she looked nothing like the wealthy wife he'd met at that dinner party.

She wondered if Michael Warner would even remember her. Seated next to her, the import-export tycoon had seemed impressed to learn she spoke five languages. Little did he know that his harmless remark about constantly needing good people with language skills would result in having her show up on his doorstep less than a year later. Kailey didn't know what he imported or exported, or anything else about his business. It made no difference. She just needed a place to go where she could get a job and earn some money in a hurry. She had no family to turn to, and hadn't dared go to any of her friends — it would have made it too easy for her husband to find her. Michael Warner was her only prayer. She wished she weren't such a mess. It was important that she look her best when she went to talk to him. *Beg him* is more like it, she thought grimly. But all she had with her were the clothes on her back, so they would have to do.

Bonnie woke up, crying. Kailey quickly scooped the baby up and rocked her. Hearing her child cry always broke Kailey's heart.

"It's okay, darling, Mommy's here." Kailey held Bonnie upright in her arms, patting her back gently and pacing around the room. Usually the movement of being walked soothed the little girl. From her chair, Nina watched, expressionless. My precious sweetheart, Kailey told the baby silently, it's just you and me now. . . .

Bonnie cried more loudly, her tiny face growing bright red. She looks so unhappy, Kailey thought miserably. Just then, Bonnie spit up the milk she'd been fed only ten minutes before. It spread quickly, warm and wet, over the shoulder of Kailey's silk blouse. The action seemed to relieve whatever discomfort the baby was feeling. She stopped crying and was soon asleep again in Kailey's arms. Satisfied that Bonnie was all right, Kailey laid her back down on the bed. Poor little thing, she thought, gazing at the baby's tear-stained face, all that driving had to upset her stomach eventually. Finally, she forced herself to turn away, glancing down at her stained blouse.

"I guess I should get this cleaned off," she said to Nina in as cheerful a tone as she could manage. "First, let me jump into the shower for a minute and then you can wash and get some sleep. Why don't you get Bonnie's things out of the car?"

"Yes, Mrs. Hawkes, fine," Nina answered, barely a trace of an accent still remaining in her speech. In her two years in the States, Nina had taken great pains to remove any traces of the small town in Norway where she had been raised. Her carefully imitated American speech and dress came directly from listening to Elvis Presley and watching Sandra Dee.

When she arrived in America, Nina firmly believed this was going to be her land of opportunity, the way it had been for so many others. Her life back home had been okay, she supposed. Her family was neither rich nor poor. They lived a comfortable life, but it was far too boring for Nina. She believed she was meant for something better, something more exciting. And she was certain she was going to find it in America.

She wanted to become wealthy, so wealthy she could go wherever she wanted and spend the rest of her life just having a good time. But she was beginning to wonder when her big break would come. So far, she'd spent two years taking care of other people's children, and it was a thankless task. Sure, she'd taken a few things here and there from the homes of her employers, some silver, a few small pieces of jewelry, a little loose cash. It wasn't as if they would miss the items or the money — they had so much, they hardly knew what to do with it all. But it was certainly no way to get rich, she could see that. Still, it looked as if things might be about to change.

Nina picked up Bonnie and rocked her, smiling reassuringly at her employer as Kailey peeled off her clothes and headed into the bathroom. Listening to the shower running behind the bathroom door, Nina surveyed her surroundings. The rich Mrs. Hawkes could afford to stay in any hotel in America, yet she had chosen this dump in a desolate spot. Nina was now sure her guess had been right; Kailey Hawkes was running away from her husband. And she was so frightened of him that she had hurried off without even packing a suitcase, just grabbing the baby and hastily stuffing some of her things into a canvas bag she'd pulled from the closet. So frightened she had driven close to eighty miles an hour, not even stopping to eat anything until they had put nearly eight hours between themselves and New York. Nina had quickly realized that if she didn't offer to do some of the driving, Mrs. Hawkes would keep going until she fell asleep at the wheel and killed all three of them.

During those first couple of days in the car, Nina had been furious at the way her employer just expected her to come along on a minute's notice and travel three thousand miles, stopping only to grab a quick meal or buy food and supplies for the baby. It was outrageous. But she'd kept her feelings to herself. Something was odd about this whole situation, Nina could see that. Mrs. Hawkes had been so frantic and afraid. She hadn't even questioned why Nina happened to be in the process of packing her own suitcase when Kailey had come looking for her.

Of course, Nina thought, Mrs. Hawkes probably hadn't known that she had been fired by Mr. Hawkes only minutes before. It had been just her rotten luck that she happened to be passing in front of Cameron Hawkes when one of his gold cuff links fell out through a hole in her skirt pocket. It didn't take him long to figure out that she'd stolen the pair of them. He was such a hard guy, she was surprised he didn't call the police but only dismissed her with a few sharp words. Then Mrs. Hawkes had appeared at Nina's bedroom door and told her to get her things together as quickly as possible, they were going to stay with relatives for a few weeks. Nina didn't understand what it all meant, but she knew better than to question this stroke of good fortune.

Now, here they were, in the middle of nowhere, hot, tired, grimy, and—Nina was willing to bet—getting down to their last dollar. She'd heard about this kind of thing before. The wife runs away and winds up with no money, no husband, no job, just a screaming baby to feed. Mrs. Hawkes had obviously never taken care of herself a day in her life. She doesn't even know how lucky she is, Nina thought. She's barely older than I am and she's already got that rich husband. Well, Nina wasn't about to sit around and be the helpmate to this spoiled fool while she discovered she'd made a stupid mistake.

Yet the situation might not turn out badly after all, Nina had realized that morning as she sat, bored, gazing out the car window, watching the ribbons of miles passing. She was certain Mr. Hawkes didn't know anything about this so-called visit to relatives. Suddenly, it had come to her. He would want his baby daughter back. And he might be willing to pay the person responsible for her return.

She hadn't yet formulated a plan, but Nina knew that if she was going to take advantage of this opportunity, it would have to be before they reached their destination. At least Kailey had told her that much, that they were headed for San Francisco. Nina didn't know what was supposed to happen there, but she had a feeling it would be too late for her to do anything. With Kailey Hawkes in the shower, this was her chance, perhaps the only one she would have. Hurriedly, she took Kailey's wallet from the bag tossed carelessly on the bed. Just as she'd suspected — only fifty dollars left. Mr. Hawkes had probably already canceled the credit cards. She took out the money, lifted Bonnie from the bed, and, picking up her suitcase, turned to go.

The car keys were on the night table. Nina reached out, then paused as she saw what rested next to them. Mrs. Hawkes never removed the pendant she wore around her neck, but had taken off her watch and ring before getting into the shower. The ring was a magnificent emerald-cut diamond, set off by two baguettes, glittering in its platinum setting. Still holding Bonnie, Nina slipped it on her own ring finger. It was a bit loose.

There was no one outside, just the same fierce heat of the afternoon sun. Nina walked quickly to the Jaguar, and hastily strapped Bonnie into her infant seat on the passenger side. Then she slid behind the wheel. She had never driven such a fancy car until this trip, but after the past few days, she felt completely comfortable with it. As quietly as she could, she started the engine and pulled out of the parking lot. When the motel was out of sight, she put her foot down harder on the gas, and the gleaming red car shot forward. For a minute, Nina gave herself over to the thrill of driving the Jaguar, imagining that she was the owner of the beautiful machine. Such a thing might be possible now — if she were smart enough to pick the right amount of money when she spoke to Cameron Hawkes. Not too high, but not too low, either.

Nina's reverie evaporated as Bonnie woke up and began to cry again.

"You hush," Nina said sharply, keeping her eyes on the road. She needed to think. She certainly wasn't going to drive all the way back, and she didn't have the money to fly from California to New York. Let Cameron Hawkes take care of the arrangements, she decided. What she needed was a phone. She would also have to stop and get some things for Bonnie; there were only a few diapers left in the car and the baby was going to need milk and more food.

Nina passed a town. She didn't want to stop there; it was too close to the motel. Now the road was practically deserted, with few buildings and no people around. She saw a small church up ahead. Driving around to the back, she parked where the car would be out of sight from the road. Perhaps she could find a telephone inside.

Bonnie was still crying. Nina grabbed a bottle and took the baby inside. Normally, Bonnie cooed and gurgled all day, with barely a cry unless she was ill or hadn't been fed. She really was an easy child to care for. Nina sighed. She did *like* the baby, more than the other ones she'd been stuck with since she'd come to the US. But that was no reason to pass up what might be her one big chance. In fact, she was doing Bonnie a favor, sending her back to her rich father.

She pulled open one of the tall wooden doors and stepped into the cool darkness. The church was small and looked at least fifty years old, with a simple altar. Shafts of sunlight filtered through the stained-glass windows, crisscrossing the pews. The baby became quiet, as if she somehow knew not to make too much noise in this place. Nina went to the front pew and sat down, cooing softly to Bonnie to keep her still.

Strains of music were barely audible, and Nina could make out the sound of a country song. Off to one side was a half-open door, through which she saw a nun seated at a desk. The nun, with an open book before her, was peering out at Nina to see who had wandered into the church in the middle of this stifling Tuesday afternoon. Apparently satisfied, the nun smiled at Nina, then leaned over and adjusted the dial on a radio, turning off the music before going back to her reading. The church was silent.

For a moment, Nina was amused by the idea of a nun listening to cowboy songs. Then she reminded herself why she was here. Time was passing, and she had to move quickly. A young woman with a baby in a red Jaguar wasn't exactly hard to spot.

Nina's gaze wandered back to the nun. I bet there's a phone in that room, she thought. But it was hardly the kind of conversation she wanted to hold in front of another person. She thought for a few seconds more, then, still carrying Bonnie, walked to the doorway. The room appeared to be the church's office, with book-lined walls and an enormous wooden desk. Everything was old and broken down, Nina noted, except for the magnificent cross that hung on the wall behind the nun.

The older woman looked up at the girl, her expression neutral.

"Excuse me, Sister," Nina said haltingly.

"Yes, what is it?" the nun replied in a soft voice.

"Could you — would you — please do a favor for me. I'm so sorry to ask, but . . ." Nina trailed off and turned her face away, as if she were troubled. She bit the inside of her cheek as hard as she could, bringing tears of pain to her eyes.

"What is it, my dear?" the nun repeated patiently.

Her eyes glistening, Nina looked woefully at the older woman. "My husband . . . he — I'm so ashamed to say it. He's so big, and very strong . . . and now he's hit our little girl. I want to take her away, far away, where he can't hurt us anymore."

"What are you saying?" Alarmed, the nun stood up and came closer to Nina. "You've been hurt?"

Nina nodded silently. She was warming up now, and let a small sob escape. "If you could just watch my baby for a few minutes. I have to get some things together. Then I'll come for her and we can get away. I'll never forgive myself if I stay and let him hurt my little girl."

"Child, isn't there some other way to work this out with your husband?"

Nina widened her eyes as if terrified by the very idea.

"You don't know him, Sister. If he finds me now, he'll kill me. He's a monster. Don't make me go back to him. *Please help me.*" Nina's face crumpled.

"I really think you should consider some other way. . . ." The nun's reluctance was apparent.

Nina turned sad eyes on the woman. "You're the only one who can help me now."

Nina had no way of knowing it, but with those words, an image — unbidden, unwanted — appeared before Sister Marie Frances, the image she had been trying to shake for nearly twenty years. It was of Grace Dukes, one of the members of her church back in Maine. Grace had come to seek comfort and advice from Sister Marie one day, confiding that her husband often beat her. She had been deathly afraid, and wanted to find a way out of the small town where they lived to escape from him. But Sister Marie had convinced Grace that her marriage vows were sacred, that she had to make more of an effort to work things out and to trust in God. Two weeks later, Grace ended up in the hospital with three broken ribs, a fractured pelvic bone, and internal bleeding. The doctors told her she would never be able to have children.

Sister Marie had never forgiven herself for what happened to Grace Dukes. Although she never discussed it with anyone else, her views on marriage changed after that. She no longer believed that God meant for women to endure such brutality at the hands of their husbands. Right or wrong, she had stopped counseling troubled women to go home and pray for answers. Instead, she suggested they seek professional guidance along with the wisdom of God. She could never make up for what happened to Grace, but she could keep from being responsible for its happening again.

Still, it was another thing to become involved like this in helping a woman run away. That was probably going too far. Well, she decided, she was going to do it anyway.

"All right, don't worry." She put an arm around Nina's shoulders and they walked together toward the doors leading from the church. "Do what you have to do, and come right back. I'll be praying for you in the meantime."

The two women stepped outside into the sunlight, as Nina, sniffling, gave over the baby, who stared curiously at Sister Marie in her big black wimple.

"Thank you," Nina said, handing the bottle to the nun. "It will only be for a little while."

Sister Marie followed the young woman around to the back of the church and watched as she got into the bright red automobile. As the nun turned and went back inside, heading for her office, the baby in her arms smiled and reached out with tiny hands, trying to grasp the crucifix hanging from the long chain around her neck. The nun returned the smile happily. Sitting down again in her hard-backed chair behind the desk, she began to sing a lullaby, her voice ringing out clear and sweet through the darkened church.

Nina got back onto Route 1, heading south. Without Bonnie, she could get to the next town and take care of what she had to without being detected; she hoped it wouldn't be too far away. Feeling around on the seat beside her, she found the sunglasses she had left there earlier and put them on. California was the first place in which she felt really comfortable since coming to this country. The mountains and the sea — and everything so big, so open. *This* was America. If she'd only known, she would never have wasted her time in New York.

She would have liked to pull over and admire the view. It was beautiful, a twisting two-lane highway carved into the side of the Santa Lucia Mountains, the road seeming to jut out over the sparkling blue of the Pacific. She felt exhilarated. A bright blue sky above, not a cloud to be seen, and a fiery ball of a sun. With all the windows open, there was even a breeze, cooling her off as she drove. Hugging the edge of the winding road, she admired the magnificent view of rock and water.

Gradually, Nina became aware of a car behind her, a big, dark blue sedan. It had come into view about half a mile back, negotiating the highway's curves at a safe distance. But it seemed to be coming closer. Too close. There was no place to turn off or let it pass. Annoyed, she went faster, holding the steering wheel more tightly. Damn idiot Americans, she thought. But she was used to driving at high speeds; back in Europe, everyone drove fast. She could handle this.

Glancing quickly at her rearview mirror, she saw there were two men in the car. They were asking for trouble, driving like that. What was wrong with them? She tapped the brakes, hoping the sight of her red lights would get them to slow down. Perhaps they didn't realize what they were doing.

They came closer still. Nina began to honk furiously, trying to signal them to stay back. Forced to go even faster, she found herself veering slightly. She struggled to keep away from the road's outermost edge on the right side—there were no barricades to protect her. If only she could move into the other lane. But the road's sharp curves made it impossible to see if there was any oncoming traffic.

She began to sweat as she grew more afraid. The blue car increased its speed, pulling up right behind the Jaguar. Nina gasped. Were they trying to run her off the road? She was going as fast as she dared; she knew that one false step could take her out of control. Her knuckles were white as she clutched the wheel. Then she felt it, a sharp jolt as the sedan smacked into her.

"Guð hjelp meg!" she cried out. Along the edge of the road, she saw a spot where she might have pulled over to let the other car pass, but she was going too fast and couldn't take the chance of making it onto the small patch of dirt. Again she felt the blue car battering her. It was as if the other driver were toying with her, ramming hard into the rear fender. She was panting, being thrown forward and back with each hit, desperately trying to follow the treacherous road.

"STOP, STOP!" she yelled.

Suddenly, the sedan swerved to the left, and smashed into Nina's left rear fender just as she was bearing around a curve. She screamed, a long, piercing wail, as the Jaguar sailed off the edge of the highway.

The bright red car seemed to rest for a moment in midair, poised high above the sweeping vista of mountains and sea. Then it dove down gracefully, hitting the boulders below with a thunderous crash. Looking back as they drove on, the two men in the

sedan could see it roll over and over down the jagged rocks, loose
objects being hurled out through the open windows. Still som-
ersaulting toward the water, the car exploded into flames. It was
a moving fireball, black smoke rising in its wake, until it came to
rest just short of the water's edge.

The fire burned, long, thick fingers of flame crackling loudly
at first, then eventually lower, quieter, until they died down altogether. After that, there was only the blazing sun beating down,
and the occasional cawing of seagulls as they swooped and rose.

Kailey Hawkes was feeling guilty. She had meant to take only a
brief shower. But the cool water had been so wonderful, so re-
freshing after their grueling trip, she'd been unable to resist just
standing beneath it dreamily, letting the stream of water massage
her and wash away the horrors of these past few days — if only
for a few minutes.

Finally stepping out of the soothing water, she wrapped herself in the skimpy motel towel and emerged from the bathroom
to let Nina have her turn. She was alarmed to find the room
empty. Nina must have gone out for something to eat, Kailey
thought, and hadn't wanted to leave Bonnie unattended. Still, it
was unlike the girl to go off without saying anything.

Unsettled, Kailey sat down on the edge of the bed and began
to towel-dry her long brown hair. She could feel the accumulated
effect of so much driving setting in. Her eyelids were heavy. She
would sleep like a log tonight. Then, an odd thought occurred to
her. Nina had said that she hadn't brought any money with her.
How was she going to pay for whatever it was she was buying?
Kailey reached out to see if she had helped herself to any of the
dwindling cash in her wallet.

The wallet was completely empty.

Kailey's stomach lurched. Something was wrong. She looked
in the zippered side compartment, where she always kept a twenty-
dollar bill in case of emergencies. Good, at least that was still
there. Nina must have missed it.

Next to her purse, Kailey noticed her watch and moved to

put it on. Whatever was happening, she wanted to be dressed and ready to handle it. She would go to the front desk and ask the man there if Nina had left a message for her. Her hand on the watch, Kailey froze. Where was her diamond ring? And the car keys? She whirled around, her heart rising in her throat. Nina's suitcase was gone.

Kailey shut her eyes, a terror mounting in her that was almost more than she could bear. Nina had Bonnie. And Nina wasn't planning to come back.

"Oh, no, please no . . . ," she whispered.

Frantically, she tore off the towel and grabbed for her clothes. Stepping into her shoes, she yanked on her skirt and, still buttoning her blouse, raced across the parking lot, heading toward the front desk. Her fright increased as she saw that the car was gone. But as she approached the glass door entrance, she stopped. Asking if anyone had seen her missing baby and au pair would attract attention to her. She couldn't do that. Dear Lord, she thought, realization sinking in, I can't even call the police. They might contact Cameron. That was a risk Kailey couldn't take.

She ran back to her room, trying to stave off her growing hysteria. Maybe she had misunderstood somehow, it wasn't what she thought, and Nina was trying to call her. Kailey stepped inside the room. Silence.

She couldn't just sit there doing nothing. Finding a pad, she scribbled down the telephone number to the room and stuffed the piece of paper in her bag. Then she hastened out once more. It hadn't been that long. They couldn't have gone too far, could they? She would get to the town nearby and see what she could learn.

Kailey half-walked, half-ran along the side of the road, hoping a car would come by so she could hitch a ride. But she was alone, the sun beating down on her mercilessly. Rivulets of sweat ran between her breasts, and her blouse was soaked, stuck to her back, the milk Bonnie had spit up on it sending off a foul odor. Pebbles and dirt were getting trapped in her pumps, which were hardly suited for walking on these roads, but she didn't stop. It was another ten minutes before she saw a few shops ahead. She hurried into a small grocery store and asked for a telephone. Luckily, Nina had left the loose change that was lying in the bottom of her purse. She put a dime into the pay phone and dialed the motel room number. *Be there, be there,* she prayed silently. Six rings, seven rings. Nina hadn't returned.

Hanging up, Kailey rushed back out. Passing the gas station, she rounded a corner and saw the town's long main street spread before her. The street sloped down and then up again, following the natural basin shape of the ground on which it was built. From where she stood, Kailey could see all the way to its end. Pausing, she scanned the few parked cars along the blocks, anxiously looking for her Jaguar. There was no sign of it.

She walked along, peering in store windows. They could be right under my nose, somewhere in this town, she kept telling herself. But as she approached the end of the strip, her sense of dread returned, and her hands shook as panic started to claim her.

There was a diner across the street. Kailey dug around in her bag for another dime as she went inside. A radio was playing rock music at full volume. The skinny teenager who stood behind the counter was pouring the last remnants of ketchup from old bottles into newer ones. There were no other customers.

"Where can I make a call?" Kailey asked urgently.

He interrupted his activity just long enough to point toward the rear of the diner. Kailey made her way to the phone and dialed the motel room again. As the music blared, she could hear the ringing at the other end. Once. Twice. Three times.

We have a special news bulletin. The voice booming from the radio intruded on Kailey's thoughts. *Police report that a car has gone over the edge of Route 1 three miles south of Monarch Heights. It is not yet known how many people were in the red Jaguar.*

Kailey wasn't even conscious of the receiver slipping from her hand. Unseeing, she leaned against a wall, struggling to fight back the waves of nausea threatening to engulf her. It was her car they were talking about on the radio, she just knew it. Please, God, don't do this to me, she begged silently.

Another song had begun to play on the radio. Kailey saw the

boy behind the counter staring at her, obviously wondering what was wrong. She straightened up and tried to think clearly.

"I need a cab. Where can I get one around here?"

"Number's on the wall next to the phone, lady," he answered, his tone bored now that he saw she was all right.

Waiting in front of the diner, Kailey told herself over and over that all of this was a mistake. That somewhere along the line, she had simply gotten confused, misunderstood something Nina had told her. When the taxi pulled up, she instructed him to drive along Route 1 until she told him to stop. As they pulled onto the mountain road, she continued to reassure herself. This accident had nothing to do with her; she was being ridiculous.

It was easy to locate the site of the crash. Kailey saw the spinning red siren lights atop four police cars and an ambulance crowded onto the narrow strip. At least half a dozen policemen were standing at intervals along the road, warning cars of the blockage ahead and carefully directing them safely around it.

She had the cab driver pull onto an overlook, a small shoulder on the road about fifty feet from all the activity. Telling him to wait for her, she continued on foot, trying not to think about anything at all. She would know soon enough.

As she approached, Kailey told herself not to look, not to see what was out there over the side. She would ask someone what was going on, act as if she were a passing motorist. Just a few yards away now, two policemen were talking. One held a partially burnt piece of metal, which she could see was a license plate.

The part that had escaped the flames was yellow with dark trim. A New York plate. Her car had New York plates.

Taking a few steps closer, Kailey was able to make out three numbers, the only ones that were still legible: 793. The first three numbers of her car's license plate.

She whirled around to look over the side. All the way down by the water's edge was a huge, black carcass of metal. It was far away, but not so far that she couldn't sense how powerful the blaze must have been to transform an automobile into that charred skeleton. Nothing and no one could have survived a fire like that.

Kailey felt herself slipping to the ground. There was a tall cypress tree right near her and she clung to it, fighting to stay upright as her eyes roamed the rocks below. Scattered in a wide trail leading down to the shoreline were different objects, difficult to make out beneath the sun's glare. They must have been thrown clear of the car as it rolled downward. She shielded her eyes, trying to distinguish what they were.

A pair of sunglasses lay dashed on one of the rocks, its broken lenses reflecting the bright sunshine. There was the red canvas bag she had used to carry Bonnie's things. Some of its contents were flung nearby — a couple of diapers, a stuffed bear, and an array of baby clothes.

Just a little farther away, she saw it. Bonnie's pink-and-white blanket, the blanket her baby loved so much. She would hold on to it most of the day, and always slept with it clutched against her velvety-soft cheek.

"Nnnooooo . . . ," Kailey moaned, covering her face with her hands.

"Miss, are you all right? Where's your car?"

A policeman was approaching. He must have seen her standing there, watching. Kailey raised her head at the sound of his voice, but something else caught her eye. Several drivers had parked their cars so they could get out and stare at the wreckage. Another car had just joined them, a dark blue sedan. Kailey watched two men wearing sunglasses get out of it and peer over the side of the cliff. She saw them exchange a few words.

It wasn't possible. She squinted, ignoring the policeman who was asking her if she needed help. Then one of the men, the taller of the two, took off his sunglasses and rubbed his eyes. Kailey gasped in fear. It was John Trumbull. She was right, then. The other one was Zack Moore.

Both men worked for her husband.

Instinctively, Kailey took a step to the side so the policeman would shield her from their view.

"I'm fine, officer. I'll be going back to my car now." She summoned up what was left of her will to give him a small, reassuring smile.

He nodded, satisfied, and walked off. Kailey pressed up

against the cypress tree, praying the two men wouldn't notice her. As they got back into their car and drove in the opposite direction, she sank down to the ground.

Of course, Cameron had sent his people after her. She had assumed that by taking the back roads and getting so far away, somehow she would be safe. It had taken them a while, but they'd caught up with her; they'd probably been looking on all the routes heading out of New York. He had warned her. It was clear from his words that he would never let her go, never permit her to expose him. He hadn't even waited to see if she went through with it. He'd sent his goons after her. To kill her. To kill Bonnie.

But someone made a mistake. Nina was dead instead of her. And Bonnie. She was dead as well. That part they had gotten right.

Sobs of rage and grief welled up in Kailey. Only a vicious animal could kill his own child, his own baby.

"You bastard!" she screamed at the open sky, tears pouring down her face.

It was her own fault. She shouldn't have run off like that. She knew Cameron well enough, knew he wasn't someone to toy with. But, dear God, who would have believed — ?

She should have. Because Bonnie would be alive now. I killed her with my selfishness, my stupidity, Kailey thought, her body rocking back and forth as she wept. If I hadn't been so self-righteous, so certain it was my duty to turn him in, this wouldn't have happened . . . if only I'd realized what Nina was up to . . . if I hadn't turned my back on Bonnie for those few minutes, hadn't left her alone in the room with Nina . . . Her anguish was unbearable.

"It's all my fault," she whispered tearfully to no one.

Two other policemen walked by Kailey. One of them was holding a small object: ". . . diamond ring in the dirt," he was saying to his companion. "A big one, too. With that piece of the New York plate, we should have an ID in a few more minutes. Not that many red Jags on the roads. Some guy with his family was coming around the curve just as the car hit. A young brunette, he said. They could hear her screaming all the way down."

Kailey stood up. Of course. The police would think that she was the one killed in the car, along with Bonnie. No one knew anything about Nina's being with her. Even the motel manager hadn't seen Nina; she'd been outside in the car.

In a few more minutes, Kailey Hawkes would be officially dead.

Sister Marie Frances was pacing back and forth in her office, tenderly rocking the sleeping baby in her arms. Over three hours had passed since that pretty young girl had asked her to watch her infant for a few minutes. She'd given her the milk a while back. Surely the child should have been fed again by now.

The nun sat back down in her chair. The baby had been an absolute delight all afternoon, other than one patch of crying. But that had lasted only a few minutes. She was such a sweet thing, Sister Marie thought, gently stroking the infant's soft hair. But where on earth was the mother? Enough was enough. There were other things still to be done today.

Frustrated, the nun reached out and switched on her radio. She smiled as the country music came on. Funny how much she loved that music, considering she'd grown up on the coast of Maine, far from the land of rodeos and pickup trucks. When the news came on, she listened with only half an ear. Then, abruptly, she turned toward the radio's dial, as if by looking at the machine she could better understand what she was hearing: "... *with certainty so far is that a young woman was driving and apparently lost control of the red Jaguar three miles south of Monarch Heights. Police are still at the scene of the crash, but confirm there are no survivors. ..."*

Sister Marie sat, stunned. The baby's mother had driven off in that fancy red Jaguar. And Monarch Heights was right nearby.

It had to be.

A great, heavy sadness descended upon her. She looked down at the baby in her arms. Just like that, the child's mother was gone. In a split second the baby's life was forever changed. She would never know the love a mother could give. Sister Marie only hoped the baby's father had enough love in his heart to help his child live with the loss.

The baby's father. With a start, she suddenly remembered why she'd been watching the infant all afternoon. That young woman had been trying to run away from the father. She said he had beaten her, had even hit the little girl. He shouldn't be left alone with this child.

You have no right, she admonished herself silently. It's not your place to decide whether parents deserve their children. But even as she thought it, Grace Dukes's face flashed before her, her eyes purple and swollen from the beating she'd received at the hands of her husband.

No, she decided, standing up and walking out of the room toward the church's altar. God had placed this child in her hands for a reason. She wouldn't give her over to a brutal father. She wouldn't take the baby to the police, just so they could hunt far and wide until they found him. This little girl was entitled to a better life than one of violence and abuse.

She put the baby down on the front pew, then turned and knelt before the altar. There was an orphanage in Hampton about seventy miles away. She would leave the baby there. No one need ever know there was a father somewhere, not if he was the awful man that poor young girl had described.

It was the right decision. It was God's will.

Sister Marie crossed herself and began to pray.

Chapter 1

1 9 6 5

Kailey Davids stared at her reflection in the gilt-edged mirror. Her thick chestnut hair, parted on one side and held on the other by a tortoise shell barrette, fell in waves down to her shoulders. The deep blue of her dress plus a touch of mascara brightened her large green eyes, and a hint of blush accented her high cheekbones. That was it. More makeup would only attract attention, and that was the last thing she wanted.

How many people could I fool, she thought, if I just sat here like this. Anybody could walk through my room, admire my canopy bed, ask me questions about the quilts on the wall and how I liked high school and why I applied to Wellesley; if I never got up, if I never tried to walk over and shake their hands, all they'd see is a normal eighteen-year-old girl. They'd have no way of knowing about my leg.

Even as she sat perfectly still, her right leg throbbed, not painfully, just enough to keep Kailey aware of her shame. It became unbearable to keep catching sight of herself in the mirror, so she turned the cushioned boudoir chair to face the windows. Disgusted by her self-pity, she got up and walked over to the windows that faced onto Fifth Avenue. The sun was beginning its descent. Soon it would be time to leave for Radost, the club her parents owned on Fifty-third Street between Madison and Park. How exciting that used to be when she was a little girl. How aptly named it was, she'd always thought, Radost, the Russian word for joy, evoking romantic evenings in mysterious foreign places.

Her first memory of Radost was a Saturday morning when she was five years old, the day the club was to celebrate its seventh anniversary. No customers were there yet. Just she and her parents, who were quietly talking in their native Russian as they went about their work. Instead of the deep drumbeats and snazzy saxophones that dominated the evenings, from a small portable radio came the beautiful harmonies of Beethoven and Brahms. Sonia, her mother, was in slacks and a sweater, with no makeup and none of the animation that accompanied her nightly role as doyenne of New York's leading nightspot. That day she went through the same routine she performed every Saturday morning, surveying the room, taking stock of what was needed. A new tablecloth, twenty new glasses, two cases of vodka, whatever was in short supply for the upcoming week's business. She moved quietly, jotting down notes.

Daniel, Kailey's father, was never that quiet. Even as he looked over the receipts from the previous night, he hummed along with the radio. It was his love of classical music, he'd always claimed, that had gotten him through Auschwitz. In those years, he'd sung the music inside his head, analyzing for his secret pleasure the scales, the dissonance, the rhythms of his favorite composers. Now, with the help of WQXR, he sang out loud, making the Emperor Concerto more emphatic, Petrouchka even sweeter.

That morning was the first time Kailey remembered performing what was to become her Saturday morning ritual: setting the tables, careful with the many forks, the confusing array of spoons. Years afterward, she realized she had always done it wrong, that the tables must have been reset later. Yet her parents had nothing but praise for her. She was their only child, their baby, she could do no wrong.

If only I could go back to being five, Kailey thought, as she sat down in the rose-colored chintz window seat, the cozy nest in which she'd spent thousands of hours. She stared out toward Seventy-third Street, then across Central Park. In the last rays of the sun, she could almost see across to Ethical Culture, her old school. At least I had one good year there, Kailey thought bitterly, tucking her bad leg under the copious folds of her blue silk dress.

The night before her seventh birthday popped into her mind. How excited I was then, how certain that every day would be exciting, a new adventure. What a fool, she thought, remembering.

Kailey Davids was a happy six-year-old girl, "cooperative and smart," according to her first-grade report card. And she had not one but three best friends, Judy, Sissy, and Melinda. Her parents had planned a special birthday party for Kailey the Saturday night in early September just before school was due to start again. They would bring the four little girls to Radost, provide them with Shirley Temples and wicked desserts, even take them backstage to meet the popular singer who was the evening's entertainment.

Kailey thought about nothing else but her birthday for weeks. She was so proud of her parents, so eager to show Sonia and Daniel off to her friends in the glamorous surroundings of their nightclub. Her mother had gone through so much when she was younger. Now she chose nightly from an array of black cocktail dresses, always adorned with the simplest but most expensive jewelry — two opera-length strings of fine pearls, a bracelet made up of square diamonds, earrings with a diamond center surrounded by a crush of pearls. She no longer bore the emaciation of her war years, but retained the lanky frame on which clothing hung as if the couturier had had her body in mind at the moment of design. Sonia defined New York style in the mid-fifties. But she also defined kindness and decency. If other New York hostesses simply attended fund-raisers and contributed huge amounts to charities, she was the one who would show up in hospital rooms of employees or acquaintances, always bringing lavish gifts, often paying medical bills anonymously. Elderly Russians, musicians down on their luck, so many would be surprised when they discovered that their huge bills had been covered. They could only wonder if it had anything to do with the sophisticated, soft-spoken woman who had dropped off the latest novel or the pretty nightgown.

Daniel, too, had grown in those good years. The nightmares of the war were gone, and his effervescent personality had reemerged. His joy in his family and in the success of his club was infectious. Kailey knew how special he would make her birthday on Saturday night, not just for her but for all her friends. She could envision how, one by one, he would dance with them, making Judy giggle, shy Sissy speak up, and Melinda, occasionally a spoiled brat, as sweet as pie. Each one would feel like a princess. As Kailey herself did every day.

If she had one complaint it was that her parents worried about her too much. She was never left alone, and even a cough could bring forth worried looks from Sonia or Daniel. The slightest murmur of unhappiness would bring obvious distress to their faces. Sonia and Daniel protected her fiercely, more fiercely than most of her friends' parents seemed to protect them. And sometimes she wanted to explore on her own, maybe even to be just a little bit naughty. But she never gave in to those feelings. She loved Sonia and Daniel too much to hurt them.

Kailey heard almost nothing about the years before she was born. Neither of her parents ever mentioned them. There was no talk of the Holocaust, no tales of lives lost or dreams shattered. They were intent on shielding Kailey from anything unpleasant. No, Sonia and Daniel were going to provide everything a little girl could wish for and more. Kailey would go to the finest private schools, wear the prettiest little dresses, have her parents' full attention regardless of the demands of Radost.

Despite her parents' refusal to speak, Kailey found out about Auschwitz, and about her parents' sisters and brothers who used to be alive and weren't anymore. She even knew there'd been an Aunt Kailey, for whom she was named.

Kailey found out all this not from her parents, but from Mrs. Gold, the elderly widow from Odessa who came to take care of her every afternoon, who filled her with stories of brave days and tragic nights. Mrs. Gold herself had been taken from Sonia's neighborhood in Odessa to Bergen Belsen, had watched her husband die even before they reached the camp. She needed to talk, and Kailey was fascinated. And so she heard about gas chambers and refugee camps. She would listen to Mrs. Gold by the hour, but even at five she knew enough not to mention it to her parents.

She certainly learned enough to get scared at night. Would I be as brave as my mother and father? What would I do if Hitler came into my room now? she would think, petrified. Sometimes, lying in her bed, she felt so frightened she would almost yell out for her mother. But she never did, knowing Sonia would only be distressed if she heard what was on her mind.

The night before her seventh-birthday outing to Radost, it wasn't fear that made Kailey cry out, but pain. It had started with a stiff neck. In fact, Kailey had been feeling a little odd for a while, weak and tired, nothing like herself. She hadn't mentioned anything to her parents. Sonia and Daniel were always so concerned about her, she hated to make them worry. But late that Friday night, her neck felt much worse and the headache that had quietly pounded at her all day long suddenly erupted into full attack. Soon she was screaming in pain.

When Sonia came running into the room, she saw tears coursing down Kailey's face, her body shaking with fever-induced chills. A frantic Sonia immediately made two calls, the first to Dr. Bergman, the second to her husband, who made it from the nightclub to their apartment in under five minutes.

It was 1954, and Sonia and Daniel knew exactly what they were afraid of. This time the enemy was not human. While Kailey lay in bed fretting because her party had been spoiled, the Davids faced every parent's greatest nightmare: polio.

Kailey got over her disappointment about the missed birthday at the club, but she never got over the effects of the disease. When Judy and Sissy were finally allowed to visit, months after she had been taken ill, Kailey was still in bed. Melinda's mother wouldn't let her daughter even enter the Davids' house. Kailey found herself awkward in front of the girls. What could she talk about? No longer was she in school, sharing classes and secrets and crushes. She couldn't play kickball in Central Park, she couldn't try on nightgowns and pretend they were evening dresses, she couldn't sit on the floor to play jacks. Judy and Sissy tried to keep up a conversation, with no success. They had been terrified by the warnings of their own parents: "Don't go too close, don't touch her." Between their fright and the awkwardness, after that there were no more visits.

Kailey began to pass the time studying languages. She knew Russian, her parents' first language, plus a lot of Yiddish, which Sonia and Daniel and their Odessa friends fell into in emotional moments. Lying in bed during those long days, she picked up French from a Haitian nurse assigned to her care and a smattering of Portuguese from another. Kailey had time, too much time, and she filled it by reading the books her parents would buy for her, most in English but many in those other languages.

It was Benjamin Gottlieb, Sonia and Daniel's partner at the nightclub, the man who had survived Auschwitz with Daniel — a fact Kailey learned not from her father, but from Benjamin — who went to tiny used-book stores along Second Avenue where he found old Russian records. Scratchy and filled with static, the songs would accompany the memories from Ben's childhood, stories of his mother, his father, and Daniel, his best friend, playing ball with him in the street, misbehaving in *cheder*. He gave little Kailey hours and hours every week, reading to her, helping her become fluent in Russian, bearing gift after gift. She learned as much from Ben as she did from the tutor who came in every morning once she was well enough to study.

Until Kailey's survival was certain, her mother would never stay in the room to hear the Russian music or Ben's stories. It was too much to bear. Everything had been taken from her during the war, and now Kailey might be taken as well. Only when her daughter's recovery was assured could Sonia relax. But never did she speak out loud about her past. It's too sad, she would reply brusquely when Kailey would ask. We'll talk about it when you're older. To herself she would add, when I'm absolutely certain that you're all right, that the demons who failed to kill me haven't returned to claim you.

Her daily pep talks to Kailey were always on the subject of how exciting it would be when she returned to school. You'll go back, she'd say, and you and your friends will pick up right where you left off. By the time Kailey was allowed to go back to Ethical Culture, two years had passed. Judy had moved to Connecticut, but Kailey couldn't wait to see Sissy and Melinda. She worried about what to wear on her first day back, what she would talk about with Melinda and Sissy, whether they would have the same table in the lunchroom, still have crushes on the same boys.

On a Monday morning in September, soon after her ninth birthday, Kailey was taken to school by both her parents. She made them stay in the cab as she got out on the corner of Sixty-third Street and Central Park West; after all, she was a big girl now. She could make her own way. The clothing decision had been tough, but she decided on her new gray felt skirt with the poodle on the front.

The entrance to Ethical Culture was just a few feet away, with scores of children greeting each other after the long summer vacation. She saw Melinda almost immediately, with Sissy right behind her. Then they saw her and smiled in welcome.

Until she began to walk toward the steps. Since her illness they had never seen her out of bed, and Kailey's limp surprised them. Even worse was the moment she reached the bottom step. They stared at her as she extended her hand toward the railing, carefully holding on as she ascended one level at a time, slowly, so very slowly.

She could see the horror on their faces as they said hello awkwardly, their eyes furtively going toward her leg. Kailey knew just what they saw. She was a cripple, a misfit.

To complete her humiliation, Kailey found herself back in

the second grade. Thankfully, it wasn't for long. When the school administrators found out how much she had done during her time at home, they quickly moved her up to the fourth grade. But the damage was done. Judy might be in the suburbs, but Sissy and Melinda seemed just as far away. They were in different classes, sat in different parts of the lunchroom, shared their secrets with each other and the new friends they'd made over the past two years.

She was so happy when one of the boys in her class was especially nice to her during a geography lesson, pointing down to Antarctica when she mistakenly reached up to the Arctic Circle during a pop quiz. Looking for him after class to say thank you, she was mortified to see him limping along the hallway, obviously imitating her for the amusement of several of their classmates. After that, Kailey didn't trust herself to make any new friends.

Her mother hated to see Kailey alone every afternoon and all weekend long. She insisted that Kailey could conquer her self-consciousness. You were always popular, she would say to her, always at the center of things. Why, you're a beautiful girl. If your friends have changed, perhaps they're jealous.

No, Kailey would answer, certain her mother was merely humoring her. Who would be jealous of her?

But Sonia felt it was all within her daughter's control. That limp is barely noticeable, she insisted, and you can make it disappear completely. You will study dance every day with Madame Theresa, and I promise it will be gone. Kailey complied, but she knew the limp would remain no matter how many pliés she managed.

Meanwhile, Sonia and Daniel did their best to fill in where friends should have been. Her mother would pick her up from school every afternoon, and the two would stop for a chocolate milkshake on their way to Madame Theresa's. There, Sonia would encourage Kailey. By the time she was fifteen and a sophomore at Nightingale Bamford, her mother claimed the limp was a thing of the past. But Kailey knew better.

Daniel usually took Saturday and Sunday afternoons off to spend with Kailey. He planned trips all over New York. One day, they would walk up and down City Island in the Bronx. The next, they would explore every corner of Chinatown. The Brooklyn Museum, the Cloisters, Prospect Park, the carousel in Central Park, the row houses of Queens, small white-framed cottages on Staten Island, the grim buildings comprising Co-op City. Not an inch of New York went unexplored by Kailey and her father.

But Kailey still felt safest in her window seat, even all these years later. Her parents had done everything they could to make her feel normal. By now, she could almost predict word for word the ways Sonia and Daniel would try to reassure her. You look like a princess, they would say, making a fuss over her dress or her hair. At eighteen, Kailey had grown accustomed to her flaws. Her mother and father wouldn't even admit the flaws existed.

Despite her parents' encouragement, Kailey was still without friends. Tonight, with Radost hosting its greatest celebration, she would be on her own, no date, no girlfriend to accompany her. But, she reminded herself, at least this time she was going to be allowed to stay until the nightclub closed. Never before had Daniel and Sonia let her remain past eleven. Fears for her health had merged with their natural protectiveness to make them very strict about such things.

But tonight was special. Benjamin, Daniel's business partner and oldest friend, was leaving New York. After almost twenty-five years as a widower, at last he had met the right woman and fallen in love. Risa Cirillo, a vivacious dark-haired widow who was co-owner of an expensive boutique in Rome, had caught his eye at a party. An animated evening of conversation had led to just three weeks of whirlwind courtship. But Ben was unfazed by the suddenness of their attraction. After so many years alone, he knew exactly what he wanted.

Buy me out, let me begin a new life with Risa in Europe, he'd begged Sonia and Daniel. Tearfully, they'd agreed.

We'll give you the greatest send-off New York has ever seen, Daniel insisted. All our friends, all our favorite customers, with the finest Champagne, the richest caviar. And the club will be closed; no money will change hands. This will be our gift, Sonia's and mine, our way of wishing you happiness in your new life.

Preparations had been going on for a month, with flowers and decorations brought in and special entertainment planned for Benjamin's pleasure.

Kailey looked at the clock. Six forty-five. They would be leaving for the club soon. Sonia and Daniel had spent all afternoon at Radost making sure everything was set in motion. She'd heard her parents come home half an hour before, water running in her parents' tub, the quick reminders back and forth as Sonia and Daniel dressed, eager to return for a final check. Kailey knew her mother would come in to see her in only a few minutes. She drew herself up, leaving the window seat for a final turn at the mirror. As she picked up her brush, she heard her mother's soft knock.

"Come on in, Mom."

Sonia entered and smiled as she surveyed her daughter's appearance. "You look lovely."

"I'm ready." Kailey hurried to her closet, and pulled out both a black silk blazer and a coat. "Which one?" she asked, holding each of them up for her mother's perusal.

"It's a little chilly," Sonia replied. "Maybe the coat's a better idea."

Kailey started to pull the coat off the hanger, but her mother held up a hand to stop her.

"No need to rush. Your father's on the phone with Benjamin and it sounds as if they'll be a while." She sank down into the cushioned chair just across from her daughter's bed.

Kailey sat down on the bed itself. "You look tired, Mom. Really pretty, I mean, but kind of sad."

"It's going to be strange without Ben. He's been such a big part of our lives." Sonia leaned forward and reached her hand out to move an errant wave away from Kailey's face. "I feel as if I'm losing more than a friend."

"Perhaps it reminds you of the old days." Kailey knew her mother was unlikely to pursue the subject, but wished with all her heart she would.

"You're a smart girl, Kailey. I was just thinking of Ben as a boy in Odessa." Sonia lapsed into silence as her face softened with memories she obviously wasn't planning to share with her daughter.

But Kailey sensed an opportunity. Maybe, just maybe, she could finally get her to talk about her family, maybe even about the war. "Mom, how did you meet Ben? And Dad? How did you and Dad get together?"

"Oh, the stories are so old. You couldn't possibly care about those things." Sonia attempted to gentle her daughter out of her curiosity, away from the memories that had lain untouched for so long.

Kailey took a deep breath. "I'm eighteen years old, and I'm leaving for college in a few months. Uncle Benjamin is going away for good. Don't you think I'm old enough to hear the truth?"

Sonia was surprised to hear indignation in her daughter's voice. She'd never meant to insult Kailey or treat her like a baby. She and Daniel had decided it would be wrong to fill the child with so much heartache. But Kailey was completely healthy now, and almost an adult. She had a right to the past; after all, it was her family too. Sonia tried to figure out where to begin.

"Your father and Ben and I . . . it was the three of us, practically from the start."

Kailey leaned forward in fascination.

Sonia smiled at the girl's eagerness. Softly, she went on.

Daniel and Sonia held hands as they walked through the park. Neither of them heard the hostile whispers of the trio of teenage boys watching them pass. *Evrey*, Jews, they might have heard if they had been paying attention, but they were too engrossed in their own world. It never occurred to them to be fearful. Sonia's father was at the financial center of both the Jewish and Russian Orthodox communities in Odessa, with connections to the wealthiest citizens of each. So vast was his fortune, so deep his ties to both worlds, he felt he could ignore the early rumblings about what was happening to Jews in Nazi Germany when disturbing news from Europe first began filtering through the town.

Daniel's upbringing was more modest. His grandfather, his father, and all his brothers were tailors. They were not wealthy like Sonia's family, but they were well educated, voracious readers of politics and history. Less observant in religious matters, they were open to the stirrings of socialism so prevalent in the Odessa Jewish community. Daniel's father, Isaac Davidowich, was temperamentally unsuited to sitting still all day, stitching hems and cutting patterns. Outgoing and idealistic, Isaac craved activity, craved the presence of people around him, arguing, laughing, dancing. So at the age of twenty he established the Radost café, a noisy, small room that quickly became a mecca for the politically active young people of Odessa.

The pull of socialism was strong, and every night the talk would revolve around Trotsky and Lenin, riches and peace for everyone. Freedom and economic equality, that's what Isaac Davidowich wanted for his wife and their five children. He knew in order to find those things he'd have to emigrate to England or the United States. Many of the men went on ahead, but Isaac wouldn't leave without his family, and saving up enough money for passage for all of them took time.

The wedding of Sonia and Daniel would also have to wait. Inseparable since they had met when they were ten, at sixteen they decided to marry. But a public announcement was out of the question. Not until Sonia's older sisters were betrothed could the couple share their happiness. That was the custom, and if Daniel might have ignored it, Sonia, the youngest of three girls, would have died before she hurt her sisters' feelings. Besides, as she would whisper to Daniel in their secret place in the park, they were young, they could wait a couple of years. Their bodies ached for each other, but hidden embraces were all they allowed themselves.

Just a year later, Sonia was certain the waiting was soon to end. Within months her sisters would be spoken for. Her oldest sister, Kailey, had fallen in love with a young rabbi. And Esther, the middle daughter, had her eye on Saul, the boy in the next house who was just her age. As tiny children, Esther and Saul had played together; when older, they had ignored each other,

Saul claiming to despise the girl, as boys were apt to do. But this was changing, Sonia could see it. She knew his eyes followed Esther when she passed by. There would be a "Hello" and "What do you think of the day?" where before there had been only a disdainful silence.

At night, alone in her bed, Sonia would listen to her sisters giggling and fighting on the other side of the room, as she longed for Daniel and silently built their future in her mind. They would marry, have two boys and two girls, and never sleep apart again. No more nights without him. No more waiting. It was all going to work out according to God's plans.

But Hitler's plans were faster than God's. The Germans marched in and Sonia's father's wealthy Christian contacts seemed to evaporate. Some were too frightened to be of help; others had already been rounded up themselves.

For Isaac Davidowich, it was the end of his belief in the goodness of mankind. Trotskyites, Leninists, Orthodox, atheists, they were all Jews and the time for hope was over.

Nor was there time for Sonia and Daniel to marry before they were shipped off to Auschwitz. Then there were the years of living through the wholesale slaughter, first Daniel's brothers and sisters, then all four of their parents, finally Sonia's two sisters.

Kailey, the oldest sister, had become like a mother to Sonia. This is for you, *zeese schvester*, she would say as she shared her rations with her little sister, ill for the third time that winter with bronchitis. But it was Kailey herself who succumbed to pneumonia just two months before Auschwitz was liberated by American soldiers. When Sonia emerged from the camp in June of 1945, she made two vows. The first was to find Daniel, who had been moved to a different camp two years before. Was he even alive? She would find him if she had to travel from town to town for the next fifty years to do it. The second vow brought tears to her eyes every time she thought about it, even years after it had been fulfilled: when she and Daniel married, they would have a daughter named Kailey. A baby would be born who would honor her sister.

The vows were easier to achieve than she had dared hope.

Sonia and Daniel found each other in a refugee center on September 19, 1945. By September 22, they were married. Daniel's best man was Benjamin Gottlieb, the only other person they knew from Odessa to survive the years in Auschwitz. Benjamin's young wife had died early in the war, and they became a threesome, Sonia and Daniel and Ben. When they arrived in the United States in 1946, they arrived together. When the name Davidowich was altered by officials at Ellis Island to Davids, Daniel was just as glad. To start his new life he would have a new name.

Daniel decided to open a small club to provide a place where other Russian émigrés could congregate in New York City. It would be a place where his sleepless nights — filled with Nazi ghosts and longings for his parents, his brothers and sisters — could be filled with music and laughter. He founded it with Sonia and Benjamin, and he called it Radost, just as his father had called his own club.

The nightclub took off. In the early years the clientele was limited to other Russians, old friends from Odessa and other European survivors. But soon a younger crowd caught up with Radost. Rich young New Yorkers loved the fancy veal dishes and succulent borscht. Pouring vodka from the bottle placed on every table, they decided the European clientele was intriguing. They might not have understood the conversations in Russian and French, but they appreciated how much fun it all was. The music was extraordinary, the food and drink were copious and delicious, and soon the club was always crowded. First, it was actors and actresses, eager for a slightly avant-garde experience, a place that was new and hot. But as the club caught on, as customers started to book tables days, even weeks, in advance, politicians and wealthy New Yorkers followed. Soon the club expanded, taking over the brownstone next door to create an enormous space, with tiers of tables going up the sides and a huge dance floor that always seemed full.

In the midst of Radost's success, the real miracle took place. A baby arrived, the girl Sonia had hungered for. Radost was indisputably New York's most popular nightspot, and Sonia and Daniel had the beautiful baby daughter of their dreams.

"The day we learned you had polio was the day I stopped believing in God." Sonia's voice was practically a whisper. She was remembering the two years Kailey spent in bed, the constant fears for her daughter's life. Then came the agony of watching Kailey's emotional pain long after the physical damage was repaired. Seeing her daughter still in that emotional pain today caused Sonia great sadness. This was Kailey, her flesh, her beloved.

"The success, the money — I could do without them in a minute, Kailey. You're the only thing that really matters."

Radost was lit up like a birthday cake when Kailey and her parents arrived. The large room was usually smoky and dark, conducive to slow dancing and hidden caresses. But for Benjamin's party the tiers of tables were brightened by huge lamps, catching the gleaming white of the tablecloths, the sparkle of the crystal.

"It looks gorgeous, Daddy," Kailey exclaimed, walking slowly around the bar. Platters piled high with pound after pound of the pinkest smoked salmon and deep bowls of black and red caviar dominated a big round table that had been set up in place of five or six small ones.

"Your mother and I didn't want people confined to their tables tonight. There are too many old friends coming, people who haven't seen each other in years. We figured everyone would want to mingle before dinner is served. Then we'll sit down for speeches and toasts." Daniel was beaming. He loved entertaining large groups of people, especially his friends.

"Tonight there are no customers. Just those we love."

Kailey sighed. "But tomorrow, there'll be no Benjamin."

"There will always be Benjamin, darling. He'll simply be in Rome. A telephone call away."

Kailey smiled at her father. She knew him so well. Now he was caught up in the excitement of the celebration. Later on, when everyone was gone and they were back in their apartment, it would be Daniel whose eyes would fill with tears at the thought of his partner leaving, Daniel who would probably contrive a trip to Rome within the next couple of months.

But this isn't the place to be sad, she realized, as Ben entered with Risa Cirillo. Kailey had met his fiancée only once before. As heartbroken as she was to see Benjamin leave, she couldn't help but notice how he and Risa looked at each other, how they seemed connected even when they weren't right next to each other. Not that they spent much time apart. Kailey's parents had been slightly horrified at first observing the way Ben and Risa touched each other all the time. But Sonia and Daniel had grown used to it, and now it made them smile in appreciation. If Ben was leaving, at least he was going off in loving hands.

Kailey knew she'd never find anyone to love her that way. No man in his right mind would fall in love with a girl like her.

Hugging her unhappiness like a cloak, Kailey made her way to a small table from which she could watch the hordes of people beginning to arrive. The band had swung into action, and people were dancing with gusto. It all seemed wondrous to Kailey, the music, the heady perfumes and stylish clothes. This was a special night, and people had dressed for it. The president of the City Council sported a red plaid bow tie, contrasting whimsically with his tuxedo. Surrounding him were two reporters from *The New York Times* and one from CBS sniffing around for early rumors of the bond issue that was coming up later that week. Nearby she spotted a well-known sculptor in animated conversation with the managing director of Lincoln Center.

The younger women all seemed to be wearing skinny black dresses. Kailey recognized several of them from magazine covers and movies. She watched the dance floor in fascination as a woman whose face she knew from a soap opera seemed to pour herself all over her date. She found it mesmerizing, the pretty blond woman with her tall, handsome escort. He's more beautiful than she is, Kailey thought, noting his deep tan and blazing blue eyes. She imagined how it would feel to dance with someone like that. To move gracefully and lazily around the room on a sea of sensuality.

Startled, she realized the man was watching her. He must

have known what was going on in my mind, she thought, frozen with embarrassment. She longed for the sanctuary of the women's lounge, but dared not move. The man was still looking at her, almost smiling at her. The last thing she wanted to do was limp off right under his gaze.

She saw him disengage his girlfriend's arms from around his neck and steer her toward the bar. But he didn't follow. Instead, he made his way right to Kailey, his eyes never leaving hers. When he reached the table, he smiled and put out his hand.

"You're the most beautiful woman in this room. Will you dance with me?"

Chapter 2

He'd been watching her all night. Earlier in the evening, while his date attempted to insinuate herself around his thigh, Cameron Hawkes was barely paying attention. He was hypnotized by the sight of Kailey Davids.

Probably just a teenager, he thought, enjoying the play of the club's spotlights on her poreless skin, the gold highlights in her chestnut hair. Daniel Davids' little darling. Gets everything she wants all the time and always has. Cameron felt momentarily sympathetic toward the woman in his arms. At least Marissa Clay has worked for everything she has, he thought, considering the long hours she put into her rigorously maintained figure, her carefully made-up face, and the soap opera that had made her a household name. Then he laughed at himself for his moment of generosity, thinking how she was about to blow it all on her very costly heroin habit.

"What's the matter with Marissa?" her tight-assed producer, Hal Dwyer, had asked him as Dwyer and his wife stood with Cameron in Marissa's living room waiting for her to emerge earlier that night. "She's asleep half the time and wired the other half. If you're the one supplying her, you'd better cut it out." Dwyer had stood straight in front of Cameron, attempting to look him in the eye, which wasn't easy, given Cameron's eleven-inch edge in height.

The producer's inability to pull this off gracefully amused Cameron, a fact the other man obviously realized, as he added words meant to instill terror. "I swear to God, if she goes down, I'm going to make sure you go down with her."

Cameron felt not fear but outrage. The prissy son of a bitch, he thought, but he managed to answer in a cool executive tone. "I'm the founder of the Little Angel Baby Food Corporation," he answered. "The only drugs my company is thinking of going into are baby aspirins."

In fact, the truth was he *had* been Marissa's supplier. But that was more than two years ago. His drug-dealing days were almost over, not that it was any of Hal Dwyer's business.

He never should have let Marissa talk him into coming to Radost with her, Cameron thought. Not that he didn't like the place. It was a nightclub he frequented often. Every time he walked in he saw congressmen, corporate chairmen, Hollywood producers. Being around all the power in that room made him feel as if he owned New York. Back in Wyoming, where he came from, people were always making a big deal about the mountains, the blue sky. To him, that was nothing. This club, with its perfectly dressed women and wealthy men, the expensive Russian paintings on the walls, the white and gold rows of tables that looked like a wedding cake — this was Cameron's idea of beautiful.

He'd loved the notion of the private party, invitation-only to New York's leading citizens. It was too bad the invitation belonged to Hal Dwyer. And it was too bad the woman on his arm was

Marissa Clay. She was on her way down, no matter how pretty she was or how popular her junky soap opera. Cameron recognized the signs all too well. Marissa was exactly the kind of woman he was determined to get away from. He was going to be straight and respectable. And rich. Very rich. He was going to walk into places like Radost on his own invitation and be treated as if he belonged.

Cameron took his eyes off Kailey for a moment and considered her father. Daniel Davids. Now there was a guy who commanded respect. He was just what Cameron intended to become. Every time Cameron visited the club, he would reach the same conclusion: Davids had New York City in the palm of his hand. He never would have walked around midtown Manhattan for an hour, the way Cameron himself had done when he first came to New York, bypassing signs saying "Avenue of the Americas" as he searched for Sixth Avenue. Nor would he have thought Top of the Sixes would be just as impressive to a movie star as Lutèce, another early blunder. He shuddered to think of some of the mistakes he'd made when he arrived in the city from the West. But now he knew better.

Cameron Hawkes was determined to become a leading member of society, and what he wanted at his side was a woman who was a class act, a woman just like Kailey Davids. He was fascinated by her. He'd never seen her here before, but he realized early on that she was Davids' daughter. He'd overheard her father bragging about her. *A gorgeous little girl,* Daniel was saying to some guy as he pointed to Kailey. Not so little, Cameron had thought. All grown up.

Why wasn't she enjoying herself more? he wondered as his eyes returned to her, still alone at the back table. She was a beauty, and she didn't look as if she even knew it. She didn't look as if she knew anything. What a kick it would be to teach a girl like that.

Marissa pulled in closer, trying to regain his attention. Cameron had always attracted women. At six-foot-two, he exuded casual assurance, with a seemingly low-key style that had been so typical in Wyoming, so unusual in the East. He also had a kind of focus, a powerful combination of urgency and intimacy that made him irresistible. Whatever he was saying, it seemed the only subject worth talking about; when he directed his attention to someone, that person felt he was the only one in the room. Attentive, hungry, sexually charged, Cameron had already worked his magic on showgirls and movie stars on both coasts. His bronzed skin tonight reflected the two weeks he had just spent in Los Angeles charming the pants off Dorrie Gordon, Paramount's contender for star of the century. Cameron doubted she'd last the decade, given her penchant for sudden fits of depressed self-absorption, but Jesus, she was beautiful. And at least she knew how to act in public.

Marissa was becoming annoying. Other couples were beginning to notice her obvious efforts to melt her body into his. The last thing he wanted was to be part of a spectacle in the middle of the dance floor. She might be a star, but tonight she was no asset.

Purposefully, he managed to force a few more inches between them. He tried to be nice about it. Basically he'd felt sorry for her when she'd begged him to come. She knew she was near big trouble, and she'd wanted him to keep her straight. And he'd agreed. But it had been a mistake. She had always been weak, and it looked like tonight would be no exception. They'd slept together a few times in his early days in New York, back when he still supplied individual users. Now he had nothing to do with actual sales; his operation was much bigger than that. But just this once, just for this party, he'd decided to be seen with her again. Watching her in action, he realized no one could keep her straight. Marissa Clay was on her way out, and it wasn't his job to keep her company.

Suddenly he was overwhelmed by disgust for her. She was old news, dirty. Exactly what he had worked so hard to get away from. Losers, victims. People like Marissa made him look backward, to Wyoming, to his past. He thought of his waitress mother, with a cup of free coffee for all the truckers who passed by on the interstate; during the day, it was smiling and flirting, but almost every night, she'd pick up a few extra bucks taking the customers home. He thought about the countless times he'd had to endure the sounds of a drunken stranger, weaving through the house on the way to his mother's bedroom. He would bury his head under his pillow in a desperate effort not to hear anything more. In the morning, his eyes would bore a hole into his cornflakes as he pretended not to see the tens and twenties being pressed into his mother's hands.

By the time he was thirteen, Cameron was working his way out of Wyoming. He'd begun by selling drugs to friends, even to the drivers who stopped at his mother's diner. He soon earned his way out of Laramie, and continued to earn big in New York. It didn't take long before he found himself with more money than he could easily hide from the IRS. So he established the Little Angel Baby Food Company. It was a perfect cover, a perfect place to launder funds.

For three years, that's all it was. But recently the baby food business had become so profitable on its own, he realized it could be his sole source of earnings. All his life, he had ached for respectability. Now here it was, almost by accident. He took the company's success as a sign: it was time to stop dealing drugs. Neither Hal Dwyer nor anyone else was ever going to accuse him of that again. He was going to be cleaner than clean. And he had a plan up his sleeve to make sure he stayed richer than rich.

But rich wasn't everything. Even money couldn't buy what Daniel Davids had. Look at the people he'd gotten to show up tonight. Newsmen, government officials, business leaders, entertainers. The Davids were always at the center of the social scene, heading up charity balls, mentioned daily in the columns. This was the cream of New York society and Cameron wanted to be one of them.

He couldn't stop staring at the Davids' daughter. Understated, elegant, wealthy without being showy.

Cameron turned Marissa away toward the bar, instructing her to wait for him. He concentrated completely on Kailey Davids, knowing she was looking at him, holding her eyes as he made his way to her table.

"You're the most beautiful woman in this room. Will you dance with me?"

Cameron noticed how flustered she was, not quite agreeing, but unable to say no. Silently, he willed her to stand, then guided her to the dance floor. She felt wonderful in his arms. Clean and graceful and young. Cameron held her close, but not close enough to frighten her. He would have to take time with this girl. She deserved a lot of time, he thought, drinking in her freshness. He would take as much as she needed, and he would teach her everything she needed to know.

They didn't speak as they circled the floor, nor did they say a word as he led her back to her table. But as he helped her to her seat, he whispered words no one else was meant to hear.

"My name is Cameron Hawkes and in a few months you'll be Mrs. Hawkes."

He ignored the shock written on her face as he lightly brushed her cheek with his hand and turned back toward the bar.

Marissa was furious when he got back. Keeping her voice low, she insisted Cameron take her home. Not until they were in a cab flying down Park Avenue toward her apartment did she open her mouth.

"You think you're hot stuff, getting it on with that little kid," she screamed. "I know who you are. I know what you do."

I know who you are. I know what you do. The words enraged him, emboldened him. Covering Marissa's mouth with his hand, Cameron pushed her onto the floor of the cab. With his other hand, he loosened his belt and unzipped his fly. Marissa tried to pull herself up, struggling wildly as he positioned her mouth directly over his penis, which had been half swollen since his dance with Kailey Davids. He kept Marissa's face trapped in his hand, waiting to loosen his grasp until she heard what he had to say.

"Who I am is a man with a lot of white powder in my pocket. What I do is up to you. If you work very hard, you might be lucky enough to get some of it."

Not until Marissa had stopped fighting him did Cameron take his hand away from her face, guiding her lips roughly over his penis. "Make me happy, Marissa. Make me very happy."

Her soft mouth found his organ, first licking the tip, then taking as much of it into her as she could manage.

Cameron felt pleasure and disgust in equal measure. What a whore she was. He pumped himself hard against her lips, purposely banging the back of her head against the seat of the cab. Her words came back to him. *I know what you are. I know what you do.* Why were those words so infuriating? Suddenly he knew. In his mind he was nine years old. It was Christmas morning, and he'd gone out on the street to escape the fat, sweaty trucker whose loud grunts of pleasure he could hear clearly from his mother's bedroom. But the street was no escape. All the kids in the neighborhood were out, each one holding a shiny new toy, one of them astride a red bicycle, ribbons still tied to the handlebars.

No toys for Cameron, they'd said, their voices heavy with insinuation. Your mom probably couldn't take time out from her part-time job.

My mother is a waitress, he'd tried to explain. She works full time, every single day.

Your mother is a whore, they'd yelled, forming a circle around him. We know who she is. We know what she does. They shrieked the same words over and over, closing in together, keeping him in the middle of the circle until he started to cry.

Marissa's the whore, he thought, watching her bare knees scraping the floor of the cab as she sucked at him furiously. *I know what you are. I know what you do.* She would never say those words to him again. He moved his hands to her neck, pushing her head firmly against the rear of the driver's seat and ramming himself toward the back of her throat until she could barely breathe.

"Work for it," he whispered hoarsely as he came, still holding himself tight in her mouth, smiling as he heard the sounds of her choking.

Chapter 3

―――――

"It's Cameron Hawkes again," Sonia Davids' voice rang out from the telephone in the den to Kailey's bedroom.

Kailey stopped writing in mid-sentence. "I can't talk to him right now, Mom. Please tell him I'm busy or something, okay?"

The Wellesley course catalogue fell from her hands. Her class selections would have to wait until her hands stopped shaking. She could hardly believe the effect it had on her each time he called. In the weeks since the party at Radost, Cameron Hawkes had called every night. Usually the phone had been answered by Mrs. Alvarez, their housekeeper, occasionally by Sonia or Daniel. Just the night before, Kailey had actually answered herself, but had chosen to pretend she was a maid. *Miss Kailey is away on a trip. She's not expected back for a couple of months.*

Well, Kailey acknowledged, he obviously hadn't been fooled.

Sonia walked into her daughter's room, a questioning look on her face. "What's the matter, darling? Why won't you talk to this man?"

"I don't know . . . I mean . . . he just makes me nervous." Kailey was floundering for something to say to Sonia, but the real reason was clear enough. He was so incredibly attractive, he terrified her. *I've never had a date in my life, never even had friends. What would I say to him? How would I act? I'd embarrass myself within five minutes.* She knew exactly what her problem with Cameron Hawkes was, but she could never explain this to her mother.

"Honey, your father and I know Cameron slightly from the club, and actually he's much too old for you. Why don't you just say that to him and then he'll stop calling. Besides, you're leaving for Wellesley in the fall. Tell him that, too."

Maybe I don't want him to stop calling, Kailey thought to herself, but she didn't say that to her mother, who was on her way back to the den. Kailey began pacing around her room. This is crazy, she thought. My mother is absolutely right. I should just tell him to stop calling. But the thought of picking up the phone, of talking to him, petrified her.

Cameron had become obsessed with Kailey Davids. He would lie on his bed at night, imagining the feel of her skin, the knowing pleasure he could bring to her innocent eyes. He would imagine scenarios where he and Kailey were sitting in Daniel and Sonia's living room, surrounded by a select few of their famous and powerful friends.

So you're the brain behind Little Angel Baby Food, Daniel might say to him. Fine business you've started.

Carl Edwards, New York City's comptroller, was often seen with Daniel. Maybe he'd be invited. We need young men like you, Edwards might add.

Cameron knew his phone call had been answered by Kailey herself the night before. He could tell from her voice, her nervous stammer at hearing his name. Away for months! What kind of idiot did she think he was?

As annoyed as he felt, he had to admit it turned him on. He couldn't remember the last time any woman had said no to a date with him. And that soft voice of hers on the phone. It reminded him of how pretty she was, of that shy quality that set her apart from the actresses and models he usually dated. He'd actually enjoyed dancing with Kailey, and he could swear he'd gotten to her.

Cameron looked at his watch. It was six o'clock. He came to a decision. Kailey, sweetheart, you don't know it, but this is going to be your lucky night.

Kailey had finished writing a letter to Ben and Risa, and was reading a book when the doorbell rang at eight-thirty. Her parents had left for Radost at seven, and Mrs. Alvarez had gone a few minutes later. It must be one of the building staff, Kailey thought, since the cautious doormen always rang up when strangers arrived.

She'd showered earlier, and put on an old cotton flowered nightgown. Pulling on her flannel robe, she hurried to the front door and opened it a few inches, just enough so she could find out what was going on. Night visits from building staff were most unusual.

Cameron Hawkes placed his foot in the space she'd provided before she even realized who it was.

"Honey, I think it's time you talked to me," he said gently, pushing the door open the rest of the way and walking into the foyer.

Kailey was too stunned to speak. Finally she whispered, "How did you get in the building?"

Lightly running his finger down her cheek, Cameron chose not to answer her. He was amused as he took in her outfit, the old flannel robe, the baggy cotton nightgown, her hand still clutching the mystery she must have been reading. He removed the book, carefully folding over a corner of the page she'd been on, and placed it on a nearby table. Then he took her hand and led her slowly to the living room.

"What's the problem, honey? Why aren't you taking my calls?"

Again the endearment. Again the caring voice that registered within Kailey like an explosion of heat. She didn't know how to answer. His intensity frightened her, but it thrilled her too. She felt as if she were alone on the planet with this impossibly handsome man, and she had absolutely no idea what to say.

Cameron gave her no time to think. "Kailey—" his voice conveyed urgency—"you are going to your room to get dressed. Then we're leaving. Whenever you want to come home, you tell me, and I'll take you right back, I promise. But right now, it's time to go. So run along and get dressed. Nothing formal necessary." He laughed as he said this, indicating his own blue jeans and a yellow cotton shirt.

Kailey walked to her room as if she were in the middle of a dream. She pulled on a pair of black linen slacks and a white sweater, quickly swiped at her hair with a brush and applied a touch of lipstick. She barely even looked at herself in the mirror before returning to Cameron.

"Good, honey. You look like an angel."

Kailey blushed at the compliment, then reddened more deeply as he took her hand.

"Have you eaten dinner?" he asked. "I'm starved, myself." He was leading her out the door as he spoke.

"No, I haven't eaten," she said in a hoarse whisper.

"Let's just go to Phebe's," Cameron said casually as the elevator arrived.

Kailey had no idea what he was talking about, but was too scared to expose her ignorance. She nodded in agreement.

Cameron had left his MG right in front of the building, watched over by Martin, the evening doorman. Only later did Kailey realize how large a tip Cameron must have slipped to Martin for his unannounced entry upstairs and temporary parking service. At that moment, she was simply being taken by Cameron in whatever direction he chose to go.

Their destination turned out to be an informal café on Fourth Street and the Bowery. Kailey knew the Lower East Side from her days of traveling the city with her father, but she was completely unaware of its nightlife. In the evenings, it was the hub of Off-Off Broadway theaters, of hippies hanging out along the sidewalks passing joints of marijuana good-naturedly among crowds of people, of loud radios blaring the Beatles' "Rubber Soul" album from fire escapes above the street.

Phebe's was the unofficial center of the theater crowd. Cameron's entrance elicited hellos from different corners of the room, but he barely acknowledged the actors he knew. He kept his attention on Kailey, as she was all-too-uncomfortably aware, his eyes never leaving her face.

He waited to speak until the waitress had taken their order, but he continued to convey that sense of urgency which never seemed to leave him.

"Okay, Kailey. Time's up. Why have you been refusing to talk to me?"

Kailey felt caught in his gaze. She couldn't lie to him.

"You frighten me," she began.

His sweet, slightly amused expression urged her on, releasing her from her embarrassment. She even found herself smiling as she went on. Sitting there with him, her terror began to fade. "You scare the living daylights out of me, if you want to know the truth."

Cameron treated her words seriously, although a smile continued to play at the corners of his mouth. "Fair enough. Here's what we're going to do about that. I'm going to tell you all about myself. Then you're going to meet all my friends, and they're going to tell you about me. Then you're going to stop being scared." Abruptly, Cameron stopped smiling. "And then we're going to get married."

Kailey's fear returned full force, but Cameron went right on, as if they were a long-time couple sharing a much-repeated, re-

laxing evening. He had rehearsed this version of his childhood so
many times since he first met Kailey it practically felt like the
truth.

"I was born in Laramie, Wyoming, twenty-eight years ago.
My mom was a waitress and my dad died when I was too young
to remember him. I went to Cody Elementary School and Laramie
High School, and I played pretty good basketball and pretty lousy
football. I'm an excellent skier, an average mountain climber, and
I'm handy with a tent."

Kailey's head was spinning. Wyoming? Skiing? Mountain
climbing? This man was from a different world. What was he
doing with her?

"This is the scar I got opening a can of Spaghettios when I
was seven," he said, displaying a small, white mark on the inside
of his wrist. "And this is where I got four stitches." He pulled his
brown hair away from the side of his head just over his right ear.
"Billy Soderstrom's contribution to my career in Little League,"
he added by way of explanation.

The waitress returned to their table with cheeseburgers and
two bottles of Heineken. Cameron took a bite of his burger, then
continued his litany of self-description.

"The cheeseburger is my favorite food." He appeared to re-
consider. "No, maybe steak. No, definitely the cheeseburger. I
like the Yankees, the football Giants, certainly not the baseball
Giants, the Knicks, bicycling in Central Park, walking on the
promenade in Brooklyn Heights, pinball machines, the Who, the
Stones, and the Jefferson Airplane."

He looked at Kailey, waited to see if she would respond, then
went right on. "When I was five, I wanted to be a fighter pilot
or a forest ranger, but when I was ten I changed my mind. See,
I had this science teacher named Mr. Foster who did experiments
like making little bombs in class, so I decided to become a scientist
instead." Cameron was rolling now. Kailey clearly wasn't expected
to break into his monologue, which lasted a full fifteen minutes,
and seemed to cover every moment of his life.

He was being outrageous, and Kailey was loving it. She
stopped being frightened somewhere between Cameron's decision

to be a great writer upon reading Jack London in tenth grade and his trip to Mardi Gras freshman year at the University of Wyoming. By the time he got to the only part of his recitation that was even partly true, his starting up the Little Angel Baby Food Company, she was completely charmed.

Cameron asked nothing of her that first night. Not only didn't he expect her to talk, but he demanded nothing of her physically. He often touched her hand as he spoke, but his only affectionate act was a light kiss on the lips when he dropped her at the door of her apartment.

"I'll pick you up at seven tomorrow night," he said as if they'd already agreed on it. "Maybe I'll get tickets to *The Fantasticks*, okay?"

The next night they saw the musical in Greenwich Village, followed by dinner at O'Henry's. Two nights later, Cameron drove her to a huge Italian restaurant in City Island. Kailey had been there with her father, but never at night, never for a candlelight dinner accompanied by several glasses of wine.

Day after day, week after week, Cameron pursued her. Some afternoons they would walk around Central Park, just talking. Kailey had never known anyone who listened with such intensity. It was as if every word she said was crucial. Evenings, he introduced her to the New York she'd never experienced outside of her visits to Radost. They went to Lutèce or Le Cirque for dinner, then danced at the Copa or the Blue Angel. She saw practically every show on Broadway, plus the out-of-the-way downtown theaters she had never even heard of before. La Mama, the WPA, jazz at Birdland, drinks at Twenty-One, brunches at the Carlyle. Just as her father had introduced her to New York, borough by borough, step by step, now Cameron made her feel as if she owned the city.

Kailey could see that his extraordinary attention concerned her parents. As she was getting dressed to go to the Village Vanguard one night, her mother walked into her room and started to ask about Cameron. Yet, after the most general questions — Are you having a good time, dear? Is he an interesting person? — she seemed to think better of it. Over the first weeks of their dating,

Kailey overheard enough whispered exchanges between her mother and her father to know just what was really going on. Cameron Hawkes made them nervous. He was older, a stranger, and a Christian stranger, at that. Yet they were so excited to see Kailey happy, to see her having fun for the first time in years, they didn't dare voice their reservations.

It was a full two weeks before Cameron did more than kiss Kailey good night. Even then, as their mouths explored more deeply and their hands began to learn each other's bodies, he never pressed her to yield more than she was willing. He had no intention of scaring her away with demands that were too strong.

By the time Kailey and Cameron had been seeing each other for a month, her desire had grown as strong as his. But still he wouldn't make love to her.

"Not yet, darling," he would murmur as they sat in his car in front of her building after an evening out. His hands would caress her breasts, roam under her skirt and between her thighs, excite her until she cried out for release. "I want you to be completely comfortable when we make love. I want the first time to be the most magnificent of your life."

In fact, Kailey was already more comfortable with Cameron than she'd ever been with anyone. Even her parents had never known the extent of her fears, the depths of her loneliness. The only thing she withheld from him was her terrible secret. She never told him she'd had polio, never mentioned the throbbing, the malformation that so mortified her. She always made it her business to wear skirts at mid-calf, saying that miniskirts just weren't to her taste. But the last week of August, she was no longer able to hide behind her wardrobe.

"We're going out to East Hampton tomorrow," Cameron cheerfully informed her as he dropped her off one Friday night. "A friend of mine is giving a dinner party, so we'll spend the day on the beach and change at his house."

Kailey was speechless. All Friday night, she tried to figure out how she could keep her leg hidden. Please make it rain, she prayed as she lay down trying to get to sleep. But the next morning dawned bright and warm. Cameron picked her up at ten, and by twelve-thirty they were at the beach. She had a long beach dress on over her bathing suit. Cameron immediately dove into the ocean, urging her to join him, but she demurred.

"I'm a lousy swimmer, especially in those big waves," she said, pretending to be fascinated by the *Life* magazine she'd brought with her.

When Cameron returned, wet and energized from the briskness of the water, Kailey feigned sleep on their oversized beach towel. Cameron dried himself off and lay on his back, taking in the sun. After a few minutes, he noticed the beads of sweat forming on her forehead. He sat up and looked at her closely. Shaking her lightly, he said, "Honey, you must be roasting. Why don't you take that thing off and at least step into the water? You don't have to break through the waves; just cool off a little."

Kailey was miserable. She knew she couldn't pretend to be asleep until sundown. It was time to face the music. God knows it had been wonderful while it lasted. She sat up and took a deep breath. "Listen, Cameron," she began, "there's something you better know about."

Slowly she rose up off the blanket and pulled her beach dress over the top of her head. She continued to stand there as she pointed to her left leg.

He whistled in appreciation. "Those legs deserve that buildup," he joked as he stood up and gave her a long kiss.

"You don't have to pretend." Kailey sat back down, dejected.

Suddenly Cameron realized something inexplicable was going on. "What's the matter? I'm not getting this."

"You don't have to be nice about it," she said quietly. "I had polio when I was a little girl, and this is what's left. That's why I look this way and that's the reason I limp."

Cameron was stunned. Her legs were fine. Perfect, in fact. "Kailey, I don't know what you're talking about. You don't limp and your legs are beautiful."

He knelt, raising her face in his right hand, forcing her to look straight into his eyes. "You walk like a ballet dancer." Then he lowered his hands to her leg. Inch by inch, he explored her thigh, her knee, her leg, her foot. "There's nothing wrong with your leg. Nothing. Nowhere. Now tell me about the polio. How old were you? Wasn't it too late to get polio? Were you in the hospital for a long time?"

Cameron threw question after question at her, forcing her to tell him everything about those two years. Finally, Kailey acknowledged how awful it had been. Her parents' pain had been so deep, she'd never felt free to complain about her own anguish, about how bitter she was when the Salk vaccine was tested successfully so soon after she came down with the disease.

"I never quite understood why you seemed so solitary," he exclaimed after she was finished. "Now I do."

He lay back on the towel and took her into his arms, holding her hard. There was such a scared little girl in there behind the overpriced perfection. Cameron was surprised at how protective he felt. So he hadn't been the only one hiding behind secrets. Somehow this made her seem even more desirable, more real.

For once, his words were heartfelt. "You are the loveliest, the prettiest, the most perfect woman I've ever met."

Kailey lay in his arms. In her mind, she could hear her parents telling her the limp was gone. They'd been saying it for years, but she never believed them. Now she had laid bare her greatest fears, and they had vanished. She was overcome with relief.

Cameron had met Kailey's parents at Radost a few times before he started dating Kailey. Since becoming involved with their daughter, he'd actually seen very little of Sonia and Daniel. When he went to pick Kailey up, it would usually be after her parents had already left for the club. A couple of times he'd said a brief hello, but never much more than that. Two days after the trip to East Hampton, Kailey asked if he would come to their home for dinner.

"My parents want to get to know you," she explained almost shyly. The notion of sitting between her parents and Cameron was pretty strange to her. "You're such a cowboy, and they're so, well, so *Russian.*"

Cameron laughed at her nervousness. "What are they going

to do, dance the kazatzke all over the living room and then enlist me in the Communist Party?"

Kailey laughed, but she wasn't entirely sure it would be a happy occasion.

"Don't worry, honey," Cameron reassured her. "They love you and I love you. We'll all do fine, I promise."

Actually, Cameron wasn't so sure himself. He knew the Davids weren't likely to be thrilled about their relationship. He was fairly certain Daniel and Sonia would have heard nothing about his drug business. Little Angel was quite a successful company by now, and his reputation as a shrewd businessman should please them. But Kailey was their little princess, and he was ten years older than she was. And there was his religion. Nominally he was Protestant, not that he'd ever spent a minute in a church. That was one thing his mother had neglected that he'd never missed. He'd never even met a Jew until he got to New York, but from what he'd heard since then, they tended to be fussy about the people their daughters married. And marriage was just what he intended.

Kailey was the woman he needed: young, malleable, and attractive. She would look perfect beside him as he made his place in the world. And he had begun to enjoy her company, to look forward to seeing her, to making love to her.

He also wanted to have Daniel Davids as a father-in-law. Marrying Kailey was like being issued a permanent, indelible stamp of respectability, and getting a gorgeous, unexpectedly passionate young partner as a bonus. But Cameron wasn't certain of the Davids' approval. He knew he had to cement Kailey's commitment to him, just to make sure. As he thought about it, he figured out exactly how to do it. A single well-placed phone call was all it would take.

On the day of the Davids' dinner, Cameron picked up Kailey at three in the afternoon.

"We're doing something special today," he said, nuzzling her neck as he took his place behind the wheel of the MG.

She kissed him on the lips, asking what it was he had planned.

"Did I ever mention my friend Bernard Holder?"

Kailey was impressed. "Bernard Holder the designer?"

"The very one." Cameron knew she'd love it. Holder was one of the elite fashion designers of the day; his suede miniskirts, fringed vests, and multicolored silk caftans had changed the face of sixties fashion. Girls on college campuses all over the country were wearing inexpensive rip-offs of Holder's designs. The real thing cost thousands. The whole country drooled over them in four-page ads run every month in *Vogue* and *Mademoiselle*.

"If you want to pick up a little something, I'm sure Bernie will give you a great price. We go way back." In fact, they went way back to Holder's excessive affection for hashish, which he had almost, but not quite, conquered, no thanks to Cameron.

"His place is on the fourth floor," he informed Kailey, as they entered the lobby of 530 Seventh Avenue.

The moment they entered the showroom, Kailey caught her breath. Everywhere she looked, she saw beautiful things: rich, black suede maxi-skirts, flowing satin blouses in deep iridescent colors. Most of it was too stylized for Kailey to imagine wearing herself, but it was dazzling to look at.

Cameron announced himself to the receptionist, and they were ushered into Bernard Holder's office almost immediately. At first, Bernard directed his remarks to Cameron, but his eyes followed Kailey as she walked around the room, looking carefully at the numerous garments draped and hung casually all over the place, as Bernard had invited her to do. Cameron had asked him for a favor, but this would be no favor. Kailey Davids was a natural model. That body. That face. She must be about five-eight, he thought to himself. Probably a size seven. No, maybe a five. She'd be perfect.

After a few moments of conversation with Cameron, Bernard couldn't hold himself back. "Miss Davids, I have a proposition for you."

Kailey turned to him in polite attention.

"My leading model just informed me that she's pregnant. By next week, she's going to be unable to fit into my clothes, and I have a major show in Paris the second week of October. Would you consider it?"

Kailey was completely bewildered. "Would I consider what?"

"Modeling in my Paris show. We have another in New York one month after that; then in six weeks there's Houston."

Why, he's serious, Kailey thought, astounded. "Me? Model? I don't know what to say. I've never even considered such a thing." She thought about how much she wanted to reveal to Holder, but with Cameron's approving eyes on her, she forced herself to speak up. "Perhaps you should watch me walk for a while," she suggested in a small voice. "I was ill as a child and . . ."

Holder brushed away her doubts. "Don't be silly. I've been watching you walk for the last five minutes. You move beautifully. You must have studied dance as a child; it shows in your carriage."

What left Kailey breathless was the casual quality of his response. So Cameron hadn't been lying. All these years, her parents weren't just making her feel better. Bernard Holder hadn't thought about his remarks for even a second. Maybe she really was, well, pretty.

"You were right," Holder said, addressing himself to Cameron. "She's gorgeous, just right."

Kailey was stunned. Cameron had arranged this. He really thought she could model. He really believed she was beautiful.

"So, Kailey, how about it?"

Bernard was more insistent this time, but it was a little too fast for her. "May I think about it for a day or two? This is just so . . . I don't know . . . so out of the blue."

"Of course. Call me by Thursday."

Kailey couldn't contain herself. After the visit to Holder's showroom, she and Cameron drove back to the Davids' apartment, where Sonia and Daniel had a bottle of wine waiting.

"Mom, Dad, you won't believe what happened this afternoon." Kailey enthusiastically told them about Bernard Holder's astonishing job offer.

Daniel looked troubled. "But, darling. You're due to leave for Wellesley soon. You have four wonderful years ahead of you."

Sonia was not at all sure she wanted her daughter to give up an education to model clothing. But she was proud of Kailey's beauty, and now Kailey might finally be able to recognize that beauty herself. Sonia had watched her blossom in the past couple of months. Cameron Hawkes was not Sonia's idea of an appropriate boyfriend, nor modeling an appropriate career, but the joy on her daughter's face made her soften her response.

"Perhaps you could arrange to model for Mr. Holder over your summer vacation, dear. Maybe even at Christmas or spring break."

Daniel saw the glow in his daughter's eyes begin to fade. He hated to disappoint her. This conversation could wait. Maybe later he could even figure out some compromise. He turned to Cameron and changed the subject, asking him if he was enjoying the wine. Sonia followed his lead and suggested they sit down to dinner. For the rest of the meal, they made small talk with Cameron, every now and then throwing in a gentle question about where he was from or what he did for a living. Somewhat to Daniel's dismay, Cameron's answers were intelligent and funny. And his love for Kailey was obvious. Daniel had never seen his daughter as a woman, had never pictured her as half a couple. But to Cameron Hawkes, that was clearly what she was.

As dinner ended, Cameron asked Kailey to show him her room.

"Let's see if you're as sloppy as you claim," he said teasingly as they walked out of the dining room. He trailed slightly behind her in the long hallway, taking in every inch of the huge Fifth Avenue apartment, the deep-carpeted floors, the many pictures of Kailey as a baby lining the walls. To Cameron it was a short course in how to live like a wealthy Manhattan family. If he had his way, it was a lesson he would be able to put to use very soon. Cameron followed Kailey into the large bedroom. He was curious to see the place that had nearly been her prison for two years of her life; he had the feeling this was where she was most likely to agree to what he wanted.

He took her hand and sat her down on the canopied bed. "You know, honey, your parents have a point about Holder's offer. In fact, I have a much better idea. Close your eyes."

Sitting down next to her on the bed, he pulled a small velvet box out of his jacket pocket. Instead of opening it, he kept it in his palm, running it down her neck, her arms, her breasts. The softness of the velvet aroused Kailey as she tried to figure out what was happening. Finally he leaned over and kissed her, stroking the inside of her mouth with his tongue.

Kailey felt unbearably excited. Being here in her own room, sitting on her own bed, she felt terrible and wonderful all at the same time. Suddenly, good sense took hold and she pulled away.

"Cameron, we can't do this here." Her voice was breathless. His voice was a mere whisper. "We can if we're married."

Kailey was stunned as he took her hand and wrapped it around the velvet box, covering her hand with his as he opened it and took out a square-cut diamond ring.

"This way you can go to school at Barnard or NYU, or, if you want to model, you can do that instead." He spoke softly but urgently.

Kailey felt bewildered, as if she were trapped in a dream. She had no idea what to say. She didn't even believe it was really happening, that she hadn't made it all up. Yet there it was, the ring, gleaming, sparkling. And there was Cameron. The man she loved. No, she suddenly realized. The man she was going to marry.

Within minutes, they broke the news to Kailey's parents. Sonia was shocked, heartsick. Cameron Hawkes was too old for her daughter. Daniel's thoughts flew to the rumors about Cameron, some kind of shady activities, nothing specific, just a certain look on some people's faces when his name came up. He was polished, and he must be well off, seeing the places he'd taken Kailey in the past few months, but there was something not quite right about him. And both of them had always assumed Kailey would marry someone Jewish. They weren't especially religious people, but the war, the years in the camps had left them hungry for Jewish grandchildren, for a Jewish son-in-law.

Both of them tried explaining this as tactfully as they could. Although Cameron picked up their doubts about his activities, the intimations flew right over Kailey's head. Even the remarks about his age and his religion barely penetrated.

"I'd like both of you to tour the Little Angel offices," Cameron suggested to the Davids. "Please, the factory as well. You should know more about my business." He didn't address their unasked questions, the vague allusions to hazy rumors. He simply maintained a polite and respectful demeanor, the slightly fawning posture of a man who wanted to marry their precious daughter.

Kailey had been silent as Cameron and her parents spoke. She had no desire to go to Wellesley. In fact, she couldn't even imagine taking the job with Bernard Holder. Perhaps she would enroll at NYU to satisfy her parents, but none of that was real anymore. The only real thing in the room was Cameron, how much she loved him, how much she wanted to live with him, to sleep beside him, to make love in the sanctity of marriage. He was the one person in the world capable of making her happy, of enabling her to shed the years of agony and self-consciousness. He was her other half, her soul mate, the one person who listened and really heard. For the first time in her life, she felt whole.

Chapter 4

"I've been Mrs. Cameron Hawkes for exactly five hours, Kailey thought happily as she lay in her bubble bath amid the luxury of their suite at the Hotel Pierre. At eight that evening, Cameron had stepped on a glass, the final act in the traditional Jewish wedding service he had agreed to have. Kailey felt like the princess at the end of a fairy tale as she heard Cameron puttering around the suite's bedroom. Her thoughts floated through the images of the day, the beautiful white peau de soie dress she'd worn, the way Cameron had looked at her as her father escorted her down the aisle, the sight of Ben and Risa, who had surprised all of them and flown in from Rome.

What a shame Cameron's mother had fallen ill in Wyoming and been unable to make it, she thought, letting a little more hot water into the tub to bring the bubbles back to life. Cameron had given the Davids a small list of guests he wanted to include, employees at Little Angel and a number of business acquaintances. None of his friends from Wyoming were available to come such a long way. Too bad. I'd love to know what he was like when he was a baby or a little boy, she reflected. In her mind, she drew pictures of what he must have looked like at fifteen or sixteen, tall and gangly in a high-school letter jacket, shyly picking up a date for his prom. No, she thought, Cameron was probably never shy. I bet he was the heartthrob of every girl in Laramie. I guess I'll have to wait until I meet his mom to find out.

Kailey closed her eyes and again relived the moment she and Cameron had stood before the rabbi. Cameron had been bewildered at the array of traditions Jewish weddings called for, the *huppa* over their heads through the ceremony, held carefully by four family friends, the breaking of the glass, the Hebrew prayers. But he had been a good sport about all of it. In fact, he had mingled freely with a lot of her father's friends, apparently comfortable with the older businessmen and politicians he'd never met before, interested in everything they'd had to say.

Kailey carefully avoided thinking about the weeks she'd spent arguing with Sonia and Daniel before the wedding. Even as her father prepared to walk her down the aisle, she could see the doubt in his eyes.

"He's too old, too sophisticated for you, darling," had been Daniel's constant lament since they'd become engaged. "Why not wait, go to college, meet some other boys, boys your own age."

But she had refused outright, and as she heard Cameron knock on the door to the bathroom, she knew she'd done exactly right.

"Are you ever coming out, or are you planning to spend our marriage in the tub?" His voice turned more serious. "Are you scared, baby?"

Kailey didn't know how to answer him. They had never made love, not in all the time they'd been together. He'd insisted they wait until they were married. Yes, she supposed she was a little scared. But she was excited, too. She'd trusted him with everything she had. Even the throbbing in her leg had disappeared since they'd gotten engaged. Cameron's love had allowed her to see that it had actually been in her mind all along. He'd made everything all right. She felt certain he would make tonight all right too. In his arms she would be safe for whatever lay ahead.

The sound of the door opening filled her with anticipation. Cameron, only his tuxedo pants left on, came over to the side of the large bathtub, and seated himself on a wide cushioned stool. Beneath the elegant black trousers, his feet were bare. Her fears evaporated as she looked at him.

"You didn't answer me. Are you scared?" He picked up a washcloth from a small shelf over the tub, filled it with soapy water, and began running it from her toes up to her thighs.

Kailey sighed in contentment. "I'm too happy to be scared."

Cameron began to run the washcloth over her shoulders, then down her chest. He dipped the cloth back into the water, then eased it over each soapy breast, until her nipples were taut. Kailey found herself forced to lower her body in the tub and widen the space between her legs as Cameron's washcloth made its way over the tops of her thighs down inside to the place between them. Caressing, kneading, he rubbed the cloth over her mound, then more intensely over her pubic lips. Increasing the weight of his hand on the cloth, he didn't rush, but just continued to exert an even pressure, over and over, until Kailey thought she would explode.

After Cameron felt her tighten in climax, he stood up and lifted the large white towel next to him. Her body was still shuddering as he lifted her out of the tub and wrapped her in the towel, drenching his pants. He carried her toward the bedroom, drying her in his arms as he walked. Kailey felt like a baby, like a woman, like a seductress and a powerless child all at the same time as he placed her gently on the king-size bed. She watched him remove his pants, and she saw that he was already aroused as he lay down on top of her, kissing her neck, her lips, her breasts in his urgency.

She felt excited all over again, not at all fearful when she entreated him to come inside her. When he did, lifting himself up slightly as he guided his penis into her, she felt a moment of searing pain, quickly followed by a rising joy unlike any sensation she'd ever known. Cameron moved slowly, expertly leading her toward ecstasy with his long, slow thrusts. When she began to peak, he jammed himself up hard inside her, filling her body completely, making her cry out.

As Kailey let go, she felt every demon of her childhood go too. She finally believed herself to be the beautiful girl Cameron kept telling her she was, healthy, vibrant, and strong. And happy. So very happy.

Cameron had enjoyed every moment of his wedding. Striding to the left of the Pierre's main lobby, up the stairs to the large room where drinks and appetizers were being served before the ceremony, he felt like a conqueror. He strolled around the room easily, chatting with the deputy mayor, the president of Foxtell International, the treasurer of a large shipping concern. No longer was he daunted by moments of uncertainty. If he didn't already know what someone was talking about, he would learn it. His own accomplishments had to take him only part of the way; his status as Daniel and Sonia's son-in-law would do the rest.

He knew full well that his in-laws weren't thrilled by their daughter's new husband. Despite months of politeness, his eager interest in every word the Davids had to say, even his agreeing to the old-fashioned ceremony with its foreign, elaborate rituals, he knew he'd made little headway into their affection.

Well, screw their affection, he decided. He was their son-in-law, like it or not, and he intended to cash in on every minute of it.

He'd carefully sidestepped Sonia's request for his mother's address and phone number when he'd said she wasn't going to be able to come to the ceremony. The decision not to tell his mother about the wedding had been easy to make. One five-minute conversation between her and Kailey would falsify every claim he'd ever made, betray every memory he'd ever pretended to have. If Sonia and Daniel got even one look at his mother, they'd know exactly what kind of woman she was. They were sharp, the Davids, they'd never be fooled. Well, he'd make sure they'd never get that chance.

The wedding was more than he could have hoped for, with two huge rooms at the Pierre reserved for the celebration. Cameron had looked approvingly at the grand ballroom where the dinner reception was held, the tables set with ornate shining silver and beautiful white china plates, the huge floral arrangements perfectly centered.

The table area in the main ballroom was surrounded by an elevated, gold-draped mezzanine, making it seem as if the guests below were onstage. A fifteen-piece orchestra played all night. In the middle of a dance with his mother-in-law, Cameron caught sight of his reflection in one of the many mirrored panels along the walls. He saw himself under the hanging crystal chandelier, splendid in the new tuxedo that had set him back nearly five hundred dollars. On one side of him was the schools chancellor and on the other Mort Jacobs, the founder of Babes in Toyland, the country's most innovative children's gift distributor. He's somebody I definitely want to know better, he said to himself, guessing that somewhere down the road there could be big business for Little Angel with a smart guy like Jacobs.

Cameron was fascinated with the vision of himself in the mirror, sensing the admiration in the eyes of the men dancing alongside him. His place in New York City and Little Angel's place in the business firmament had been cemented that night. He was sure of it. All those years he longed for respect. Now he would never have to worry about it again.

The hours after the wedding was over were just as memorable. Kailey had proved quite exciting. Taking a girl her age, a virgin, and teaching her to make love was always electrifying. For him, despite his sexual experience, that remained the moment of purest pleasure.

And Kailey had proved to be passionate, more passionate than he would have guessed. She had been so timid when they'd met. All those years she'd wasted imagining she was crippled, all of that had erupted into extraordinary sensuality. Her body was lean and athletic from her years of ballet. He even found himself turned on by how thoroughly she adored him. In the past, it had been annoying when women liked him too well, stuck too close. It was different with Kailey. Every time she held on to his arm, he felt the pleasure of what she brought with her, her father's power, her family's firm place in the city. But it was more than that, he admitted to himself. During the months of courtship, he had actually begun to love her.

"Your wife's on line three, Mr. Hawkes." The secretary's voice was soft as she stood in the doorway. Cameron lifted his hand in a gesture Marianne knew meant "Tell them to call back in ten minutes." Whenever he was on the line with Mort Jacobs, he refused other calls, even Kailey's.

Marianne stood her ground. "Mrs. Hawkes said to tell you she's in a phone booth, and that it's urgent."

"Well, tell her to call me back from another booth in a few minutes. *This* is urgent." Cameron went back to his conversation with Mort Jacobs without another word.

In the months since the wedding, Cameron had taken advantage of all that the Davids' name could offer him. He'd had lunches, dinners, and drinks with an assortment of city and state officials, plus a host of business executives. Little Angel was about to become his only source of income, and Cameron was taking no risks with its ongoing success. He was out of the drug business almost completely, with all his cash channeled back through Little Angel. As Daniel's son-in-law, setting the groundwork for legitimate growth was proving very easy. Cameron had visions of Little Angel's expansion, of its becoming the industry leader in sales. He even kept track of the elegant little phrases Kailey brought home with her from her language classes at NYU. One day soon the company would go international and the more he knew, the better.

For the moment, Jensen, Incorporated, was the only company that might be competition for market share. But Cameron wasn't worried. And he didn't need any help dealing with Jensen, not even from Daniel. He knew exactly what he was going to do with his competition, had been planning it for a long time. Just the day before, he had finally managed to get hold of a list of all Jensen employees. He was certain his plan would work, but the choice of someone to help him implement it was crucial.

Agreeing to meet Mort Jacobs for drinks Thursday night, he hung up the phone and scanned the list of Jensen personnel yet again, then put it down. No, he thought. He had months to defeat Jensen, as long as he needed. Why not take someone he had reason to trust and place him within the Jensen production plant. That was a much better idea. Cameron started considering the people closest to him, trying to decide who would be best. His train of thought was interrupted by his secretary.

"It's your wife again. She's on line two."

"Put her through, Marianne." Cameron picked up the phone on his desk. "Yes, honey," he said almost brusquely, eager to get back to what he was doing. He forced himself to pay attention to Kailey. She rarely bothered him in the office. It must be something important.

"Cameron." Her voice was breathless, excited. "I've got some amazing news. Could you come home a little early tonight?"

He'd been counting on late hours that night to solidify his plans for Jensen, but he kept his voice as patient as he could. "Can you tell me what's going on right now? I'm in the middle of some important things today."

He could sense Kailey's indecision on the other end of the phone. Obviously whatever she wanted to tell him meant a lot to her, and she was generally careful not to interfere with his business. She had proved to be exactly as thoughtful as he had guessed she would be.

"Well, Cameron, okay. Here goes." Kailey waited a couple of seconds, then plunged on. "Which would you prefer, a boy or a girl?" She giggled with pleasure.

So Kailey was pregnant. Cameron's initial response was revulsion. He'd never liked children, never given them a thought.

But he took hold of his emotions quickly. It wouldn't do to sound negative right now. A real conversation would have to wait until he got home. His voice was neutral when he answered.

"I assume that means we're having a baby."

Kailey didn't attempt to suppress her elation. "It certainly does. In exactly six months."

Cameron was in no mood for banter. "We'll talk about it later. I've got to go now; I have people in my office waiting for me."

He heard the disappointment in her voice as she said good-bye and hung up, but he had no intention of making her feel better, not yet at least. His affection for Kailey had grown since their marriage. When he whispered "I love you" each night before they went to sleep, he found that he meant it. But a baby. The thought of his wife's beautiful body distended and bloated was disgusting. And a howling infant didn't sound much better.

Then he considered the situation more objectively. Daniel and Sonia were still not crazy about him. Not that he ever caught them deliberately trying to turn Kailey against him. But there were lingering doubts, he could tell. If he were the father of their grandchild, they would be connected by blood — and he knew how much that would mean to them.

Besides, he thought, this will be the perfect opportunity to move. From the time he first arrived in the city, he'd looked with longing at the blocks of apartments on Fifth Avenue in the Seventies and Eighties. He could well afford one, and he damned well wanted one. He'd mentioned it to Kailey before the wedding, but she'd been against it. Too grand for us, too big, she'd said. He could have pushed her into it, but now he was glad he'd waited. By the time he bought the co-op he wanted, she would think the idea had been hers all along, that they needed more space for the baby.

Fine, he decided. We'll move and I'll hire some girl to take care of the kid and keep it out of our way. The more he thought about it, the better it sounded.

When he got home that night, he brought with him three dozen roses. He could tell Kailey was relieved. He must have really thrown her off balance this afternoon, a fact that filled him with pleasure. That was exactly the way he wanted to keep her.

The following months were filled with activity. By the beginning of Kailey's third trimester, Cameron had found an au pair from Norway, an eighteen-year-old girl named Nina. She claimed to know a lot about babies, had references from her last job with a family in Westchester, and, best of all, she had no immediate plans for college or travel. It was important to Cameron that he find someone who'd stay longer than the one school year or so to which most European girls were willing to commit. He didn't want his home life interrupted any more than it had to be.

When it came to where they were going to live, Kailey suggested a house in Connecticut, pointing out how nice it would be for the baby to have a backyard and safe streets for a bicycle. Cameron was impatient with Kailey's fantasies. As far as he was concerned, she had watched too many corny movies when she was a kid. He had no intention of moving out of Manhattan. In fact, he knew precisely which Fifth Avenue building he wanted, a fifteen-story gray structure built in 1917, complete with flying buttresses and leaded glass windows. He could name ten different men who lived in that building, all of whose names he saw daily in *The New York Times.*

Cameron went around with real estate people for several weeks, but he decided early on that this was the only place for him. He made a generous offer on a nine-room apartment on the twelfth floor, with windows facing south and west, straight across Central Park. He was careful and thorough in the assets and liabilities statement he had to present to the co-op's board of directors, listing his earnings from Little Angel, plus a wealth of blue chip stocks, municipal bonds, and mutual funds. Between his laundered drug money and the legitimate income from Little Angel, Cameron had made himself an extremely wealthy man. But New York co-op boards were infamous for their whimsical decisions. In addition to the rigorous examination of his financial assets, he and Kailey would have to go through an interview with the building's board of directors. As self-confident as Cameron had become, he remained somewhat nervous about their acceptance into the building.

On a Tuesday evening, Cameron and Kailey arrived for their interview with the board. As he had instructed her in advance, Kailey remained quiet, while Cameron adroitly fielded question after question. Approval was never given at the interview, but Cameron knew that the decisive phone call would come from Herb Taylor, the real estate agent, by the next afternoon.

Cameron was in a meeting with his production executives when the call came. A nervous smile played on his face as he lifted the receiver.

"Hi, Herb. I hope you're calling with good news." His voice sounded confident and charming, but Cameron's face crumpled in disbelief as he listened to Herb's words. The executives who sat waiting to continue their meeting were shocked when he exploded at them a moment later.

"Get the hell out of here," he yelled, not even bothering to cover the phone as he vented his rage. "And close the goddamn door behind you."

Cameron couldn't believe what Herb Taylor was telling him. "What do you mean we were turned down!"

Taylor tried to placate Cameron. "You know how quixotic co-op boards can be. They never really tell you why they decide one way or another. Legally they don't have to. It could be anything from your investment choices to something as simple as not liking your face."

A sense of dread began to build in the pit of Cameron's stomach. What if the board members had somehow gotten wind of his drug business? How could he find out if that were true?

Herb Taylor had no idea of what was going through Cameron's mind. All he heard was silence, which finally impelled him to raise the subject he wished he could avoid. He knew exactly why the Hawkes had been turned down, and if he wanted to end up with a commission from Cameron, he had better let him in on certain things he didn't seem to know.

"Let me ask you something," Herb began gingerly. "Isn't your wife the daughter of Daniel Davids, the owner of Radost?"

"You know she is." Cameron's annoyance was plain. "What are you getting at?"

"Of course there's no way to prove this, but some of these buildings on Fifth Avenue, well, they're not exactly open to certain kinds of people. People like the Davids, for example."

"Taylor, what the hell are you talking about?" Cameron demanded impatiently.

"They're Jewish. Your wife is Jewish."

Cameron was shocked. Without another word he hung up the phone. So fancy buildings in New York don't sell to Jews. It had never occurred to him that Kailey's religion might prove a liability to him.

What a fool I was, he thought bitterly, to have counted on the Davids. They must have known how thoroughly screwed he'd be by marrying Kailey. She must have known as well. Pretending to be so high-class, so la-di-da. She'd held out the promise of respectability to him and then snatched it out of his hands. How could she have betrayed him like that? He might as well be back in Wyoming; as far as his position in New York went, Kailey and her parents had shipped him right back to square one.

Cameron spent the rest of the day in a rage. Bringing his production team into his office again, he cross-questioned them on everything from the unit cost of their three-ounce jars to their expectation of an extra day off over the Christmas weekend.

He didn't let them out of his office until almost seven that night, two hours after Kailey's phone call reminding him that they were due at her parents' house for a dinner party. Screw the Davids and screw their dinner party, Cameron thought, bringing his feet up and laying them across his desk. He imagined the scene at his in-laws' apartment, his wife looking like a whale with that huge pregnant belly, foreign accents all around the table. Until today, Cameron had been impressed by the wide array of people represented at Sonia's dinners. Now the thought disgusted him. Foreigners. Jews. Cameron couldn't believe he'd let this happen to him. All his life, everything he wanted had been denied him. I haven't learned anything, he thought, sickened by his own stupidity.

Abruptly, he brought his feet to the floor. I know exactly how to make myself feel better, he thought. He pictured his petite, red-headed secretary, with her firm behind and moist lips. He knew Marianne would still be working at her desk, as she was under strict instructions never to leave before he did. Deciding not to use the intercom, he walked to the door of his office instead. Opening it, he smiled at the girl.

"It's late," he said, grinning at her. "You must be starved. Why don't we run down to the Four Seasons and do something about that?"

Marianne looked at him in surprise. Cameron Hawkes had never been anything but businesslike in the year she'd worked for him. Every day she'd been there, she'd thought about how great-looking he was, building fantasies around his finally noticing her, paying her some real attention. And now it was actually happening.

It took her only a few seconds to take her handbag out of her bottom drawer and hurriedly pull some lipstick across her mouth. "I'm ready," she said eagerly, already out of her chair.

Kailey kept checking her watch every few minutes. She couldn't imagine what had happened to Cameron. Her parents' guests that night included some old Russian friends; their lawyer, Frederick Wolf, and his Spanish wife; and a man she'd never met before, an importer from San Francisco named Michael Warner. She was seated between Warner and the empty chair that waited for Cameron.

The conversations flowed in English, in Russian, in Spanish, with Kailey helping to keep the talk going smoothly. Michael Warner watched her closely.

"How many languages do you speak?" he asked admiringly over dessert.

Kailey waved away his intended compliment. "It's a hobby of mine," she said modestly.

"No, really, I want to know," Warner pressed her.

"Well, I've been taking French and Italian at NYU, and I can dredge up a little Portuguese if I have to," she finally answered. "So, with Russian, I guess that makes five."

Warner was impressed. "Boy, could I use someone like you in my business," he laughed. "If you ever move to California, give me a ring. We're always desperate for multilingual people. I'll make you rich, I swear."

Kailey laughed along with him, but inside she was frantic. What could have happened to Cameron? Her parents too were looking at the clock every few minutes. Finally, Sonia drew her aside.

"Where is Cameron? Did he mention anything about being so late?" Sonia's concerned tone gave no sign of how furious she was at her son-in-law. Taking in her daughter's distress, she knew instinctively it would do no good to indicate that to Kailey.

"Mom, I'm going home. I'm sure everything's fine. He probably just forgot. He must have had some important work to do and didn't want to be interrupted. In fact, he must be home right now, wondering where I am."

Kailey knew she wasn't making much sense, but she desperately needed to get out of her parents' apartment. It was too hard to keep up a smiling face, and her parents distrusted Cameron enough already. "Please make my apologies for me, okay?" She looked imploringly at Sonia.

"I don't like your leaving alone. Let me come with you. After all, if anything's wrong, you'll need me." The sight of her daughter's anxiety was unbearable to Sonia.

"No," Kailey insisted, going to the closet for her coat. "I'll call you if anything's the matter, I promise." Quickly, she ran to the front door and let herself out, leaving her mother no time to argue further.

Kailey felt frightened all the way home in the cab. Finding their apartment empty, her fear grew. By the time Cameron walked into the house at four in the morning, she had called the police and several hospitals, a fact that drove him into a paroxysm of fury when she told him.

"How dare you check up on me," he thundered in a voice Kailey had never heard.

"Sweetheart, I was just so worried," she tried to explain, but he walked away from her, slamming the door to the den behind him.

She felt absolutely powerless in the face of his anger. His disapproval was like a physical blow to her. Sobbing and shaking, she lay in their bed, wondering how to make things right once again. Cameron was her whole world. She felt the baby kicking inside her. Usually that filled her with delight. Tonight it reminded her of how ugly she had become. Since she had begun to show in her fourth month, her husband had barely touched her. I'm disgusting, she thought, the familiar feelings once again spreading through her. Suffused with self-hatred, she never even thought to ask Cameron where he'd been.

Chapter 5

Kailey stood in the door-
way of the kitchen watching Nina feed rice cereal
to the baby. When Cameron hired the au pair two
months before Bonnie had even been born, Kailey
thought he was being foolish. We can hire a nanny
for a couple of weeks and then I'll take over, she
had said at the time. In retrospect, she was glad
Nina was there. She wondered what she would
have done if she hadn't had help since Bonnie's
birth. With the terrible events of the past few
months, Kailey would have been lost without
Nina.

Kailey remained silent. If the baby knew she
were there, she would push the spoon out of Nina's
hand and scream for her mommy. Ordinarily,
Kailey loved feeding her daughter. But right now,
she needed time to get ready for her lunch date
with Frederick Wolf, her father's lawyer.

I wish I could stay here with her, she thought, watching Bonnie giggle with delight as Nina switched from the bowl of bland cereal to a jar of sweet strained applesauce. Four months old, Bonnie had turned into a baby, no longer a docile, sleepy infant. Now she laughed and smiled, was aware of every movement around her. With her dark brown hair and light blue eyes, she was unusually pretty. Kailey had thought so from the minute she was born, but as she led the baby on her daily walks in the park with complete strangers grinning at her and pointing her out to their friends, Kailey felt satisfied it was not just a mother's prejudiced eye.

She would have loved to put Bonnie in the stroller and walk her through the park right now. It was the middle of May, and the sunny sixty-five-degree temperature and blooming trees made Central Park especially inviting. Not today, Kailey thought. Nina would have to be the one to push the stroller around the boat pond or the zoo.

I wonder what's so urgent, Kailey mused, as she looked at the clock and hurried into the bedroom to change for her lunch date. Frederick had insisted on meeting her at the Cornell Club, where there would be "a quiet place to hash things out." What an odd phrase, Kailey had thought. What more was there to hash out? All the legal matters had been taken care of. The only thing left was the grief, but Frederick could be no help there.

Kailey felt tears forming in her eyes as she took her linen suit off its padded hanger and stepped into it, fumbling with the zipper on the skirt and buttoning the fitted jacket over her silk blouse. Will I be crying for the rest of my life, she wondered as she smoothed the skirt over her hips, a sob welling up. Although she was running late, she suddenly found herself crying so hard she had to sit down for a few minutes. She couldn't stop thinking about Sonia and Daniel. Why couldn't they be coming to have lunch today with Frederick, as they had done so many times over the years?

Finally, she made her way to the bathroom sink, wet a cloth with cool water and held it against her reddened eyes. From the kitchen, she heard Bonnie's squeals of pleasure. Perhaps Nina had finished feeding her and had handed her one of her favorite stuffed toys, or was dressing her to go out. Getting ready to leave the apartment always filled the baby with anticipatory glee. Oh God, what a wonderful time she would have had with her grandparents, Kailey thought, tears welling up again.

It was in the middle of a busy Saturday evening at Radost, just a few weeks after Bonnie was born, that Daniel suffered the stroke that killed him. Although he was immediately rushed to Mount Sinai Hospital, he died within hours. Kailey thought her heart would break when the doctor delivered the news to her and her mother, both of them waiting anxiously outside the Intensive Care Unit. But Kailey's own sadness was nothing next to Sonia's. Unlike her daughter, who was sobbing openly, Sonia sat on the hospital couch silent and stonelike.

Kailey put her arms around her mother, praying she could bring some kind of comfort, but Sonia was incapable of giving or taking anything from anyone. She was silent through the funeral at Riverside Chapel, silent through the days of sitting *shiva*. While hundreds of friends came with food and candy, with memories of Daniel they wanted to share, she sat in the room saying nothing.

When Sonia died of a heart attack just two months later, Kailey was devastated but somehow not surprised. Sonia and Daniel had spent a lifetime together. They had loved each other through childhood, through Auschwitz, through the successful years in America. Kailey believed her mother simply didn't want to be alive without her husband. For her mother's sake, Kailey could almost be glad. But for her own, it was a loss so terrible she had no words to express it, no way to make sense of it.

Was there some law decreeing that people must suffer for great happiness? Kailey was beginning to believe it was true. Bonnie's birth in January had been the happiest moment of Kailey's life. Not even her wedding had provided the depth of joy she experienced as she gave a final push and, watching the overhead mirror in the delivery room, saw her daughter emerge. Sonia had gone with Kailey to her Lamaze classes, Cameron claiming to be too busy to attend, and it was Sonia who was there with her at the birth. The delivery room nurses had cleaned the baby and wrapped her in a blanket. Then they gave her to Kailey.

As soon as she felt the weight of the small bundle in her arms, Kailey was flooded with love. She had thought her passion for Cameron and her feeling for her parents were what love was about. Giving birth to Bonnie was completely different. Their connection was visceral, as if the baby remained a part of her body. Kailey couldn't take her eyes off the soft pink skin, the perfectly formed fingers, the rosebud mouth already making sounds and issuing demands. When the nurses reached out to reclaim the baby, she had trouble letting go.

Four months later, Kailey still felt the same way every time she looked at Bonnie. She would hear her daughter laughing as she lay alone in her crib early each morning, cooing at the musical mobile of tigers and lions Ben and Risa had sent from Rome. During her morning bath, Bonnie would pull herself up to a sitting position, holding tightly to Kailey's fingers. When Kailey lifted the baby to change her diaper or feed her, Bonnie would pull her mother's hair with strong fingers, grab at her earrings, her sunglasses. The baby had begun to utter sounds that were almost words. "Da, da, da, na, na, na," Bonnie would chirp happily. Was she saying Daddy? Kailey would wonder. Ironic, she thought in unbidden moments, since Cameron spent so little time with his daughter. In fact, he spent almost as little with Kailey.

She reflected on how much Cameron seemed to have changed since she'd gotten pregnant. Early in their marriage, he'd been loving, passionate. He claimed to be happy about her pregnancy, but in fact he almost never got home before midnight. As Kailey's belly had grown with every passing month, his interest in her had diminished proportionately.

When she finally found the momentary courage to ask him what was wrong, his answer was an abrupt dismissal. "Don't you see how busy I am? How can you bother me with this nonsense right now?" Shattered, she never asked again. Instead, she cried herself to sleep every night as she waited for him to come home, never complaining about his absences, fearful of driving him farther way. When the baby's born, she assured herself, things will go back to the way they were.

But Bonnie's birth hadn't made much of a difference, at least not at first. Cameron visited Kailey in the hospital each day, but briefly. Nor had he been able to stay for the actual birth, although he came later that night with a huge spray of roses. Sonia and Daniel found his inattentiveness odd, but Kailey refused to answer their questions or listen to their complaints about him. He's overwhelmed at the office, she claimed. You can't imagine how sorry he is, how loving he is to the baby and me. It felt awful to lie to her parents, but she was too terrified to admit to her own disappointment. It might push him even farther away. Her demands might make him stop loving her completely.

Kailey suffered through those months. The fear that Cameron no longer cared about her was torture. He was the one who'd brought her to life. She would die without his affection.

Until Bonnie. With the birth of the baby, everything changed. For the first two weeks, Kailey's ecstasy over the birth pushed all thoughts of Cameron's indifference to the back of her mind. Then, to Kailey's surprise, when Daniel died, Cameron's love for her seemed to come alive once more.

Throughout the funeral service at Riverside and every minute during the five days of *shiva,* Cameron stayed by her side. He handled the details of the burial on Long Island and the obituary in *The New York Times.* He even chose to throw a shovelful of dirt into the grave, the Jewish custom for those closest to the loved one. On the second night after Daniel's death, Kailey woke up out of a dream, shaking. Cameron came awake, began to comfort her, and suddenly they found themselves making love avidly, passionately, as if no rift had ever existed between them.

With profound relief, Kailey turned over all the details of her parents' estate to her husband. Even before Sonia's death, it had been hard enough to cope with her grief; with both of them gone, she had no idea how to handle their Fifth Avenue apartment, the running of Radost, the particulars of the Davids' will. And Cameron had come through brilliantly, taking the weight of responsibility off her shoulders.

He still paid less attention to Bonnie than Kailey wished he would, but she felt sure that too would change as the baby got older. A lot of men were uncomfortable with babies, she told herself. She had faith in her husband. When Bonnie was old enough to walk into his arms, Cameron would never be able to resist her.

How my mother and father would have spoiled her, Kailey thought wistfully, as she folded the wet washcloth over the towel rack. Then she rushed downstairs. Frederick was waiting for her, and she knew it was something important.

Kailey looked at her watch as the cab pulled up in front of the Cornell Club. Despite the hundreds of people walking around in midtown during lunch hour, the club was almost empty.

Frederick Wolf was waiting for Kailey near the entrance, barely accepting her kiss on the cheek, holding himself stiffly when she tried to hug him. Odd, she thought, apologizing for being more than twenty minutes late.

"I'm so sorry, Frederick," she said for the third and last time, as the maître d' seated them near a window.

Frederick neither accepted nor rejected her apology. He continued to maintain the formal distance that had been there since she'd arrived. Ordering a dry vodka martini for himself and a club soda for Kailey, he was looking expectantly at her, not even the smallest smile on his face, as if he were waiting for her to say something.

"Frederick, is something the matter?" Kailey was beginning to feel uncomfortable.

His expression turned to disapproval.

"Is something the matter?" he repeated dryly. "Frankly, I feel you owed it to me to tell me before. As someone who's known you since your birth, I shouldn't have been the one to call you." His voice was cold.

"Frederick," Kailey's voice revealed her bewilderment, "I don't have any idea what you're talking about. Is there something wrong with the will?"

The lawyer was finally unable to contain himself. His voice filled with rage, and he smacked his hand down on the table. "Don't insult me further, Kailey. You know damned well that's not my concern anymore. I can live with that, although I think your parents would be horrified to see you fire one of their best friends." He took a sip of his martini, willing himself to calm down. "What I cannot live with is your wholesale destruction of their entire dream. How could you do it? How could you sell Radost?"

Kailey tried to absorb everything she was hearing. "Please slow down. I can't follow a thing you're saying."

Frederick searched her face. Suddenly he realized she might be sincerely confused. "Kailey, do you know that Cameron is using another law firm for settling your parents' estate?"

Numbly, she shook her head no.

"Well, my dear, perhaps you also don't know that he sold the nightclub yesterday. Noone Brothers, the realty firm, is building a high-rise after they knock down the building. As of about a month from now, Radost will be razed to the ground."

Kailey felt sick to her stomach. She thought of the Saturday mornings she'd spent at the nightclub when she was a little girl, when both her parents were alive, when life seemed filled with warmth and fun. How could Cameron do this without consulting her? Never mind that, how could he do it at all? I should have paid attention, she thought. Then it never could have happened. I would never have allowed it.

Why had Cameron needed to do it? Kailey tried to imagine what could possibly have caused her husband to do something so rash, something that would cause her so much pain. Radost was irreplaceable. And the blow to Frederick. What could Cameron have been thinking?

Dimly, she recalled how months before, in the depth of her grief, he had pushed some papers in front of her. She'd had no idea what she was signing. Well, now she knew. She had signed away her control of her parents' estate, and Cameron was selling it all off, piece by piece. He must have realized how strongly

Frederick Wolf would feel about such an action, so he had summarily fired him.

Kailey was embarrassed that her surprise was so evident to Frederick. But that embarrassment was nothing compared to how she herself was feeling about Cameron. Miserably, she thought of her parents' warnings. Had they been right about him all along?

Kailey had to say something to Frederick, but the words were hard to find.

"I'm sorry. Obviously, I didn't know anything about this. As far as I'm concerned, you're my lawyer, and by the end of today, I'm going to get to the bottom of this." She pushed her chair away from the table. "Pardon me for leaving in the middle of lunch, but I must see Cameron right away."

She could read the doubt on Frederick's face as she kissed him and turned to leave. And when she arrived unannounced at the Little Angel offices, she realized the lawyer had been right to be skeptical.

She had to wait fifteen minutes until Cameron finished a meeting. Then, as she faced him across his desk, he was unapologetic. She so rarely came to his office, he must have known how urgently she felt about all this. Yet he acted as if it didn't mean a thing.

"I sold it for millions," he said, referring to Radost as casually as if he were talking about a painting or a chair.

"That was my parents' whole life," Kailey cried, her face flushed with a fury she'd never felt before.

"Darling," Cameron said without much warmth, "if you didn't trust me to make the correct decisions regarding these matters, you shouldn't have turned them over to me in the first place. After all," he added in a patronizing tone, "if you're unwilling to deal with your own mess, you don't have much right to criticize the person you leave holding the bag."

"Stop treating me like a five-year-old." Kailey's voice rose dangerously. "You had to know how strongly I would have objected to selling Radost. I insist you buy it back right now, before they destroy it. And you must rehire Frederick. He's always been my parents' lawyer." Kailey flushed, but stood her ground.

Cameron remained seated and cool. "Wolf isn't the only law-yer in New York. As far as I'm concerned, he's over the hill. Mike Harris, his replacement, is doing a much better job. Besides, if your parents had wanted him badly enough, they'd have made him co-executor. They didn't choose to do that, so I have to believe it didn't really matter very much to them."

Cameron got up from his chair, and walked over to put his arm around Kailey. "As for Radost, I'm sorry, dear. Perhaps I should have told you about it, but there's nothing to be done. Stop worrying about all this, honey. We'll talk about it later. Right now, I've got a telephone meeting with the LA office."

Kailey couldn't believe it. First he had humiliated her, and sold off her last tie to her parents, and now he was dismissing her. It was like dealing with a stone wall. Tears began to stream down her face. It was all she could do to keep from screaming.

Pretending not to notice, Cameron led Kailey toward the door, signaling to his secretary to accompany his wife out to the elevator. Kailey was caught off guard. She was furious, but making a scene in front of Marianne was unthinkable. Turning her back to the door, she grabbed a tissue from her handbag and tried to keep her lip from quavering.

"Will you be home by six?" she asked in as normal a voice as she could manage. "There's more to talk about, Cameron. This discussion is not over."

"I'll try, Kailey. If I can't get there by six, I'll aim for seven. Don't worry."

Kailey felt miserable as Marianne shut the door behind her. She had seen the look on the woman's face as Cameron spoke. It was obvious even to his secretary that he had no intention of being home on time. How do I proceed? Kailey wondered listlessly. Dejected, she walked outside and hailed a cab. Maybe she'd think of something to do, but for right now, she needed to get home to Bonnie. Holding the baby was the only thing that could make her feel better.

For weeks, Kailey remained angry, but she had to admit that Cameron was trying to make it up to her, even if he didn't come right out and admit he was wrong. Although he never exactly apologized, he took to calling often in the middle of the afternoon just to say hello, played with Bonnie, and seemed to care more about being a family.

But it was when she saw her husband in a crisis that she began to forgive him completely. It was during one of his midday calls that he mentioned the problems at the Jensen Baby Food Company. Some LSD had been found in their strained carrots, and an infant was dead. As Kailey heard later on the five o'clock news, police had no idea how the substance had worked its way in, nor did they know whether a whole batch had been poisoned or merely one jar.

Cameron and his people found themselves on a twenty-four-hour workday, filling in with Little Angel on the grocery shelves where Jensen products had been removed. Cameron spent every day running between his Manhattan office and production headquarters in White Plains. He also managed several appearances on the morning talk shows, reassuring parents of the general safety of the baby food on their shelves. He was impressive on the air, a clear leader in his field.

For two straight days, he didn't have time to come home even to change clothes. Finally, on the third day after the crisis started, he returned around two in the morning, falling immediately into a deep sleep. The next morning Kailey found herself in his arms, making love even before she was fully awake. In spite of his exhaustion, Cameron was passionate and strong.

She luxuriated in his affection. As she lay in his arms, she realized that, for the first time since her lunch with Frederick, she wasn't angry with her husband. In fact, she found herself proud of him. Selling Radost had been a mistake, but whatever his flaws in judgment, he was a man who could triumph in a crisis. If anything, he seemed energized by it.

"Can you stay home for a while today, get some rest?" Kailey held him gently, almost willing him back to sleep.

"No," he answered, kissing her on the lips and easing himself out of bed. "I've got another morning in White Plains and meetings with the people from Kroger's all afternoon."

Suddenly, Kailey remembered what day it was. The cocktail

party the mayor was giving for Soviet Jews was being held at Tavern on the Green at seven that evening. It had been one of the causes dearest to Sonia and Daniel, and tonight's event had been planned for months. Virtually every city and state official was invited, and even the vice president was due to attend. Kailey had been asked to deliver a few words on behalf of her parents. Cameron was supposed to accompany her, but she realized that what he was doing was far more important.

"Honey, at least you can skip the party later. I'll be fine by myself." She had followed Cameron out of bed and was picking up the articles of clothing he had carelessly heaped on the floor the night before.

He turned toward her, incomprehension written all over his face. Obviously, he had completely forgotten about the party, and she didn't blame him a bit.

"Soviet Jews, honey. Remember?" Kailey ran her hand down the length of his back. "Don't even think about it."

She had no way of knowing how much he'd been looking forward to meeting the government people and business leaders expected there. His answer surprised her. "No, Kailey. I wouldn't miss it for the world. I might be just a few minutes late, though, so why don't I meet you there."

Later that day, Kailey realized how nervous she was about speaking in front of so many people. Perhaps some exercise will distract me, she thought as she completed her hair and makeup just before six o'clock. The restaurant was in Central Park near West Sixty-seventh Street, only a ten-minute walk from their apartment. She had plenty of time.

In mid-August there were hundreds of people in the park, walking home from work or playing softball in the fields. Kailey strolled past the boat pond. She knew every inch of Central Park; it had been one of her father's favorite places. Checking the time, she realized she could go out of her way a little bit and follow the path she loved most. Heading downtown, she made her way toward the carousel.

It was still light at six-thirty, and she enjoyed the sight of couples hand in hand, the business people dressed in neatly pressed suits, carrying their attaché cases, hurrying home. The carousel was closed for the evening, and the area around it more deserted than the boat pond had been. Cutting across the lawn just south of the carousel, Kailey was startled to spot her husband. Cameron was standing with a man she'd never seen before. He was medium height, maybe somewhere in his forties. His hair looked too black, as if he dyed it, and his skin was dead white, set off by black horned-rim glasses. It was as an odd combination, a memorable face.

She walked up to the pair and took Cameron's hand. Startled by her presence, he immediately cut short his conversation with the man and led her away.

"Who was that?" she asked casually, as they walked toward the West Side.

"Just some guy asking for directions." Abruptly he changed the subject. "So, are you ready for your speech? Why don't you rehearse it with me? It will relax you, you'll see."

Kailey was sure her husband's conversation with that man had been about something more important than directions. They had been standing so close to each other, speaking so quietly. But she wasn't about to question him. Things between them were finally coming back to normal, and she had no intention of making waves. If Cameron didn't want to identify his friend, so be it.

Kailey was proud to walk into Tavern on the Green with Cameron, to show him off to friends of her parents from years before. It seemed as if everyone in New York was there, at least all the people who had loved Sonia and Daniel. Not only had the businesspeople come, but all over the room were dancers, writers, artists, people speaking Russian. By the middle of the evening, it seemed as if every one of them had taken Kailey aside to reminisce about the first years of Radost, when her parents had provided their meeting place, their home away from home. By the time Kailey walked up to the podium, she didn't even feel nervous. "If my mother and father were here tonight," she began, but her next words were drowned out by applause.

Only much later that night, when she was waiting for Cameron, who was chatting with a congressman and several of the event's sponsors, did she see Frederick Wolf standing farther down the narrow corridor, gazing at her husband with distaste. Kailey hurried over to say hello. She had never meant to lose contact with Frederick, but with her schoolwork and the baby, there never seemed to be time to call. No, she admitted to herself. That wasn't the real reason. She was embarrassed. She had made a promise and had been incapable of making it come true. Radost was gone. She hadn't been able to stop the sale. The building had been razed. Now her parents' dream was a boarded-up construction site, just as Frederick had known it would be.

Kailey steeled herself. Frederick had been a part of her life since she was a baby. If he was angry with her, she'd just have to face it.

"Frederick." She said his name softly as she walked toward him, her uncertainty obvious even as she raised her face to kiss him tentatively on the cheek.

"Hello, darling." Frederick's voice was grave but warm. She felt his affection as she used to, before she had let him down so badly.

She hadn't decided what to say, but the words began to tumble out. "I'm so sorry about everything. Radost, not calling. Being such a disappointment . . ."

Frederick stopped her with a smile. "Kailey, dear, there's nothing you could have done." Raising his hand to the back of her neck, he ruffled her hair affectionately, just as he used to when she was a little girl, but quickly his expression turned more serious.

Glancing back toward where Cameron was still enjoying his conversation, Frederick lowered his hand to her shoulder and held it tightly. He began to speak, earnestly and quietly, into her ear, careful that no one else hear what he had to say.

"Kailey, I'm terribly worried about you. I don't think you really know the man you married."

Kailey pulled away. She couldn't face Frederick's dislike of Cameron, not now when everything was finally going so well.

Frederick saw how little she wanted him to continue, but he couldn't stop now. This was too important.

"I see you don't want to hear this, but you have to. That

baby who died last week. I know enough about your husband's company to know he'll benefit from this."

"Cameron's been working day and night since that happened. He's exhausted," she said defensively, unaware of where Frederick was headed. His next comment was completely unexpected.

"I think perhaps Cameron was involved in that poisoning," Frederick whispered.

"How can you suggest such a thing!" Kailey's outrage was clear. "What could possibly make you think something like that?"

"Kailey." His tone was gentle. "I won't be the only one to suspect such a thing. The police routinely investigate anyone who profits from a crime, and Little Angel has to be profiting greatly from the events of the past few days."

Kailey felt like slapping him. What he was suggesting was monstrous. But she controlled herself. Frederick was an old friend, and he had a grudge, an understandable one even. He would have come to his senses by the next time she saw him, he was bound to. And next time she wouldn't let so much time go by. His ridiculous accusation was probably as much about her lack of attentiveness as it was about his hatred for Cameron. She began a polite good-bye, but Frederick stopped her before she turned away.

"Kailey, please take this seriously. Your husband is a man who knows exactly what he wants and goes for it." His eyes strayed momentarily toward the elite group assembled around Cameron. "Please, dear, think about this."

"Frederick, I refuse to listen for one more minute." Old friend or not, he had no right to say these things.

Kailey pulled away once more, this time turning her back to him. As she began to walk toward Cameron, she heard Frederick's voice behind her.

"Mona and I are leaving for a cruise later tonight, but we'll be back in two weeks. If you need me, I'll always be here for you."

Kailey was furious when she returned to Cameron's side, but within minutes she had calmed herself down. Frederick was an old man now, holding his grudges hard.

By the time they had returned to the apartment later that night, Kailey felt only sadness for Frederick. For her own part, she was relieved. Her speech had gone fine, and Cameron's mood remained buoyant. When just a few minutes later he announced he was returning to the office, Kailey was disappointed.

"I understand you feel you have to, but can't you get at least a few hours of sleep before you go back?"

"I'll be right beside you when you wake up," he answered. "I have a couple of hours' work to put in. Honestly, I might be home even sooner."

She knew she'd never fall asleep after Cameron left. She was too wound up from her evening's performance even to read a book. Idly, she turned on the TV, switching channels until she came to the eleven o'clock news. The Jensen baby food story was still being featured. A Channel Four reporter had gone to the Jensen factory in south Jersey, and was delivering his report from the packing room.

Kailey watched with some interest, wondering how Jensen's plant compared to Little Angel's; she remembered so well the day she and her father had visited Cameron's White Plains facility just after her engagement. At first the camera was focused on the reporter's face, but soon it panned a line of four or five employees on the assembly line. Then the camera lingered on one of the men setting empty jars on a conveyer belt. Suddenly she sat bolt upright. She knew that man. The camera never strayed from his face as the reporter went on talking. It couldn't be, she thought. I must be crazy. She got up from the bed and stood directly in front of the television. That was definitely the same man she'd seen earlier tonight with Cameron. She was sure of it. What in heaven's name could it mean?

She was unable to stop the questions coming into her mind. If the man on the television worked for Jensen, what had he been doing in the park with Cameron?

She worried about it all the next day. Finally, late in the afternoon, she picked up the phone and dialed the number for the Jensen Corporation. Hesitantly, she asked to be connected to the packing room. When a woman's voice came on, she asked to speak to the man with the glasses and the black hair, the one who'd been singled out on Channel Four the night before.

"Oh, I was watching NBC too. That was Alfred Bankes." The woman's voice had become cheerfully intimate. "Hold on. He'll get a real kick out of being noticed."

Just a moment later, another voice came on.

"Bankes," he identified himself abruptly.

She couldn't think what to say next, but finally she decided to stick as closely to the truth as possible. "I think you're a friend of my husband's. Cameron Hawkes."

The phone was slammed down so solidly it sounded like an explosion in her ear.

Why would Alfred Bankes hang up on her like that unless he had recognized Cameron's name? Could there be some connection between them? Did that mean her husband might have had something to do with the problems at Jensen?

Just as Frederick had suggested.

Kailey found herself shaking. A baby was dead. It could have been Bonnie. She couldn't bear it. Impossible, unthinkable.

When Cameron returned from work that night, she pretended to be asleep. She couldn't find the words to ask him about what she'd seen. In the morning, she feigned sleep once again as she heard him awaken. She listened to him take a shower, then have some kind of conversation with Nina.

As he reentered their bedroom and picked up his briefcase, she realized he would be leaving the apartment soon. There was the sound of the front door closing. Cameron was on his way to the elevator; he would be gone in a few seconds. She had to know the truth. She had to speak, no matter what the cost. Quickly, without even throwing a robe on over her nightgown, Kailey ran out after him, catching him, his hand on the elevator button.

"You don't have to be up this early," Cameron said, his tone as affectionate as it had been the night before.

"I have to talk to you," Kailey said, fighting back her fear, trying to stay composed. "I saw that man on the news last night . . . the one you were talking to in the park. He works in the

Jensen factory." Kailey stopped for a moment. She couldn't seem to form the words.

"Cameron, did you have anything to do with that baby, the one who died?" Kailey's hands were trembling, but she managed to look her husband in the eye.

Cameron grabbed her arm roughly and pulled her back into their apartment, making sure the door to Nina's room was closed before he answered her. His voice was a biting whisper.

"Where did you get an idea like that?" He tightened his grip on her arm. "Now you listen to me. If you interfere in any way with my business, you'll be sorry. I promise you'll regret it." He released her hand and walked back to the front door, stopping to look at her once more. He seemed to be contemplating something. When he spoke again, he whispered words of pure evil. "And you won't be the only one who's sorry. Bonnie will be sorry too."

Kailey felt her body go cold, wildly hoping she hadn't heard him correctly, that she'd somehow misunderstood. Even as she'd questioned him, even as her logic was telling her he was guilty, she hadn't really believed it. Yet it was true. Cameron was a murderer.

Bonnie will be sorry too. Kailey shuddered as those words repeated themselves over and over in her mind. Cameron wasn't just threatening her. He could hurt Bonnie. Kailey thought about Cameron's ruthless disregard when he sold Radost, when he fired Frederick. She recalled how serious Frederick had been last night, when he warned her about her husband. If what Frederick said was true, Cameron could kill Bonnie without a moment's hesitation. It was that thought that finally prompted Kailey to action. Whatever she did, wherever she went, she had to get the baby out of here right now. She would call Frederick. He would be at his office. She started for the phone, but suddenly stopped. He'd been leaving on a cruise, she remembered. Two weeks? Three weeks?

What's the difference, she realized. She had to do something right now, right this minute.

"Nina," she said urgently, hurrying to the au pair's room, "we're going away for a while." She faltered, wondering what excuse to give. "We'll be visiting some relatives and we have to leave right now. Can you pack a bag while I get Bonnie ready?"

As Nina nodded, Kailey raced into Bonnie's room and threw a small box of diapers plus two pairs of overalls and a couple of T-shirts into a red canvas bag. She knew she had to be quick, but she didn't want to forget anything that was absolutely necessary. She hastened around the room, picking up the baby's pink-and-white blanket and several of her favorite stuffed toys. Bonnie was lying in her crib, watching every step her mother took. She smiled widely as Kailey lifted her out of the crib. Kailey thought about what else she might need, and ran toward the kitchen, adding a baby bottle and a few jars of baby food to the bag.

She was terrified that at any moment Cameron might reappear, and she didn't want to stop to pack anything else. After a quick call to the garage to have the car brought around to the front of the building, she threw some clothes on and hurried Nina and Bonnie out of the apartment. Within ten minutes of Cameron's leaving, the three of them were driving off in the bright red Jaguar.

I don't even know where I'm going, Kailey thought in a frenzy as she sped up Madison Avenue. Without thinking much about it, she headed for the George Washington Bridge, taking Route 80 west.

Who can I call, she wondered as she sped along the highway. The people she really needed were Sonia and Daniel. With them gone, there were only acquaintances. Even if someone agreed to help her, Cameron would easily find out where she was. No, she had to get as far away as possible. So far away that he couldn't lay a hand on the baby.

She struggled to concentrate. If she went to the police, Cameron would find a way to fool them. He had grown so powerful since their marriage. With her parents' help he had become friendly with too many influential people for her to believe even the police could keep her and the baby safe.

As they drove west through New Jersey, Kailey turned the situation over in her mind. She had only a couple of hundred dollars with her, and using her credit cards would make her traceable. Money was soon going to be a problem, and she would have to find some way to take care of Bonnie.

Then she thought of Michael Warner out in San Francisco. She'd met him at her parents' dinner party while she was pregnant, and he'd made such a fuss over her fluency at foreign languages. She remembered his saying he was desperate for people like her in his import business. Well, she prayed he'd been serious, because it looked as if he was her only hope.

If she drove straight through to California, if she took back roads and traveled quickly, Cameron would never find her. And he would never think of her going as far as California. Maybe Michael Warner would come through. Then she would have some money and the safety of three thousand miles between her and her husband. She couldn't allow herself to worry about Michael Warner, or whether he would even remember her. It didn't matter. All that mattered right now was having someplace to go.

Kailey was so frightened of being followed she didn't even slow down long enough to buy a map until she reached the middle of Pennsylvania, nor did she think to stop for anything besides gas for the car until Nina complained of being hungry. Even then, they ate sandwiches as they drove rather than dawdle inside a restaurant. With Nina spelling her at the wheel while Kailey fed Bonnie or caught a little sleep, they made it to California within four days. The heat and humidity had followed them all the way across the country, and both Nina and Kailey felt filthy and exhausted. When Nina begged to sleep in a motel for just one night, Kailey knew she had to say yes, finally opting for a tiny place only hours from their final destination. I owe it to both of them, Kailey thought as she left Nina and Bonnie in the car at the far end of the lot and walked to the motel office.

Kailey bit her lip as she stared at the motel registration pad. *Name and address.* She couldn't seem to focus. Think. *Think,* she told herself sharply.

The man behind the desk rustled some papers.

"That'll be twenty-five dollars. Cash or credit card?"

Chapter 6

———

Benjamin Gottlieb could hardly believe Kailey was alive, right here in Rome. He and Risa had seen the small article in the *International Herald Tribune* only hours before. WIFE AND DAUGHTER OF EXECUTIVE KILLED IN CRASH, the headline had read. The accompanying photo of Kailey had reduced him to bitter tears. His call to Cameron in New York moments later revealed that Kailey's husband too was beyond grief.

Then, amazingly, Kailey had turned up at their doorstep, disheveled and obviously exhausted. Overjoyed, Ben had lifted the phone, immediately beginning to dial Cameron's number, but Kailey's reaction stunned him. She'd grabbed the phone out of his hands, insisted that he and Risa tell no one she was there, not the American

Embassy, not their closest friends, and especially not Cameron.

The Gottliebs were shocked by her request. They'd tried to reason with her, bully her even, but her stubborn insistence convinced them to do exactly as she begged them. All she would say after getting them to agree was that she was very tired, and could she please stay with them for the night.

Could she stay with them for the night? Why, she was practically his daughter. What could have happened in California? Ben couldn't begin to imagine what the truth might be, but he had to trust Kailey's instincts. She'd seemed perfectly normal when he'd returned to New York for Daniel's funeral, just as she'd been the four or five times he'd spoken to her after Sonia died. However crazy Kailey's request seemed, he had to respect it. Whatever the real story was, his instinct told him it was something terrible.

Risa, too, was dying of curiosity, but one look at Kailey had convinced her that questions would be futile, maybe even dangerous. Thank God the girl was alive, but so fragile, so wounded.

What could have happened, Ben and Risa asked each other in hushed whispers after Kailey had been led to the guest room and settled in with a cup of tea and some sandwiches. Risa hardly knew Kailey, yet she too had noticed the terror on the girl's face. Long into the night, the Gottliebs debated what they should do. Call a doctor friend of theirs? Try to force Kailey to discuss whatever had happened? By three in the morning they had given up, deciding to wait and talk to Kailey again after a good night's sleep.

In the guest room Kailey lay in bed, wide awake and staring into the darkness. *Cameron will never stop until I'm dead. He warned me not to do anything, and I didn't listen. Because of my stupidity, my daughter is dead. Now it's my turn.*

She rolled over, gazing out the window at the stars in the night sky. She almost looked forward to Cameron's catching up with her. At least her pain would be over. She could stop seeing Bonnie's torn blanket on the rocks, stop hearing the screams her daughter must have unleashed as the car started to go over the cliff.

Cameron's men would never be identified by the police any more than that Alfred Bankes person Cameron had hired to do his dirty work in his competitor's factory would ever be caught. No, her husband was too powerful, too clever to get caught.

And with Bonnie dead, it didn't matter anymore.

Suddenly she felt overwhelmed with self-loathing. *If only I'd run to the police right away, told them what I knew.* But she had to face the truth. When she'd stood at the scene of the accident, she was paralyzed with fright. Within seconds, she realized that if she didn't get as far away as possible, she wouldn't live to face anything again.

Her trip to Rome had been fraught with terror. She barely remembered how she located the pawnshop that gave her the money for her flight in exchange for the diamond pendant her parents had given her for her sixteenth birthday, the one piece of jewelry she never removed, even in the shower. She'd gotten less than it was worth, but it was enough to get her on the plane. She hadn't dared call Ben and Risa from the United States, somehow certain that would enable Cameron to track her down. Every time she had to show identification, she felt as if someone were following her. The passport inspector, even the flight attendant seemed ominous. Would they call Cameron the moment she passed through?

That's crazy. I'm safe now where no one can get me. Kailey rubbed her eyes. Here, thousands of miles away from New York, she could explain everything to Ben and Risa. With their help, she could notify someone in the United States. The police. No, maybe the FBI. Ben would know what to do.

She remembered the feeling she'd had at the scene of the accident. Would anyone ever believe what she had to say? Well, what possible difference would it make if they didn't? They couldn't bring Bonnie back to life. At least she knew what she had to do and, finally, she was ready to do it.

Relieved by her decision, Kailey relaxed into the soft mattress, finally able to close her eyes after so many hours of terrified wakefulness.

Bonnie's imagined cry jolted her awake. Kailey was dazed from the dream in which her daughter still seemed agonizingly close. Tears poured down her cheeks until she finally had none left to cry. She got up and sat down by the window, waiting for the sun to rise.

At eight o'clock the next morning, Risa retired tactfully to the bedroom, and Kailey sat facing Ben across the breakfast table. After all that had happened, she was surprised to find that the details of the past few weeks took only moments to tell. The poisoned baby food, the horrible journey across the United States, Nina's flight, Cameron's final revenge. Ben looked shocked and gray with concern.

Kailey was too overwrought to sit. Pacing in front of Ben, her head high, she was finally able to say the words she'd been too frightened to think about the night before.

"It's time to call the police in New York and California. He can't be allowed to get away with this, no matter what he intends to do to me." Kailey paused. "My daughter is dead, and he has to answer for it."

Ben rushed over to comfort her. "Oh, my baby, of course I'll phone immediately. I think the FBI is a better place to start than the police in New York or California." He saw the remnants of fear in her eyes. "You'll be safe here with us. Nothing can happen here, nothing more that man can do to you."

Ben eased Kailey down into a chair and strode across the room toward the telephone, thinking it through out loud. "Now let's see, what time would it be in Washington? Should I wait a few more hours until the regular forces are on duty, or is it better to start them on it immediately . . ."

His musings were interrupted by Risa's explosive entrance.

"Ben, put that phone down. I was listening to you from the next room — I'm sorry, but I was just too worried not to. And," she said, holding out the *International Herald Tribune* in front of him, "thank God I did."

She held out a small article on page three. "Read this," she insisted.

MAN QUESTIONED IN BABYFOOD MURDER
DIES SUDDENLY

Alfred Bankes, former employee of the Jensen Baby Food Corporation, was found dead today in his home in Astoria, Queens.
Questioned in connection with last month's poisoning, which resulted in one baby's death and eight more severely injured, Bankes
had revealed nothing to police, but had become a leading suspect
according to the New York Police Department.

Ben devoured the piece, then handed the paper to Kailey.

"Is this the man you were talking about, the one Cameron
hired?"

Kailey scanned the piece. The sight of Bankes' name so far
away from New York frightened her all over again. "That's him."

"Do you think Cameron is responsible for this?"

Kailey nodded.

Ben kept silent. The last thing she needed to hear was fear
creeping into his voice. She must have been exactly right. Cameron
must be just as dangerous as she'd thought.

Ben stared at the phone. Suddenly he felt less sure of himself.
Could he really keep Kailey safe from such a man? After all, under
American law someone like Cameron, with so much money and
the best legal advice, could be free on bail for months, years even.
In fact, he was so smooth, so convincing, who knew what a jury
might think of him? Perhaps Kailey's original terror had been well
founded.

"Darling —" he looked at his wife — "I want you to forget
everything you've heard, everything you think you know. It would
be too dangerous for Kailey to do anything but stay here with us.
We can tell people she's my niece." He glanced at Kailey. Was it
a lie? He'd loved her as long as she'd been alive. She was the
closest he'd ever come to having a daughter. There was no way
he would allow her to risk her life.

Kailey was staring at him in horror. "Ben, if you think you
can keep me from calling the American authorities, you're wrong.
I should have reported Cameron right away. There's no way you
can stop me from telling what I know."

Ben loved her too much to let her win. Knowing it was unfair, he played the only card that could possibly stop her. "The moment you pick up that phone you put Risa and me in danger." His voice broke, but he struggled to go on. "Bonnie is dead. If you call the police, we could all be killed. Surely you can't allow that to happen."

"Ben, you don't know that." Kailey's voice was desperate. "How can I let him get away with this? How could he possibly find me here?"

"The only reason he hasn't found you yet is he believes you're already dead. When he learns you're alive, he'll know exactly how to find you. And when he finds you, he'll find us."

How can you ask me to do this? How can I live with myself if I listen to you? All this and more Kailey wanted to scream at Ben. But the look of fear on Risa's face as she turned toward her husband demonstrated just how selfish those questions would be.

Chapter 7

———

"**T**ry to be a brave girl, sweetheart," whispered Ruth Mitchell, kneeling before the tearful five-year-old and putting her arms around the child to pull her close. "We'll be thinking of you. Remember we all love you."

Susannah Holland buried her face against Mrs. Mitchell's broad shoulder and hugged her tightly. She was trying desperately not to cry. Behind her she could hear the two younger Mitchell children sniffling softly as they waited their turn to say good-bye. Feeling her foster mother's hand stroking her long brown hair, Susannah shut her eyes tightly and wished one more time that this wasn't really happening.

"Do I have to go?" She raised her head and blurted the words out. "I promise I'll be good if you let me stay with you."

Ruth felt as if her heart would break. She

smiled sadly. "Oh, honey, you've always been good. You know if I could keep you here, I would."

They all heard the honk of a horn. Through the window, Ruth saw a tall, thin man in a suit get out of a car and come up the short walk. There was no more time.

Holding both of the little girl's hands tightly, Ruth kissed her on the cheek. If only she could think of some way to keep Susannah with them — but she'd racked her brains for the past six weeks and knew it was hopeless. She had no idea how she was going to care for her own three children now that her husband was dead. It had been difficult enough to make ends meet with both their incomes. Her job in the supermarket wouldn't begin to cover expenses. Even with the money the state provided for foster care, the added strain of keeping a child who wasn't hers would be unfair to all of them. Still, Ruth Mitchell would have tried to make it work. But as soon as the state learned of her husband's death, she had received a telephone call informing her that Susannah would be transferred to another foster home; the decision was out of her hands.

Ruth disliked self-pity, but for a moment she gave herself over to it. God, why do you have to take away my husband and this child both, she asked silently, a tear escaping as she allowed herself one last long hug. For a brief second, she remembered back to the time she and her husband had decided to bring another child into their home. They had certainly had their hands full caring for their own, but they both agreed there were too many unloved children in the world, and they wanted to do something, however small, to help. Taking Susannah in had seemed like a perfect solution: though the state's money was never enough, it helped make it possible for them to give a home to an orphaned baby.

Yet all their good intentions had resulted in today's pain. In the four and a half years Susannah had been with them, the Mitchells had come to love the pretty little girl as if she were their own. Even as a baby, Susannah had been so winning, so eager to love them and feel their love in return. Those big blue eyes and sweet smile had easily won the hearts of the whole family. And

she was growing up to be so warm and caring. Ruth had watched
her at preschool, sharing her lunch, so friendly with all the other
children. At home, she would happily do anything asked of her,
always wanting to help.

Standing up, Ruth wiped her eyes with her hand. She was
a big, sturdy-looking woman, but right now she felt frail. I must
be strong for Susannah, she thought.

"Okay, sweetie, everybody else wants a kiss and I shouldn't
keep you all to myself."

Susannah hung her head as she turned to say good-bye to
the others. Twelve-year-old Sam Mitchell put his arms around
her awkwardly and gave her a gentle squeeze. "Bye, Sooze," he
said softly. "We'll miss you."

"Bye, Sam." Her answer was barely audible. She broke away
and turned to nine-year-old Lily. There was a knock on the door.
Ruth Mitchell opened it to let in the man who had come for
Susannah.

"I'm from — " he started to say.

Ruth held up a hand. "Just a minute more, please," she said
gently.

Susannah watched, her eyes large with fright. She grabbed
onto Lily as if that might somehow stop her from being taken
away.

Lily's face was wet with tears. "Bye. I love you." She kissed
Susannah and hugged her.

"I love you, too," Susannah said, her voice wobbling. "Write
to me, okay?"

Timmy Mitchell, seven, came over to them gravely. "Here,
we want you to take Otto."

Susannah looked at him. He was holding out the white stuffed
toy seal his father had given him two years before. Tom Mitchell
had rarely taken a day off from his fishing-boat charter service,
but when he could get some time to himself, he loved to take the
family over to the enormous Morro Rock, where they watched
the otters play in the water. Eating potato chips and drinking
lemonade, the children would laugh and point as the otters basked
in the sun's warm rays, floating on their backs like fat, satisfied

tourists on the beach. Mr. Mitchell had bought the stuffed seal and presented him to Timmy two Christmases ago. It wasn't *really* an otter, Tom Mitchell had said, rolling his eyes and making them laugh, but what did these toy people know about what was important—besides, they could pretend.

Otto was usually kept in a place of honor on the old sofa in the living room. By now, he was more gray than white, and had lost most of his whiskers and one of his glass eyes.

"For me? Really?" she asked in disbelief.

Timmy nodded. Susannah took the seal and clutched him to her. "Thanks, Timmy."

Growing impatient, their visitor stepped forward. "You'll have to come with me now, young lady. Your new foster parents are anxious to meet you."

Ruth Mitchell put an arm around Susannah's small shoulders, trying not to watch the tears streaming down the child's face. She kept her voice cheerful. "We'll all write, and you call us anytime. Your new home will be wonderful, I promise."

Ruth had packed Susannah's belongings into two suitcases, which stood by the door. The tall man picked them up, and Susannah followed him outside into the bright California sunshine. He opened the car door for her. Looking up, she saw the Mitchells huddled in the doorway of the small yellow house. Mrs. Mitchell waved and blew her a kiss. Susannah waved back, then turned away and climbed into the front seat.

The drive from Morro Bay to San Luis Obispo was a brief twelve miles, but it might as well have been twelve thousand to Susannah. Through the car window, she watched the small town slipping by. She couldn't remember the six months she knew she had spent in an orphanage not too far from here, but she'd been only a baby then. This had been her home ever since, and she loved it. Sitting up as high as she could in her seat, she could see the water. She imagined the white sand of the beach under her feet, remembering the picnic she and the Mitchells had gone on just a week before Mr. Mitchell's heart attack. They had spread a blanket out and were just getting down to eating when two big black Labradors had come bounding up, running across their lunch, scattering sand everywhere. Mr. Mitchell and the children had all laughed, but Mrs. Mitchell was annoyed. Finally, she had to give in and laugh along with the rest of them.

There was Morro Rock off to the side, huge and dark, a light mist surrounding the bottom. The second biggest something-or-other in the world, Mr. Mitchell was always telling them. It was Saturday, so soon there would probably be lots of tourists wandering around the path, feeding the otters all sorts of junk food. She looked down at Otto. Don't worry, she reassured him silently. Our new home will be wonderful. I promise.

The silent blackness of the bedroom was pierced by a shaft of light as the door opened. Lying in her bed, Susannah froze, waiting.

"Are you asleep yet?" Mary Rule's voice had the thin, reedy quality of old age, but there was an underlying strength to it. "Remember, tomorrow I'm going to show you how to run the vacuum cleaner."

"Yes, I remember." Susannah kept her voice cheerful.

Apparently satisfied, the older woman said nothing else, but shut the door. Susannah heard her slow shuffle down the hall to the bedroom she shared with her husband. The house was quiet again.

Susannah stroked Otto's head, hugging him to her as she had every night for the past three weeks since she'd arrived here. She had told herself over and over that things would get better, that Mr. and Mrs. Rule were just old, and needed time to get used to her. Again she wondered if some mistake had been made, if somehow she had wound up at the wrong house. The Mitchells had been like regular moms and dads, but these people were as old as Granny and Grandpa, Mrs. Mitchell's parents. They were shriveled and skinny, with thin white hair. Why would they even want a child in their house? Besides, Granny and Grandpa had been so nice; the Rules weren't nice at all.

Without realizing it, Susannah gave a small sigh. She knew it was wrong to think such things. Mary and Arthur Rule had taken her in, given her a home. Who knows where she would be if they hadn't been willing to help her? They made it clear she was costing them a lot of money, and she knew she should be grateful. But it was just so different here. Back at the Mitchells' she had had chores — all the children did — but they were divided up, and everybody took turns setting the table, washing the dishes, helping make the beds, each child doing whatever they could manage at their age. Here, there was only Susannah to do the chores, and some of the things she had to do were awfully hard.

Each day in her new home was pretty much the same as the one before. Today had been no exception. When the alarm clock next to her bed went off at six o'clock, Susannah had jumped up immediately, made her bed, then washed and dressed herself. It was hard for her to get the tangles out of her wet hair and comb it into a ponytail, and she could see it didn't look quite right. Slowly, she struggled with her buttons and shoelaces. When she was finished, she went down the narrow hall to the kitchen, where she poured a bowl of cereal. The Rules had eaten their breakfast earlier, and she could hear them in their bedroom, getting dressed, as she ate. She washed her bowl, along with the other breakfast dishes left stacked in the sink. After that it was time to leave.

Susannah didn't go to kindergarten anymore; Mr. Rule told her it wasn't necessary. When she was old enough, she could start first grade. She had no idea how far away that was, but she loved going to school, and hoped it was soon. Now she spent the days with her new foster parents at Rule's Pharmacy on Chorro Street. The store was very old, its narrow aisles crowded with all kinds of bottles and boxes. Mrs. Rule spent her time at the front of the store behind an enormous cash register, waiting on customers or, when it was quiet, writing in a tall green ledger book. Mr. Rule was usually behind a counter at the back of the store, mixing up medicines.

Susannah was expected to amuse herself quietly in a small curtained-off storage room. There the Rules had provided her with a few toys and a couple of coloring books from their rack of crossword puzzles, comics, and magazines. Sometimes she would peer out from behind the faded curtain and watch what was going on. There were a lot of tourists passing through to see the famous mission and the old stores, to go to the nearby beaches or visit the university. They would come in, laughing and talking loudly, the cowbell over the door jingling cheerily as they entered. They bought suntan lotion, bathing caps, cold remedies. Susannah especially liked to watch the families, how the parents and children acted with one another. When a family seemed happy, for the moment she would be happy too. She hated it if the parents were short-tempered or indifferent to their children.

Not all the customers were tourists. Lots of the local people shopped there as well, some of them going directly to talk with Arthur Rule, handing him notes explaining what pills they wanted or asking his advice about some pain they had. Things always got busy around lunchtime, so the Rules would wait until two o'clock before sitting down in the stock room for ten minutes with Susannah to eat the sandwiches they had brought from home. If anyone came into the store, Mary Rule would go out front to wait on them. The three ate quietly, the silence coming as a surprise to Susannah, used to a noisy table full of family members all talking and laughing at once. The older couple hardly ate at all themselves and the portions were small and thrifty; back at the Mitchells', food was heaped upon plates, and everyone had seconds. Susannah always chewed her ham or bologna sandwich slowly, trying to make it last. Sometimes she got an apple or a box of raisins as well.

The days were long, but even when they closed up at six o'clock, there was more to be done. The three of them would get into the Rules' old black car and drive around town, delivering small bottles of medicine to different houses. At each address, Arthur Rule handed Susannah a brown paper bag and told her how much money she was supposed to collect from the people inside. She got out and rang the doorbell, always a little bit afraid at these strange places. Sometimes the people in the houses gave her extra money, a dime, maybe even a quarter, telling her to keep it for herself. But Mary Rule had instructed her to give them anything she got, so she always handed it all over to her. Heading back to their house when they were done, they often passed a pretty green place Arthur Rule told her was called Mitchell Park. She would watch it go by, thinking of the Mitchells, and for a second it would make her feel better, as if they were here with her.

Back at home, the three of them ate dinner, usually some sort of meat Susannah didn't recognize, with peas or boiled potatoes and applesauce for dessert. Susannah hated the food, but didn't dare say anything about it. After the meal, Mrs. Rule cleared the table and washed the dishes, while Susannah sponged the kitchen counters and wiped up any spills on the floor. After straightening up her room, Susannah went out to say a polite good night, then put on her pajamas and crawled into bed, exhausted from the lonely boredom of her day.

Hugging Otto, she told herself it was important that she be good and help out in the house. After all, the Rules were old and sick, as they kept reminding her. They both had something awfully wrong with them which made their bones hurt all the time, something that sounded like Mr. Rule's first name, Arthur, something -itis, but she didn't know what it was.

She wanted real parents. She wanted her own parents. Where were they, and why didn't they come for her? Over the past three weeks, she had found herself thinking about them every night, trying to figure out why they left her at that orphanage with only a note beside her. It was such a nice note, Mrs. Mitchell had once told her, asking that someone please take care of this baby and love her. But it didn't even have her name on it. Susannah Holland was just a name someone at the orphanage had made up for her. If her parents wanted her to be loved, why didn't they tell anyone her name?

Who were they? She had always wondered, but she had been happy with the Mitchells, content to be a part of their family. Now she was desperate to find her real mother and father. Last week, she imagined them as a prince and princess, forced to leave their country without her when something terrible happened. Night after night, she had gone over her fantasy, embellishing the details until it was just right. Tonight she wondered if her mother might have been a kind and famous actress, killed in some horrible accident or by a long illness. Her handsome father was too broken-hearted to go on, flinging himself into a swirling, black river.

Maybe, she thought, they were just two regular people, good and loving, wonderful parents who somehow lost her. She was certain they would want to find her if they could. Somewhere they're out there, she decided, crying and unhappy because they were apart from her.

She whispered as softly as she could. "Good night, Mommy. Good night, Daddy."

Then she rolled over and cried until she fell asleep.

One morning the following week, just before they left for the drugstore, Mary Rule handed Susannah an envelope. It was a letter, already opened.

"This came for you yesterday," she said.

Susannah pulled out the contents. There was a red piece of construction paper with a crayon drawing. She realized right away that it was from Timmy Mitchell. In one corner it showed three big circles with eyes and frowning mouths. From the curls on one of the heads, she could see that was supposed to be Lily, so the other two must be Sam and Timmy. In the opposite corner there was a face with long brown hair and a smile, surrounded by lots of little hearts. That, she saw, was Susannah herself.

A white piece of paper with Ruth Mitchell's writing was clipped to the drawing. She looked at Mrs. Rule.

"Would you please read this to me?"

Pulling her glasses down from the top of her head, Mary Rule took the letter.

" 'My darling Susannah,' " she read, her voice expressionless, " 'We all miss you and think of you often, but we know you are in a new place and it will be much better for you. As you know, things have changed a lot since Mr. Mitchell died. Now there will be another big change for us. We are moving to Harrisburg, Pennsylvania, so we can be near my sister and her husband. You never met them, but they are very nice people. All the children send you their love, and we promise to write to you. Please write back to us. Our new address is below.' " Mrs. Rule's eyes skipped down the page. " 'Be a good girl. I love you. Ruth Mitchell.' "

Susannah quietly took the piece of paper back. "Thank you."

She went into her room and carefully put the drawing and letter into the two-drawer chest over by the window, laying them flat beneath her socks and underwear. Pennsylvania. She had no idea where that was. Now the Mitchells were really and truly gone.

That day at the drugstore, Susannah found it especially difficult to sit quietly. Long finished with the coloring books, she was bored with the same few toys. She decided to investigate what was in some of the cartons piled up around her. Standing on a chair, she looked in the box on top of the nearest pile. Her eyes opened wide. It was full of toys, just waiting to replace the stock already out on display in the store. If she was very careful . . . She reached inside and pulled out a big blue-and-orange truck.

Getting down from the chair, she squatted and began to roll it along the floor, softly making engine noises. She pushed it faster, curving it around in circles, picking up speed. Intent on the truck, she didn't see the chair until she'd banged her head on it and sent the truck right into one of the legs. Slightly stunned, she rubbed her forehead and looked down. The front of the toy was dented and one of the orange wheels had come off. At that moment, the curtain was pulled aside and Mary Rule peered down at her.

"What was that noise?" she demanded.

Susannah looked up at her, but said nothing. The woman quickly took in the scene and pursed her lips in anger, then turned and left. Later, as Mr. and Mrs. Rule sat down for lunch, Susannah was surprised to see only a small apple at her place setting.

Mary Rule was watching her. "Where do you think the money comes from to pay for that truck you broke?" Her tone was cold.

"I don't know," Susannah answered, her voice little more than a whisper.

"From our pockets, that's where." The woman bit into her bologna sandwich. "Maybe next time you'll think twice about destroying things that don't belong to you."

Susannah ate the apple, sitting quietly until the Rules had finished eating and gone back to their customers.

Mommy, Daddy, do you see me? she asked silently. Please come for me.

It was later than usual when they closed up the drugstore that night, and the sky had already turned dark. Seeing Mr. Rule holding four small paper bags with their yellow prescription receipts stapled on, Susannah realized they still weren't on their way home. Her heart sank. Breakfast had been at six-fifteen, and she'd had only that apple since. The hunger pangs in her stomach had been growing stronger all afternoon. By now her head was hurting from lack of food. Four deliveries could mean more than an hour before they got back to the house. Tears of frustration stung her eyes.

Arthur Rule stopped the car in front of a large white house with a long flower-lined walkway leading to the front door. Susannah took the bag he handed her. She went up the walk and rang the doorbell, repeating to herself over and over "five dollars and fifty cents" so she wouldn't forget. An elderly woman opened the door and smiled at the little girl.

"Oh, my pills. Thank goodness. Come in for a minute while I get my wallet," she said, ushering Susannah into the foyer.

A delicious aroma of food filled the air. From where she stood, Susannah could see a gray-haired man sitting in front of the television set, watching the news as he ate his dinner from a snack table before him. Another snack table was set out in front of the chair next to him, where his wife must have been sitting when Susannah rang the doorbell. Susannah's hunger intensified as she took in the smell and watched the man cutting up a thick slice of rare roast beef. Just then, the woman returned and counted out the correct amount of money.

As she turned to go, Susannah noticed that the kitchen was through the doorway to the left. She was suddenly struck by an idea.

"Excuse me, ma'am," she said politely, "but may I use your bathroom?"

The woman smiled at her. "Certainly, dearie. It's through the door there."

Susannah headed in that direction, but waited in front of the bathroom door, watching as the woman rejoined her husband in the living room. Satisfied that they were both once more engrossed in the news, Susannah hurried into the kitchen several feet away. There it was: a big, juicy rib roast sitting on a cutting board on top of the counter. Her heart was pounding wildly but, terrified as she was, she acted quickly. Standing on her toes, she picked up the large carving knife next to it and carefully cut off a thick slice of meat. At that moment, she was thankful that her chores at the Rules' had taught her enough to handle such a big knife.

She stuffed the meat into her skirt pocket. As soon as she got home, she would wash the skirt out in the bathroom sink to eliminate any trace of the smell that might linger.

"Thank you very much," she called out to the couple as she headed for their front door, so afraid her voice trembled. "I can let myself out."

The woman turned in her chair and smiled again at her. "You're very welcome. Good night."

Grateful for the darkness outside, Susannah waited a moment for her heart to stop banging. She walked as slowly as she dared down the long path back to the car, wolfing down the meat as she went. It tasted wonderful. She smiled, her stomach finally satisfied.

"What took you so long?" Arthur Rule asked in a peevish voice as Susannah opened the rear door and climbed in.

She handed the money to Mrs. Rule, then sat back. Now she understood. She would have to take care of herself. All alone. She couldn't expect anyone else to help her. But no matter how bad her life was with the Rules, she would make it come out all right. And one day, she would find her *real* parents. Then everything would be the way it was supposed to be.

Chapter 8

Cameron smiled in satisfaction as his eyes opened. He looked around the room, still strange to him, given how little attention he'd paid the night before. Tish and he had never spent much time at her parents' Greenwich estate, but the guest room bore out every fantasy he'd carried around for the months they'd been dating. White lace curtains fashioned the May sunlight into golden stripes across the foot of the bed. Dogwood trees in full bloom peeked through the windows. The Malmquists had left copies of *Great Expectations* and *Treasure Island* on the plain oak bedside table for the pleasure of their guests. The polished parquet floor was bare except for an elegantly faded blue Persian carpet lying between two wing chairs covered in a heavy floral pattern. Everything he saw reflected generations of wealth and ease.

He lifted his eyes to the sunshine and stretched to his full height under the white percale sheets. A fine place for a wedding, the right kind of place. Sixty or so people in the garden, a string quartet playing Mozart and Brahms. Not like that damn festival at the Pierre where his first wedding had been. Cameron grimaced at the memory. The huge crowds of people, dancing and eating until the crack of dawn. How little he had known then, all impressed with Kailey's father, with his political cronies and his foreign friends. No class, no style. No taste.

Not like this. Over one hundred acres of prime Greenwich land, trees that dated back to the American Revolution. Hell, the family practically went back to the *Mayflower*. And it was exactly what he deserved. His satisfied smile began to sour as images of Kailey early in their marriage came into his mind, long-buried memories of the time she seemed like a beautiful princess out of a fairy tale. He caught himself immediately. Sure, Kailey was beautiful, but so was Tish. And she knew precisely how a woman should act. Kailey was so helpless, especially in the beginning. She never seemed to learn the rules — how to run a big house, how to handle the help properly; she was always ironing a blouse herself or running off to the supermarket for something. She was too, well, *interested* in things, too friendly, with the neighbors, with the maid.

He thought of Tish's cool blond beauty, the face so classy it demanded not one touch of makeup. From the night he met her at a business associate's dinner party the previous year, his attention was held by her graciousness and poise, her gentle laugh, her ability to draw him out, making certain not to disagree with him. She was so feminine.

He'd been so naive when he selected Kailey for his wife, assuming she'd be his ticket into society. Now he understood — Kailey could provide access only to Jewish social circles, to the nouveau riche. Tish was the real thing.

He forced his feet to the floor and pulled his long body out of bed. If Kailey weren't dead, he'd have had to divorce her. Frowning at the thought, he made his way to the window, looking out through the trees across the huge expanse of green lawn. Tish was like this house. Understated but lovely. That's what the rest of his life would be. His illegal activities were over. His baby-food company had been transformed into the Hawkes Corporation, every penny it made legitimate. And today, his personal life was about to match his professional success.

He had no intention of rushing the day's events. No, every minute was to be savored. He caught sight of a finch pecking at one of the bird feeders set up in the branches of a white birch. Barely discernible a hundred yards or so behind the tree was the white clapboard chapel the Malmquists had used every Sunday for generations. Today, he would attend the only religious service that could possibly matter to him — his wedding to Tish Malmquist Gardiner, the culmination of months — no, years — of careful planning.

The silent perfection of the morning was suddenly punctured by the sound of a bicycle horn, blaring again and again as Tish's eleven-year-old son from her first marriage, Evan, rounded the side of the house and began to circle the yard, faster and faster, pushing harder at the horn with every curve he turned.

What an annoying brat, Cameron thought, as he opened the window and called out. "Stop that racket, Evan. You'll wake everyone in the house."

The boy glanced at him, but didn't even bother to slow down, shouting back loudly, "Mom and Grandma are already eating breakfast, and Granddad is playing golf. The only one sleeping is you."

With that, the boy followed his path around the sitting area outside Cameron's window and pushed on toward the chapel. As he rode away, he looked back over his shoulder at Cameron only long enough to add, "But I guess you're already up."

Rage swept through Cameron like a forest fire, but he quickly willed himself back to calm. A few months more, he thought, and I'll be able to solve the Evan Gardiner problem.

Evan continued his noisy ride to the chapel, then stopped at the sight of delivery trucks pulling up the driveway. Leaning on the handlebars, he watched the parade of floral arrangements being placed around the east lawn. Ten round tables had been put there the night before, and were now being covered with white tablecloths. He'd seen his grandparents entertain a couple of other times since he and his mother had come to live with them, but nothing like this.

Usually, he was bored by such events, but he didn't feel bored today. More like furious. This was the day his Little League team could have regained first place, and he was the player they counted on the most. And he wasn't even allowed to go for a few innings before the stupid wedding ceremony started. But it was more than just that. Ever since his mother had started dating this Hawkes guy, he'd been afraid that she would end up marrying him. Why couldn't she see what a scuz he was! When they first started going out, Cameron acted real nice to him, always talking to him and bringing him stuff. But Evan wasn't stupid. He could see that this guy was a fake from a mile away, nice in front of Mom or Grandma, bringing him a ten-speed bike, a radio, a tennis racquet, but cold and mean when they were alone. Evan couldn't believe his mother. She couldn't see what was happening. But he could. Cameron Hawkes hated him. No question about it.

Evan began pedaling toward the long curved driveway, quietly and slowly. He couldn't stop worrying about Cameron. The guy had plans for the future, and Evan was sure they didn't include him. He knew his mom loved him, but he had the feeling that after the wedding this afternoon, things would never be the same.

The rush of longing came unexpectedly. There in his mind's eye was the picture of his father, running behind him, holding onto the back of the bicycle seat, teaching him how to ride in the park a few blocks from their house in Alexandria. Bill Gardiner had been so proud when Evan mastered it so quickly. He remembered riding away on his own almost immediately, then returning to find his parents kissing. He'd been mortified at the time; now it filled him with a feeling so sweet it was painful.

Evan was only eight when his father died but he remembered everything about him — how he looked, how he sounded, even how he smelled. He could picture him on their trip to the Tetons the summer before he died, riding up the funicular. Evan would never have said anything out loud, but he'd been scared stiff rising up so many thousands of feet over the vast mountain range. His father had put his arms around him as they stood together in the small cable car, describing some of the rock formations and flowers, talking about the founding of Jackson Hole just a few miles away until Evan was too interested to feel frightened anymore. Bill Gardiner had that effect on people; he made them laugh and forget the stuff that scared them. Especially Mom, Evan realized. When his father was alive he would laugh her out of her frightened moments.

Since his death, Mom had been quiet all the time. Moving back in with her parents seemed to have taken the spirit out of her. Evan could see her pulling back further and further into herself. Not that she didn't get along with Grandma and Granddad. Grandma was always doing something in that efficient way of hers. Superchief, Granddad called her. She would walk a couple of miles every morning, make lists of activities over her six-thirty breakfast and spend all day accomplishing whatever she set out to do. It probably was just easier for Mom to let Grandma do everything.

Evan would try to cheer her up, try to get her moving. So would Grandma and Granddad, in their own understated way. But he watched his mother fade month after month. In fact, it was only when this Hawkes guy showed up that she began to get a little spirit back.

At first Evan was glad to see his mom smiling again. She was up earlier in the morning. She and Grandma would go around together, both of them energetic and cheerful. He knew his mom felt better, and he was prepared to like Cameron Hawkes. Until he met him.

He might only be eleven, he could tell that Cameron was a phony. Evan could swear his grandparents agreed with his assessment, although they never said anything.

"Give him a chance," his mom would respond when he'd try to explain to her what was so clear to him. "He's been awfully generous and good to you. The bike, the day trips. He wants to adopt you, honey. He loves you."

His mom was so sweet, so hopeful. But what a sap. Cameron didn't love him. He wondered if Cameron even loved his mother.

Evan pedaled furiously down the gravel driveway. Slowly his anger melted into fear. He could take care of himself, no matter how far away Cameron managed to send him. But his mother was a different story. Who's going to watch out for her? he worried, honking furiously as he again circled the guest room window.

The persistent sound of Evan's bicycle horn rang through the open windows of the dining room. Oh God, he'll wake Cameron, Tish thought, torn by the obvious distance between her fiancé and her son. Things had been so easy when Bill was alive. Her parents had hated it when she married a lumberman's son from Oregon, but how wrong they'd turned out to be. Everything about her life with Bill had been wonderful — their tiny cottage in Virginia, Evan's birth, the slow but steady growth of Bill's client list as his reputation grew. He had begun to be known as an independent and highly ethical attorney, the smart, decent guy people wanted on their side. Even the big companies and government agencies he fought against on behalf of his clients had begun to hold him in high esteem, recognizing a worthy opponent.

Everything, even those things her parents had warned her about, turned out just right. Money had stopped being a problem, they'd made good friends, Bill had been an ideal father to Evan, and with almost a decade of marriage behind them, Tish and Bill had remained passionately attracted to each other. Then the hideous moment when at only thirty-five Bill suffered a heart attack, instantly fatal, turning Tish's life into a nightmare.

With mortgage payments and private school bills, and no one in line to continue Bill's law practice, Tish found herself unable to cope. Within weeks, she had moved back to Connecticut, back to the smoothly run estate of her perfectly-turned-out parents. The town had always treated her father like an honorary king, and his air of impersonal generosity and friendliness helped keep that attitude alive even now that he was near eighty. And he'd been decent enough to his daughter. It was just that there never seemed to be any difference between his feelings for her and his feelings for the complete strangers to whom he was so terribly gracious.

As for her mother, Anne Malmquist could be found heading every volunteer drive, teaching flower arranging to the younger women who lived in the housing developments she privately referred to as "ticky-tack," shopping for several elderly outpatients from the local hospital, remembering birthdays of people she hardly spoke to. Never stopping, always giving, always cheerful, Anne Malmquist was a role model for everyone within a fifty-mile radius. But all of her energy and efficiency made her daughter feel inept and alone.

In fact, the only time her parents had seemed to notice Tish was when they threatened to cut her off for marrying Bill Gardiner. When Bill died, and Tish had moved back into the house with Evan, her parents hadn't referred to their previous disapproval, and Tish was grateful. But they hadn't said much about anything else either. Certainly her unhappiness as a recent widow and her fears for Evan's future had gone unmentioned. When her mother spoke, it was about the new buds she'd noticed on her morning walk or the shrubbery on the west lawn.

Tish looked across the table at her mother, who was reading the *Times* as she finished her cinnamon toast. Anne Malmquist had already showered after her two-mile walk, outlined the order of service to the wedding caterer, and personally overseen the delivery of floral arrangements. At eight in the morning, her day was in high gear.

She envied her mother's purpose, but Tish wished just this once that her mother's executive brilliance in the domestic sphere might extend to real emotion. Somehow all that drive managed to leave Tish feeling stranded, and right now she needed a friend.

"Mom," she said hesitantly, "I know you and Dad weren't happy about Bill and me, but what about this time? Neither of you has said very much."

The expression on her mother's face was frightening. Rarely

did the older woman register strong feelings, but the naked hostility was all too obvious.

"You didn't care what we thought the first time, Patricia," she said coldly, "so why would it matter to you now?"

Tish held out little hope of her mother's sympathy, but this was too important; she tried again. "Please, Mother, whatever our disagreements about Bill, I'm very concerned about Evan and Cameron. I've been so lonely . . . well, I'm afraid I might have made a hasty choice."

The last thing Anne Malmquist intended to do was coddle her only child. Three years ago, they had taken her back in, and now they were making her another wedding, a magnificent one. Tish had made her biggest mistake years before, marrying that nobody. Now the girl was on her own. At least this time, she had picked a man who could pay his way. Carefully folding her linen napkin on the table in front of her and pushing her chair away, Anne regarded her daughter with polite disinterest.

"You're a grown woman now, dear. I'm sure whatever you decide will be fine." With that, she left the dining room, listing to herself the numerous tasks she had to perform before the noon ceremony was due to begin.

Tish stared at her cup of coffee, wishing out loud it would turn into wine.

"You drink entirely too much as it is." Her mother's voice surprised her through the doorway. That wasn't exactly the kind of attention she'd been asking for, though actually Tish agreed with her; she'd been drinking a lot since Bill's death. But being caught made her feel like a naughty child.

His hair still wet from the shower, jeans and a red crewneck sweater emphasizing his good looks, Cameron came into the dining room. "Just some toast, please," he said to the butler, as he leaned over to give Tish a kiss.

"How did you sleep?" Tish smiled up at his touch, hoping he hadn't heard her mother's comment.

"Fine," he replied, taking the chair next to hers and pouring himself a cup of coffee from the silver urn in the center of the table. "That is, until your son began his symphony."

Tish laughed. "I'm sorry, darling. Did he wake you?"

"I guess I should be grateful he didn't murder me in my sleep."

Cameron saw at once how relieved Tish was that he was joking about it. His relationship with her son had never been good. Evan had taken an instant dislike to him, which was to be expected. He could see her hoping it would soften, that the boy's resentment would fade. But obviously even Tish knew that wasn't happening. Since the announcement of their wedding, Evan had been openly hateful. Cameron sensed that this was the moment to speak.

"You know, Tish, perhaps we should take his behavior a little more seriously." He reached for her hand as he spoke. "It's bad for a boy, being so close to his mother. He should be away, growing up around other boys. That's what a good prep school is for."

The indecision in Tish's eyes was plain. Cameron could see the pull between what her son wanted and what her new husband would need. It was time to throw in all his ammunition.

"Darling, I want Evan to be my son too. I want to adopt him, to give him the father he lost."

Tish was moved by his words. "Oh, Cameron, I've wanted so much for the two of you to love each other. Bill was a hero to him." She stopped when she saw the small look of irritation at the mention of her first husband's name. Somehow whenever she felt most loving, she seemed unable to express it without doing something wrong. She cleared her throat and tried again to let him know how happy he was making her. "If the three of us are a real family, I'll be the happiest woman in the world."

Cameron smiled at her. "I promise it, darling. Evan deserves his own friends, his own activities. He can never do that with you around; he feels too responsible for you."

He watched her take in the truth of his words. Now, if he could move her one step further. "The biggest favor we can give Evan is to send him away to a great camp and a great prep school. He'll make friends who'll last him a lifetime. Living with his grandparents, spending all his time with us, it's just not fair to him."

Tish felt so torn. What was the right thing to do? Everything had been so easy when Bill was alive. Now each decision seemed monumental, impossible. It made her breathless with anxiety. "I'll think about it later, honey," she said, pushing her chair back and walking into the kitchen.

Cameron laughed. "You'll have other things to think about later, dear. In about four hours, we'll be standing in front of Reverend McNaught, saying I do."

"We certainly will," Tish answered softly.

Chapter 9

"**B**y 1986, Compass Systems will have surpassed every other American computer service in terms of economy and service. By 1987, it will make even the Japanese companies pale not just in those terms, but in quality as well." Delmore Byar leaned into his audience so enthusiastically his highly polished black tassled loafers were almost perpendicular to the floor. In the enormous living room, his booming voice seemed to bounce off the domed ceiling.

Kailey translated the message of the enthusiastic young engineer from Chicago to the largely Italian crowd in a more modulated tone, pausing after each phrase and making Byar's statements more palatable to the Roman businessmen gathered in a large circle around him. Business in Rome was conducted in a different rhythm, marked by courteous speech and personal charm. The glitz of a Los Angeles trade show or a bombastic television campaign would be wasted here. Kailey didn't think much about the actual words she was translating, yet she conveyed the speaker's intention with intelligence and seriousness. Since her three years of training at the *Istituto Internazionale*, her natural facility with languages had enabled her to make a steady income. She was one of a small number of Americans working in Rome as interpreters, and now she had proved her usefulness to the point that she was busy nearly every day. Hired on a free-lance basis by American companies, news magazines, even the American Embassy, which was sponsoring today's event, she easily altered the aggressive spiels of energetic American companies to the more elegant and reserved style of the Italians.

Byar was winding down his presentation, and Kailey's translation of his final sales points evoked scattered applause around the room. As several of his listeners came forward for informal discussion, Kailey began to inch toward the doorway. She looked around for the butler who had taken her coat when she arrived, but he was nowhere in sight. The hosts tonight were close friends of Ben and Risa Gottlieb, and Kailey herself had been in this apartment many times, so she decided to retrieve her own coat.

The massive living room led through an equally massive dining room, an only slightly smaller sitting room, and around to the family quarters, where James Interro, the Deputy Chief of Mission, and his wife, Gillian, spent most of their private time with their three small children. Kailey had gotten to know Jim and Gillian fairly well, but before this she'd stuck to the formal entertaining rooms. As DCM, Jim Interro and his family were automatically housed in one of Rome's grandest apartments. There was a price, though — namely, having to give party after party on behalf of American companies, to be gracious and welcoming to an army of strangers. Within their own rooms, though, Kailey saw how they really lived as a family. In the area that had been screened off from the party, she saw toys and dolls strewn all over the couches and chairs. The furniture here was worn and decidedly American.

Past the long racks holding all the coats was an open door

to a small bathroom, where Kailey spied two little girls, perched precariously on the closed toilet lid, applying lipstick and eye shadow as they admired themselves in the high mirror. Each was dressed in a fur coat, obviously taken from one of the racks.

Kailey felt caught between laughter and sadness as she took in the scene. They must have been six or so, just the age her daughter would have been, one blond, one dark, both in party dresses under their borrowed splendor. Kailey might have laughed delightedly watching the two play grown-up if she hadn't felt as if her heart were breaking. She was prepared for the dreams that still haunted her almost every night — Bonnie in her crib as she remembered her, Bonnie as she might have been at three or at five if she had been allowed to live. Kailey was used to that pain; she expected it. But coming upon these little girls without warning was too much. She just couldn't bear it.

Forgetting about her coat, Kailey turned to go. Just then, she heard a man's voice coming from the hallway.

"Becky, BECKY! Where are you? It's time to get going."

Kailey turned back to the children and, sure enough, one of them had dropped the lipstick she was using and was wiping at her face with a towel. She watched the child climb down and run past her toward the hallway.

"I'm here, Daddy. I'm all ready. We were just playing. I wasn't doing anything wrong, honest I wasn't."

Her ingenuous denial made Kailey smile in spite of herself. As the girl's father marched his daughter back toward the bathroom, Kailey could see that he was smiling as well.

"Perhaps if you return that very expensive coat and wipe the showgirl makeup off your face, I'll buy that part about your not doing anything wrong."

Suddenly the man caught Kailey's eye in the bathroom mirror. "Well, hello," he said easily to her reflection. "I see we have a witness."

With those words, he removed the fur from his daughter's shoulders and hung it carefully on a padded hanger, inspecting it for a few seconds to make sure no lasting harm had been done.

Kailey felt awkward, as if she'd been caught observing something she had no right to see. Quickly she found her black wool jacket, and began to walk out of the room without even stopping to pull it on.

The man recognized her immediately as the interpreter, and he couldn't imagine why this competent young woman should suddenly seem so ill at ease. Looking more closely at her, he realized she was quite pretty, and familiar somehow. The reporter in him was aroused; he was damned if he was going to let her get away so fast.

Shifting his position so he stood between her and the door, he held out his hand, preventing her from leaving. "You're the translator, right?"

Kailey nodded.

"I'm Max Canfield, and the hooligan is Rebecca Canfield."

The little girl giggled at her father, while her friend joined them in the bedroom, demanding equal attention.

"I'm Courtney Interro and I live here." The girl's voice left no doubt as to who was in charge on these premises.

Kailey was desperate to leave. She'd worked three jobs that day, the first at the airport at six in the morning, and now, after the late party, her fatigue had left her even more vulnerable than usual to the feelings these little girls evoked in her. And this man, so vibrant, so *American*, felt a little too familiar for comfort. Yet she realized she couldn't leave without replying, so she put out her hand.

"Kailey Davids. How do you do."

"Why, you're American. How did you come to be a translator for an embassy event? I thought these jobs were always filled by Italians."

There was nothing Kailey wanted less than a long discussion of her interpreting skills. "Just luck, really," she said briefly.

Again the man stood so that to pass him would be awkward, almost rude. "You know, you look familiar. Not just from today. I could swear we've met before."

"I don't think so."

"No, I'm sure we have. In fact, I bet it was right here at one of the Interros' parties."

"That could be." Kailey edged around him as she gave her neutral responses, but Max Canfield wasn't making it easy.

Max had begun to enjoy this game. Just as he could get answers out of heads of state who hadn't intended to say anything, he wasn't about to let this woman go before he got what he wanted. And right now what he wanted was to figure out what was bothering this exceptionally attractive girl.

"Perhaps it was at the Halloween party last year? Or maybe Thanksgiving?"

"I don't think I was here for either of those parties," she responded politely, trying to maneuver past him.

Kailey wasn't the only one dying to get out of the room. Rebecca Canfield was impatient. This was supposed to be her time with her father. Playing with Courtney Interro while Daddy worked was one thing; now she wanted to get home and have him all to herself.

"Daddy, can we have hamburgers for dinner?" Rebecca considered this her trump card. With all the fabulous food in Rome, hamburgers were the one thing her father loved that he rarely got to eat. She didn't like them particularly herself, so on the occasions her father ate at home, she usually forced pizza or yet another plate of pasta on him. But right now even a hamburger would be okay. She wanted her father, and she wanted him alone.

Max was much too involved in his flirtation with Kailey to even hear what his daughter was saying. *Why is this woman so eager to get out of here?* No wedding ring, none of the feel of having to get home to someone, that aura he had learned to sense in his years as a widower.

"You worked awfully hard in there tonight, and you must be starving. Why don't you join us for a little dinner? I'll get you home early, I promise."

"Daddy!"

Kailey could hear the frustration in the little girl's voice.

"Thanks, but I can't tonight," Kailey said, touched by the relief she saw on Rebecca's face.

But Max remained oblivious to his daughter's drama. Not so fast, he thought, still blocking the doorway. "Well, that's fine.

We'll do it some other night. Now, I'll just drop you wherever you're going."

"No, really, that's not necessary. I live only a few blocks from here, and I can use the walk."

Max pointed out the large window. "It's pouring," he said. "You can't possibly walk in this weather."

Dismayed, Kailey realized he was right. The rain was coming down in thick sheets, flooding the rounded driveway visible from where she stood. Besides, riding with them would also give her another few minutes with Rebecca. Kailey had hardly been able to take her eyes off her. Bonnie would be almost the same age. Would she be as mischievous, as energetic? Would she have displayed that same open yearning for her father if Cameron had been a man like Max Canfield? Kailey shuddered involuntarily at the thought of Cameron. Quickly she agreed to leave with the Canfields.

In the car, she was silent, but Max filled the spaces easily, talking about himself and his career as bureau chief for *Time* magazine's Rome office. He'd been widowed when Rebecca was born, and had accepted the assignment in Europe only a few months later. During the ride to Kailey's apartment, Max again invited her to join them for dinner, but she demurred.

He accepted her refusal gracefully, but teasingly insisted she take a selection of old issues of *Time* piled up in the back seat so she'd think about him in the coming weeks.

The phone was ringing as Kailey walked into her apartment. She was relieved to hear Ben's voice.

"Come on over, darling. There's a veal chop on its way to the oven and it has your name on it."

Kailey couldn't help laughing. The sound of his voice was just what she needed tonight. But even the thought of Risa and Ben couldn't pull her out of herself.

"Sorry, Ben, but the veal chop will have to assume some other identity. I'm staying right where I am."

She could hear Risa encouraging him in the background as he repeated his invitation, but finally Kailey convinced him of her seriousness, and they hung up.

Kailey undressed as soon as she got off the phone, and climbed in to her bed, not even stopping to eat anything. She still felt unsettled by her encounter with Max and Rebecca. Too distraught to sleep, she began to browse through the copies of *Time* that Max had given her.

Kailey read the *International Herald Tribune* regularly, so the news itself was familiar. But the American magazine's slant was different from the global focus to which she had become accustomed. And the people named in feature articles were completely unfamiliar to her. Only six years away, and so much has changed, she thought, tossing the issue she was reading aside and picking up one from just two weeks before.

Suddenly an image appeared that wasn't foreign at all. It was a large black-and-white photo of Cameron Hawkes, plus three full columns of a business report. There he was, smiling confidently from the page. For one crazy moment, Kailey felt he was there in the room with her, smiling at her alone. Gathering her wits, she read the article frantically, barely breathing until she reached the end.

The photo showed Cameron in front of Little Angel's new warehouse in Dallas, Texas. As the article explained, this was major economic news. Little Angel had become the number-one baby-food manufacturer in the country. According to *Time,* the warehouse opening would add millions of dollars to the Texas economy. And just four months before, he had donated two million dollars for a new wing to the children's hospital in Fort Worth. There was another man in the picture, alongside Cameron. Reading the photo's caption, she saw that it was the Texas lieutenant governor, only too pleased to be standing next to the state's financial benefactor.

So Cameron had succeeded in every way. The money was his, the power was his, the fancy friends and national respect. He had walked away with everything. The thought of it filled her with rage. She imagined herself going to the phone, telling someone — anyone — everything she knew.

But just as quickly she realized how fruitless it would be. If she had feared his power before, now he was practically a national icon. Sick to her stomach, she realized that Ben and Risa had been right years ago. No one would believe her, and who knew what he could do to her with all his newfound power.

Sleep that night was impossible. In dream after dream she relived her life with Bonnie and Cameron. There was Bonnie, peacefully breast-feeding in the early hours of the morning with the sun just beginning to rise over the New York skyline, Bonnie again, a couple of months older, lying awake in her crib, giggling as she reached for the colorful clowns of the mobile dangling above her.

Then there were the dreams about Cameron. In Kailey's uneasy sleep he was chasing her down a long hallway, a knife in his hand, and she was just a few yards in front of him, the distance between them quickly closing.

But the most disturbing dream of all came just before dawn. Cameron became her husband as he had been, not the man who murdered people, but the lover who touched her sexual core, who excited her for the first time.

Kailey felt betrayed by her dreams, and forced herself out of bed and out of the house well before five in the morning. She walked quickly over the *San Pietrini,* the tiny square cobblestones that covered most of the ground in Rome. The front of the Spanish Steps was deserted, devoid of the huge crowds that gathered every day. Fifteen minutes later she found herself in the Piazza Navona. It, too, was empty. No groups of youngsters eating *gelato* or fashionable women drinking tiny cups of espresso. Exhausted, Kailey looked for a place to sit down, noticing that the tables and chairs always crowded together during the day had been stacked on the sides of the various *gelaterie.* She walked over to one of the three fountains in the center of the piazza, and gratefully seated herself on the short wall surrounding one of Bernini's white stone masterpieces. She ran her hands over the cool hard surface, as if the solid mass could ground her, could make the pictures she had carried from her dreams go away.

Finally the images of Cameron and Bonnie faded, but in their place came the unsettling thought of Max Canfield and his adorable little daughter. No, she thought, never again would she allow herself to get so dangerously close to a man. If this kind of pain was what it would bring to her, she had no intention of inviting that in. And if there was pleasure to be missed, so be it.

Less than a month later, thoughts of Max Canfield made her refuse an invitation from Jim Interro for his Fourth of July celebration. Although she hadn't admitted it to Max, she *had* gone to many of the Interros' American parties. Perhaps she'd even seen Max among the crush of people always in attendance. But she had no intention of attending another party there and possibly running into him. When Gillian invited her to a good-bye lunch in early August, however, she figured it would be perfectly safe to accept.

Although Jim, as second in command at the American Embassy, was not allowed to lend his name to private organizations, his wife, Gillian, had been active in an international human rights organization called the World Peace Foundation since they'd been stationed in Rome. Along with Ben and Risa, Kailey, too, had become actively involved in the same group. Meeting with Gillian over the years, spending long afternoons mailing off hundreds of letters to various governments around the world where political prisoners were being brutalized, Kailey and Gillian had become friends. Kailey didn't feel ready for an intimate friendship, but Gillian was an expert in the instant, affectionate camaraderie that foreign service personnel had to count on if they expected any companionship at all as they moved around from posting to posting.

Kailey felt unexpectedly sad when Gillian informed her that she and Jim would be leaving within the month. Jim's tenure as DCM was almost up and he was due back in Washington. Gillian would be taking the kids back to the small house they owned in Bethesda even before Jim followed them, so the girls would feel comfortable by the time school started.

Jim Interro had been one of Kailey's favorite employers, easily throwing off the formal behavior necessary in public when the two saw each other privately, and she knew she was really going to miss him. She wasn't looking forward to Jim's successor, who was due to start the following month. An older, more conventional diplomatic type had been given the post, and his reign would probably usher in an era of more pomp and less good sense.

Not that it would really make much of a difference to Kailey. After her rigorous training at the language academy and the expert way she'd performed since, she'd had little trouble establishing herself. In fact, the demand for her services was growing. She found herself turning some jobs down. When she heard that the Interros were due to return home, she realized with relief that if Jim's replacement proved difficult, she could simply choose other work.

Gillian sounded philosophical about their impending move. In Washington, Jim would once again be a mid-level functionary within the State Department. Perhaps another glamorous posting would come their way, perhaps not.

"What do you think the kids make of all this?" Kailey asked, as the two sat down for their farewell lunch, indicating the valuable paintings lining every wall and the two butlers just entering with elegantly arranged plates of seafood salad.

"Well, Leila knows what real life is like. You know, at nine, they take in everything. And after all, she remembers living in Bethesda before we were posted to Rome. For Courtney, I don't know, it may be a rude awakening, finding out that she's the one responsible for making her bed and clearing the table." Gillian lifted her eyes to the ceiling. "I don't know how she'll take the change in housing. Our entire home could fit in the living room here."

Gillian took a bite of salad, still thinking about her younger daughter. "I think the kids have always known that these years are a kind of make-believe. The real problem for my little one is going to be losing her friend Rebecca. She practically lives here. They've been inseparable for four years now."

Kailey changed the subject quickly from Rebecca Canfield, moving on to the World Peace Foundation. "Is there an active unit in the Washington area?" she asked.

But Gillian was more interested in discussing the Rome branch of the organization, for the first time sounding critical of its most active member, Carlo Giantonio, a close friend of Ben and Risa's whom Kailey had never warmed to either.

"Honestly, Kailey," Gillian confided, "no matter how many hours he spends talking about human rights, it's hard to believe he really cares much."

Gillian warmed to her subject until Kailey suddenly noticed the time out of the corner of her eye. "Oh God, it's almost three. I have a job at the embassy in twenty minutes."

Reluctantly the two women walked back through the huge living room, through the formal sitting room, into the enormous entrace foyer. Just as they were saying their final good-byes, the doorbell sounded. At the first ring, Rebecca Canfield came bounding out of the bedroom area on the other side of the foyer.

"Daddy, Daddy!" The little girl ran up to the entrance and threw open the tall heavy doors as if they were made of paper.

To Kailey's dismay, there was Max Canfield, who smiled as soon as he noticed her standing there. "Well, what do you know, it must be my lucky day."

What can I possibly think I'm doing?

Kailey stared miserably at the untouched slice of *pizza con funghi* lying across her plate. Max's voice continued in his intimate tone, as if she were staring into his eyes, inhaling his every word.

"So when Fran died, I asked my editor if the magazine could send me to Europe, away from all of it. It was just too damn sad. And Rebecca and I have done pretty well." Max's voice took on a professional tone. "You know, labor costs in Rome are higher than anywhere else in Italy, but next to any city in the USA, it's almost nothing. . . ."

His voice went on and on, but Kailey could hardly follow the words. She had allowed herself to be coaxed into dating Max, at first because it had been too embarrassing to refuse with Gillian standing right there, then because Ben and Risa had insisted she go out one more time. *You deserve some fun. You need it.* They refused to leave her alone until she said yes.

That's the real problem, she admitted to herself. She actually liked Max. It was fun to stroll in front of the Pantheon after dark accompanied by a handsome man, part of a couple within the sea of married Italians who gathered there to pass a pleasant evening. Fun to listen to him talk about *Time* and the interesting political stories he'd covered since he'd been in Europe. More than that, she admitted to herself, it was heaven to hear him talk about Rebecca — what the six-year-old did in school, who her new best friend was since Courtney Interro had moved away, what games she'd learned from her new baby-sitter.

She hoped Max didn't notice her fascination with Rebecca. Kailey had decided that, if at all possible, she would never spend time with Max when his daughter was with him. It was too painful. She couldn't bear the nightmares she would be inviting about Bonnie if she allowed herself to become attached to an adorable little girl the same age. Besides, with Max's busy schedule, there wasn't much time for father and daughter. The last thing Rebecca needed was some woman sharing the all-too-occasional spotlight. Kailey had noticed the girl's attachment to Max immediately. "How do you manage to get enough time with her?" she'd asked him the first time they'd gone out.

His answer had sounded casual enough. *Oh, she's such an independent kid. And besides, everyone here is ITALIAN. They adore kids. For the last few years, between Courtney and our housekeeper, I think Rebecca was happier when I wasn't around.*

Kailey had laughed as she was meant to do, but she knew how much pain had to lie behind his words. He loved his daughter; it had to be awful losing a wife so young, then having a job that kept him so busy he barely had a weekend free for Rebecca.

Kailey heard Max's voice shift back to the intimate, seductive tone that was making her feel as if she couldn't breathe. The photograph of a friar digging into a plate of fettucine, the signature of La Sacrestia's colorful menu, seemed to be swimming in front of her eyes, the turquoise tiles on the wall shimmering in the dim light. *So that's the real problem. You're attracted to Max. You want him as much as he wants you.*

Kailey allowed her eyes to travel over his face. The clear eyes, the confident manner. It was exciting to be with him, to have his arm casually draped over her shoulders, to smell the unfamiliar after-shave lotion as he leaned across her to open the car door. More than exciting to feel connected to someone. Risa and Ben were like parents to her. But that was different. This was a *man*.

Like Cameron. The thought made her shudder.

"Are you okay?" Max was instantly alert.

"I'm fine. Really."

Max noticed the uneaten pizza on her plate. "Listen, I've been doing all the talking, and you're still not doing any eating."

"I'm not very hungry. How about taking a walk?"

"Sounds great." Max was happy to comply. He found this woman enigmatic. Maybe a walk would help her relax.

Within minutes they had become part of the swarm of people roaming through the Roman streets. Walking slowly, Max took her hand, sending a chill of pleasure through Kailey. How long had it been since she'd felt that? After a while, they found themselves in the Piazza Navona, and as if by magic, Max stopped in front of the very fountain where Kailey had sworn to keep him away.

But in the moonlight, Max's hand brushing hers, his other beginning to stroke the side of her face, Kailey felt her resolve slipping. As his mouth came down over hers, she couldn't protect herself from the feelings he evoked. His lips were soft at first, gently exploring her mouth. But gradually the kiss deepened, his tongue insistent. And she found herself all too willing, her arms winding around his neck, her breasts arching into his chest.

Later that night, when he lay with her in her spartan apartment, she took pleasure in his rough passion as her sheets and blankets fell to the floor. It had been so long since she'd had a man beside her, years of loneliness. His mouth engulfed her mouth, his tongue along her throat, her breasts, her stomach, evoking sensations she never thought she'd feel again. When he moved his body over hers and entered her, she gasped, then clung to him as he pounded into her. When they finished, she saw the scratches her nails had left on his back, as if she had tried to get every bit of him inside her.

For a few minutes she had forgotten her fears and her sadness.

She burrowed into him in gratitude. Max was not a tall man, but his body was strong and compact. Her hands roamed all over his shoulders, his belly, his arms. Only after they'd made love again did she allow reality to return.

"You should be getting home," she said gently. "Rebecca will be up early."

"Adela is more than capable of taking care of my daughter," he chuckled, taking her hand and guiding it back to his body. "I'm the only one who can take care of you."

It wasn't until Max left in the morning that Cameron's face came again into her mind, reminding her of her sadness; yet later that night, it was Max she dreamed of, happily lying in his arms, finally letting herself into the light.

She saw Max every weekend after their first night together, even a few evenings right after he'd made the exhausting weekly deadline for copy and photos to be sent by pouch to *Time* headquarters in New York. She invariably asked about Rebecca, but was always secretly relieved that Max never chose to include the child in their plans. Of course, he couldn't have known why it would be so painful for her, but nonetheless she was grateful.

Only when Max suggested a long weekend on the Amalfi coast, did Kailey finally urge that Rebecca come along. Max dismissed the idea.

"She'll be happier at home with Adela."

Kailey doubted that, but even though she had been the one to encourage it, the thought of watching the sweetly sassy little girl for three days in a row had been torture. Instead, the weekend gave Kailey a measure of happiness she hadn't known since she'd run from the United States. Hour after hour, they made love, drank wine, ate long meals of pasta and crispy shrimp straight from the sea. They talked about subjects they'd never had time for on their more hurried dates, even silly things like his passion for soccer and Marilyn Monroe in just about equal measure. He confided to her his interest in Eastern Europe, how he sometimes wished he could take a leave from the magazine and really focus on the links between the Soviets and their satellites, and explained to her how differently the Yugoslavs coped with the Soviet Union than did the Bulgarians. Max found politics endlessly amusing, and he readily entertained Kailey with a range of gossipy stories from his years as a reporter in Washington.

She enjoyed it all, but more fascinating to her was his finally opening up in a more personal way. She was surprised at his candor when he talked about his parents.

"My father's almost eighty now, not in such great health. He had a stroke a couple of years ago." Max was quiet for a moment, but when he started speaking again, it was with some bitterness. "You know, before, when he was strong, he was a pretty threatening guy, bored stiff on an assembly line. Every now and then, he'd take his boredom out on us with a strap."

Kailey was horrified, but Max laughed it off.

"It's funny now. He's almost jealous of my life. Well, he certainly didn't do much to help me make it, that's for sure."

"How about your mother?" Kailey's voice betrayed her sympathy.

Max looked pensive. "I guess she managed the best she could. But she's pretty elderly now. Doesn't say much and never did. She seems out of it most of the time."

"Maybe she's scared," Kailey suggested, not wanting to overstep her bounds, but slightly shocked by his words.

"Maybe so," Max agreed perfunctorily, moving away from the conversation with a shake of his head. "I guess neither of them ended up with the life they hoped for."

When he questioned her about her own past, Kailey was vague, quickly turning the conversation to another subject. He let her off surprisingly easily, which filled her with relief.

By the time he drove her back to Rome, she knew Max much better than she had; it was time to get to know his daughter.

"Next Friday, please bring Rebecca for dinner. I'll make a dish that children like, hot dogs or macaroni and cheese, something entirely American."

Max agreed, and Kailey spent the next few days debating the merits of french fries against the slightly healthier properties of baked beans. By the time Friday night had come, she was genuinely excited about the visit.

When Max and Rebecca arrived, Kailey had even come up with party favors for the little girl, having located a set of jacks and a Chinese checkers board in the basement commissary of the American embassy. And she was delighted when Rebecca seemed to like her, as if the child instinctively understood how pleased her father would be if she got along with this stranger.

"Let's play another round, Kailey," Rebecca said over and over as they finished a game of jacks.

Kailey was less prepared for Max. From the moment he arrived, he barely talked to his daughter, rarely including her in his conversation, never touching her hand affectionately, as he did Kailey's. She attempted to keep the talk general, on a level Rebecca could understand, but Max was consumed by an event that occurred earlier in the week in the office, something having to do with the new DCM's tactless remarks to the Italian prime minister, who had just been thrown out of office.

Bored, Rebecca interrupted several times, but Max had little patience. Finally he suggested she watch television in the other room while the adults continued to talk.

"But, Max," Kailey protested, "this is Rebecca's night out too."

Rebecca looked at her father hopefully, but Max just gave her a quick hug and ushered her out of the room.

"I have some news, Kailey," he said, drawing his chair closer to hers once they were alone. "Great news, in fact. Months ago I requested a two-year leave to travel around the Eastern bloc and research a book. I have the feeling big stuff is going to happen, and I want to be the first American journalist to get the real story."

Kailey was surprised. "You mean you've gotten permission from the magazine to do it?"

"Not just permission. Paid leave plus a book deal and a sizable advance. *Time* finally realizes how good it will be for the magazine if the Soviet Union and the satellite nations go the way I expect, and they already have the expert on staff."

Kailey couldn't even begin to focus on how much she would miss him, but the thought of how difficult it would be for Rebecca

to travel around Albania and Poland for months on end was immediately apparent to her. "But, Max—what about Rebecca?"

"Oh, I'd never bring her along. It would take away the flex-
ibility I need to do this right. She's going to spend the time back
in Detroit with my folks. I spoke to them this afternoon and they
sounded perfectly willing."

"Your folks . . ." Kailey found herself almost stammering.
"But your father is practically violent and your mother, well, she's
an old woman."

Max didn't respond.

Kailey was incredulous. What could Max be thinking?

She tried to reason with him, to explain how awful it sounded.
"What's it going to be like for Rebecca, living with people who
are strangers, old strangers, for God's sake?"

Max laughed off her objections. "Oh, Becky's a much
stronger kid than you imagine her to be. She'll love it with Mom
and Dad." He dropped his voice. "Don't say anything to her. She
doesn't know anything about it yet, and there's no reason to tell
her until just before it happens. No need to worry her."

Kailey couldn't believe what she was hearing. Not only was
he going to leave his daughter for two years, deprive her of the
only parent she had ever known, but he was going to spring it as
a surprise, not even give her the time to make some kind of sense
of it.

Kailey stared at Max, seeing him as if for the first time. What
kind of man was this? She was seeing underneath the vitality and
the sexuality. Max wasn't independent and fascinating, he was
vain and selfish. Suddenly Max began to look a little like Cameron.
Smug. Arrogant. Pleased by the very things that were worst about
himself.

And suddenly, horrifyingly, Rebecca began to look like Bonnie, her Bonnie. A casualty of a father's ambitions, sacrificed
without a second's thought.

There was nothing she could do for the child, no way she
could replace Rebecca's father any more than she could have
replaced her mother. She felt overwhelmed by powerlessness. It
was as if she were once again standing on the edge of that cliff,

looking over the burning automobile that had held her daughter.

She had to try one more time. "Max, please think about this some more. You don't understand how much Becky needs you. You're the only one she has."

Max eyed her skeptically. "You know, Kailey, it's not good for a child when you turn your life inside out for them. They get spoiled. I've done just fine, and no one ever handed me anything."

He would never understand what she was saying. Outraged, hopeless, she rose and walked to the door of the bedroom. "Honey," she called out to Rebecca, "it's time to go."

Max looked surprised; it was only eight-thirty.

"Good-bye, Max," Kailey said, her voice cool and emotionless.

"What's going on, Kailey?" he demanded.

She didn't answer. When Rebecca reached them, Kailey put her arms around the child for a brief moment.

"You're a delightful girl, and being with you today has made me very happy. Thank you for coming."

Rebecca returned the hug, bringing tears to Kailey's eyes.

Max was annoyed. "Hey, what's happening here?"

Kailey looked him in the eye. "I said good-bye. The evening's over."

Angry at being dismissed, Max turned and left the apartment without another word. The little girl was alert to the tension between the two adults, but followed her father out.

"Oh, God," Kailey breathed out loud as she shut the door behind them, "that poor little girl."

Chapter 10

The school's main corridor was filled with students talking and laughing, eager to leave as they slipped on their jackets and gossiped in groups of two and three.

Several of the younger boys were running at full speed, shouting as they raced through the crowded thoroughfare. Walking down the hall, Susannah felt herself being jolted as one of them bumped into her, knocking her copy of *Jane Eyre* to the floor. She recognized the boy; he was an eighth-grader too, and they were in the same social studies class. He didn't notice her as he sped by, and, stooping down, she saw that the book had opened as it fell so that some of its pages were crushed. Susannah was annoyed. She loved books, and tried to treat them carefully.

There was still another hour before she had to be at the drugstore, and she planned to spend it in the library doing her homework. Most of the other students couldn't wait to leave at three o'clock, but she felt happy in the peacefulness of the library. She would be left alone there, free to read about anything she wanted. School was the one place she enjoyed, the only place where she felt comfortable, away from the watchful, critical eyes of her foster parents. She did whatever she could to stretch the amount of time she was allowed to stay there. It was also where she could spend the most time with her friend, Diane. Susannah never invited her or anyone else to her house. She didn't dare antagonize Arthur and Mary Rule with the loud noise or bother of having other kids around. Besides, even though Diane knew she was an orphan, she didn't want her friend to see the run-down house where she lived, or discover how awful her foster parents were. At school, she could act as if her life were normal, as if she were like Diane and the others.

As she pushed open the big wooden door to the library, she heard someone calling her name. Turning around, she saw Mrs. Flynn, the drama teacher, beckoning from her classroom. Susannah smiled. Mrs. Flynn was one of her favorite teachers, and drama was her favorite class. She loved the hours of make-believe, where she could escape and pretend to be somebody else altogether.

A petite woman, Mrs. Flynn was friendly to all the students, both in and out of class. Her expression was warm as she closed the door behind Susannah.

"Dear, I've been looking for you all over. I've got something very special to tell you."

"Yes, Mrs. Flynn?"

"We're going to do *Cheaper by the Dozen* for the junior high spring production. You don't know the play, do you?"

Susannah shook her head. "No."

"It's terrific, the story of a big family. I think you'd be perfect for Ernestine — she's the second oldest sister, and it's a very important part."

Immediately, Susannah felt a stab of anxiety.

"We're even borrowing some children from Miller Elementary to play the younger brothers and sisters," Mrs. Flynn went on. "I'll be holding auditions for the rest of the characters, but I've decided on you and two other eighth-graders as leads." She smiled at her student. "I hope you realize what a compliment that is."

Even though she was thrilled by Mrs. Flynn's confidence in her, Susannah felt miserable. The Rules would never let her take time off from working at the drugstore to be in a school play. Just asking permission to do it could set them off and get her into all kinds of trouble. They didn't question what she did during the school day, but at four o'clock they expected her to relieve Mary Rule behind the front counter. That's how it had been for the past two years, ever since she was old enough to be trusted handling the register. There had never been any exceptions.

She spoke hesitantly. "Mrs. Flynn, thanks for asking me, but it would be kind of hard for me to stay late after school to rehearse. . . ."

"Oh, that's not a problem," the teacher responded easily. "Since we're working with children from Miller, we'll do most of it during lunchtime. We'll eat and rehearse at the same time. And we'll schedule some extra rehearsals during study hall. I'll get you a pass to be excused."

Still doubtful, Susannah asked when the performance would be. It was on a Saturday night, six weeks away. She thought that over. Saturday night after they closed the drugstore was her own free time, as long as she had finished doing her chores. Usually she spent the evenings in her room, but on a couple of occasions she had gone out with Diane to a movie, and her foster parents hadn't objected.

Mrs. Flynn went over to her desk and picked up a sheaf of papers. "Here's the script. Read it at home and let me know if you'd like to do it. I really think you'll be wonderful in the role."

Susannah didn't wait until she got home. Sitting in the library, homework forgotten, she pored over the play, growing more and more entranced. *Cheaper by the Dozen* was about a family called the Gilbreths back in the nineteen-twenties. There were twelve children, six sisters and six brothers, and the most incredible mother and father. The father was an expert in efficiency, and he had systems for accomplishing even the smallest household chores, so the children ran around like crazy getting things done in the quickest possible way. When he whistled, all twelve of them came running from wherever they were and lined up like soldiers to be counted. He brought them presents, took them for ice cream and to the movies, and taught them about absolutely everything. Mr. and Mrs. Gilbreth loved each and every one of those children, whether they fought or broke things or were bad — everyone always wound up laughing and happy. The character of Ernestine had lots to say and do, and the other family members adored her.

Clutching the script, Susannah went right back to Mrs. Flynn's classroom. She was still there, finishing up.

"I'll do it." Susannah was grinning from ear to ear as she made the announcement.

She flew out of school, and the afternoon at the drugstore, usually so tedious, sped by as she daydreamed about the part. Even Mary Rule noticed something was different.

"What are you so happy about today?" she inquired in a querulous voice.

Susannah tried to think of a plausible answer. "I got a hundred on my math test," she replied.

"Oh." Mary Rule turned away without interest.

Susannah smiled to herself. On the way over to the store, she had figured out the safest way to deal with the Rules. To begin with, the rehearsals would have to be kept secret. Only a few days before the actual performance would she tell them about the play at all; that way it wouldn't seem like such a big deal, and there wouldn't be enough time for them to dream up some excuse to stop her.

When she got home that night, Susannah decided to write a letter to Ruth Mitchell. Just as she had promised, her first foster mother had always stayed in touch; every year she remembered to send birthday and Christmas cards from their new home in Pennsylvania. Some years, she even sent presents. Susannah knew the Mitchells had very little, and she was grateful for the gifts. She realized how hard it must have been for them to spare the money, and would immediately send them thank-you notes in return. Every so often Ruth called, and Susannah would get to talk to her and the rest of the family. Susannah imagined that it cost a lot to pay for these phone calls, and wished she could make them herself, but the Rules wouldn't allow it. They didn't care if she got calls, they told her, but they would have nothing to do with throwing away their hard-earned money on a lot of long-distance chatter to people she would never see.

Susannah always tried to squirrel away something from her tiny allowance to reciprocate with birthday cards to the Mitchells. She didn't write many extra letters to them, because she was afraid of driving the family away. Too many calls, too many notes, and they might get tired of her, feel she was taking up too much of their time. But tonight she made an exception. As always, she started out by saying that everything was going well. She was very careful never to complain or give any hint of how unhappy she really was. Then she told them her news about *Cheaper by the Dozen*. When at last she went to bed, she felt content.

Rehearsals began the following week. Susannah had already learned all her lines, and was beginning to memorize the other cast members' lines as well. She didn't know the two students Mrs. Flynn had chosen to play the parents, Frank and Lillian Gilbreth, and she liked that; if she had known them it would have been harder to pretend they were really her parents. She closed her eyes and listened to everyone reading their lines aloud, imagining that this was a real family, and she *was* Ernestine Gilbreth, the freckled girl with eleven siblings. When Mrs. Flynn told them one day that the family had, in fact, been a real one and that the play was based on a book about them, Susannah rushed to the public library to find it. She read it that evening in her room. She wanted to know everything about her new family.

More and more, Susannah's thoughts were caught up with the Gilbreths. As she walked from school to the drugstore, she imagined that she was Ernestine on her way home, where her father would teach her and her siblings something about astronomy or take them for a ride in the enormous open car that would start only for Frank Gilbreth. Then the family would sit around together outside and drink lemonade, made from scratch by their mother and nothing like the disgusting mix Mrs. Rule kept in a plastic pitcher in the refrigerator during the summer. Susannah talked about the play incessantly to Diane, until her friend made it clear she was bored with the subject.

"It's just make-believe," Diane said petulantly. "Knock it off."

After that, Susannah kept her feelings to herself. But when she got into bed at night, she thought about the Gilbreths until she drifted off to sleep, and when she awoke, she could hardly wait for rehearsals at lunch, to speak the lines again that made it all the more real to her. Someday, Susannah decided, she would have an enormous family herself, maybe twelve of her own children. Why not? she thought. A house full of love and laughter, just like the Gilbreths'.

In the next weeks, nothing the Rules said or did could bother her — she had Frank and Lillian, her other, secret parents who loved her. Mrs. Flynn was delighted with her dedication to the part. Stopping Susannah in the hall at school one afternoon, the teacher affectionately put an arm around her shoulder. "You're doing a great job," she said. "You've even exceeded my high expectations."

The next day, Susannah came home to find a letter from Ruth Mitchell waiting for her. Ruth talked about how proud they all were of her for getting the part in the play. "We always knew you'd do great things, darling," she wrote, "and this is just the beginning. We'll be thinking of you on that Saturday night."

Far too quickly, the week of the performance was upon her. On Thursday she decided that it was time to tell the Rules. After she had finished washing the dinner dishes, she went into the living room, where Mr. Rule was reading the newspaper in his armchair, while Mrs. Rule sat on the couch watching television.

She took a deep breath. "Excuse me, I'd like to talk to you for a second."

Mary Rule glanced at her in irritation. "Can this wait? I'm in the middle of my program."

Susannah hesitated. But she had to tell them sometime.

"I'll be quick." The words came rushing out. "I'm in the school play Saturday night, so after I finish my chores I'm going out, just for three hours."

Arthur Rule put his newspaper down in his lap. "*This* Saturday night?"

"Yes. It's *Cheaper by the Dozen* and I'm one of the daughters. . . ." Susannah's voice trailed off as she saw the pair of them staring at her in angry disbelief.

"Have you forgotten?" Mary Rule spoke first. "Saturday night we're doing inventory at the store. You know it's always the same night every year."

Susannah felt her stomach lurch. She *had* forgotten. How could she have? Inventory was a long, arduous process, starting when they closed the store early at four o'clock and ending as late as one or two in the morning. Relieved and exhausted when it was over, she would always feel grateful it was a whole year before she had to go through it again.

"Please. This is really important." Her voice rose in panic. "I'll make it up to you in the store somehow, I promise. It's just this once and everybody's counting on me. You've just got to let me be in the play."

"We've *just got to*?" As she repeated the words, Mary Rule's tone conveyed her astonishment at the girl's audacity. "You don't seem to understand. You will not be in any play on Saturday night. You'll be at the store doing what you're supposed to be doing."

She should have known it would be impossible, that somehow she would never get away with being in that play. Susannah grew frantic. "Oh, please, I'll do anything," she said, her voice breaking.

"What you will do is inventory," Mary Rule snapped. "This is our livelihood at stake. You have prior, more important commitments to this family than to a silly little school play."

"This *family*?" It came out as a sob. "You think this is a family?"

"That's enough," Arthur Rule said sharply. "Go to your room."

Susannah obeyed. She spent the next two hours crying, praying one of the Rules would relent. But the evening passed and there was only the muffled drone of the television, punctuated by bursts of canned soundtrack laughter. At ten o'clock, she heard them turn it off, as they did every night, and go to their bedroom without a word as they passed her door.

This is what happens when other people get control of your life, she said to herself, lying across the bed and staring at the ceiling. They can do anything they want. She had fooled herself into thinking she was like the other children, that she could have a regular life. But that wasn't so. She was someone nobody wanted.

Early the next morning, Mary Rule appeared in Susannah's doorway. In the middle of buttoning her cardigan, Susannah froze, wondering what was coming. The older woman spoke briefly.

"We've decided that you can be in your little play. But we'll expect you to be at the drugstore by six the next morning to make up your share of the inventory work."

"Oh, thank you, thank you so much." Susannah didn't try to hide her relief. She had a momentary urge to run and hug Mary Rule with gratitude, but the woman was already turning to go.

"And, next time," came the parting words, "don't hide things from us. It's underhanded."

Her shoulders sagging, Susannah reflected that she would never be able to please the Rules if she lived to be a hundred. Then she broke into a broad smile, realizing she would actually get to be Ernestine. She practically ran out the door to school, eager to get the day started so she could rehearse again.

The night of the performance, Susannah felt as if she were in heaven. As Ernestine, she had the very first line of the play. A few seconds before they were due to start, with the audience still getting comfortable in their seats, she held hands with the boy playing her brother Frank, and they made their way to the center of the darkened stage, in front of the curtain. Music played softly. Standing there, waiting for the spotlight that would reveal them to the audience, she was so nervous, she was afraid she might throw up. But as soon as she began speaking, saying the lines she had memorized practically backwards and forwards, she relaxed, her confidence growing. As the two of them continued their dialogue, she could hear her name being whispered among the children in the audience. *Susannah Holland. She's in Lombardy's homeroom.* It made her feel wonderful.

By the time the curtain had risen, and she had crossed to take her place with the other characters, she was transformed, almost able to believe she had truly become Ernestine for that night. When she took the same spot in front of the curtain for the beginning of Act II, she thought she could *feel* how much the audience was enjoying her performance. Stepping forward to take her bow at the end of the play, hearing the raucous applause and cheering, she wondered if she would ever know another moment as glorious as this one.

She was still drunk with excitement when she let herself into the house later that night. Quietly, she made her way down the dark hallway to her room.

"Is that you?" Arthur Rule called out groggily from his bedroom.

"Yes," Susannah answered. "I'm back from the play. It went great."

There was a grunt of acknowledgment. "Remember, inventory at six A.M."

As she undressed and slipped under the covers, the good feelings fell away as quickly and easily as her blouse and skirt had. It was as if she were suffocating, trapped by some invisible weight. She closed her eyes and imagined the evening again, trying to recapture every second from the very beginning. By the time she had gotten to the end of the first act, she was asleep.

The next morning, she knelt in the drugstore's middle aisle in front of the shaving creams and razors, making notations on a clipboard. The Rules had joined her at nine-thirty, working in different aisles, taking their own notes. The harshly lit store was quiet as Susannah looked at the clock on the wall. Twenty to eleven. She closed her eyes, thinking about the play. She envisioned a scene in the last act, mouthing the lines she had spoken just twelve hours before.

She took a deep breath. Somehow, she had to find a way

out. She had seen another world, and that was the one she wanted to be part of. A world where people enjoyed themselves, and did fun, interesting things, and liked you if you tried hard.

Of course, she wasn't old enough to defy the Rules, and knew better than to think she could get along if she ran away now, a thirteen-year-old by herself, with no one to go to. What she needed was money, a lot more of it. That much she understood. As soon as she was a little older, she would find a job, one that would take her out of this hateful drugstore.

But money from part-time jobs wasn't enough. She had to set up a future for herself. She moved a few feet down the aisle, counting bottles of aspirin, continuing to jot down numbers. College was the answer. At college she could become something. But she wasn't foolish enough to dream that the Rules would pay for it. She would have to get the grades that could earn her a full scholarship. That was the only way she would ever be able to go.

She moved down the next aisle toward the shampoos. Okay. Now she had a plan. She would let nothing stand in the way of her schoolwork, and she would have the best grades in her class. She would get a scholarship. And then she would be free.

Chapter 11

Seated at her dressing table, hairpins clenched in her teeth, Tish Hawkes finished brushing her long, blond hair and twisted it into a French knot. Using the hairpins to secure it, she swept up a few errant tendrils, then reached for the can of hair spray. Having worn her hair this way for some fifteen years, she didn't have to pay much attention to the task. Instead, she halfheartedly contemplated what she should wear to meet her friend Winnie for lunch. It was either her beige dress with the black trim or the navy blue suit. Setting down the hair spray, Tish considered her reflection in the mirror, eyeing with displeasure the slight jowls she saw forming at her jaw, the deepening lines around her mouth. As much as she liked Winnie Brady, going out was the last thing she felt like doing. If only she could just go back to bed. Sighing, she wondered how she was going to get through another day of lunch, shopping, then home to wait for a late, silent dinner with Cameron.

That was, of course, if Cameron showed up at all. Tish never knew if he was going to make an appearance. On those occasions when she used to ask where he had been, he invariably replied curtly that he was working late or was off attending some business function. Maybe those excuses were true, and maybe they weren't. She rarely bothered to ask anymore. She didn't much care where her husband spent his time.

In the eleven years since they had been married, Cameron had managed to destroy every vestige of the love, desire, and respect Tish once felt for him. It had taken a long time, and she had resisted, fighting frantically to save their relationship. But in the end she had given up. Things had been so different in the beginning, her new husband eager to please her, loving and attentive. She supposed she should have seen his ulterior motives back then—maybe she *did* see them, but she just didn't want to admit the truth to herself. She had stood by quietly, watching his caring interest in her turn to criticism and, finally, contempt.

She wondered how she could have been so naive—or just blind—about her husband. But Cameron had already achieved so much by the time they were married, he seemed so firmly established, she never dreamed he was marrying her simply as a means to what he considered a greater success. Tish hadn't realized how desperately he craved the social standing that her family enjoyed, something she had always taken for granted, and was never particularly interested in, anyway. Her parents had a lot of important connections, and, from the first, Cameron moved to take advantage of them. He wanted to be invited to the homes and clubs of the old-money families, to befriend the men who paid to keep their names *out* of the newspapers.

Tish had willingly provided him with access to the exclusive dinner parties, the sailing and golf dates, the polo games. After all, she moved freely in this world, and her husband was entitled to become part of it if that was what he wanted. But once she'd opened the door, she served no further purpose for him except as an ornament on his arm, the final stamp of approval that he truly belonged.

It wasn't until their second year together that she began to fully grasp how alone she was in her marriage. His appearances at home had been growing shorter and more rushed, his conversations with her more perfunctory. Months went by when they didn't make love, with Cameron either away on business, working late, or unapologetically claiming he was too busy or tired. Looking back, she supposed he must have been finding his sexual pleasures elsewhere.

On the night of her birthday in late August, Tish had sat at home waiting for him. She hoped Cameron's silence on the subject indicated he was planning a birthday surprise of some sort for her. But he didn't even come home until after midnight, and he made no mention of what day it was when he joined her in the bedroom, where she lay in bed reading, disappointedly having given up on him two hours before.

Still holding her book, she'd watched him undress, his mind clearly on things other than her.

"You know, Cameron," she said softly, "today was my birthday."

He looked over at her, startled. So he really had forgotten, she thought unhappily.

"I guess it was," he replied mildly, reaching into his closet to hang up his tie on the rack inside. "Well, happy birthday."

She closed the book and put it down. "I don't mean to make a fuss, but don't you think we might have done something together to celebrate it?"

Annoyance crossed his face. "Jesus, what are you — six years old? I had an important dinner meeting tonight. I wasn't about to leave because you wanted to blow out the candles on a cake."

Tish stared at him. It wasn't that she wanted so much of his time and attention; she understood what a busy man he was. But it was apparent her husband had stopped concerning himself altogether with what she might want. She mentally began toting up the other times he had missed holidays or events that were significant to her, vague excuses always at hand. Tonight, he wasn't even pretending to be sorry.

Once her eyes had been opened, his lack of feeling for her became painfully obvious. She couldn't pretend to herself anymore. More sure of himself now that he had been accepted by so many of her family's friends, Cameron began dictating to Tish, instructing her on what dress to wear when they were going out, what not to say to someone he was in negotiations with, telling her she was gaining a few pounds, and had better get to a gym to exercise the way everyone else's wife did. He seemed to have totally forgotten that she was the one who had introduced him to the people he now considered his friends, to the vacation spots he had adopted, the sports and charities to which he now devoted his spare time. As he became more caustic with every passing month, she had to accept that he didn't love her at all, that he never had. He'd used her just the way he used everyone else around him. But she suspected he'd never divorce her; that would destroy the picture of respectability and domestic bliss he carefully painted for the rest of the world.

Tish had kept her hurt and the shame of her empty marriage to herself. But she finally decided to confide in her mother. She and Cameron were at her parents' house for Christmas dinner, an event Cameron always seemed to enjoy wholeheartedly; he would talk for hours with Tish's father, taking walks with him, further cementing the relationship that had helped pave the way to so many other valuable contacts.

In the late afternoon, while Cameron and her father were out behind the house inspecting some firewood, Tish saw her opportunity to ask her mother for advice. Anne Malmquist was busy searching for a set of Christmas dessert plates in the pantry's enormous china closet when Tish approached.

"Mother," she said hesitantly, "could I talk to you?"

"Is it important, dear?" Her mother didn't turn around, continuing with the task at hand. "If I don't find these plates, we'll be eating plum pudding straight off the place mats."

"Did you . . . did you ever have any problems? With Dad, I mean." Even though she'd resolved to discuss it, Tish's courage was suddenly flagging. After all these years, her mother still made her feel as if she were a small child.

The older woman did nothing to make matters easier now. She knelt, poking around behind the serving platters on a low shelf. "I'm not sure what you mean. You're being very vague."

"I don't know if Cameron loves me. In fact, I'm sure he doesn't," Tish blurted out.

Her mother stopped what she was doing, and stood to face Tish. She looked displeased.

"I hope you're not suggesting that you'll be packing up and coming home again. Honestly, you're about twenty years too old for this sort of thing. And you've got *two* children now to think about—last time there was only Evan. You marry a man, you stay with him. It's simple."

The words stung Tish. "I see."

"Really," her mother said exasperatedly, "we've already given you more help than we should have." Her tone grew stern. "A grown woman should stand on her own two feet. That's how you learn to survive in this world."

Tish turned away. She should have known better. Her parents would no more give her emotional support than they would financial support. She knew their ethic: no coddling, no help, everyone should pull themselves up by their own bootstraps. It was only because they feared for Evan's well-being that they had taken her back to live with them when her first husband died; if she'd been alone, they wouldn't have considered it. They'd paid the bills for him directly, but never offered her any money for herself; they simply didn't believe in it. Perhaps at their death, there would be money left in trust for Evan and Olivia, but she doubted there'd be much for her, even then. It was just the way they were. There would be no help of *any* kind forthcoming from them.

After that conversation with her mother, Tish had become resigned to her situation. She'd chosen her husband, and she had to live with him. What else could she do? But as bad as things were, they deteriorated further as the years went on. She felt invisible in her own home. Sometimes she wondered if her husband actually enjoyed the misery he inflicted on her, or if he even stopped to give it a moment's thought.

She sighed at the memories. If she didn't hurry, she would be late for her lunch date. The navy suit, she decided, entering her walk-in closet. Still, she looked through the dresses that hung along one wall, waiting to see if anything else caught her eye. The funny thing about it, she thought, was that none of the people they knew would believe her if she tried to tell them what Cameron was really like. He always seemed so charming, so warm and interested. Tish knew full well that getting Cameron Hawkes to come to your dinner party was a coup for any hostess. He had a way with people, a style polished to perfection over the years.

Of course, Tish could always have divorced him, started all over again. But the idea terrified her. She had her son to think about. Evan had gone through such upheaval, going away to prep school, making new friends, adjusting to Cameron as a stepfather. Tish had been so pleased when Cameron bought this house, their weekend retreat in Bedford. She was thrilled to have a place where Evan could be outdoors, even if it was only on his occasional visits from school. It was way too grand, a compound actually, with a main house, two guest cottages, stables, and servants' quarters. Tish would have preferred a cozy country place, but there was no point arguing with Cameron once he had made up his mind.

And she had loved watching her son play softball out back, so lean and fast, so astonishingly talented at the game. The sight had given her such pleasure. Not that she got to see it much anymore now that he was away at Yale. But she could hardly blame him for coming home so rarely. His bitterness toward his stepfather had only grown over the years; now, Evan hated Cameron. Tish tried to help them get along. But Cameron — uninterested, impatient, critical — had been no kind of father to Evan. One could hardly expect a young boy to be magically transformed into a loving son to a man like that.

Tish stepped into the navy skirt and zipped it up, then slipped on a silk blouse. She glanced at her watch. Hurrying with her stockings, she chose a pair of navy pumps and quickly put on earrings and two gold bracelets. Taking one last unhappy look at her reflection, she grabbed her purse and suit jacket and hastened out of the bedroom. The driver was already waiting in front of the house, holding the door to the shining, black Mercedes open for her. She nodded stiffly to him as she climbed in. She hated having a car and driver, and would much rather have driven herself around town. But in Cameron's view, a wealthy man's wife did not drive herself. It doesn't look right, he'd said. And he should know about appearances, she thought bitterly; they were what Cameron Hawkes was all about.

The restaurant was a few miles away. Tish leaned back into the car's plush upholstery. Today was Tuesday, which meant Olivia would be home late — she had ballet lessons at four o'clock. So she had no reason at all, not even her ten-year-old, to come back to the huge, empty house.

She wondered which was worse, having a son who despised his stepfather or a daughter who loved her father so desperately she would do practically anything to win his approval. When Olivia had been born, almost a year to the day after Tish and Cameron's wedding, she had been so happy that *this* child, at least, would have the security of a father, someone to care and provide for her. The loss of Bill Gardiner had caused Evan such pain. Olivia would be spared that. Well, Olivia was *provided* for. Unfortunately, when it came to love and caring, to warmth and affection, Cameron was no better father to his own daughter than he had been to Evan. Yet Olivia worshiped him. She was pathetically grateful for even a few minutes of his attention, which was usually all she got. Still, no matter how indifferent Cameron was to his family, Tish always felt her children were better off in a house with two parents. Divorce was out of the question. Or at least, she *used* to feel that way. She wasn't so sure anymore.

The car pulled up in front of the restaurant and Tish waited for the driver to come around and open the door for her. Hastening inside, she spotted Winnie seated at a table near the window. Winnie always got the best table. She and her husband ate here often, and the maître d' was well aware that Dan Brady was an extremely wealthy banker who often steered his friends there.

"Sweetheart." Winnie rose and kissed Tish on the cheek. "You're looking terrific."

Tish was grateful for the lie. As usual, she thought, Winnie herself looked perfect, every blond hair in place beneath a wide headband, her dress gracefully clinging to her slender body as if it were made expressly for her — which it probably had been.

"I hope you weren't waiting long," Tish said, sitting down and spreading the generous napkin across her lap.

Winnie smiled and picked up a menu. "Not at all. Dan called the house as I was leaving, so I just got here myself. I'm starving. How about you?"

They signaled to the waiter and each ordered a salad. Winnie and her husband lived just twenty minutes away from the Hawkes' Bedford house, and Tish had met her four years before at a country club dinner. Though several weeks might pass without their getting together, Tish considered Winnie a close friend. Despite her extensive array of social acquaintances, Tish didn't have many friends she could confide in; in fact, Winnie was the only one who knew how unhappy Tish was with Cameron.

As the waiter set down two Bloody Marys, Winnie asked Tish how things were going at home. Tish shook her head.

"Cameron's really getting to me," she said quietly. "I don't know how much longer I can stand it."

Winnie took a sip of her drink, then put her glass down thoughtfully. "You know," she began, leaning forward, "I was going to wait until later to say what I'm about to say, but I guess there's no point. Maybe you really should leave him."

Hearing the words spoken aloud shocked Tish. As often as she toyed with the idea of leaving Cameron, she knew she would never actually do it. She couldn't support herself, and she knew full well her parents wouldn't give her any money. And she had no job skills. Besides, it was a long time since she'd been alone.

"Honestly, what would I do?" she asked, picking up her drink. "I couldn't count on Cameron to take care of me."

"That's what I wanted to talk to you about." Winnie's voice rose in excitement. "Something occurred to me a few weeks ago and I discussed it with Dan. We have an idea. It's the key to your making it on your own."

Tish laughed. "I don't know what you could possibly mean, but I'm listening."

Winnie leaned back in her chair, smiling. "Ever since I met you, you've been famous for something. On any afternoon, anyone who comes by your house can expect to be served the most incredible tea. Those little cakes you make, your tea sandwiches — it's fantastic, and so beautifully served, with all that linen and lace."

"It's a hobby," Tish said, surprised that Winnie had taken such notice of the effort she put into serving company. "It relaxes me to do it, and I get a kick out of fussing with all the food and the china."

"Maybe so, but it's time you turned it into a business." Winnie paused. "Open up a tearoom."

"What?" Tish was taken aback. "You can't be serious."

"I mean it, Tish. You have a terrific eye for detail. You could create a charming little place in Manhattan. I'll be your partner, and Dan will put up the money to get us started. He says it could be a great business opportunity."

Tish stared at her. "I don't know what to say."

"Say yes," Winnie replied. "Sure, we'd have a good time, but this is a serious business proposition. Dan did a few projections and came up with some figures. He's willing to put up seventy-five thousand dollars and the first six months' rent. After that we're on our own — not a penny more from him. You would run the day-to-day operations, and I'd be more of the business partner. It would be great fun."

Tish smiled gratefully at her friend. "Thank you for your confidence, Winnie. That means a lot to me. But it seems impossible."

"No, it's not. You could be free of your husband, be your own boss, and start over all at the same time. That's exactly what you want. Cameron will give you alimony, so you'll be safe financially." Winnie signaled the waiter for another round of drinks. "I know you can do this. Promise you'll consider it."

Nothing further was said about the subject that afternoon. Not until hours later, when Tish was relaxing in a hot bubble bath with a glass of dry white wine next to her did she think again about Winnie's idea.

Of course she couldn't really consider such a thing. But wouldn't it be fantastic? After so many years of sitting around moping in this enormous house, she could make something of herself.

And it would be so satisfying, having her own business to run as she wished. Setting out afternoon tea was a comforting ritual for her. She'd seen it done countless times at home while she was growing up. Even as a little girl, she'd gotten pleasure from arranging her mother's sterling, the fine china, the white damask napkins and tablecloths. There was something so soothing about a proper afternoon tea.

She ran a washcloth along her arms and legs. Her body was getting so soft, she thought, betraying her at every turn. If she was ever going to take a chance, this might be the last real opportunity she would get. But was it possible to create a viable business from something as trivial as her ability to present tea? If she left Cameron, everything would be riding on it. No, it was too dangerous for a woman of her age to start over. She must be mad even to consider it.

There was a knock on the bathroom door.

"Who is it?" Tish called out.

"Your husband, if you remember who that is." Cameron's voice was angry. "I know it's unimportant to you, but we're expected at a dinner honoring Shep Lewis in half an hour, and I'm getting the strong feeling you just might not be ready."

Tish sat upright in the tub. She'd completely forgotten. Shep Lewis headed up a huge chain of grocery stores, all of which sold Little Angel Baby Food, so Cameron had bought an entire table at a charity benefit honoring Lewis for his work on behalf of cancer research. They were taking four other couples as their guests.

"I'll be right there," Tish called out, hastily stepping out of the tub, water splashing all around her as she grabbed a fluffy white towel.

"How could you be so mindless?" Cameron spat out from the other side of the door. "You do nothing all day, and you can't even manage to remember this. But what the hell do you care? The money to support you and your shopping just keeps rolling in, doesn't it? It's not your problem how it gets here."

Tish bit her lip silently as she hurriedly dried herself off. If she stayed with Cameron, this is what she had to look forward to for the rest of her life. She had never dared to think about it that way before. But she had never had another option before, either.

Tish poured a glass of champagne into a tall stem glass, then carried both the glass and the bottle into the living room, glancing out the window at the unfamiliar view. She sat down on the couch, put her feet up on a carton, and sighed contentedly. There was so much to be done in the apartment, but right now she was just going to sit down and savor the moment. She'd earned a little celebration.

Leaning over to put the bottle down on a folding table next to the couch, she yawned. This had to be the first time she had sat down all day. Not that she minded in the least; it was probably the most exciting day of her life. And now it was so peaceful and quiet, Olivia asleep in the second bedroom, no household staff to contend with. And no Cameron. Just wonderful solitude. Tish took a long swallow of her champagne. *You did it,* she thought, mentally toasting herself. You actually did it.

She rose and went over to her purse to get her small notebook. Even though she was celebrating, she couldn't stop her mind from racing. Today, she and Winnie had agreed to rent a storefront on Madison Avenue and Ninety-fourth Street for three thousand dollars a month. The location had previously housed a small coffee shop, closed only the week before and still equipped for cooking and serving food. With a little negotiating, Dan Brady had helped them buy the equipment on the premises. The East Nineties was an up-and-coming area, and the store was the ideal size for the cozy, intimate effect they wanted to create. They were on their way. The tearoom, which they planned to call Patricia's, was scheduled to open in six weeks. There was so much to be done, but she was filled with energy.

Botanical prints. She made a note. She would start shopping tomorrow. Dan Brady's seventy-five thousand dollars plus the first six months' rent would go only so far, so she had to watch every cent. She continued writing. Candlesticks, a sign for over the door, menus, sherry glasses. She paused. It would be nice to serve sherry, but that would entail getting a liquor license. Too involved, she decided, crossing the last item off the list. Did she want the restaurant to look like a library, someone's living room, an outdoor garden? Should she serve high tea, offer other kinds of foods, make it a prix-fixe menu or have everything priced individually? She scribbled more quickly.

Tish stared at her list. Not very organized. There were so many things to consider, to decide, to buy. She could feel her heart beating faster, anxiety rising as her confidence suddenly ebbed. Take it easy, she told herself, putting the notebook aside. You did all this. Got away from Cameron. Rented this apartment. Packed Olivia up and moved her here with you. You're ready for whatever comes.

It had been the most frightening thing Tish had ever done. She had been packing surreptitiously for two weeks, and then, one night when Cameron was scheduled to be away on business, she'd taken her daughter and moved into this apartment on East Ninety-second Street in Manhattan. Bless Winnie Brady, she thought again gratefully, knowing she could never have taken that final big step if her friend hadn't arranged for the apartment through a real estate agent she knew. The rent wasn't cheap, but Tish had gotten ten thousand dollars in cash advances with her credit cards, a daring but necessary risk that was certain to make Cameron livid. That money would hold her until she and Cameron could work out some suitable agreement in the next month or two. Eventually he would realize that it was the right move for Tish, that they would both be better off in the long run.

The note Tish left for her husband hadn't even mentioned

the possibility of a divorce. She wanted to, *had* to, try something new, she'd written. He would have gotten that note over a week ago, but so far she'd heard nothing. Not that it surprised her, knowing Cameron. She could envision his fury at what he would see as her disloyalty and how she was humiliating him. She was sure he was busy finding a respectable way of explaining her absence to their friends. Damage control.

Right now, she had to deal with her tearoom. That was what this was all for. And she was ready for a taste of success. Tish envisioned the gleaming sterling trays with sugar and creamer sets, the beautiful platters of tiny cucumber and watercress sandwiches, beribboned baskets of scones served with clotted cream and strawberry preserves. She picked up her notebook again. She must ask Winnie how one went about hiring a chef, a waitress, and a busboy.

Starting the next day, she traveled the streets of New York, trying to learn everything she could about her new business. Downtown, she scoured the restaurant supply district. She frequented flea markets and auctions to find tables and chairs, water pitchers and ashtrays, coat racks and table linens. Thank goodness, she thought, she'd had the presence of mind to take her own extensive collection of tablecloths and napkins when she moved out. She would never have taken anything that belonged to Cameron, but these were hers from her marriage to Bill, and they would be perfect in the tearoom. As much as she hated to give up the idea of using sterling flatware, the cost was prohibitive, so she settled for silverplate, she and Winnie spending hours poring over the different patterns in stores all over the city. Through Dan Brady's connections, they had a lawyer and an accountant, both of whom repeatedly advised them not to do most of the things they wanted to; Tish tried to follow their advice, but occasionally she knew she should listen to her own instincts and splurge on certain items. Quality couldn't be faked.

Tish was amazed to discover how efficient she really was. She called employment agencies and ran help wanted ads, hiring a staff of four, not quite believing that these people were actually going to be working for her, that she would be someone's boss.

Discovering there was trouble with the air-conditioning system, she quickly got someone to fix it. When the oven from the restaurant's previous owner turned out to be defective, she elected to replace it with a new one rather than invest in a major repair job. She surprised herself at how adept she could be in handling problems and decisions as they arose. She'd never known she had that kind of ability, and she was secretly proud.

Nearly three weeks had passed when Tish came home one night, exhausted as usual, to find a letter from Cameron's lawyer waiting for her. Just the sight of the envelope was enough to frighten her. It's all right, she reassured herself, using a letter opener to slice through the heavy gray envelope. Everything will be fine. But her heart was pounding as she unfolded the contents.

She scanned the three-page document, trying to cut through all the legal language. *Cameron Hawkes will not be providing his estranged wife, Patricia Hawkes, with financial support in any form . . . Mr. Hawkes will make no further tuition payments to Yale, Brearley, or any other educational institutions for either Evan Gardiner or Olivia Hawkes.* Tish's hands began to tremble. *Should Patricia Hawkes request a divorce, one will be granted under the condition that she receive no financial settlement or lay claim to any assets held either jointly or singly by Cameron Hawkes.*

Stunned, Tish went back to the beginning, reading the entire letter through again. How foolish she had been. She'd understood that Cameron would be angered by her departure, but she'd chosen to believe he would get over it, handle it like a gentleman. Her husband was a shark; she should have known that better than anyone. She'd been so anxious to make this move, to get away and start over that she'd jeopardized her children's future, never mind what would become of her. Of course, she could retain a lawyer to sue him, fight him for alimony or at least some form of child support, but that would take time, months, possibly years. If he chose to, Cameron could no doubt use his money to tie up the case almost indefinitely.

She crushed the letter into a tight ball. With all the expenses of her move, her original ten thousand dollars was dwindling rapidly. If she conserved very carefully, maybe she could make it go a little further than she'd planned. But the tearoom *had* to succeed. That was the only answer. She would work twice as hard, and somehow find a way to keep paying the schools, the rent on the apartment, the expenses of living on her own. Tish covered her eyes, fear striking her like a fist in the stomach. She thought briefly of going to her parents for help, but immediately rejected the idea. She could almost hear her mother's voice. *You made your own bed and now you can lie in it.* And so she would.

Her fright drove Tish on. Reading up on direct mail advertising, she hired a copywriter to prepare a mailing about the tearoom's opening. But opening day was delayed by two weeks when the wallpaper she'd gone to such pains to pick out was ruined; the paper hanger hadn't shown up to finish the job, leaving the remaining rolls of flowered paper in the basement, where they were stained by water draining from a leaky pipe.

But finally, everything was ready. Tish had been working eighteen hours a day, but as they officially opened the door for business at noon, she felt exhilarated, her fatigue completely forgotten. She and Winnie moved around the small room, continually restraightening the place settings on their twelve tables. The atmosphere was cozy, just as Tish had envisioned it, the pale pink of the carpeting and new pin-striped wallpaper warmed by the glow of tall pink candles on each table. Fresh flowers were everywhere, bright blossoms in tiny porcelain vases at every setting, an enormous arrangement of dried flowers and wisteria near the entranceway. Tish was pleased with the casual charm of the mismatched pieces of china, the heavy flatware contrasting with delicate lace table linens. The menus were satisfyingly heavy, appealing with their old-fashioned illustrations and hand-printed calligraphy.

"Do you think actual people will come in here and order actual food and pay us real money?" Tish asked her friend breathlessly, moving the crystal salt and pepper shakers on one of the tables slightly to the left, then frowning and putting them back where they were. Turning around to look at Winnie, she laughed. The truth was, she felt nervous but absolutely terrific.

Before Winnie had a chance to answer, the door opened and two women in their mid-thirties entered, their arms laden with shopping bags. They glanced around at the empty chairs.

"Are you serving?" one asked hesitantly.

Tish smiled at them. "Please come right in. Won't you let us take your coats?"

"Mommy, look at your cards. You had gin in your hand already!"

Olivia's face displayed the exasperation Tish had gotten used to in the past few months. Tish looked down at the cards she'd placed face up on the table when her daughter had announced a triumphant finale to their game, and realized that she'd indeed overlooked the fact that she held three queens, three tens, and four twos. It was hard to concentrate.

Guiltily she restacked the cards and began to shuffle. "We'll start a new round," she said, "and next time I'll win."

"But you won this round, Mommy," Olivia whined. "You just weren't paying attention."

"I'm sorry, honey." Tish was annoyed at herself. Not only didn't she give her daughter the time she deserved, but here she was, rewarding her for whining. It was so hard to discipline her now, being away so often at the tearoom. She hated to make their few hours together unpleasant. "Come on, sweetheart, let's play one more game."

"You don't even *want* to play. I can tell." Olivia looked petulant, and in one swipe pushed the whole deck of cards off the table. "I'm going to call Daddy."

She ran out of the room before her mother could say anything. What should I do, Tish thought unhappily. She hated to see Olivia misbehave like this, but the girl was right, Tish wasn't really thinking about the game. The tearoom was so demanding, it consumed all her thoughts, even when she was at home.

She sighed. Watching her daughter run to Cameron was so painful. It would just end up hurting Olivia. She always turned to her father for help, and always ended up disappointed.

As soon as the tearoom gets off the ground, I'll hire someone to help me run it, she decided. Winnie was sympathetic, but she'd never planned on spending much time on the daily operations of the restaurant; she'd made that plain right from the start. Her involvement was restricted to using her friends for things like legal advice, and conferring with Tish on major decisions.

Tish had had no idea how complicated the whole thing would be. The problems with staff alone kept her on the run all day and all night; in the first month of business alone, they'd gone through three waitresses and two chefs. Receipts were low, but that was to be expected in the beginning. All in all, the signs were good. The tables were nearly filled at lunch, and, at their peak hour of teatime, people were willing to wait nearly half an hour for a table. They'd also gotten some nice mentions in a couple of the local giveaway newspapers. They were even beginning to recognize a few regulars, customers who came in frequently, a few who showed up almost every day. If things continued to go well, they should be okay. One more month, maybe two, she reassured herself, and she could get back to the business of raising her daughter.

It wouldn't be a moment too soon. Olivia was far too often left alone with baby-sitters, or forced to make do with the short snatches of time her mother could spare. Tish saw how confused the ten-year-old was, miserable at being away from her father, annoyed at her mother's absence. She worried about Olivia's listlessness, her lack of interest in getting out of the house. When Tish urged her to call a friend, she'd always refuse, preferring to spend all weekend long in front of the television set. There wasn't much Tish could do about it; after all, she was almost never home.

Olivia reentered the room, dejection written all over her.

"Daddy was in a meeting."

She flounced down into a chair, glaring at her mother as she saw that this was what Tish had expected to hear. "He'll call back in an hour or so, you'll see."

Tish saw all too clearly. Cameron wouldn't return his daughter's call. At best, his secretary would call back, asking Olivia what she wanted. But there wasn't much Tish could do about it.

The tearoom opened for the day in forty-five minutes. She rose and headed toward the hall closet to get her jacket.

Tish didn't take any steps toward getting a divorce — there wasn't even time to think about it. She was mildly surprised that Cameron didn't either. But she could no longer use his name to get credit or cash. It was her children's schooling that worried her the most; they were safe for the upcoming semester, but after that she was staring at a tuition bill far beyond anything she was likely to come up with, no matter how successful the tearoom was. There was just no chance she would clear enough profit to pay those kinds of bills after her first year in business. But she couldn't take Evan out of Yale — he loved it there so much. And poor Olivia. Yanking her out of Brearley on top of everything else was the last thing Tish wanted to do. She took some satisfaction out of how well Patricia's *was* doing. But it wasn't enough.

Three months before the tearoom's first anniversary, Tish found out her problems were about to become much worse. She and Winnie received a letter informing them that the building housing the tearoom had been sold. The new owner was raising their rent from three thousand to seven thousand dollars per month, effective upon their signing another lease for the next year.

She called Winnie early the next morning.

"Did you get the letter?" Tish asked as soon as she heard Winnie's hello on the other end of the phone.

"What letter?" Winnie asked. "Oh, about the rent." Her voice became indignant. "Isn't that outrageous?"

"What are we going to do?" Tish tapped her foot nervously on the floor, her head aching from lack of sleep. Dan Brady had already refused her request to put more money into the business. Politely but firmly, he told her seventy-five thousand had been all he'd promised. But the bills just kept piling up. She had already been turned down twice for bank loans; there was no point asking again. The tearoom was popular, but it couldn't support that kind of rent. No matter how well they did in a week, some emergency or unexpected expense would come along the next week to eat up any extra money. She felt as if she might explode from the strain.

Winnie paused thoughtfully. "Gee, hon, I don't know what we can do. It doesn't seem to me like we can swing it."

"That's it, that's all you have to say?" Tish's voice rose in anger.

"Look, I know this is awful for you. You had a lot riding on it. But what can I do? We've gone through Dan's money and there's no more. We tried, we really did. I'm sorry for you, but I don't have any answers."

Tish closed her eyes. It had all been a lark for Winnie, really, and she had never pretended otherwise. Besides, this wasn't Winnie's fault and there was no point trying to blame her. It was nobody's fault.

"It's all right, Winnie," she said quietly. "We both did the best we could. Unless a miracle happens, I don't see any alternative but to close up when the lease runs out."

"What a shame. It started out as such fun," Winnie said sadly.

"We owe a lot of people money right now, and that will continue for as long as we stay open." Tish's mind was clicking off a list of things to do. "The staff needs to be compensated, the vendors, and so on. It wouldn't be fair not to pay all of them. That will have to be worked out."

"You're right."

Winnie obviously had nothing more to contribute to the conversation. It would be up to Tish to close up Patricia's, and to see it through to the end. Looking ahead, her heart tightened in her chest.

She tried to put it off, but she finally faced what she had to do. Late the following Friday night, when Olivia was sleeping over at a friend's house, Tish decided it was time. Taking great care with her appearance, breathing deeply every so often to keep calm, she prepared herself.

It had been so long since she had set foot in the apartment building, almost a year. The doorman greeted her with his usual expressionless nod and ushered her inside. As the elevator stopped on the fourteenth floor, Tish set her lips determinedly. She had two children to consider, and their needs had to come before her own.

The housekeeper answered the door, and though her eyebrows shot up with surprise at the sight of Tish, she said nothing other than "Good evening."

"Is Mr. Hawkes at home, Dorothy?" Tish asked, drawing herself up, hoping she appeared more poised than she felt.

"Yes, ma'am. In the study."

Tish nodded and crossed over to the study door. Before she could change her mind, she knocked quickly and entered without waiting for a response.

Cameron was seated at his desk writing, his tie loosened, his suit jacket thrown over a chair nearby. He looked up, pen still in hand, to see what the intrusion was. Their eyes met. His face betrayed nothing. Then he smiled.

"You've come to visit me," he said pleasantly, standing and gesturing toward the leather couch against the wall. "Won't you have a seat?"

He knows why I'm here, Tish thought. And he's going to make me beg. For a split second, the suspicion flashed through her mind that it might have been Cameron who was behind the purchase of the tearoom's building, that it was he who had arranged to have the rent driven up so high she would be doomed to fail. No, it was simply that he had known she would never have come to see him in person unless she was in trouble.

"Why don't I have Dorothy get you a drink. Some white wine, perhaps?" Cameron smiled. He was tan and fit as always, she noticed.

Just half an hour later Cameron strode to the door and summoned the housekeeper, who hurried out of the kitchen at the sound of her name being called. Tish, seated on the couch, guessed that she had been in there gossiping with the kitchen maid and the butler about this mysterious late-night visit by Mrs. Hawkes.

"Dorothy," Cameron said, "please telephone Olivia at Lucy Haverford's house and tell her she is to return here in the morning instead of to the Ninety-second Street apartment."

"Yes, Mr. Hawkes."

"Tomorrow morning," he went on, "I'd like you to arrange for a moving van — my secretary can tell you whom to use — to go to Ninety-second Street and pack everything up. All the clothes and personal items should come here. Send the furniture and the rest up to the Bedford house for storage."

"Will that be all, Mr. Hawkes?" the housekeeper asked.

"Yes, that's it."

Tish looked away from the sight of the two talking, suddenly so tired she wondered if she could manage to stand up. Dorothy retreated to the kitchen, while Cameron returned to his desk and picked up the telephone.

"This is Cameron Hawkes. Gavin, please," he said when his call was answered on the other end. Even though it was late in the evening, Tish knew that Cameron's lawyer would respond immediately; Cameron was one of his biggest clients.

"Gavin." Cameron's voice rose to a friendlier pitch. "Tish is back home now."

Tish wanted desperately to go to her bedroom and sleep. It was as if a fog had descended upon her, making it difficult even to think.

Cameron went on. "I need you to do a few things. To start with, break the lease on the apartment she's been living in. And see to the closing of that tearoom. I'll be paying off the business debts, and I want that done right away. Then you'll have to handle all the details of permanently closing it up. The necessary papers will be messengered over to your office in the morning. I don't want to hear anything else about this."

Tish left as Cameron was hanging up. When she got to her bedroom, she took off her clothes, went to her closet, and found a nightgown she had left behind. She slipped into the blue satin gown and got under the covers, noting that the bed seemed freshly made, almost as if she had been expected. There was one call she wanted to make. Picking up the telephone next to her bed, she dialed the intercom number for the kitchen maid.

"Alice, bring me a glass of vodka," she said calmly. "A very tall one."

Chapter 12

"Come on, Susannah, say you'll go out with Andy. I know you'll like him." Sam Mitchell pushed his chair away from the table and picked up his plate to bring it into the kitchen.

Susannah smiled, joining him in the process of clearing the lunch dishes. "I'm not sure, Sam. I'm here to see all of you, not to meet a guy."

"I don't know why it would be so terrible if you happened to meet someone you liked at the same time you're visiting." Ruth Mitchell joined in the conversation. As she stood, Susannah put a hand on her shoulder.

"Please, Ruth, sit down," Susannah said gently but firmly. "We can clear up. You've done nothing but cook and serve us all day. I don't want you going to so much trouble."

"It's no trouble, darling." Ruth beamed at her. "You have no idea how much pleasure it gives

me to do things for you. Having you with us for an entire week
is such a treat."

Lily emerged from the kitchen. "Who's ready for coffee? Mal,
I know you're good for a cup."

"Always am," her husband replied with a smile.

"Sam? Timmy?" Lily asked.

Both her brothers nodded.

"Let me give you a hand," Susannah said.

Following Lily out of the small dining room, Susannah
thought again how amazing it was that Lily, at twenty-four, already had two children. Having arrived the night before, Susannah
hadn't met the boys yet, but she imagined them as being as free-
spirited and delightful as their young mother. It was immensely
satisfying for Susannah to see first-hand how good Lily's marriage
to Mal was. She was only sorry to discover how difficult their
financial situation was. All of the Mitchells were struggling to
make ends meet, Susannah saw, with the three children doing
what they could to help Ruth out. But they all seemed happy,
nonetheless.

They were always there for each other, and they were there
for her as well. What other family with so little to spare would
have pooled their resources to send her a plane ticket from San
Francisco to Harrisburg for the Christmas holiday? Even though
the special low fare meant Susannah had to come the week prior
to Christmas and return to California on Christmas Day, she didn't
mind. She was overjoyed just to be able to see them. Although
she'd hesitated initially about skipping the last few days of classes
at Berkeley before Christmas vacation officially began, now that
she was here, she was glad she'd done it.

Lily turned on the hot water and squirted detergent into the
sink, then started to rinse the dishes. "You really should go out
with Andy Bond. I promise you, he's great-looking."

Susannah laughed. "And looks are all that count, right?"

"No," Lily responded with a grin, "but they don't hurt, either.
I've had a secret crush on him since the first time Sam brought
him around, maybe two years ago. He's great." She lowered her

voice to a teasing stage whisper. "Swear you won't tell my husband."

"What's it worth to you?" Susannah smiled, taking a box of aluminum foil from a drawer to wrap up the leftovers.

Lily laughed, flinging a handful of suds at her.

The three men at the table all piled into the tiny kitchen at once, talking loudly, their arms laden with dirty dishes. Ruth came in right behind them, directing traffic, making short work of the cleanup. Within fifteen minutes, everyone was back at the table with coffee and pie before them.

Susannah sipped at her coffee, half listening to the noisy but affectionate banter of the others sitting around her, basking in the glow of being part of the Mitchell family again, even if it was just for a little while. Despite all the letters and phone calls they'd exchanged, fifteen years had passed since she'd last seen them. It was hard to believe. She'd grown up, as had the Mitchell children. But it felt as if no time had passed, as if she'd seen them only months ago. How nice it was, she thought, that the Mitchells had all stayed in the same town until now, and could so easily get together at their mother's house anytime. And they still wanted Susannah to be with them, still treated her as one of them. She looked over at Ruth, who was offering Timmy another piece of pecan pie. Ruth hadn't changed at all. She looked the same, just as Susannah always remembered her. She was as kind and loving as she'd been when Susannah had lived with them. God, I'm lucky to have these people, she thought.

She couldn't help reflecting how different her life would have been if she had stayed with the Mitchells, instead of being forced to live with Arthur and Mary Rule. Even now, after three years away from them, Susannah shuddered at the thought of the couple, as if they might somehow reach out and pull her back to their house, to that life. She reminded herself that it was all over, that they couldn't touch her anymore. But, like a prisoner suddenly released, she still had the feeling that her freedom might be snatched from her at any second. She vividly recalled the overwhelming feeling of relief that day back in high school when she found out the University of California had accepted her for admission. When she learned that she was receiving a full scholarship, she had gone into her bedroom, shut the door, and cried with joy. She'd spent the next few months worrying that the school would call and announce there had been a mistake, that she would have to pay full tuition, or, worse, that they didn't want her at all. But it hadn't happened. September had finally come, and she had packed two suitcases and gotten on a bus north.

What a sensation, stepping off that bus at the end of the ride. She had gotten away, escaped. It wasn't that the Rules had kept her locked up, certainly not that they'd beaten her. And, unable to use the tactics that had been so effective when she was small, as she'd gotten older they'd lost much of their power over her. They could no longer deprive her of meals, or make her sit in a corner for hours when she misbehaved. Nor could they threaten to withhold the shoes or clothes or school supplies she desperately needed; she had become resourceful enough to find a way around such punishments.

But life in their house was never anything less than miserable. As the years passed, the Rules grew elderly and more frail, and with advancing years, they became meaner, more angrily dependent on Susannah. Having spent most of her life bending to their tyrannical wills, she didn't know how to stop. She cooked for them and doled out a constant stream of medications, attending to their endless aches and pains. Despite her round-the-clock labor as maid, nurse, and chauffeur, the Rules complained ceaselessly that they were fed up with supporting her, railing at her incompetence, her laziness. She was too slow bringing their pills, and she didn't care whether they died right in front of her; the house wasn't cleaned properly; her skirts were too short and the neighbors were talking about how sloppy she looked.

Yet as the Rules criticized her, Susannah blocked them out. Her detachment would infuriate them even further, as they worked themselves up to screaming the same words they always did at the end of these tirades: she didn't care about anyone but herself. Now, at last, it didn't matter anymore. Her hard work was going to take her away, and she would be able to start over. The difference was that, this time, *she* would be in control. *She* would direct the course of the rest of her life.

"More coffee, Susannah, sweetheart?" Ruth Mitchell interrupted her reverie.

"Thank you," Susannah nodded, affectionately watching the older woman refill her cup.

Unlike the Rules, who'd resented losing her services when she left for Berkeley, her other foster mother had reacted with delight and pride upon hearing about Susannah's acceptance. A week after arriving at school, she was stunned to get a letter from Ruth containing a check for two hundred dollars. The accompanying note gave no hint that she suspected Susannah's money problems; it only wished her love and good luck in this new phase of her life, and told her to use the money to buy herself something nice, something that would make her feel as special as she was.

Susannah's first response had been to send the check back. She knew the Mitchells' situation had gone from bad to worse over the years. Ruth had gotten a job in a supermarket, and didn't earn nearly enough to take care of them all. Only Sam had managed to go to college with the help of an athletic scholarship. Two hundred dollars represented a small fortune for Ruth. But Susannah quickly realized that returning the money would hurt Ruth's pride. Instead, she opened an account at a local bank, and used her first check to buy a Berkeley sweat suit, which she sent to Ruth along with her letter of thanks. Ruth got a big kick out of the present, writing back that she was looking forward to wearing it on those cold winter nights at home.

It had been the same with the airline ticket for this vacation: Susannah wanted to return it, but Ruth wouldn't hear of it. She said that seeing Susannah was for the family's selfish enjoyment. When the time came, Susannah told herself, she would certainly pay Ruth back for the ticket, but she hoped to be able to do a lot more than that; once Susannah had money of her own, she'd see to it that Ruth was taken care of financially and never have to worry about money again. God knows, I'd do anything for her, Susannah thought. Money was the least of it.

If only Ruth had been her real mother. Susannah had never

stopped fantasizing about who her real parents might be. Throughout high school, she was certain that as soon as she got away from
the Rules, she would be able to find her mother and father. Over
those years, she imagined dozens of scenarios to explain what
forced them to leave her at the orphanage. Sometimes, late at
night, she was afraid they weren't alive anymore, or they wouldn't
want her turning up at their doorstep; at other times she was
positive they must be living close by, aching for her and wondering
what had become of their little girl. If only she could talk to them.
She was desperate to know the truth about them. And she couldn't
help believing that when they saw her again, they would love her
as much as she was prepared to love them.

    Within a few weeks of arriving at Berkeley, she had hired a
detective out of the yellow pages to see if there was any way to
trace them. It had cost much more than she anticipated and used
up most of her savings. The money from her morning job in the
downtown laundry and her evening stint as a waitress also went
to cover it. She would do whatever it took if there was even a
chance she might find some clue, anything at all, that would lead
to her real mother and father.

    In the end, the disappointment had almost overwhelmed her.
The detective came up with nothing, confirming only what she
already knew: that she had been left at the Franklin Orphanage
near Hampton, California, in the summer of 1967, accompanied
by an anonymous note. There was no trail leading further back,
at least nothing he could uncover. He was very sorry, but he
doubted that anyone would ever be able to trace her parents. They
would never be found unless they chose to be.

    Susannah refused to accept that answer. She hired a second
detective, but the result was the same. Sorry, miss, I can't help
you, he'd told her. She begged him to try again, look some more.
But he'd refused, telling her he didn't know what else could be
done. She had sat up most of that night, crying with disappointment and helplessness. Finally, exhausted from her tears, she
conceded defeat. Her dream of being reunited with her mother
and father was never going to happen. She was on her own; she
always had been and she always would be.

After that, she redoubled her efforts to excel in school. If the other students spent a week writing a paper, she spent three; where others studied for a test for two weeks, she devoted four. She realized that the extra hours she put in each week were probably unnecessary, but she wasn't willing to take any chances, not when everything depended on that scholarship. Her hard work had paid off, earning her straight A's. Still, she took little pleasure in her academic success, always fearful that the next exam, the next paper might be the one where she blew it all. She couldn't let that happen. She had her life in her own hands now and she could never let go.

There was still a year and a half left to go until graduation, but she had already decided she should go on to business school when she finished at Berkeley. The competition might be stiff, but she was willing to work as hard as she had to in order to get accepted in a top MBA program. Then, she could get a decent job and the salary that went along with it. She didn't care about the money; it was the freedom and independence it brought, the power to do what she wanted with her life, to be dependent on no one. That was what her education would buy her, and she was determined to have it.

Timmy Mitchell stood up. "I'm off to Gloria's house. You want to come meet my girlfriend, Susannah, maybe have dinner with us?"

Lily answered for her. "No, she doesn't. She wants to go out with Andy and the rest of us." She turned to Susannah. "Right?"

Susannah shook her head in resignation. "Okay, I give up. But I do have that studying I should get done. . . ."

"Listen to this girl—studying on vacation," Sam said with a laugh. "I'll call Andy and we'll pick a time."

After lunch, Lily announced that she and Mal had to leave as well; a neighbor was watching their children, and they had to pick them up.

"I'm glad we'll get to spend the evening together. See you later," Lily said, hugging Susannah good-bye. Susannah had met Lily's husband for the first time that day, and she was pleased when Mal gave her a warm kiss on the cheek as he left.

When Sam said he had to go for a while, too, Ruth and Susannah were left alone. They went into the living room, where the couch and two chairs had been pushed into a corner to make room for the Christmas tree. The Mitchells had waited for Susannah's arrival to decorate it the night before, and it glowed with the warmth of the colored lights strung through its branches. Making their way through the crowded room, they sat down together on the couch. Susannah ran her hand along the flowered upholstery; it was faded and worn, but very comfortable. That was how she recalled everything in the Mitchell home: lovingly worn out and welcoming.

The older woman watched a wistful expression fleetingly cross Susannah's face. Ruth felt the familiar stab of guilt that came to her so often, the pain of not having found a way to keep Susannah with them more than a decade before. As always, she reminded herself there was nothing that could have been done; as always, it did little to make her feel better.

Ruth marveled at how beautiful Susannah had become. Thick, lustrous hair, so dark it was almost black, framed her slender oval face, and her large, long-lashed blue eyes shone with promise. Her high cheekbones set off a creamy complexion, and she walked gracefully but with an air of determination. Ruth was as proud of Susannah as if she had been her own child.

She took Susannah's hand. "It's suddenly so quiet with everyone gone." She smiled. "But it's nice to have a few minutes to ourselves. Tell me, darling. Are you happy?"

The question took Susannah by surprise. "Happy? Of course I am. Everything's going so well for me. I'll be applying to business school soon."

Ruth's eyes searched hers. "And that's what you want?"

"Yes, very much."

"I'm glad things are working out for you, darling."

Susannah didn't say anything for a moment. She didn't want to upset Ruth, but she longed to tell her the truth about what it had really been like for her after she'd left their home. It was all over now, and there was no longer any reason to keep it a secret.

"You know," she began, "things are good now. But it wasn't

like that for a long time. I never wanted to worry you, but living with the Rules was hard. They didn't love me at all."

"Oh, sweetheart." Ruth was visibly upset. "Why didn't you tell us?"

"There wasn't any point," Susannah said simply.

"What happened? What did they do to you?" Ruth asked anxiously.

Susannah thought for a moment, wanting to sum it up without disturbing Ruth even more.

"They were both old and sick, but right from the start they were just, well — mean."

"That's what I was so afraid of," Ruth said unhappily, "that they'd put you with people who wouldn't be good to you. But your letters — "

Susannah smiled to reassure the other woman. "It wouldn't have done any good to complain and worry you. Legally, they were the ones who were taking care of me. You couldn't have done anything."

Ruth shook her head sadly. "Oh God, I'm so sorry."

"Don't be. It's long past now." Susannah leaned over to kiss Ruth's cheek. "And I always had you, I knew you were out there. You can't imagine what that meant."

Ruth put both arms around Susannah, drawing her close. "I'm so sorry," she repeated.

Susannah hugged her in return, and lay her head on Ruth's shoulder. She stroked Susannah's hair. Susannah gave herself over to the feeling of being protected, loved . . . mothered. When they pulled apart, Susannah smiled again.

"Now tell me about Timmy's girlfriend."

The two women lost themselves in conversation, unaware of the hours passing. For Susannah, it was a golden afternoon. Listening to Ruth, laughing, and sharing secrets, she wished she could hold on to these moments somehow and preserve them forever.

Susannah sipped her beer, trying to hide her nervousness as Andy went on talking. Despite Lily's glowing endorsement, Susannah wasn't prepared for how attracted to him she would be. At twenty-seven, he was Sam's age, tall, with prematurely graying hair. There was something about him that Susannah liked instantly. The feeling had frightened her, and she tried to reassure herself by peering out to locate Lily and Mal on the Blue Lagoon's dance floor, Sam over by the bar talking to a friend.

"I doubt Sam will last the year at work," Andy was saying to her. He signaled to the waitress to bring them two more beers.

"You mean he might be fired?" Susannah was alarmed.

Andy laughed. "No, Sam's a great worker, the best in the factory. But he's got wanderlust. I wouldn't be surprised if he went off to Japan or Australia or someplace like that. This town is much too small for him."

Susannah picked up a tinge of disapproval in his voice. "What about you? Where would you like to end up?"

Andy smiled easily. "Right here, of course. It's my home. Harrisburg has just about everything I need. My folks, my brothers, my work, everything. I should be made foreman at the plant in another few months, so I'll be in good shape. I've got pretty much all I want."

Susannah smiled back. How nice to be so sure.

"What do you want, Susannah?" Andy played with her hand as he asked the question.

"Well . . ." She hesitated before going on, aware of the sensation of his hand on hers. How could she tell him without sounding like a snob? "I want to get my MBA and then find a decent job."

"A job, that's your big goal?" Andy shook his head. "That's fine, but isn't there anything else? Maybe something a little more pleasurable — like a husband and some kids?"

As he stroked her hand, Susannah felt her face flush. She was spared having to answer when Lily and Mal reappeared at the table.

"Come visit more often, Susannah," Lily said to her. "It's the best excuse for us to splurge on a baby-sitter and a night out."

The rest of the evening flew. Sam rejoined them and they sat around the table, talking, drinking, listening to the music. Susannah liked the easygoing way Andy kidded with Sam, his evident fondness for Lily, how he drew Susannah into the conversation if the others lapsed into talking about the factory where they all worked. When he put his arm around her as they got up to leave, it was casual, unstudied, as if it were somehow the right thing to do.

Andy drove her home in his car, pulling up outside Ruth Mitchell's house and turning off the engine.

"It's been a nice evening," he said quietly. "Very nice."

Putting his arm around her, he pulled her near and lifted her face for a long kiss. Without thinking, Susannah responded immediately, the stirrings of desire deep inside her.

Later that night, as she lay awake in bed, she thought about the kiss. She'd known so little about the opposite sex, had never had the time or opportunity to date as a teenager. I guess I've bypassed boys altogether, she thought in amusement, and gone straight to men. There was still little time for them at college, though, with all her studying and two part-time jobs. But being with Andy had felt so good, so different from everything else in her life. And here she was, as if she were double-dating with her older sister and brother, having a regular night in a local bar. It was so, well, normal, as if she were part of a regular family. Smiling in the dark, she rolled over and drifted to sleep.

When he showed up at noon the next day, she realized Andy must have had a good time too.

"Ready to go shopping?" he asked her.

"Shopping? Did we make a date for that?" Susannah was confused.

Andy grinned. "No, but it seemed like as good an excuse as any to spend time with you."

Ruth came into the room. "Hello, Andy. Can I get you something to drink?"

"No, thanks," he replied. "We're leaving in a minute to hit the stores."

"What are you two looking for?" Ruth asked.

"As usual, I've left my Christmas presents till the last minute," he said. "I'm hoping Susannah will give me a hand picking out presents for my nieces." He looked at her. "Would you mind?"

She smiled. "I'll give it a shot."

Several hours later, they returned to Ruth's house with their arms full of toys, puzzles, and books. Dropping off the packages, they went over to Lily's so Susannah could meet Lily's children. When the rest of the Mitchell family members came over for dinner, Andy stayed to eat with them all. With Susannah's encouragement, he joined the family on Sunday as well.

On Monday, it just seemed natural for Andy to come by after work. Making plans to return to Ruth's later to meet up with everyone, he took Susannah out to dinner. After enjoying two thick sirloin steaks and baked potatoes, they lingered over coffee and blueberry pie. Andy already knew that Susannah was an orphan and had lived with the Mitchells, and he asked her about the years after she'd left them. Although she told him a little bit about her past, she refrained from going into detail; somehow, she couldn't bring herself to talk much about it. Instead, she shifted the conversation to Andy's job at the factory, the production arm of an office furniture company in New York. He described the camaraderie among the people, the satisfaction he got when a project was completed, the opportunities to move into management that he saw opening up down the line.

Emerging into the crisp night air, Andy suggested a stroll to walk off dinner.

"Were you always so sure you wanted to stay here in Harrisburg?" Susannah asked him, reaching into her pockets for her gloves.

"Not always. I suppose things might have worked out differently if I'd gone to college," he reflected. "My parents didn't have the money to send me. I'd been hoping for a track scholarship, but in the end, it didn't work out."

"What are your parents like?" Susannah asked.

"My mom was the nicest lady in the world. She died when I was twenty," he said. "A couple of years ago, my father got himself a girlfriend, which is great for him. They basically live together. My brothers and I always tease him about living in sin."

"You have two brothers?"

"Three, actually. Ted left at eighteen. He's got a big job in Portland."

"And you're all close?" Susannah envisioned happy family get-togethers.

"Ted's not too good at that. But the rest of us are close, yes."

Susannah tried not to sound envious. "You must be pretty content."

"I'm content with what I have and what I'm doing. The only thing my life is missing is the right woman and some children. I love all my nieces like crazy, and I want some of my own just like those three."

He smiled at her, tilting his head forward to give her a quick kiss. "Why stop at three, though?" he went on. "Five or six sounds good, too."

In the next few days, Susannah discovered she could relax more around Andy than with any of the boys she knew at school. She warmed under his kisses, the ease with which they talked. On her last day in Harrisburg, Andy invited her to his place for a spaghetti dinner. When she said yes, she decided she was ready for whatever might happen.

But that evening, she found her stomach was in knots as he led her inside his house. It was a small one-bedroom cottage a little more than half a mile from the factory where he worked. She saw it was messy and cluttered, but clean.

Too nervous to do more than push her food around on the plate, she sipped the Chianti that Andy had poured for her and watched his expressive face as he talked, scared but also hoping he wouldn't just offer to take her home when the meal was over.

She wasn't disappointed. They brought their plates into the kitchen and were about to leave the room when Andy suddenly leaned over and pulled Susannah close. His mouth covered hers. Her heart pounded in her ears as she matched the urgency in his kiss. He slid his lips down her neck, pushing her blouse aside, his mouth hot upon her.

They slipped to the floor, their breathing coming quickly now, and she heard the snap of her blue jeans being opened, the zipper hurriedly being undone. Her limbs were like jelly. She felt his hardness against her thigh, and she suddenly tensed. Even though she hadn't sought them out, there had been so many boys asking her for dates at Berkeley, and lots of opportunities to have sex if she had wanted to. But no one ever seemed right, no one ever stirred the feelings in her that she knew should be there. With Andy, it was different. She was ready to make love, but she was also afraid.

Andy saw her hesitation, and pulled away slightly. "What is it?"

"I . . . I've never done this before." She felt so foolish.

"You've never . . . ?" He was obviously surprised. After a moment, he spoke quietly. "Do you want to stop?"

The gentle way he asked her somehow made it easier. "No," she said, "no, I don't want to stop."

Andy smiled and kissed her. Slowly, he began again, not rushing her, stroking her shoulders, her breasts, her stomach. He whispered her name as he eased her pants off and brought his hands between her legs, touching her lightly until she let herself go, carried away by the unfamiliar sensations exploding inside her. They shed the rest of their clothes and came together once more. She began to match his caresses, sliding her hand down his bare back, then farther down, feeling his desire for her in the tension of his hard buttocks and legs. He groaned and gathered her in his arms, their kisses passionate, their bodies moving faster. When he finally entered her, she cried out with pleasure.

Afterward, he held her tenderly. "You're wonderful," he murmured.

Susannah was surprised to find tears stinging her eyes.

"I'm sorry I have to go back so soon. There's only tonight," she said to him, running her hand along his arm.

"Then don't go," he said hoarsely. "Stay here."

Susannah laughed. "Okay, we'll just stay on this floor here for the rest of our lives."

Andy sat up. "I mean it. Stay in Harrisburg. We can make it on my salary. You can switch to a college here."

"Live with you?" Susannah was shocked that he was serious.

"If you want. I was thinking more about your marrying me."

Her eyes opened wide. This week had been like a dream. The Mitchells, meeting Andy, all of it. But marriage was something else entirely.

She thought about her scholarship to Berkeley, her plans for business school. If she stayed here with Andy, she could be with him, live in his house, make love like this all the time, have a family. It would be so easy, and she would be taken care of, never have to worry about anything again.

A vision of Arthur and Mary Rule came into her mind. Living their wretchedly miserable lives, forcing their values on Susannah. She'd vowed to make it herself. It would never be safe to be dependent on anyone or anything, she'd learned that the hard way. She took in Andy's face, his warm eyes. Yes, she could probably love him. But she couldn't abandon everything she'd struggled for, not even for him.

The flight back to San Francisco was almost empty. Of course, who would travel on Christmas Day, Susannah asked herself as she lay across the four empty seats in the middle of the aircraft. She pictured Ruth Mitchell with her children, no doubt drinking eggnog and opening presents right about now. Before she could stop herself, the thought flashed into her mind that they were probably having a wonderful time, even without her. She wanted to recapture the sense of security, the warm family feelings she enjoyed over the past week, but they were already fading into memory.

Biting her lip, she imagined Andy's profile, the way he looked seated beside her as he drove the car. She tried to recall his passion when they kissed, the sensation of making love with him. It had been only the night before. Why did it seem so long ago? Restlessly, she stood up and took a blanket from the overhead compartment.

It was all over now. The Mitchells, Andy, all of it. Somehow, in just a couple of hours it had already begun to feel like a dream. She was alone on Christmas, on her way back to a mountain of schoolwork. Alone, just as she had been every holiday of her life. That was real. All the rest was miles away.

Chapter 13

―――

With great reluctance, Kailey put down her copy of *Pride and Prejudice* and looked at the clock. She knew she should be picking out a dress and fixing her makeup, but it was difficult to summon up enough enthusiasm for the evening ahead to concentrate on the color of her lipstick or the anarchy of her hair. Being in large groups of people had never been easy for her, and tonight's fund-raiser would be enormous. It didn't seem to matter how comfortable she had come to feel as a sought-after interpreter. She was in her late thirties, a respected professional, yet the streak of shyness still remained. And all these years of being a loner hadn't helped a bit.

Guiltily, she admitted to herself that shyness wasn't the only reason she dreaded tonight's festivities. An entire evening of listening to Carlo Giantonio pontificate was going to be hell. She knew she ought to be grateful to him; after all, it was Carlo who had first drawn Ben and Risa into the World Peace Foundation, and it was only through their connection with the WPF that she had become involved. Without that involvement her sadness might have been completely overwhelming, even so many years later. Still she dreamed about Bonnie, but, strangely, she could deal with the occasional nightmare; it was the pleasant dreams, the long reveries in which Bonnie was alive, playing and smiling in her crib, holding her arms up to be held, winding them around her mother's neck, those were the ones that continued to hurt the most. The moment of waking from one of those dreams was just as devastating as the moment she had stood at the scene of the accident on that narrow California road.

Her means of escape was the WPF. She hadn't been able to save Bonnie, but at least there were things she could do to help other people, especially children. Every week she devoted two or three nights to the foundation, and the time hadn't been wasted. Raising money, writing letters, rounding up contributions of food and clothing, these she did with real enthusiasm. The last international letter-writing campaign had resulted in the release of three political prisoners in El Salvador. Other WPF events had raised large amounts of money and tons of food for refugees in Southeast Asia and several Eastern-bloc countries as well. Just the other day, their most vociferous member, Carlo himself, had distributed several copies of a letter from a family in Bucharest thanking him profusely for his help.

Of course that was just like Carlo. Don't just read the letter and feel grateful; make sure all your friends understand how much you're doing, how hard you're working. Carlo cared deeply about mankind. It was people he had little regard for. Her years with the WPF watching Carlo at the helm had enabled her to see him as a little less than heroic. All that knowledge, all that ebullience had begun to look more like grandiosity than generosity.

But Kailey kept her opinions to herself. Whatever she thought of Carlo, the work itself was essential. And she had to give him credit. However obnoxious he might be, he had managed to bully his fellow countrymen into a hardworking, well-run organization.

Besides, the Gottliebs adored him. At Carlo's urging, Ben had come out of his retirement and opened a coffee bar. It was there that the WPF people congregated, planning their strategies, coordinating their campaigns with allied groups like Amnesty International and UNICEF. Sometimes the WPF people would come just to socialize over a *caffè latte*, debating public affairs, even gossiping. Late in the evening they would often end up at Ben and Risa's apartment. Always, platters of food would appear, huge bottles of wine helping to keep the evening going until well into the night. If Risa provided the feeling of community and the nourishment, it was Carlo Giantonio who always held the floor, an expert on everything.

Kailey caught herself again. He really had pulled off a coup. Tonight would be Carlo's triumph, a fund-raising dinner celebrating the beginning of a five-city tour on behalf of the WPF. The tour featured a renowned French doctor from Médecins sans Frontières and then, most impressively, international singing star Preston Slater. It had taken months of telephone negotiations for Carlo to set it all up. First he'd had to agree to donate a large portion of the money to the overcrowded refugee camps set up on the Thailand-Cambodian border, the French doctor's pet cause. The WPF people had readily agreed to that. It was settling things with Preston Slater's bevy of agents, managers, public relations people, and lawyers that had taken Carlo so much time.

When Kailey first heard about the singer's being part of the tour, she found herself smiling. She could still picture her mother on a Friday night getting ready to go out, putting on her makeup, selecting her wardrobe, all the while swaying gently to the ballads of Preston Slater. Sonia Davids would never have stood on line for tickets from three in the morning on, as many of his fans did, or sent him any of the tons of adoring letters his publicity people kept in the public eye, but she certainly loved to listen to him. Slater was one of the few entertainers Daniel had been unable to entice to Radost.

Kailey couldn't remember hearing much about him in the last couple of years, but that didn't seem to matter much. Now in his late fifties, Slater still had the magic. Ticket sales had skyrocketed immediately, every venue sold out weeks before the tour even started. She couldn't imagine how Carlo had succeeded in getting such a big star to work for free on behalf of the WPF. The tour would start in Rome and finish in Paris, with stops in Geneva, London, and Frankfurt. Slater's hour or so of singing would be preceded by a talk by Jean-Paul Tranh Lassier, the French doctor. It was he who would do the pitch for money, food, and clothing. Then Preston Slater would take over. Carlo hoped that the combination of real information and big star power would raise several million dollars. Hundreds of thousands of lives would be affected if it worked according to plan.

Okay, Carlo, Kailey thought, pulling herself out of the chair and walking to the closet. You win. If you can get two busy and successful men to give up weeks of their lives, I can get myself through one long evening.

"Good evening, Jean-Paul. What a pleasure to see you again." Risa had to lean up on her toes to kiss him on both cheeks.

Jean-Paul was grateful to see a familiar face. He and Risa had met several times over the years at various political functions. He'd seen the same people over and over again, many of whom had become friends, but he'd always found Risa Gottlieb especially charming, her warmth a natural balm at events that were so serious. In her late fifties, she remained trim and attractive.

Risa escorted him into the small library, where a silver tray had already been set up with a few glasses and an assortment of beverages. "No one else has arrived, thank God, so we have a chance to catch up."

Jean-Paul laughed at her phrasing. Risa was one of the most outgoing and generous people he knew. If Carlo Giantonio was the moving force behind the Italian branch of the WPF, Jean-Paul was certain that Risa and her husband were the ones who provided the human touch, the thing that kept the loyalists coming back to work day after day.

"You love nothing better than large groups of people trooping through your home. When the others get here, you'll be in your element."

"Well, I have to admit to a certain excitement about this particular night. I do have the happiest marriage in the world, but that may not stop my heart from thumping when Preston Slater walks in."

Jean-Paul knew he was expected to smile, but he found it hard to do. Even before this dog-and-pony show had been arranged, he'd had doubts about Slater. Hospitals were rife with gossip about famous people with infamous health problems. Only a few months ago, during a research trip to the United States, he had overheard something about the singer having a problem with drugs. Jean-Paul probably would have forgotten all about it if he and Slater had never met.

Carlo's grand scheme had united them, though, and during the initial planning meetings for the five-city tour, Jean-Paul had been less than impressed with the famous American crooner. He had the self-absorption that both show people and addictive personalities so often displayed. During a break in the middle of the third planning session, Jean-Paul had been looking for some papers and unintentionally overheard Slater talking on the telephone.

"Listen. If I fail at one of these sucker events, no one will be any the wiser. If I fall on my face on the Carson show, every jerk in America will think I'm back on the powder. Jesus, I can't even blow my nose when I have a cold without worrying about a headline in the *National Enquirer*."

Jean-Paul had hurried out of the room before he had to listen to any more, disgusted but not really surprised. He'd been ready to congratulate Slater on his generosity. After all, the man must be losing hundreds of thousands of dollars in concert appearances giving so much time to this trip. The natural assumption—that Slater was devoted to human rights—would have made him very impressive; having met Slater, the real motive made much more sense. Everything about the man reeked of self-promotion.

Jean-Paul wished he didn't have to spend so much time with Slater, but the game was worth the candle. With the star's participation, they could raise as much money for the Cambodian refugee camps in five appearances as Jean-Paul himself or the WPF could in years. Even his spending a month every year running a clinic in one of the camps and donating part of his annual income to the cause couldn't accomplish nearly what the next few weeks' work would.

Risa noticed Jean-Paul's lack of response. "Is there something I should know? You're so quiet."

"No, let your heart thump away. Slater will charm you, I'm sure of it." It wouldn't be wise to share his hesitation with Risa. Slater's association with the fight for the Cambodian refugees stuck in camps would raise money for years to come. The fewer people who questioned his motives the better. It hadn't been easy to arrange for this tour, and he'd been lucky to convince Carlo and the WPF people to donate seventy-five percent of the profits to the camps. Slater was Carlo Giantonio's contribution; it would be a disservice to cast any shadow at all on his triumph.

"How are the plans for your hospital going?" Risa's voice broke in, bringing him back to the present.

"Very well, actually. What is it, three or four years since I saw you last at the Lisbon conference? We took title to three small buildings several blocks from Beaubourg. Since then I've spent most of my time trying to pick up corporate sponsors. Thank goodness, I've had some luck. One company in Japan has even agreed to a large annual donation." Jean-Paul chuckled. "I wonder what they'll expect in return."

Risa chided him gently. "Perhaps they're interested in the tropical diseases you're planning to study. After all, even some of the old things seem to be coming back. I see measles and tuberculosis mentioned in the newspaper quite often. Perhaps these companies wish to invest in the health of their consumers."

"And perhaps they think their consumers will buy more vacuum cleaners and cars and instant mashed potatoes if they read that their large corporations are dedicated to the social good." Jean-Paul laughed at his own cynicism. "Here I am on a five-city tour complaining about corporate promotion."

The sound of other company arriving interrupted them, but

as Jean-Paul sat at dinner and listened to Carlo's long toast to Preston Slater, his mind wandered back to his conversation with Risa. What burning egos all these people had. Slater and his career. Carlo and "the victims of the earth," an irritating phrase he'd used at least six times so far. Ego spoiled everything. When he was a boy in Vietnam, he saw the ego of his father's people, the French, claiming a nation that didn't belong to them. Then there was the ego of the Vietnamese, his mother's people, fighting among themselves for power when they should have been uniting against despotism, poverty, and disease.

Jean-Paul found himself smiling as Carlo's voice went on and on. Ego. He'd learned even more about it watching the power struggles within a large hospital. Doctors jockeying for eminence, researchers vying for grant money. When the Paris Hospital for the Study of Tropical Diseases opened its doors, no ego would be allowed. Not even his own.

Jean-Paul forced himself back to reality. Carlo seemed to be winding down.

"So to Preston Slater, artist and humanist, our greatest thanks."

Kailey took a sip of Beaujolais as Slater rose and started to speak. Her mind had begun to wander during Carlo's toast, and she saw that she wasn't alone. There were about thirty-five people at the long table and several of them seemed half asleep; the rest looked confused or just plain bored. She felt frustrated. The work of the WPF was so urgent, and here at this table were some of the richest and most influential people in Rome. If their interest were engaged, it could mean so much! She hoped Preston Slater would be an improvement.

"You know," Slater seemed to be looking directly at Kailey as he spoke, "human rights couldn't be more important. The right to be human, the humanity when you're right. This whole struggle is so profound, so global. . . ."

Kailey couldn't believe her ears. This man was an idiot. Clearly he didn't know a thing about the aims of the WPF. She wished she could ignore him, but the singer's eyes never seemed to leave her face. She couldn't decide which was more discomfiting, her dissatisfaction with Preston Slater or the obvious, come-on glances he was throwing in her direction.

She realized that Ben had noticed Slater's interest in her as well. What he didn't seem to be noticing was how little sense the man was making. Like a Dutch uncle, he seemed to be getting a kick out of the big star's attentions to Kailey. So did Risa, for that matter, sitting there smiling like a Cheshire cat. Well, the rest of the table might not find him quite as silly as she did, but there wasn't a chance they were being moved by this vapid speech.

She was relieved as Slater wrapped up his speech.

"As a performer, I know when the sideshow should end and the central attraction should begin. So please give the real act the same great response you've just given to me. Straight from Paris, Doctor Jean-Paul Tranh Lassier."

The group applauded politely, although Kailey could see disappointment on some faces as Slater returned to his seat. The tall, sober-looking Eurasian doctor moved to where the singer had been standing. Kailey admired his poise as he waited for silence. He was quite striking, with luxurious dark hair and an almost exotic cast to his strong-boned face. He looked presentable enough, but after Carlo Giantonio and Preston Slater, Kailey didn't hold out much hope. Still, she prayed he would be an improvement. So much was riding on this tour. Even on this dinner. To Slater it was obviously an opportunity to perform. Would the handsome doctor turn out to be equally self-serving?

"Ladies and gentlemen, I lack the theatrical ability of Mr. Slater, so I won't bore you for long." He took a sip of water before continuing. "Hundreds of thousands of Cambodians, all of them marked for death in their own country, are living in no-man's-land, in the refugee camps on the border between Thailand and Cambodia. The Thai government will not let them leave, the Khmer Rouge would eliminate them if they dared step back into Cambodia, and no other country is inviting them in. They are starving, they are suffering from disease, and every single day their situation grows more hopeless. Every dollar we raise tonight, every dollar we raise on the tour can make all the difference in the world. Another dollar, and a baby may be born alive and healthy. A dollar more may enable that baby to grow to adulthood. With the political pressure from the WPF, the medical care from Médecins sans Frontières, and the money donated by people like you, another holocaust may be averted. Thank you for your help."

Kailey surveyed the table. Every eye was on Dr. Lassier. Finally the words had been spoken simply and directly. A moment of silence was followed by strong applause. She could see several people reaching for their checkbooks, others whispering to each other, expressions of concern on their faces. Her eye continued up the line of diners. Only one person seemed to be unaffected by Dr. Lassier's speech. Preston Slater smiled broadly at her. A few moments later, she was dismayed to see him walk over to where Ben was sitting and whisper in his ear. She was uncomfortably sure his words had something to do with her.

She couldn't imagine what they were plotting, and she wasn't about to find out. Slater was due to entertain the guests with a couple of songs later in the evening, but Kailey had no intention of remaining for his performance. Quickly, she got up from the table. The night had been a success. A lot of money would be raised. The tour would undoubtedly be successful. For all of that she was grateful. But she was relieved that for her the night was blessedly over.

She was still asleep when Ben and Risa called her at seven-thirty the next morning, both of them chattering at once on different extensions, excitement making them interrupt each other like children.

"Kailey, darling," Risa's voice finally prevailed, "we have wonderful news for you."

Ben immediately took the conversation away from her. "Guess who's going on tour?"

"Who?" Kailey pulled herself up to a sitting position. Perhaps that would encourage her brain to start.

"You are!" Ben's voice was triumphant.

"What?" Kailey was confused.

Risa took the reins as her voice bubbled in pleasure. "Preston Slater needs an interpreter, and when he heard that you were the best in Rome, he insisted that you join him."

Kailey couldn't believe they wanted her to do this. "Please, Risa, there are hundreds of interpreters in this city. I'm much too busy to even think about spending that much time away. Who would do the economic conference next week at the embassy or the IBM event at the ambassador's house in two weeks?"

"Well, you see," Ben's voice returned, "you're hoist on your own petard. There are hundreds of translators in Rome. You just said so yourself. Anyone can take over for you at those events. But you're the only person Preston Slater will think of having."

"Oh, Ben, you just don't understand what you're asking. I find Mr. Slater quite charmless, I'm afraid."

"Well, he finds you dazzling, and you haven't dated anyone since Max Canfield." Ben suddenly realized he had hit a sore point. Quickly he changed his tack. "You're long overdue for a vacation."

Ben was making this so hard for her. Didn't he realize how difficult a five-city tour would be, constantly on call to a man like Preston Slater? Once more she voiced her objections, but Ben interjected once again.

"Honey, if you don't agree to accompany Mr. Slater, I'm afraid he'll back out of the trip completely. I'm sorry to use blackmail, but so much depends on this tour. If you can bring yourself to do it, please agree to this. Preston Slater is just used to being a star; you can deal with him easily enough. And really, the few weeks away will be good for you."

Kailey debated saying no, but quickly realized she couldn't. She thought of the Cambodians strung along the Thai border. What she was doing was whining, and she would stop it immediately. She rose from her bed and picked up the travel alarm she used every morning.

"Okay, you win, Ben. I've practically started to pack."

Chapter 14

"**K**ailey-cookie, tell the man I prefer the one with the silver face over there on the left." Preston Slater pointed to the expensive watch on the outer corner of a large tray, putting his arm around her shoulders.

Holding back her annoyance, Kailey moved out of reach. *"Combien, Monsieur?"* she asked the jeweler.

"Quinze mille francs, Madame," the Swiss watchmaker whispered, barely looking at Kailey as he answered her question. He was rendered almost speechless by the international celebrity standing right there in his shop. *"Pour Monsieur Slater,"* he added, speaking slowly as if somehow the singer might understand with more time between syllables, *"seulement douze mille francs."*

"The watch costs twelve thousand francs, Preston. He has taken three thousand off the price in honor of your fame." The sarcasm in her voice was wasted on the singer, to whom an *hommage* of a mere twenty percent was nowhere near honor enough.

"See if you can get it down to around seventy-five hundred." Slater's hand again moved toward Kailey, this time brushing the hair back from her forehead and traveling slowly down her cheek.

"Damn it, Preston," she said, swiping his hand away, "this isn't an Egyptian bazaar and I'm not a toy. Are you seriously interested in this watch or are you just amusing yourself?"

Kailey could no longer keep the frustration out of her voice. Slater had been pulling these stunts ever since the tour started, wasting people's time, taking advantage of his fame without giving a moment's thought to anyone else's agenda. And pawing her every chance he got in situations where putting him off would cause the kind of public embarrassment the World Peace Foundation could ill afford on this heralded tour.

She tried once again to keep her voice even as she spoke to him in low tones. "This is one of the finest stores in Geneva, and Monsieur Wachtel has other customers to attend to, so if you're not interested in the watch, let's stop wasting his time."

"Tell him he's charging far too much for it." Preston had no intention of stopping. He loved getting Kailey excited, watching the color rise in her cheeks. It had taken several days to engage the interest of this beautiful woman at all. Now that she was paying attention, anything felt good, including anger. No, he thought, especially anger, as she pushed his hand away once more and began to walk out of the store.

He watched her pause, addressing her good-bye not to him but to the jeweler.

"Monsieur, je vais penser à la moutre et je reviendrai. Je vous remercie pour l'aide et les renseignements que vous m'avez fournis."

Preston understood every word of her brief, apologetic conversation, but he had no intention of letting Kailey find out that his own French was flawless. The game of cat and mouse was too much fun, Kailey pretending to be frustrated, he wearing her down with his charm. He loved it when the women played a little harder to get.

Kailey saw the smirk not quite hidden at the corners of his mouth and turned away, unable to stand him for a moment longer. "You know, Preston, it's almost five. Why don't you go back and take a rest for a while before tonight's performance? The hotel's only a couple of blocks from here." Again she succeeded in the tiny victory of a normal tone of voice.

"Kailey-cookie, come back with me and I'll go to bed right now." Slater held his arms out like a two-year-old who wanted his mommy.

Did he set out to annoy her, or could he possibly believe he was adorable, that she would be swept away by the irresistible Preston Slater? Kailey didn't really want to know. She was sick of him, and longed for a couple of hours by herself.

"I'll meet you in the lobby at six-thirty. That should give you plenty of time to get to the theater and warm up." Without waiting for a response, she marched forward quickly to prevent him from following.

Relieved at the notion of freedom, she was unprepared for his sudden reappearance when she stopped at a traffic light two blocks farther down the large shopping street. He must have sprinted down the narrow street behind the large boulevard she was on to catch up with her like this, and she could see from the look on his face that he expected to be congratulated for his ingenuity.

"You see, Kailey, you can never get away from me." With those words, he lifted her off the ground and planted a kiss at the base of her neck.

The action galvanized her. "Get your filthy hands off me and leave me alone."

Seemingly chastened, he put her down.

She looked him in the eye. "I'll pick you up at six-thirty. Good-bye." She knew this scene would be repeated many times in the next couple of weeks. Well, she didn't have to think about that right now. She was entitled to a couple of hours on her own and she wasn't about to waste them.

This time he didn't follow her, as she walked along the street, completely alone for the first time in a week. Thank God, she thought. Since she'd left Rome there'd always been someone there. To save money for the WPF, she'd shared a hotel room with Slater's keyboard player, Meggie Capstone. And that was fine. Meggie kept mostly to herself, and the odd breakfast or lunch they shared together proved pleasant. But it left Kailey with no time by herself. And dealing with Preston Slater was proving to be a task that required virtually all her effort.

From the moment she signed on in Rome, Slater requested her presence every hour of the day and night, for shopping, for menu translation, for keeping crowds away. Kailey quickly caught on to the fact that he deliberately set out to attract people, then called on her to find a means of escape. Now that they were in Geneva, she also suspected that he spoke French very well. Every now and then she would catch him following a conversation, nodding yes or no at the appropriate time. Not that there was any way to prove it. But they had only one day left in the city; it was easier to just go on with what seemed more and more like an annoying charade.

Still, all of that seemed minor compared to the night after the first concert in Frankfurt. Three hours after he had hit the last note of *"Danke ʃchön,"* an experience that left the German audience standing and applauding for fifteen minutes, the police had picked him up on the autobahn going over one hundred miles per hour. When Kailey was summoned to the police station out of a deep sleep, the grim-faced officer in charge showed her a list of laws Preston had broken behind the wheel, starting with speeding and ending with an alcohol level so high it was amazing he was capable of driving at all.

He was lucky; the policeman was a great fan of American music, and Preston Slater was Officer Schneider's favorite singer. With a great flourish, the officer tore up the indictment and ushered them out of the station. On the way back to their hotel, Kailey was amazed to hear Slater's version of the events.

It'ʃ ʃo irritating to be recognized all the time, to have to be on your beʃt behavior, to have to be nice, even to Officer Schneider, the last two words spoken in a broad German intonation.

Kailey couldn't believe her ears. Not one word of gratitude, not even a sigh of relief! Sternly she reminded him that an officer who was less of a fan could have had him thrown in prison for drunken driving, but clearly he wasn't even listening.

The next morning, when the chambermaid reported to the concierge that Slater had painted a mural on the walls of his hotel room — it was such an *ugly* room, he whined to Kailey when she was called to the front desk — she began to realize that he would never listen. The man was a completely self-centered, overgrown baby. The most frustrating part was how he loved his pranks, looking at Kailey after each incident as if she were his mother, about to hug him and congratulate him on being such a charming cutup.

Kailey had gotten him out of Frankfurt immediately, leaving thousands of marks to smooth their departure, and prayed that Geneva would bring better behavior. But he was no better there, and from the day they arrived, his sexual advances had only intensified.

"Kailey-cookie, you're the most gorgeous woman I've ever known, and I'm so lonely," he crooned in her ear as they arrived at their adjoining rooms, his hands attempting a journey over her body.

By this time she had stopped being surprised by anything he might do. In fact, Slater's solution to her putting him off had almost amused her. When she went out to the corridor late one night for some ice, she saw two young women — identical twins, she realized, as they passed — leaving Slater's room, one of them still adjusting her waistband.

Kailey focused on the tiers of beautiful buildings and blossoming trees that lined the graceful shoreline of Lake Geneva. Without even realizing it, she had circled around back to the neighborhood of her hotel. She wasn't ready to go in yet, so she walked down toward the water, hoping for thoughts worthy of the spectacular scenery. But once again, she was haunted by Slater.

In Rome and Frankfurt, he had been infantile and unashamed of it. But here in Geneva, she had begun to see aspects of his character that he tried to keep hidden. At almost every meal, someone else was forced to pick up the check. Here was an American millionaire cadging free lunches from his translator, his backup singers, anyone he could find. There was always an excuse — he didn't have his credit card with him, he had to make a phone call just as the bill was arriving — but somehow he managed to avoid being the one to pay.

She looked at her watch. Five-thirty. Only one hour before she was due back. If she returned to her room, Slater might hear her next door and come up with some reason why her services were needed immediately. That was out of the question. She decided to have a coffee at the hotel's elegant bar before returning to the fray. Within moments, she had her *café-crème* set before her and was finally relaxing into the luxurious surroundings.

"Madame."

The sound came from behind her. It took a few seconds for Kailey to realize that the man was speaking to her. Turning around, she saw Jean-Paul Lassier, the doctor whose introductory words about the Cambodian refugees had stirred great emotion at every concert so far. He was holding a cup of coffee in his hand. Kailey had hardly spoken to him; the one time they'd begun a conversation he'd been called to the phone.

"Do you mind if I join you?" He stood politely at his table, waiting to move until she nodded.

"It's nice to see you, Doctor Lassier."

"Please, it's Jean-Paul."

"Well, then, I'm Kailey."

"So, Kailey, how is it going for you with the *enfant terrible?*" Jean-Paul spoke English well, the slight trace of an accent making the words seem more intimate somehow. "I gather he would keep you very busy if he could. Even busier than you are already."

Kailey was alert to the irony in his tone. Lassier had kept to himself during most of the tour, yet the doctor had seen the real Preston Slater more clearly than some of the others on the tour. She continued to be amazed at how many of his players and backup singers supported his worst habits, even at the expense of their own pockets, as if he really did deserve royal treatment. But Lassier was sharper than that.

"It's kind of you to notice, but I'm surprised you have time to think about my daily tasks. You seem quite busy yourself, with your phone calls and your notebooks." Kailey smiled as she said it. In his hand was the notebook he'd obviously been writing in before he noticed her.

"Well, that's far too true. Your friend Carlo promised me a vacation, but it's not turning out that way. I have a project back home that's just coming to a head. I'm afraid this past hour is one of the few times I've had to sit and do nothing."

Kailey cringed at the description of Carlo Giantonio as "her friend," and quickly moved the conversation back to Jean-Paul's work. "May I ask what kind of project you're working on?"

"Of course. Some years ago, I became aware that Paris had no hospital specifically for the tropical diseases that travel between France and the Far East — even after all those years that the French occupied Vietnam. What I'm interested in is the spread of disease across the two continents." He caught himself. "No, it's really three continents, once you include the United States."

Kailey nodded as Jean-Paul took a sip of coffee. "I must be boring you to death," he said. "I'm sorry."

"Why no, not at all. Frankly, it's the first interesting thing I've heard in weeks. How on earth did you get stuck on this tour?"

Jean-Paul laughed. Turning his large brown eyes to Kailey, he looked at her intently, his arched eyebrows raised quizzically. "I, at least, get the time to do what I need, and to do it by myself. How did you become the baby-sitter for *le petit prince*?"

Kailey explained briefly how Ben and Risa had roped her into the tour. Then she pressed Jean-Paul further about his work; in the next hour she found out a great deal. He'd been born in Saigon to a Vietnamese mother from an upper-class family and her Parisian husband, one of the consultants sent over by France in the early nineteen-fifties. When Jean-Paul was ten, his father had moved the family to Paris.

"I was given every privilege a boy could ask for," Jean-Paul explained. The finest *lycée* had been followed by the Sorbonne, medical school, even several years of residency in a New York hospital.

"I never thought much about Saigon, no more than the average rich Parisian boy. I was spoiled, selfish. A little like Monsieur Slater, really," he admitted, smiling. "Now I feel terribly guilty for those years." His voice turned grave. "It took too long for me to realize how much I owed to my mother's people."

"What finally made you see this?" Kailey wondered.

"Well, American television, for one thing. During my years at Mount Sinai, right there in the middle of beautiful Fifth Avenue, I would turn on the television and see my countrymen being slaughtered." He sounded not self-pitying, but ashamed. "I left New York and worked in Saigon as a medic for a couple of years, but when the war ended there was little more I could do. Hanoi wasn't about to let any outsider help, not even someone who had been born there."

He smiled in resignation, then went on. "I did travel back to Southeast Asia, and on one of those trips my friend Henri Stern took me to Thailand. We'd gone to medical school together. Henri was active in Médecins sans Frontières, a group of doctors who volunteer all over the world. It was Henri who introduced me to the Cambodian refugee camps."

Kailey was shaken as he described the horrors he'd found there. When he had learned about the camps, Jean-Paul had gone to work immediately, scrambling for drugs, treating scores of people every day he was there.

"I was well into the work on my hospital in Paris, so I couldn't spend as much time as I would have liked with Médecins sans Frontières. And, of course, I have patients in my private practice in Paris to consider; I couldn't just abandon them. But every year I return to Thailand for at least a month. Not even the hospital in Paris stands in the way of that."

Kailey was mesmerized by Jean-Paul. After these weeks with Preston Slater and the interminable evenings listening to the pontificating Carlo, she had almost ceased to believe that a man of strength and dedication could still exist.

And humor. He was funny in an appealing, self-deprecating way. She looked closely at him, at his deep brown eyes and thick dark hair. His high cheekbones and the slight arch of his eyes suggested his Asian heritage. He was self-possessed and strong, this handsome doctor. Was he in his late thirties? A couple of years older, perhaps?

Kailey flushed as she realized he noticed her staring. "I'd better get upstairs," she said as casually as she could, trying to cover her embarrassment. "I have to meet Preston in a few minutes."

Standing quickly, she intended to walk away from the table, but was stopped as Jean-Paul leaned over to kiss her on both cheeks. It was not the polite brush of his lips on her cheeks that left her shaken, but the lingering touch of his cool fingers caressing the naked underside of her wrist. She was electrified as his fingers slid up her arm, stopping in the vulnerable place inside the elbow. Suddenly she felt like a shy teenager. Was something happening between them, or was she making this up?

Daring to look him straight in the face, she saw the intensity in his eyes. There was a question there, not the adolescent whining of a Preston Slater but the open longing of a fully grown man.

Stunned at the sound of her own voice, she heard herself saying, "Perhaps we can meet after the concert tonight."

Jean-Paul nodded yes, and walked out of the bar ahead of her. It was several seconds before she was released from the invisible hold he'd had her in, before she could remember she had to collect Slater and return to the real world.

"But you promised, Kailey-cookie," Preston Slater moaned as Kailey began to thread her way through the crowds in the men's department of Harrod's. "You said you'd stay with me until I found something I liked."

"Preston, we've been here for an hour and a half. You've seen a hundred beautiful things."

Kailey took a quick glance at her watch, a motion not lost on Slater. Suddenly the mock-pathetic tone of his voice changed to a petulant five-year-old's.

"If Doctor Smarty-pants can't wait to see Florence Nightingale, that's just too bad."

Kailey had come to learn that only two modes of behavior worked with Preston Slater: humoring him or responding with complete outrage. It seemed a little early in the day for outrage, so she forced a smile and said, "You're my only priority today, Preston. I'm just a little tired. Maybe we could go back to Brown's and have a real English tea. You always like that, don't you?" My God, she was practically cooing, but if it worked it was worth it.

Slater could tell that he had pushed her as far as possible. It had been fascinating in the last two weeks, learning to gauge the exact minute, the exact phrase that would catapult her over the edge. But that wouldn't be any fun right now. She would just storm out, and he didn't feel like being alone. Meekly, he agreed to return to their hotel. But even as the doorman at Brown's was graciously shepherding them in, he seized the opportunity to complain about the size of his room.

"It's like a railroad car, for God's sake," he exclaimed loudly as the elevator operator took them up to the fourth floor so Slater could take a quick shower before tea.

Kailey was mortified. She thought she'd grown numb to his atrocious behavior, but at this small, elegant hotel, his reputation as the Ugly American was even more obvious than usual. It was bound to get all over the London tabloids. If Slater wanted to end his international career, she couldn't have cared less. But right now, everything he did reflected on the tour. It seemed wiser not to say anything while they were on their way up, but as soon as the operator closed the elevator door behind them she aimed her words at him.

"Preston, you cannot be rude in England without millions of people reading about it. Please, if you aren't concerned about the WPF, think of your audience tonight. If they walk in angry, you're the one who'll pay the price."

"Okay, Kailey."

He sounded contrite, which probably meant he wanted something. She braced herself.

"Kailey-cookie, will you wait for me while I get ready for

tea? You know I can't bear to walk into a room alone." He leaned down and started rubbing his head up and down against the hollow of her neck. "Pleeeeease."

She thought she would scream, but she suspected that was just what he was going for. Only two more performances, she said to herself. She knew she was going to end up humoring him, but she needed at least a few moments alone or she might really end up giving him a smack. Which, she realized, he would probably like.

"Preston, leave your door open, and I'll join you in two minutes."

"Thank you, Kailey," Slater purred.

Kailey walked to her room at the other end of the hall, and checked the telephone for messages. Sure enough, the light was on.

"Doctor Lassier will meet you in the bar of the Connaught after the show." The operator's words brought a smile to Kailey's lips. Just the sound of his name filled her with pleasure. They had been spending as much time as possible together each day, although with Preston Slater on the scene that didn't amount to very much. Kailey was amazed at the singer's perspicacity. From the evening she'd had her first drink with Jean-Paul, Slater had known something was going on. And the smell of competition had brought out the worst in him. Now virtually the only time he wasn't demanding her presence was the two hours he was onstage singing.

Not tonight, Kailey thought happily. She knew that Slater would prefer spending his time after the show without her. It was at an earlier concert in Geneva when a whiskey-voiced starlet had swept backstage, insisting he join her *samedi soirée* when they reached her "little British island." Kailey had watched Slater taking in her prominent breasts and long legs.

I wonder what he'll have in his bag of tricks at tea, she thought, giving in to the fact that it was time to pick him up. But when she got to his room, the door was ajar, and he was still in the shower. She decided to call Slater's hairdresser and makeup

people, and double-check with the theater people that Perrier, not
Evian, was to be left in his dressing room. Who would have
predicted that an interpreting job would include such menial functions, but she had learned that it was easier to deal with problems
before they occurred.

As she waited for the backstage phone to be answered, her
gaze fell on an open drawer in the desk. A black silk shirt lay
folded neatly, pinned, in fact, she realized as she looked more
closely. Hanging off the cuffs was a Harrod's tag, the price in
pounds translating to just under two hundred dollars. Funny, she
thought, I don't remember Preston's buying anything this
afternoon.

It somehow reminded her of a similar moment in Geneva.
Slater had shown up wearing cuff links she could have sworn he'd
admired in Monsieur Wachtel's jewelry store. When she'd questioned him, the singer had said that he'd already owned them.
There had been no reason to question him further. But now she
wasn't so sure. Slater had never bought a single thing in any
store they'd visited. She'd had a hard time figuring out why
someone who never spent any money loved taking so many hours
to look at expensive things. Feeling like a thief, she pulled open
another of the drawers. Sure enough, there were five or six ties,
each bearing a Harrod's tag, plus a beautiful glass plate. She
recognized that, too. It was from the elegant antique shop right
around the corner from the hotel, at which they'd stopped this
morning.

The bastard was shoplifting.

It would serve him right if I called the police, she thought.
But, of course, she couldn't. Hearing the shower go off, she
rounded up the items Slater had obviously taken. She'd just have
to return them to the stores they'd come from, and make some
kind of lame explanation.

I'll end up in jail myself, she thought ironically as Slater's
voice rang through from the bathroom.

"Kailey-cookie, can you bring me a towel? I left all of them
on the bed."

Within one week, I'll never have to see this man again, Kailey comforted herself. Then she picked up a towel and heaved it through the open bathroom door.

The Paris sun woke Kailey before seven. Her first thought was that there was only one more concert left. Then there would be no more baby-sitting, no more returning stolen objects to mystified store owners, no more tipping hotel employees long after Slater had made use of their services. No more "Monsieur was horrified when he remembered" or "embarrassed to be without small bills."

Kailey loved the view from the Meurice. Even Slater had had no complaints: room service breakfasts were perfectly cooked, his single room had been upgraded to a suite when the manager had personally seen to his arrival, and the women who worked there were stylish and seemingly adoring of the famous Preston Slater. Not that he had rewarded them particularly. As usual he hadn't parted with a dime since they'd arrived. It amazed her that the staff stayed as polite as they did as long as they did. The benefits of fame.

Time to shower, she realized, looking at the gold clock on the mantle. One more day of window-shopping, one more day of guard duty. One more day.

The good mood lasted until Kailey reached Slater's room thirty minutes later. The door was open when she arrived, but as she entered she realized the maid was cleaning the bathroom. Slater must have made it to the dining room by himself. Turning to go, she was stopped by a box lying on top of a dark walnut chest. She recognized it immediately. Slater had requested an empty gift box from Boucheron, the wildly expensive jewelry store near the Place Vendôme. "I want to play a joke on a friend," he'd explained endearingly to the dapper salesman who had, to his eventual frustration, shown the singer practically everything in the store. Kailey had kept an eagle eye on him after that, but hadn't seen him do anything out of the ordinary.

Have I become paranoid or could my worst fears be justified?

she wondered. Looking quickly to see that the chambermaid was still occupied, Kailey opened the box. Sure enough, inside was the magnificent ruby necklace she had seen Slater eyeing as he pressed the salesman to the next object. When had he managed to steal it? She looked at the price tag still affixed to the delicate clasp and did some quick math. Oh, God, the thing cost well over four thousand dollars. There was no way she could return this as she had the smaller items he had taken. The people at Boucheron would never believe her.

"Madame, je m'excuse."

The chambermaid startled her. Kailey placed the box back where it had been and mumbled a quick good-bye. What could she do, she wondered as she rode the elevator to the lobby. First she would find Slater. And then what? Should she confront him, demand that he be the one to go back to Boucheron? Fat lot of good that would do. In London, he had charged over a thousand dollars' worth of clothing in the haberdashery near Brown's and left word that the WPF would be footing the bill. When she explained that personal expenses had been no part of his agreement, Slater had simply refused to meet his obligation. "I'm worth it," he'd stated imperiously, refusing to discuss the subject any further.

So would he own up to stealing the necklace? No way. There he was, eating a magnificent breakfast in the ornate dining room. A heaping basket of croissants and brioches, several pots of assorted jams, a large platter of eggs with sausage, bacon, and ham piled on top — he had denied himself nothing this morning.

"The manager has offered us *le petit déjeuner* to honor our choice of his hotel," Slater said in perfect French to Kailey as he waved at the empty chair opposite him.

"Your language skills have improved remarkably since we were in Geneva," she said sarcastically.

"De rien," he replied, smirking spitefully. Slater had given up feigning ignorance. It was their last day together; he had other fish to fry.

Not bothering to notice whether Kailey was eating, he pushed his chair away from the table. "I have work to do this afternoon.

Perhaps you and the house physician can finally have a day all to yourselves." With that, he swept out of the room, as usual without leaving a tip.

At least it's the last time, Kailey thought as she took some bills from her purse and laid them on the table. She felt empty, not from hunger but from her problems with Slater. And there was no way to see Jean-Paul this afternoon. He was far too busy now that he was here in Paris, dealing with the final arrangements for his hospital.

On her way out of the dining room, she thought about how she should spend her day. Suddenly she felt angry at herself. Here she was in Paris, and she hadn't seen anything but the insides of stores. Well, she was damned if that was enough. Getting into the elevator, she had the pleasure of planning an entire day by herself. First the Louvre, then the Rodin Museum, she decided. And maybe lunch at L'Ambroisie. She would deal with Preston Slater and his attendant problems later.

And for several hours, she allowed herself to enjoy Paris. Realizing she was closest to the Rodin Museum, she made her way there. She intended to spend only an hour or so, and was shocked to realize almost the whole afternoon had flown by, most of it spent in staring at a Camille Claudel sculpture of a man and woman locked in a passionate embrace, which was located in one of the smaller rooms.

When she returned to the hotel at four, the enormity of Slater's crime shocked her all over again. Finally, she realized what she had to do. She would reclaim the necklace. If Slater ended up on the front page, so be it.

It was no problem getting the key to his suite. The manager had grown used to the notion of Kailey as part of the Slater entourage. He explained that the singer had had one guest just an hour before, then had left, "humming magnificently" as he walked down the front steps out into the sunshine.

Kailey kept an appreciative face for the manager's description of Slater's happy-go-lucky day, but when she let herself into the room, and looked at the place the necklace had been, she found instead four thousand dollars in cash. It took only a few seconds to figure out exactly where the money had come from. It wasn't just "a guest" who had visited Slater. It was a fence. A bearer of cash for goods. So that was the singer's real goal. She wondered how many things he had managed to sell before she had caught on.

Kailey stood there, deep in thought. Then, scooping up the four thousand dollars, she walked to her own room. Let's see, she mused as she began dividing up the bills; certainly that nice chambermaid deserved a few hundred. And the bellman who had hung all Slater's suits the day they'd arrived. And that nice watchman at the back door of the theater; surely he could use a large tip from the good offices of Preston Slater. She laughed out loud as she imagined how vociferously people would thank him later that night, after she had made her rounds armed with his cash. She might thank him herself, given how large the donation was that he was about to make to the WPF.

Jean-Paul splashed cold water all over his face. Thank goodness, the tour was over, and he was in his own home. Tonight was the very last time he had to solicit funds, the last time he had to be a public minstrel instead of a physician. Not that he had felt much like a doctor in the past year or two. Starting up the hospital had turned him into a full-time manager, and he wasn't all that sure he liked it. Raising money, spending countless hours with the architect, soothing ruffled feathers half the time, trying to rouse people the other half—these were not the actions of a man practicing medicine.

You wanted that hospital for very good reasons, he reminded himself, and now you have to deal with every aspect of it. Even the concert tour, coming as it did right on the heels of the hospital's opening, was worth it. Millions of dollars had been raised. Thousands of Cambodian refugees would eat, and get medicine and shelter. A lucky few might even get to bribe their way out of the camps, into one of the nations that paid so much lip service to helping them. The ringing of the telephone interrupted his train of thought. After perhaps his thirtieth conversation of the day regarding the hospital's opening, he hung up. He felt like taking the damn thing off the hook. No more phone calls from disgruntled lab assistants wanting more space, from Taggert at Oxfam decrying the hostility of the Americans or Shields from UNICEF complaining about the lack of generosity on the part of the British. Tomorrow night, he would leave for Thailand, ready once again to take on real medicine.

But tonight was strictly for Kailey. He glanced at his watch. There had been some kind of unpleasant conversation going on with Slater that kept her from leaving with him right after the concert, but she should be there any moment now. Interestingly, he'd seen from Kailey's face that whatever was going on this time was more fun for her than it was for *le chanteur*. Perhaps she was finally giving him what he deserved. Certainly Slater had looked miserable. And Kailey looked just the least bit smug. Well, good for her.

She deserved the world, this woman, not an imbecile like Slater. Jean-Paul had found her fascinating from the first time they'd met. He'd watched her when he'd spoken at the Gottliebs' table. She seemed to hear what he was saying, to understand the desperation of the situation.

And, of course, she was so beautiful. He had to laugh at himself. He had noticed that long before her intelligence and sensitivity had struck him. But it wasn't her beauty that so intrigued him, not even her compassion or her endless efforts on behalf of this tour. No, her most arresting quality was that extraordinary strength offset by such fragility. Kailey could handle Slater, that overgrown brat, she could speak any language and command the attention of any room. She even had a formidable temper. Yet, like a perfect crystal goblet, at any moment it seemed she might break in half. It wasn't clear what might cause her to shatter, but whatever it was, he had no intention of letting that happen.

He had taken it so slowly with her, never sure exactly how far he should push her. She seemed almost haunted, wounded by something. Did it have to do with the husband and child she'd lost? She hadn't offered any more information about them, yet underlying even the mention of them seemed to be some terrible secret. He felt closer to her than he had to any other woman, yet they'd never even made love. Never even really kissed.

Perhaps he could have penetrated all those mysterious layers, if only there had been time. But Preston Slater had made certain there never would be. Once he discerned a relationship between them, he wouldn't let her out of his sight. Well, as of right now, that was over. From the second Kailey arrived until he took off for Thailand tomorrow, they would be blessedly and completely alone.

His housekeeper, Madame Richoux, entered the large drawing room carrying a tray with a variety of hors d'oeuvres. "For you and the mademoiselle," she said, grinning widely. "Perhaps soon she will be a madame."

So, the canny Madame Richoux thought he was ready to marry. Well, perhaps she was right. The thought intrigued him. Who would have believed it? Certainly not Madeleine or Françoise, the two women with whom he'd spent the most time in the past ten years. Four years with each of them. Was there some alarm that went off exactly four years after a relationship started when a woman started to notice that something was missing? "You're never here. And even when you are, your thoughts are elsewhere." So said Madeleine. Four years later, Françoise had used almost the identical words. But with Kailey, it felt different. What a fascinating thought, to be married to her, to have her near him every morning when he woke.

The ringing of the telephone interrupted his musings yet again. He heard the voice of Pierre Sanois, his chief administrative aide, even as he was lifting the receiver.

"Jean-Paul, les techniciens du laboratoire ne commenceront pas à travailler prochainement. Ils sont d'accord pour le salaire, mais ils trouvent que les bénéfices ne sont pas suffisantes. Je te téléphonerai encore, mais je crois qu'il faudrait que tu viennes bientôt."

Kailey was led in by Madame Richoux before he had a chance to answer. He smiled weakly at her, then asked Pierre to hold a moment.

"Kailey, I'm afraid I'll probably have to go to the hospital to talk to the laboratory assistants. There's some problem with benefits, and if it doesn't get resolved, the hospital might not open on time. I'm sorry, but our evening's likely to be cut short."

Her graceful nod of acceptance didn't hide her disappointment. Looking at her, inhaling that hint of perfume that always signaled her arrival, Jean-Paul realized he couldn't let her just walk out of his life. He would be in Thailand for a month, so this would probably be the last he saw of her. No, he thought. That's just not possible. Saying a quick good-bye to Pierre, he hung up abruptly and walked over to where she stood. For a moment, he just looked at her. Then he lifted his hand to her cheek, trailing it down her neck, brushing past her breasts and coming to rest on her narrow waist. Pulling her close, he kissed her slowly and deeply. He felt her hand on the back of his head, her fingers in his hair as she responded to his kiss.

He couldn't bear the barrier of her clothing. He opened the covered buttons of her cream-colored silk shirt and ran his hands across the white lacy bra she wore underneath. He heard her gasp in response as his hands finally touched the naked flesh beneath. Lowering his head, he brought his mouth to her right breast, teasing the nipple with his tongue.

He brought his face up to hers. Without a word they sank down on the couch, kissing again, softly, then more urgently. His hand traveled over her body, finding its way under her skirt, cupping her mound. He pulled away the lacy underpants she wore and, as if by accident, his fingers slid inside her, moving, caressing, turning her to liquid heat. He heard her moan as he stopped and stood up, gazing down at her magnificent body, so sweetly inviting. Reaching up, Kailey hurriedly helped Jean-Paul shed his clothes. As he stood above her, she raised herself up on her knees, discovering his smooth chest, the hardness of his buttocks, the backs of his thighs. She wanted to feel every inch of him, to give him pleasure and take pleasure for herself. She'd never felt desire like this, so powerful, so consuming.

Jean-Paul eased her skirt off and together they lay down, staring into each other's eyes, both of them barely breathing as he found his way into her. Slowly they began to move together, exquisite torture, each movement a flood of sensations. Their motions became faster, fevered, building until they could stand it no longer. At the same moment, they both felt the explosion of pleasure, the brilliance of release as they held fast to each other.

They lay on the couch in silence, too sated to speak. But suddenly Jean-Paul knew what to do. He lifted his head, and his voice was ragged as he looked into Kailey's eyes again.

"Kailey. You must come with me."

"If you like, Jean-Paul, but I don't think I have that much to add to a labor negotiation." She laughed, her happiness from their lovemaking in her voice.

Jean-Paul laughed with her. "No, darling, not tonight." His voice grew serious again. "I want you with me in Thailand. Please, come with me tomorrow. The accommodations won't be much, but I promise you'll never be bored."

She felt the joy before she could say the words. To be with him alone, to see his face as she woke up each morning. It was as if a whole new life were being offered to her.

"It was a haven in the midst of a battleground. You can't imagine how beautiful Phnom Penh was before Nixon started his bombing." The old man didn't bother to hide his bitterness. "We all made it through the time of Lon Nol, that American stooge. But my wife was diabetic; she didn't survive the forced evacuations of Pol Pot, our very own Hitler."

Kailey watched the circle of Cambodian refugees surrounding them mouth the name in silent unison. *Pol Pot.*

The man continued, but now the anger was mixed with tears. "My little daughter came through all that. It was the famine of 1980 that finally killed her. And now there is nothing." The man suddenly looked straight at Kailey. "Tell that to your democratic government."

Kailey walked back slowly to the shack that served as their medical headquarters. She needed to see Jean-Paul, to watch him work, to believe that hope was still possible. They'd arrived in

Thailand at the camp Jean-Paul returned to each year only that morning, and it seemed every person she spoke to had another terrible story. She had known so little about the fate of the Cambodians who'd managed to get out, paid too little attention to the occasional news stories. In retrospect, her selfishness made her shudder.

Jean-Paul had explained the rudiments of the situation while they were on the plane. During the years of war between the United States and Vietnam, Cambodia had managed to remain a peaceful oasis in the midst of a firestorm. But some North Vietnamese installations had been set up on the border between North Vietnam and Cambodia, and the United States began bombing, following that with the installation of the government of Lon Nol. Subsequently, Pol Pot and the Khmer Rouge took charge, and began ejecting people from their homes. Entire hospitals were cleared out, families were split apart, hundreds of thousands died as the cities were emptied out completely.

Forced labor, starvation, mass terror, these were the trademarks of the Pol Pot regime. And when the Vietnamese invaded Cambodia after the end of their struggles with the United States, it was no better. In 1979, just as the Vietnamese defeated Pol Pot and the Khmer Rouge, scattering their remnants into the countryside, the worst famine in Cambodian history began. With the lingering terrorist attacks of the Khmer Rouge, the brutality of the Vietnamese conquerors, and the starvation, life in Cambodia became a living hell.

Those Cambodians who managed to escape went to Thailand, right over the Cambodian border. But here, they were stuck in camps. The Thai government agreed not to send them back to Cambodia, back into the midst of the violently warring factions, only because an alliance of democratic nations pledged to take care of them. Each nation sent a little money, but none would accept them as citizens.

And all around the camps lay danger. The Khmer Rouge, still supported by China, had established itself in small guerrilla units along the border. Then there were the forces of Hun Sen, the Vietnamese-backed new leader of Cambodia. The "lucky" escapees who made it to Thailand faced daily acts of terrorism along with starvation and rampant disease.

Kailey was overwhelmed by sadness, especially when she saw the children who lived in the camps. Most walked barefoot over the unpaved roads to tents and bamboo huts. The effects of malnutrition, malaria, and tuberculosis were evident everywhere. It was especially heartbreaking in such a beautiful people, their grace and politeness obvious even here.

Arriving at the medical facility, Kailey saw Jean-Paul just finishing his examination of an old woman. When he was done, they found themselves alone for the first time since they'd arrived.

Jean-Paul saw how exhausted she was. "Let's have some tea," he said softly, guiding her toward the small room that functioned as his temporary home, located just behind the treatment area. He placed a kettle of water on the primitive stove, then sat down next to her on a narrow cot, putting his arm around her.

"I'm sorry. I never should have urged you to come. It's too sad for you here." He gently lowered her head onto his shoulder, stroking her hair back from her forehead.

Suddenly she sat up straight. Too sad for me, she mused. How could any sadness *I* might feel be too much in the midst of this suffering? She pictured the refugees with whom she'd spoken during the afternoon. The woman whose husband was killed by a terrorist just after they had passed across the Thai border, the child whose left leg had been amputated when he was only four, the man who'd lost his mother during the forced march, his wife to a sniper's bullet the next day, his daughter to pneumonia two months later. All these years, she had been clinging to the tragedy of Bonnie's death, while all around her tragedy renewed itself daily. And these people went on, always looking toward tomorrow.

It was as if a twenty-year curtain of sorrow had parted, revealing light for the first time. Haltingly she tried to explain how she felt to Jean-Paul.

"For years now I've existed in the shadows, certain that everyone else really lived while I just hung on. Coming here with you, talking to the people here . . . they face death every day, they have nothing, yet they go forward, they still try."

What had happened to keep her so closed off for so long? he wondered, taking in the sadness in her large green eyes. Come only so far, and not an inch farther. That was the message she gave out, without ever having to say the words. But it wasn't enough for him. If she wanted the privacy of her past, so be it. But her future lay with him. He felt it. He knew it.

"Don't just hang on, Kailey." Jean-Paul turned her face toward his. "Go forward with me. Marry me."

Her flood of laughter took her by surprise as much as it did Jean-Paul; after so many years, her happiness came as an explosion.

"Does that mean yes?" he asked her, smiling.

Kailey gazed at him tenderly. "Oh, darling, yes."

Crowds of sightseers and workers surged through the Rue des Archives, making it almost impossible for Kailey to reach the front door of the main building. Her month in Thailand had left her unprepared for the Paris throng. Finally she made her way, pausing before the entrance. Her heart swelled with pride.

Today was a milestone: the opening of the Paris Hospital for the Study of Tropical Diseases. Jean-Paul's years of work were finally a reality. Since they'd returned from Thailand the week before, he had been there until eleven or twelve each night, finishing the seemingly endless tasks that had been interrupted by his month of service in the refugee camp. Kailey strode inside and was immediately impressed by the organization already in place.

Then again, she realized, everything about Jean-Paul had come as a pleasurable surprise. Even after a month of constant companionship, he never failed to impress her. The two of them together, making love, even just talking, seemed to make one entity, as if half of each of them had been missing all these years.

But their tiny universe had in no way prepared her for the public Jean-Paul. When the WPF tour had gotten to Paris, she'd been busy watching over Preston Slater, seeing Jean-Paul only onstage and in the privacy of his apartment that last night. But being with him every day now, she realized that here at home, he was treated to almost as much attention as if he were a pop idol or a movie actor. She'd been shocked by the appearance of newspaper reporters when they'd arrived at the airport, and she had avoided cameras every day since. If the private Jean-Paul were modest and considerate, it seemed to the public he was a wealthy, brilliant bachelor, a hero whose every move was of interest.

Even today, a swarm of paparazzi aimed their lenses in her direction as she approached the hospital. *"La fiancée de Lassier,"* she heard them murmuring. Kailey thought instantly of Cameron. He had been on her mind ever since she'd seen the first photographer trying to get a shot of her. Would all this public attention expose her? Could he possibly find out all the way from America that she was alive?

As she walked down the long corridor leading to Jean-Paul's office, Kailey pushed her fears aside. She had allowed no one a full view of her face. And so what if someday her picture appeared? She would be with a man of stature. Cameron couldn't touch her ever again. Relaxing, she began to notice the activity in each room as she passed by. This was the section where most of the laboratory work went on. Dozens of men and women in white lab coats — bent over microscopes or conferring in small clusters — attested to the fact that even on this first day, the work had truly begun.

At the end of the corridor was a passageway leading to the other two buildings. One was the in-patient section, where by the end of the month there would be over five hundred beds, all filled. Next to it was a slightly smaller structure, the outpatient clinic and emergency room. Jean-Paul's office was located at the very back of the laboratory facility. As she walked through the glass door with Jean-Paul's name labeled in elegant black letters, she saw that here, at least, it was clear this was the hospital's first day. Two large filing cabinets lay on their sides, and the desk was buried beneath a foot-high pile of the papers that belonged inside it.

At least in this endeavor Kailey realized she could help. She began to separate the papers and folders into organized piles; Jean-Paul would be able to file them as he wished. As she combed the mass of papers, she came upon the newspaper clipping that must have run that morning. Scanning it, she translated the French words. Suddenly, she stopped, rereading the sentence she'd just completed. There it was, right in the middle of the third paragraph, the corporate sponsors that had enabled Jean-Paul to get the hospital off the ground.

The Hawkes Corporation. Right at the top of the list. According to the article, Cameron Hawkes had promised five million dollars, far more than any other American sponsor, almost as much as the most generous French organizations.

Kailey sank into Jean-Paul's chair. She knew what that would mean. Jean-Paul met constantly with international leaders, not just doctors or government types, but businessmen. Aside from all his meetings, there were the numerous social occasions men in his position were forced to attend. One of these days, it would be Cameron sitting next to her at a dinner. Even if she could prevent that, as Jean-Paul's wife her name was bound to come up at the hospital. It didn't matter how many photographers she had ducked so far, he was bound to see her eventually.

And what then? He would assume that she had told Jean-Paul everything. Cameron couldn't possibly live with that. So now, both she and Jean-Paul would be in danger. She knew Cameron. He would stop at nothing.

Even if Cameron's only reaction were to withdraw his funding, Jean-Paul would lose his hospital. It couldn't continue without the money from Hawkes.

She had to leave Paris, and bitterly she realized she couldn't even tell Jean-Paul why. She could imagine his words if she told him why she was going. *I will never let anyone hurt you. You are safe here, and so am I.* But she wasn't safe from Cameron, and neither was Jean-Paul. Not if she remained. All those years of work would be ruined; his dreams would come to nothing. She couldn't do that to him. She loved him far too much.

Kailey waited until they were home to say something. Even then, she found it hard to begin. It was Jean-Paul himself who got her to speak.

"You haven't seemed happy all day, darling," he noted, taking her hand. "What's the matter?"

The lies came hard. Hesitating, Kailey began the words she'd taken hours to prepare.

"I can't do this, sweetheart. I don't want to marry you."

Stunned, Jean-Paul stared at her. His voice was a hoarse whisper. "You don't love me, then?" He almost couldn't bear the pain, even as he was saying the words.

"I do love you." Kailey couldn't lie about that. She followed the admission quickly with her planned speech. "It's this life I can't bear. After Thailand, where I felt so necessary every minute of the day, I can't stay here and be just a wife."

Jean-Paul's shock was obvious. "Just a wife. Is that how you think I'll see you?"

"No, of course not." Kailey found the strength to make her words sound convincing. "*I* see it that way. Back in the camp, I was doing something worthwhile. I'd like to go back, to continue the work I started, raising money, finding food and supplies, even helping in health care." Kailey knew her words sounded artificial, but it was the best she could do. "You taught me a lot in the past month. So many people need my help."

He gripped her hand more tightly. "*I* really need your help, dammit."

"Yes, but you'll be fine without me." Kailey fought back tears as she spoke, willing herself to sound firm.

Jean-Paul's tone betrayed his fury. "You love me, yet you want to leave me. Not to marry me, not to live with me, not to be with me. I don't understand — not a word."

"I'm sorry, Jean-Paul. If I stay here, I'll be just the sort of useless appendage I was in my first marriage. I'll shop, I'll accompany you to fancy dinners, I'll look nice and make nice friends and talk nice talk." She lowered her face so he couldn't see her anguish. "In Thailand I can achieve something."

Jean-Paul dropped her hand abruptly and began to walk out of the room.

"I'm sorry there isn't enough achievement in building a life together," she heard him say bitterly as he closed the door behind him.

Kailey left a few minutes later. She had no idea of where she was going. What possible difference can it make, she asked herself as she walked through the dark Paris streets.

Chapter 15

Susannah finished making the bed, and quickly straightened up the room, hanging a pair of pants in the closet and putting her blue sweater in the bottom dresser drawer. The years of being punished for the slightest messiness as a child had translated into a deeply ingrained habit of neatness. Pushing open the curtains, she looked out the window. It was a sunny Saturday morning, much too nice to spend inside studying. She had that economics test coming up, but she had already overprepared.

Grabbing her camera and the zoom lens, she yanked a denim jacket from the closet and headed out. She settled the camera strap more comfortably around her neck as she emerged onto 110th Street. The temperature was in the high seventies, one of those rare days when the air is exactly right, a warm breeze gently blowing. She closed her eyes for a few seconds to enjoy the feel of the sun's rays on her face. Her second winter in New York was fast approaching, and she was relishing these last weeks before the cold set in again.

It was a Central Park day, she decided, perfect for a visit to the playground at West Eighty-fifth Street. Briskly, she walked down Broadway, observing the Columbia students, the older men and women, and the young families who were out strolling, taking advantage of the weather.

The light at Ninety-fourth Street turned red as she approached, and she waited at the curb. Everything was going well, no question about it. Here she was at Columbia Business School, having just started her second year, in exactly the position she wanted to be. She had completed her first year with top grades, and her professors knew and liked her. She was active and busy, balancing her studying with a part-time job at a brokerage house, a good place to learn about finance. Because of the long hours she had to put in at work to earn the tuition money she needed, she wouldn't graduate from Columbia in the usual two years, but she expected to be able to finish in three. If she kept up her grades and did well in her interviews, she shouldn't have a problem coming up with one of the better jobs after graduation, maybe in a bank training program or with a consulting firm. She was dating here and there, mostly boys from her classes, a couple of men she'd met through work. But none of them stirred anything in her, none of them made her feel anything beyond a casual enjoyment of their companionship. Still, she was trying. Everything was going according to plan. The only problem was that she was miserable.

She'd been so clever, so smug with her decisions, her blueprints for the future. Go to grad school, get a big job, earn enough money to be independent. It had never occurred to her that the plan might require her to become someone she didn't want to be. The truth was she hated business school. Doing the work wasn't the problem. But she had no interest in what she was studying. And, worse, it frightened her to realize she could wind up locked into a life that wasn't what she wanted at all. A life without any creativity in it, no fun, no challenges. Plain and simple, a big bore.

At Eighty-sixth, she turned and strode over to Central Park West. There was a playground near the park's entrance and she stopped to watch the children, her eyes searching out possible shots.

This had been the big surprise, her photography. Susannah had known nothing about taking pictures, and for a long time had never even used the camera Ruth Mitchell had so generously given her as a college graduation gift. Then, one Sunday afternoon, she'd wandered into a gallery featuring an exhibit of black-and-white photographs. She lost herself in the pictures, staring into the eyes of the men and women who looked out from their places on the white gallery walls. She wondered what made a good picture, and how the photographer knew this was just the right composition and lighting, or exactly the right moment to push the shutter.

Later that week, she got out her camera for the first time and read the instructions that came with it. She always enjoyed looking out from her window over Riverside Drive, the sun playing on the Hudson, flooding the sky with color at sunset; it was a good place to start. Buying two rolls of film, she went down to the water at five o'clock, and shot all seventy-two pictures, experimenting, varying the shutter speed, focusing on different points, walking a few blocks every so often to change the scene. It was a bitingly cold, bright day, and she wanted her pictures to capture the hard light, the crispness in the air. Diverted by two children jumping rope, she snapped pictures of them as well. But when she got the prints back, she was disappointed to see that the day's vivid colors hadn't come out the way she remembered them, and the children's flushed cheeks somehow didn't come through. A number of the photos were completely out of focus. She obviously had a lot to learn.

School left her little spare time, but she took out a few library books on photography, trying to find out something about it. In January, she enrolled in a course that met on Thursday nights. The extra time put added pressure on her, but she didn't mind. Slowly, the world of f-stops, focal lengths, and depths of field began to open up to her. Whenever she could manage, she walked around in different neighborhoods, shooting whatever caught her eye. People, animals, architectural details — she tried to capture it all. Every so often, she spotted someone with a particularly interesting face hurrying into a restaurant or stepping out of a car, and she would quickly snap a few shots, enjoying the challenge of having only seconds to get her picture. But time and time again, she found herself drawn to taking pictures of children: a group of little girls in their parochial school uniforms, a lonely child on the playground swings, longingly watching the soccer game going on without him, a little boy dressed up for church, clutching both his parents' hands as they hurried down the street.

She took another photography course, and over the summer, treated herself to a good zoom lens. As soon as she got a batch of prints back from the lab, she would carefully scrutinize them, trying to figure out how to make them better. It wasn't until the end of August that she grudgingly admitted to herself that she had improved a little bit.

The whole thing was ridiculous, she thought. Here she was, in the enviable position of studying at a prestigious university, ready to embark on a serious career, and all she wanted to do was take pictures. She would rather be out with her camera than learning about macroeconomics or accounting or marketing. She didn't give a damn about those things. But how could she give it up, walk away from all the hard work she had already put in, the promise of her future? It was crazy even to think about that. For ten years she had struggled to follow her plan, studying, winning one scholarship after another, always keeping her nose to the grindstone. Now, finally, she was inches away from achieving her goal. Yet she couldn't seem to remember what the point of it all was.

Strolling through the playground's slides and tire swings, she caught sight of an elderly man sitting on one of the benches reading a book. There was something about him that made her stop. Tilting her head, she studied him, wondering why he seemed so familiar. As she moved closer, it came to her. It was Horace Sheffield, the historian. He was famous for his writings on World War I, practically a legend back in her Berkeley classes. She'd heard him speak once on campus — a rare treat, since he was a virtual recluse.

She knelt on the far side of the playground, fumbling to get the lens cap off her camera, hoping he wouldn't spot her and leave. She took fifteen shots in quick succession, zooming in for some, letting others reveal him from the distance. Her heart was beating wildly. She often took pictures without the subject being aware of it, but this was different somehow. Even though he was known to the public, she knew Horace Sheffield never posed for photographs. He wouldn't have permitted her to take them, no matter how innocent her purpose.

As always, Susannah felt a sense of accomplishment when she finished shooting. To capture a moment in time, maybe even to show someone or something in a way it hadn't been shown before — she was enthralled by it, in love with the whole process. God, how she would like to forget about business school, and just spend every day wandering around with her camera. But pictures wouldn't pay the rent.

It was nearly four o'clock by the time she got back home. She stopped to pick up her mail, inserting the tiny mailbox key and flipping open the metal door to the box marked 4A. Inside was a pile of envelopes and she quickly sorted through them. Junk mail and bills. She was inside the elevator, the door closing, when she saw that the last letter in the batch was addressed to Marlene Fuchs, apartment 3A. Normally, she would have left the letter in the lobby for the mailman to redistribute. Already on her way up, she reached out and pressed three. It would take only a minute to drop it off herself.

The name on 3A was Frost, not Fuchs. Susannah rang the bell and waited. Silence. Ringing again, she was about to slip the letter under the door when it swung open. Standing in front of Susannah was the most beautiful woman she had ever seen. Somewhere in her twenties, tall and statuesque, with voluptuous curves, she had flaming red hair and catlike gray eyes. Clearly in a rush, she was buttoning her blouse and trying to tuck it into her short leather skirt with one hand, while her other hand held two high-heeled black shoes, which she dropped noisily to the floor. Her beauty was so overpowering, it was as if everything around her receded into the background. Susannah couldn't help but stare for several seconds, the thought flashing through her mind that she herself must look like a complete mess after her day in the park.

The woman smiled at Susannah. "Hold your goddamn horses," she said pleasantly. "I was getting dressed and I'm late."

She turned away, stepping into her shoes as she continued to tuck in her blouse, apparently unconcerned whether the total stranger standing in her doorway was going to enter or not. Susannah held out the letter.

"I'm Susannah Holland. I live upstairs, and this was put into my mailbox by mistake. It's for a Marlene Fuchs."

The woman took the envelope, glancing at the return address. "Jamie, of course." She looked back up at Susannah. "My smart-assed cousin in LA thinks it frightfully amusing to keep reminding the world of my real name."

Susannah had to smile. "So I guess this is the right place."

"It is," she replied, a musical lilt in her voice. "I'm Marlene Fuchs, as my delightful cousin Jamie would like you and every-one else to know. My stage name and, as of six months ago, my legal name is Bibi Frost."

Her stage name. An actress. Of course, Susannah thought. With that face and that body, how could she be anything else?

Bibi — or Marlene — turned away once more, reaching for the lipstick that was on a nearby table and starting to apply it as she peered into a small mirror. The lipstick was the same bright orange as her hair. She was so beautiful there wasn't even any point in being jealous, Susannah thought as she watched her.

"I'm sorry to be rude," Bibi gestured with her lipstick, "but I'm in a terrible rush. Thanks for bringing by the letter."

"You're welcome." Susannah gave her a last smile and walked away as the door closed behind her. Boy, you never knew who lived in your building in New York.

She hurried back upstairs and quickly changed her clothes. She had a date that night with Mack Wilson, a student at Columbia who was in her marketing class. He was pleasant, and nice looking enough, but he didn't have much of a sense of humor. Still, she hoped Mack would be more fun than the man she'd had dinner with at V & T's the week before; he'd spent the entire evening talking about his former girlfriend.

The next day, she was at home, guiltily avoiding her schoolwork and reading a book on Diane Arbus when the bell rang. Opening the door, she found Bibi Frost standing there in a wildly flowered kimono and pink high-heeled slippers with maribou trim. The perfect outfit for an actress on a Sunday morning, Susannah said to herself, amused.

"I didn't know your number, so I just popped up," Bibi said apologetically. "I'm sorry about being so abrupt yesterday. I was on my way to an audition, and I was late. I'm *always* late. Come down for a cup of coffee, and let me make it up to you."

"That's really not necessary." Susannah wouldn't have minded a cup of coffee, but she really had to get down to studying.

"Come on, come on." Bibi waved her hand impatiently, ignoring Susannah's reluctance. "I have croissants."

It took only another moment for Susannah to change her mind. But Bibi was already halfway down the hall by then, her kimono billowing out around her long legs as she hurried toward the elevator, her high-heeled slippers clattering on the old tiled floor.

Like the rest of the apartment, Bibi's kitchen was overflowing with an odd assortment of things: mismatched dishes, trays, bottles and jars, and an endless variety of old biscuit tins, which, she explained to Susannah, she collected. The effect was something like an antique store, bric-a-brac in every corner, a treasure perched on every shelf. In walking the brief distance from the door to the kitchen, Susannah observed scripts and sheet music in tall, precarious stacks on the floor, dozens of framed photographs collecting dust on a cherrywood end table, and clothes strewn everywhere. Thinking of her own overly tidy apartment, she found herself admiring the freedom of spirit that somehow seemed reflected in all this mess.

They sat at the large kitchen table, and Bibi poured out freshly brewed hazelnut coffee into delicate china teacups. Susannah watched as her hostess slathered raspberry preserves all over a croissant, then took a satisfied bite, gesturing for Susannah to have one herself.

"So, who are you, what do you do?" Bibi asked suddenly, just as Susannah was taking her first bite of the buttery roll.

Her mouth full, Susannah paused before speaking. In those few seconds it occurred to her that she was tired of giving the usual, automatic answer.

"Well, let's see," she said once she had managed to swallow. "I'm at Columbia, at the business school. It's my second year. But I don't know. I'm . . ." She trailed off.

"Don't know what?" Bibi prodded her, looking interested. "You don't seem all that pleased about it."

"No, I am. It's great." Susannah hesitated. "You want the truth? I'd rather take pictures for a living. That's what I really love to do." She sat back, surprised at having blurted this out to a stranger.

"Well." Bibi raised an eyebrow, but said nothing more.

"I know, it doesn't make any sense," Susannah went on. "You can't make a living as a photographer, and no one in their right mind would drop out of business school when they're halfway done."

Bibi poured Susannah another cup of coffee. "I'm not the one who said it doesn't make sense. And who told you photographers can't make a living? Okay, so maybe half, three-quarters of them starve to death. But some of them do all right."

Susannah laughed. "Good odds."

"Okay, but why would you stay in grad school if you don't like it?"

"You don't just walk away from this," Susannah said strongly, as if trying to convince herself. "I've got school loans to repay, and I'm on track to a good, secure job."

"A good, secure job," Bibi echoed, wrinkling her nose in distaste. "You make it sound so incredibly appealing, like spending your life in a padded cell strapped to a chair. But, of course, I'm the wrong person to ask. Actors don't know anything about secure jobs."

Uncomfortable with the subject, Susannah asked Bibi about her acting.

"Ah, yes," Bibi said dramatically, as if she were about to reveal a great secret. "Little Marlene Fuchs was always singing and dancing for her parents' dinner guests back in Akron. Now she's alone in the wilds of New York, acting her heart out for fat old producers who don't care about anything but getting laid."

Susannah laughed again. She liked Bibi's style.

"I've actually done a fair amount of performing by now, mostly theater, and I'm studying at the Neighborhood Playhouse. You know, I think I've got some talent." Bibi looked serious. "But that doesn't mean anything. You need luck, being in the right place at the right time."

"If you're really talented, don't you believe you'll make it one day?"

"Talent isn't enough, they must have taught you that much at business school. Of course, you've *got* to believe you'll make it, you're nowhere without that. But you have to keep getting out and doing it, meeting people, practicing your craft, getting better. If you sit around and wait for things to come to you, you're a fool. You've got to *make* it happen. And every time it does, every time I get onstage, there's nothing like it."

Susannah was startled by Bibi's passion. That's what I thought I was doing, she reflected silently, making it happen. But she would never describe her own life with such enthusiasm. Maybe she'd been making the wrong things happen.

They sat and talked for close to an hour. Bibi told Susannah about a blind date she had the night before with a blond actor named Kurt.

"He seems much nicer than anyone I've met in the past few years," she said. "You know, I've dated some real losers."

As she elaborated on the long list of rotten boyfriends she'd had, Susannah wondered why a woman as gorgeous as this one would let so many guys walk all over her. When she finally stood up to go, Susannah realized how much she liked this woman. It would be nice to have a good friend right here in the building. Or anywhere in New York, for that matter.

Back upstairs, she tried to settle down to her accounting homework, but she found herself thinking about their conversation. Bibi didn't seem to have much money, yet she'd made it clear that she would never give up acting. The only thing in Susannah's life that created that kind of excitement was her photography. Up until now, she had just assumed it was a hobby, a distraction. What if she were to take it more seriously? What if she actually let go of the idea of getting her MBA, and attempted to make it as a photographer? She thought back on all those horrible years when Arthur and Mary Rule had control of her life. She'd vowed she would never be that powerless again. Dropping out of the MBA program for God knows what was inconceivable.

In the next two months, Susannah and Bibi spent a lot more time with each other. When they were both around in the evenings, they would go out for a hamburger, or cook dinner together. At the same time, Bibi was falling in love; her blind date, Kurt, was turning out to be more than a nice guy. In October, Kurt went on the road with a production of *Barnum,* so Bibi was free a lot more often. If Susannah could spare a weekend afternoon, they might go to a museum or a movie. One Sunday they rented roller skates and spent the day careening around the Columbia campus.

Walking down the street on the West Side or eating at the local restaurants, the two of them attracted a good deal of attention, an elegant brunette with sparkling blue eyes and a sexy redhead with long legs. Bibi had a wicked sense of humor, and Susannah watched her in admiration, knowing she could never get away with saying the outrageous things her friend did. Yet, despite her magnificent face and her quick wit, Bibi proved to be insecure. Before each audition, she would call Susannah and ask her to come by to approve her hair and clothes. No matter how much Susannah reassured her that she looked gorgeous, Bibi would insist on combing her hair differently, changing her eye makeup, putting on another outfit. But, she said, it was completely different once she got in front of a camera or an audience; that was when she felt really alive and unafraid. How come she always *seemed* so self-confident, Susannah asked her, even when she wasn't performing? When they were out, talking to people, Bibi could be the life of the party, completely self-assured.

"Act 'as if,' " Bibi had told her. "It's an old lesson I learned at AA. No matter how scared you are, you act as if you haven't got a care in the world. It's amazing how well it works."

"AA? Alcoholics Anonymous?" Susannah asked, surprised.

"That's right," Bibi answered. "It's six years since I've had a drink."

Susannah was flattered that Bibi had confided in her. She had never felt as comfortable with a friend as she did with Bibi, and it was nice to see that the feeling was mutual. She decided to tell Bibi about having been left at an orphanage, and how awful it had been to be taken away from the Mitchells. For the first time, she talked about growing up with foster parents who treated her as worthless and lazy, about how desperately she wished for her real parents.

"I felt so unwanted," she explained to Bibi. "I just wanted someone to love me. The Mitchells had, and I couldn't understand why I had to leave. It was as if everybody else was allowed to have people love them except for me."

Bibi sat listening quietly.

"More than anything," Susannah said, "I wanted my parents. If only I could find them, I thought everything would be all right. I'd have a happy home, I'd be loved. Nothing ever hurt as bad as finally having to admit that would never happen."

Bibi nodded in understanding. She seemed to know there wasn't anything to say that could really help. But Susannah had never told anyone the truth about those feelings. She was amazed at how good it felt to bring them out into the open.

Bibi always encouraged Susannah to spend more time on her photography. Eventually, Susannah was relaxed enough with her to show Bibi some of the pictures she'd taken. Bibi told her they were good, really good. She didn't press Susannah directly about pursuing it full time; she had her own unsubtle way of making her viewpoint known. Occasionally, she ran into Susannah coming down the block with a briefcase, dressed for her part-time job at the brokerage house in low-heeled pumps and a business suit. Bibi would smile widely.

"A good, secure job," she would say, echoing Susannah's words, looking her outfit up and down and nodding in exaggerated approval.

"Go to hell," Susannah would answer, laughing.

In November, Bibi's cousin Jamie came from Los Angeles for a week-long visit, and the three of them had dinner together several times. Susannah liked Jamie immediately, just as she had Bibi. Twenty-seven, attractive, and unabashedly homosexual, Jamie was a movie buff with an infinite store of Hollywood trivia. He had no idea what he wanted to do with his life, and had bounced around in several jobs before becoming a tour guide at Universal Studios. He talked in the same frank way as Bibi, whom he insisted on calling Marlene, and had the same wickedly sharp tongue; it was easy to see they were related. They insulted each other constantly, but it was obvious how close they really were.

During the last week of December, the two women were in Bibi's bedroom, Susannah leafing through a magazine as Bibi rummaged around in her drawers for something to wear on a date with Kurt, who was finally back in town. She had tried on virtually everything in her closet. Surveying the mess she had made around her, she sighed.

"I've got to get my life together. And I've got to get some new pictures. Of course, the pictures are more important than getting my life together. You can't go to auditions without good ones."

"What's wrong with your pictures?" Susannah asked.

"Oh, they're old, outdated, and the biggest problem is I don't have any more."

"Why don't you get some new ones done?"

"Why indeed." Bibi raised one eyebrow as if she disapproved of the answer she was about to give. "Money, as always. Filthy lucre."

Susannah looked at her. "You, know, Bibi, they might not be perfect—or even very good—but I'd certainly be willing to shoot some photos of you. If they work out, fine, use them. If not, you can go to a professional and pay to have them done."

Bibi took a sip of the club soda she'd poured earlier, setting her glass down on the cluttered bureau in a spot already covered by dozens of marks left over from other wet glasses. "Would you? I was hoping you'd offer, but I didn't want to ask."

Susannah was surprised. "Don't be ridiculous. It'll be a challenge for me."

The following weekend, Susannah brought some of the lamps from her apartment down to Bibi's and hung up a beige tablecloth as backdrop. Bibi sat in front of it, tilting her face according to Susannah's instructions, as Susannah moved the lamps around over and over, experimenting with light and shadow, taking a few pictures, then starting again. She kept telling Bibi it probably wouldn't work, that she needed better lights and she didn't know what she was doing with the ones she had, anyway. Bibi replied airily that she was just going to ignore her; the pictures would be sensational, she had no doubt.

When the prints came back from the lab a few days later, Bibi was delighted. They were just fine, she said, as she'd known they would be all along. Susannah herself was amazed that they came out as well as they did. She supposed Bibi was too good a subject for anyone to ruin, even an amateur like her. She went back to the library, taking out more books on lighting, trying to figure out how she could have done it better.

Early the following Monday morning, Susannah was at home, reading the newspaper and lingering over coffee before starting her statistics assignment. Her classes didn't begin until eleven that day, so she thought she would try to get some work done at home first. Flipping through the paper, she stopped suddenly at the obituaries. Horace Sheffield, the historian she'd photographed in the park back in September, had died. Immediately, she noticed that the picture accompanying his obituary was blurry, obviously taken when he was a much younger man. Couldn't they find any recent shots of him, she wondered, as she read the columns describing his life. When she was finished, she thought for a few minutes, then got up and pulled the telephone directory from a shelf above her desk.

In her photography class, she had once gotten into a discussion with another student about photo research agencies. These agencies, the student explained to her, kept all sorts of photographs, filed and cross-referenced under every conceivable category. They were used by advertising agencies, publishers, television producers, anyone who had the need for a particular picture. Clients called up, explained what they wanted, and were shown different shots that might meet their requirements. They selected the one they liked best and paid a fee for using the picture; the original photographer was paid a fee as well.

She tried to remember the names of the agencies the student had rattled off. One was coming back to her. Heaven something, or some word like that. Paradise, that was it. Paradise Photos. She flipped open the telephone book and found the number.

"Paradise Photos, good morning."

"Good morning." Susannah was suddenly nervous. "I don't know if this is of any interest to you, but I have some photographs, recent ones, of Horace Sheffield."

"Who?"

"The historian. He died yesterday. His obituary is in the paper."

"Hold on, please."

Susannah waited. Making this call had been a mistake; she was wasting her time.

A deep male voice spoke tersely into the telephone. "This is Jack Traldi. How can I help you?"

She took a deep breath. "My name is Susannah Holland. I took some shots of Horace Sheffield a few months back, and I wondered if by any chance you might be interested in them."

"Are you a photographer, Miss Holland?"

"Yes, I am." She wondered if he would somehow know she was lying. "Sort of."

He laughed. "Well, I've gotten two calls today for something on this guy, academic journals wanting a shot taken within the last forty years. I guess old Sheffield didn't pose much. Anyway, if you've got something, bring it in and we'll have a look."

"Right now?" Susannah asked, startled.

"Why not?" Jack Traldi said gruffly and hung up.

She shouldn't be doing this, she thought, hurrying over to her filing cabinet. She would be late for class. All her prints and negatives were neatly labeled and tucked away in folders. She pulled out the one marked *Sheffield, Horace/Central Park*. Grabbing her coat, she was downstairs and racing for the subway within five minutes.

Paradise Photos was on Twenty-sixth Street, just a few blocks from the subway stop. She practically ran into the building, knowing that it would be a close call if she was going to get back uptown by eleven. Nothing would come of this anyway, she thought, annoyed at herself, just a lost morning when she could have gotten through that statistics chapter.

She entered the office, seeing the rows and rows of tall filing cabinets, apparently full of photographs. There were five people in the big open room, most of them talking on the telephone as they jotted down notes or worked at computers. She walked over to the person sitting closest to the door, a young man about twenty.

"I'm here to see Jack Traldi."

He gestured toward an office off to the left. Thanking him, Susannah knocked, then entered as she heard the same deep voice she had spoken to earlier, telling her to come in. The dark-haired man seated behind the desk looked to be in his thirties and wore wire-rim glasses.

"Yes?"

"I called before, about the pictures of Horace Sheffield. Susannah Holland."

"Oh, right." He stood up and came around the desk to shake her hand. "Let's see what you've got."

Returning to his chair, he flipped through her pictures. Some showed an old man on a park bench, his dark suit contrasting sharply with the bright blue of the sky on that warm September day. But in others Susannah had zoomed in on his face, and caught a dignified and studious man, quietly contemplating his book.

Jack Traldi looked up. "Okay, Miss Holland. I think we can work something out."

Susannah was so surprised she barely heard him as he described the minimal fee she might receive if one of her photographs was used by their clients. But on the subway ride home, she couldn't keep from smiling. She was selling one of her pictures.

"Sorry, Horace," she whispered, feeling guilty that she was so happy, making money from his death, from pictures she shouldn't have been taking in the first place.

When she got back to her building, she went straight to Bibi's apartment. Her friend hugged Susannah excitedly when she heard the news.

"I told you, I told you," she yelled, pounding her fists on the kitchen table. "You can do it. You're just too stupid to realize it."

"Thanks so much," Susannah answered dryly.

"Okay, okay, you need to put together a portfolio. Something to make you stand out." Bibi covered her face with her hands, deep in thought. Susannah smiled at her theatrics.

Suddenly, Bibi looked up, a big grin on her face. "I have the answer."

"That's great," Susannah laughed. "Your audience waits with bated breath."

"Nudes. You're going to do nude photos of me." She nodded as if it were settled.

"What?" Susannah was genuinely taken aback. Despite her curves and customary short skirts, Bibi was actually quite modest. "Bibi, don't be silly."

"Why is that silly? Art shots for your portfolio. I trust you, I know they'll be in good taste. Ansel Adams, Stieglitz — and Susannah Holland."

Susannah laughed, but she was touched. "You'd pose to help me?"

Bibi shrugged, affecting an air of tired arrogance. "You're too pathetic to get your own career going without me. I'm simply going to *have* to step in."

For the next few weeks, Susannah prepared. It was the first time she'd let anything come before her schoolwork, but for once, she didn't care. At the library she read whatever she could find on shooting nudes. She'd invested in a tripod and a few lights and stands, but now she bought more equipment and a proper off-white backdrop. At home, she set everything up so she could practice. As a stand-in for Bibi, she used clothing in pale colors tied around pillows, experimenting with different types of film, shutter speeds, and lighting.

She and Bibi agreed to hold their session on a Sunday night. Beginning at six o'clock, Susannah made three trips between their apartments, ferrying all her equipment down to the third floor and nervously setting up. She tried to take her time and get things just right, while Bibi, wearing only her robe, watched quietly. When Susannah was finished, she turned to her friend, about to tell her they might as well get on with this fiasco, that she was as ready as she'd ever be. Bibi was a vision, her hair fanning out around her shoulders like a flame, her face perfectly made up. But it struck Susannah that Bibi was nervous too. She looked almost fearful.

At that moment, Susannah realized she could no longer behave like an amateur. This was a big favor, and she should treat Bibi with the professionalism she deserved. Bibi was willing to trust Susannah. *Act as if,* she told herself.

"All right, we're ready." She spoke calmly. "We won't shoot anything for a while. Just try a few positions until we come up with one we both like."

Bibi must have heard the authority in Susannah's tone, because she seemed to relax as she crossed the room.

"Let's do it," she said cheerfully, letting her robe fall to the floor.

As Susannah looked through the lens, she stopped seeing Bibi. Instead she saw curves and planes, light and shadow. She shot nearly two hundred pictures in three hours, stopping only when she saw that Bibi was exhausted. It was after one in the morning when she got home, but she was too excited to sleep. She lay in bed until the sun came up, knowing beyond the shadow of a doubt that this was what she loved.

On the day Susannah brought the pictures back from the lab, she sat down at her desk and took a deep breath before opening up the large gray envelope. Slowly, she pulled out the proof sheets and looked them over, examining every image.

Susannah didn't have to be told they were good. She knew they weren't perfect — far from it — but even she could see that they captured an object of true beauty and preserved it, simply and with dignity. In some of the photographs Bibi looked like a magnificent statue, while others made her seem alive, as if she might jump off the paper.

She brought the contact sheets downstairs and handed them to Bibi. Wordlessly, Bibi sat down and went through them. Susannah waited nervously.

When Bibi finished, she looked up.

"Magnificent" was all she said. It was more than enough for Susannah.

She left Bibi and went out for a long walk, still holding the proofs. This is mine, she thought happily. This has meaning, and I did it. And she was going to keep on doing it. *This* was what it felt like to have power over your own life. *This* was what it felt like to *be* somebody. It was as if years of trying, of struggling so hard and so joylessly, were slipping away.

Chapter 16

Susannah got out of the subway at Sixty-eighth Street and headed down Lexington Avenue. The December night was cold, and she walked briskly, pulling her long black coat tightly around her. At Sixty-fifth Street she hurriedly turned the corner. Jack and Claudia Traldi's brownstone was just a few doors in, toward Third Avenue. She'd been there once before for a dinner party, and the evening had been slightly intimidating, a roomful of impressive names from the world of photography and art, all talking shop. Judging by the bright lights, music, and noise emanating from the beautifully preserved gray building, tonight's party was going to be just as splashy. There were limousines parked up and down the block, the chauffeurs standing around talking.

Pausing in the vestibule before ringing the

intercom bell, she smoothed her hair and braced herself. She hadn't wanted to come in the first place; she was already tired and the night hadn't even started. Only a few hours before, she'd gotten off a bus from Harrisburg, where she'd spent three days with Ruth Mitchell. It had been so terrific to see Ruth again. Sam had moved to Canada, but Susannah had been able to visit with Lily and Mal, and Timmy as well. She'd considered calling Andy to say hello, but dropped the idea when the Mitchells told her he'd gotten married to a woman who also worked at the factory; he already had a son, and another child on the way.

It was a long trip to Harrisburg, but she was glad she'd made it. Ruth was so caring, so full of love for Susannah. Still, the hours sitting on the bus back had left her exhausted, and she would have much preferred spending the evening at home with some pizza and a good book. Besides, her general rule was never to go out on New Year's Eve if she could avoid it. She hated feeling obligated to have a great time, everyone trying so hard to make it the best night of the entire year. But she couldn't refuse Claudia. They had become friends over the past seven months, ever since Jack had hired Susannah at Paradise Photos and she had begun seriously pursuing a career as a photographer.

As hard as she had expected it to be, breaking into professional photography was far more difficult than Susannah had envisioned. She knew she needed a rep, someone to act as her agent and get her work, but it seemed impossible to get a rep without having work to show them, and equally impossible to get any work without having one. The biggest piece of luck that had come her way had been the afternoon she spotted two female rock stars coming out of a department store together. The photo she had taken of them, carrying lots of shopping bags and laughing, had been picked up by *Rolling Stone* and a few other music publications, and the picture was now on file at Paradise Photos. But that wasn't much to show for seven months of trying. Slowly, she was building up a portfolio. In fact, her book was full. But she wasn't satisfied with it. She wanted every single shot to be perfect.

Still, it was exhilarating, the freedom of having left business school, determined to devote herself to what she loved. At the same time, though, if not for the job at Paradise, she would be in trouble. When she'd dropped out of business school, Jack Traldi was one of the first people she'd called. She had told him her story and how much it would mean to her to find a way to be around photographers and pictures all day. There hadn't been any openings at the agency, but only four weeks later one of the staff members left, and Jack remembered her. The job didn't pay much, he told her, and she was far too qualified, but he understood what she was trying to do, and if she still wanted the job, it was hers.

Grateful for the break, Susannah tried to make the most of it. She studied the photographs in the files and tried to absorb the workings of the business, listening to Jack and the others negotiating deals, trying to figure out why clients picked one photo over another to communicate their message. She was barely able to get by on the salary, but she didn't mind; she was used to scrimping.

Susannah gave the intercom bell a light jab. If she hadn't been so fond of Claudia, she thought, wild horses couldn't have dragged her downtown to this party tonight. She hoped she looked all right, having taken a half hour to settle on the tight black skirt and lacy black camisole, with sheer black stockings and heels. Her hair had grown to nearly the middle of her back and cascaded luxuriously over her shoulders. The only jewelry she wore were long, dangling earrings of small gold coins that jingled lightly when she walked. Catching her reflection in the mirrored wall, she had to smile, thinking that a year ago she would have dressed for this party in something far more conservative — a simple black dress, probably, and some pearls. Being around the photographers, art directors, and models she encountered these days had definitely changed her style.

A butler opened the inner door to the Traldi brownstone. Handing him her coat, she stepped inside, gazing at the way the town house had been transformed for the evening. Hundreds of tiny white bulbs of light were strung along the ceilings and walls, casting a soft glow everywhere. Loud rock music accompanied the noisy chatter of people having a good time, punctuated every so often by squeals and shouts of recognition. The guests, she saw, wore everything from T-shirts and jeans to black tie.

It looked to Susannah as if there were at least two hundred people here. She wondered how many more were roaming around on the two floors above. Spotting Jack and Claudia across the room, she worked her way over through the crowd.

"You made it." Claudia shouted to make herself heard. She gave Susannah a hug. "You look gorgeous, even more gorgeous than usual."

Susannah kissed her cheek. "Thank you. Nothing could have kept me away," she shouted back. "The place looks incredible."

"Do you have a drink?" Jack raised his hand high above the heads of the guests around him and beckoned to a waiter. "What would you like?"

"White wine would be great."

At that moment, a short, rotund man appeared, taking Jack by the arm and causing both Jack and Claudia to turn away for a moment. Susannah recognized the man as the owner of a major gallery, and slipped off so the Traldis would be free to talk to him. It took a few minutes of being jostled at the bar to get a glass of wine. With her drink in hand, she turned and surveyed the room once more, suppressing the urge to check her watch. I must have put in a good ten minutes here, she thought. Only another three hours to go until midnight and then I can leave. *Stop it,* she admonished herself. She had sworn she was going to give it a chance.

She went up the narrow carpeted stairway, excusing herself as she wove through the guests talking on the steps. The landing on the second floor was also wall-to-wall people, so she continued up. Some of the men smiled at her and said hello. She smiled back but kept on going. The walls of the staircase were covered with photographs, some of which she knew were very valuable. She stopped at the top of the stairs to study the two hanging there, one a portrait of a flapper in the nineteen-twenties, another of a small town sometime in the late fifties.

There were only ten or so people up here, she saw with relief.

Looking around, she saw a pretty young woman sitting on a window ledge talking with a man in a tuxedo. His back was to Susannah. The woman was laughing. As Susannah watched her, it struck her that she was trying to seem very gay and carefree, probably to impress the man she was with. He leaned over and put his face close to hers. The woman smiled and nodded, then stood up, heading toward the stairs. As the man turned to watch her go, he caught Susannah's eye.

He had black hair and piercing dark eyes. Still holding her gaze, he smiled, the dazzling white of his teeth set off against his dark skin. She felt an odd sensation, a sudden leap in her stomach. It had been a long time since she'd had that feeling. The woman he'd been talking with brushed past Susannah, then stopped and turned to face him again.

"You'll be along?" Her accent was British.

He looked at her and nodded. Satisfied, she went downstairs. His eyes came back to Susannah's face, studying her. She was unable to move. He crossed to where she was standing.

"My name is Peter Manzoni." He had a deep voice. "Forgive me for staring at you like that. But I'm sure you're used to it."

She took a step back. Being that close to him was making her nervous. God, he was attractive.

"I'm Susannah Holland." She couldn't think of anything else to say. "Are you a good friend of the Traldis'?" How trite. She could have kicked herself the minute it was out of her mouth.

But he was smiling again. "Actually, I'm a very good friend of Jack's. We've known each other since we were kids. I'm just wondering why you and I have never met if you're one of their friends as well."

It dawned on Susannah who this man was. Jack was always referring to his childhood buddy Peter, and had described him to Susannah as his good-looking single friend, the one who had all the women. The word "good-looking" doesn't even come close, she thought. Drop-dead gorgeous is more like it. For a split second, she imagined how it would feel to kiss him, to loosen his tie and pull off his perfectly tailored jacket and the starched white tuxedo shirt beneath it. She was stunned by her thoughts, and by the sudden burst of heat that rushed through her.

"I work for Jack, actually, at Paradise." She wasn't going to lose her composure and act like a fool. "You and he used to shoplift together as little boys, right?"

The man before her laughed easily, his eyes crinkling. "Jack talks too much. But, hell, that was a million years ago." He looked at the nearly empty glass in Susannah's hand. "Can I get you something else to drink?"

"Isn't someone waiting for you?" Susannah gave a slight nod in the direction of the stairs where the woman he'd been with had gone. Why did I do that? she wondered. Now he'll remember and leave.

"No, no one's waiting." Peter looked her squarely in the eye and smiled. They both knew he was lying. Susannah smiled back, her fatigue forgotten.

"There's another bar on the second floor," he said, gesturing downstairs. He took her glass, his hand brushing hers lightly. The sensation was electric. She led the way down, her heart pounding. What was it about him that was making her feel like this?

He handed her glass to the bartender and asked for another white wine. Then, as they watched the drink being poured, Peter turned to her abruptly.

"You know, if you're really enjoying this, that's fine. But I think I've had enough. I know of some great parties."

"You're leaving?" Susannah kept her tone light, hoping there was no trace of the disappointment she felt in her voice.

"Only if you'll come with me."

The image of Jack and Claudia flashed through her mind for a second. They'd be upset if they discovered she hadn't stayed for more than a half hour. Well, she was going anyway.

"My coat is downstairs," she answered.

"Just give me a minute to say good-bye to someone," Peter said. "I'll meet you out front."

Susannah watched him walk away, obviously going to extricate himself from the woman he'd been with upstairs. She felt a twinge of guilt, then shrugged.

Once they were both out on the sidewalk, Peter held up his hand. Susannah couldn't figure out what he was doing until she saw a dark figure halfway down the block detaching himself from a group standing on the street, signaling back with a quick wave. It was one of the chauffeurs. The man got into a parked limousine, and pulled the car up directly in front of Peter and Susannah.

"Where to next, Mr. Manzoni?" he asked once they were comfortably settled in the back.

"The Corridor, Harry." Peter turned to her, lightly taking her hand. "Have you been there?"

"No, I don't think so," Susannah said casually. She'd never even heard of the place.

The Corridor turned out to be a nightclub, apparently a very popular one. A large crowd stood on the sidewalk. Susannah watched as Peter greeted the doorman with familiarity, then pressed two twenty-dollar bills into his palm as they were swept past the people waiting to be let in. The club was dark and smoky but lively, brimming with rich-looking, well-dressed New Year's Eve revelers. A live swing band played, and the dance floor was packed with couples. Peter led Susannah to a small table and held her chair as she sat down.

"This used to be a restaurant," he explained, watching her look around. "Recently, a couple of guys I know bought it and turned it into a club. They've been incredibly successful."

A waiter appeared at their table with a bottle of champagne. He poured them each a glass and discreetly placed the bottle into a bucket on a tall stand to keep it chilled. Peter lifted his glass in a toast.

"I generally hate New Year's Eve, but this one is going to be special, I can see that. To a beautiful woman and a beautiful night."

A tingling sensation spread through Susannah as she sipped the champagne, but she knew it wasn't from the drink. He was looking at her so intently. Something was happening, something she had never experienced before.

A sandy-haired young man, one of the club's owners, stopped by their table to say a brief hello before moving on. Then, she and Peter began to talk. He was in real estate, he said, and hinted at a boat and a small house in the south of France. When Susannah told him she had no family, he responded that he knew what it was like to be without parents; he had lost both his father and mother a few years before.

When the band played a slow number, he asked her to dance. It felt to Susannah as if they were floating. Peter pulled her close. The nearness of his face, his lips made her weak. It was all she could do to stop herself from kissing him, from blurting out that she wanted him. But she saw she didn't have to, that he knew how she felt, that he felt the same way. When the music stopped, they stayed where they were. Peter wrapped his arms around her and brought his mouth close to hers, pausing for a brief moment of exquisite torture. Then, he pressed his lips against hers. Susannah's eyes closed with pleasure as the heat she'd felt before flooded through her once more.

They sat down at their table and talked for another half hour, and were back on the dance floor when the clock struck twelve. The crowd cheered as confetti flew. Peter touched Susannah's hair, now sparkling with the glitter that had fallen onto it.

His voice was a whisper, yet she had no trouble hearing him despite the noise around them. "Happy New Year. It's going to be a wonderful year, isn't it?"

He leaned in to kiss her deeply and passionately. She wrapped her arms around him. The best year ever, she thought.

Peter stayed with her that night and the next. For Susannah it was as if the other experiences she'd had with sex had never happened. Making love with him was everything she hoped for. His kisses were hot and demanding, his desire for her intense. She felt herself consumed by him, everything blocked from her mind but the feel of his body against hers. His hands and mouth were everywhere, his experience in bed obvious as he brought her to climax over and over.

They spent all of New Year's Day in bed, with Peter getting up only to throw on his tuxedo to run downstairs for bagels and orange juice. He was so sexy, all disheveled like that, Susannah thought as she watched him come back into the bedroom, unshaven, his white shirt open at the collar. As he hurriedly stripped off his clothes, she found herself wanting to make love again.

The next morning Peter left at seven, saying he had to get home to change for a business meeting. He had dismissed the limousine, which turned out to have been rented, so he went off to catch a cab. Susannah, exhausted but happier than she could ever remember being, showered and got dressed for work, humming and whistling. She was late, and didn't even have time to make the bed, but she didn't care.

Jack was busy with a client that morning, so she didn't have a chance to see him. It was no surprise, though, that Claudia Traldi was on the telephone by ten o'clock.

"Good morning and Happy New Year, angel face," she said affectionately.

"A very happy New Year to you, too," Susannah answered cheerfully. "Thank you so much for having me to your party. It was great."

As she had expected, Claudia didn't waste any time getting to the point. "Great? You weren't there an hour. Somebody told me you left with a man. Who was it? Anybody good?"

Susannah wanted to giggle. She knew she was being ridiculous, a child, but she couldn't help it. "Somebody very good. Your friend, Jack's pal Peter Manzoni."

There was silence on the other end. She heard Claudia take a drag on her cigarette and exhale slowly.

Susannah didn't like the quiet on the telephone. "You know Peter, don't you? God, he's incredible."

"I just hope you know how to handle him."

"What do you mean? What's wrong with him?" Susannah's voice rose.

"He's a wild ride." Claudia paused. "He's gone out with an awful lot of women."

Susannah felt herself growing annoyed. "Claudia, just because he's gone out with a lot of women doesn't mean anything. He's gorgeous — how could he *not* have dated like crazy?"

"It's not just that. I know he's Jack's friend, but there are some things about him I don't trust."

"Like what?" Susannah asked.

"It's nothing I can put my finger on," the other woman replied. "But I'm afraid he could be trouble for you."

"Come on, Claudia," Susannah said. "That's not much to go on. I'll be fine."

"Okay." Claudia was clearly unconvinced. "As long as you can handle him."

Susannah didn't answer. Why was Claudia trying to ruin the best thing that had happened to her in ages?

"At least be very careful," Claudia pleaded.

Susannah's voice became polite. "Thanks for your concern. I'll speak to you soon."

She hung up, immediately feeling guilty at having been cold to Claudia. But she was furious that her friend couldn't have kept her opinions to herself. Even if it's only for a little while, she told herself, I'm going to have this man and I'm going to enjoy him.

Over the next month, Susannah was able to reassure herself that Claudia had been completely wrong. Peter was the perfect lover, warm and passionate. They spent every night together, and he constantly brought her flowers and small gifts. If she could have changed anything, it would have been her sense that she wasn't giving him as much sexual pleasure as he gave her. He seemed more interested in satisfying her than himself. When she tentatively voiced her thoughts, he replied that she was the sexiest woman he'd ever met, that no one could make him happier. At the end of their second week together, she was amazed when he told her he loved her, and knew they were going to spend the rest of their lives together.

It didn't take long for his belongings to start making their way to her apartment. He said he was having some work done on his own apartment on East Seventy-second Street, and didn't want to bring Susannah to see it until it was finished. She was disappointed, curious about what kind of place Peter lived in, but she agreed to wait. Aside from that, the only matters he kept to himself were his business dealings. Sometimes he worked late at night, and occasionally would go away on business for days at a time. But he explained that he was under a lot of pressure, and the last thing he wanted to do when he came home to her was discuss real estate.

Quickly, she was caught up in the whirlwind that was his social life. Every night for weeks, they would meet his friends and eat out at the trendiest restaurants, go to the hot new clubs, stop in at parties. Sometimes Jack Traldi was at these gatherings, and Susannah tried to adjust to dealing with her boss on more equal footing. She was surprised to observe how blatant Jack's social climbing was, how actively he pursued those who could be of use to him professionally — and ignored everyone else. Peter, on the other hand, seemed to know everybody in New York, and, from what he told her, was involved in a wide variety of development deals with lots of different people. He used some of his contacts to help Susannah as well, introducing her to gallery owners, to a man who wrote for an art magazine, and to several people who collected photographs for investment purposes. One woman bought a print from Susannah, and paid her three hundred dollars for a shot of two four-year-old twins on a seesaw.

Susannah was often exhausted by the pace of their social life, although every so often Peter would come home and announce they were staying in, plopping down in front of the television with no explanation. She would scramble to cook some dinner for them. She tried to be ready for whatever kind of night it was going to be, although she was puzzled as to why Peter never told her in advance what to expect. She wasn't about to criticize him for it, but secretly, she thought he could be a bit selfish. He just assumed she would be prepared for whatever type of evening he felt like having.

Peter had been intrigued to learn that Susannah knew Bibi. Their first week together, he noticed the framed photograph on the living-room bookcase of Bibi and Susannah smiling happily. Bibi's cousin Jamie had taken the picture when he was here on a visit, just a month before the release of the movie that made Bibi a star.

It had all happened so quickly, Susannah still couldn't make sense of it. Bibi had landed a small part in a film around the same time Susannah left business school. Flying out to Los Angeles for her five days of shooting, she had been such a big hit with the director that he instructed the screenwriter to expand her part. Even before the movie came out, word had gotten around about Bibi's talent and luminescent beauty, and the offers started. Over the past year, she had completed shooting on three more films, the first of which had already been released. It had gotten rave reviews, and made an enormous profit at the box office. Advance word on her next film indicated that it was likely to follow suit. As Bibi told Susannah, she was suddenly bankable, the magic word in Hollywood.

Bibi was renting a house in Malibu, though she kept her old apartment in Susannah's building, and tried to come back to New York when she could. Susannah was sorry to see those visits were becoming fewer and fewer. But they spoke on the telephone at least twice a week. Bibi never stopped telling Susannah how grateful she was to have her as a friend, someone she could rely on for the truth, who wouldn't treat her like some bimbo movie star, the way so many of the people she was meeting in Hollywood did. She was frightened by so much success so fast, and it was Susannah who helped her keep her feet on the ground.

Susannah promised Peter she would introduce him to Bibi the next time she was in town. She had already told Bibi all about Peter. Bibi was thrilled. She said she couldn't wait to meet the man who had finally melted the ice maiden's heart. But when Bibi returned to New York that March, Peter was away on a business trip. Although Susannah was disappointed that she couldn't bring them together, it was a treat for her to spend time alone with her friend again, just as they had before everything in both their lives changed so much.

Bibi was more beautiful than ever. Her hair was longer, falling in casual waves, and her pace seemed slower. Kurt had moved to Los Angeles to be with her, and his career was picking up too; he had already landed guest spots on two television shows. She told Susannah things were even better between them; she couldn't believe her luck. Susannah tried to convince her that it wasn't luck, but Bibi just rolled her eyes.

Back at the apartment, Bibi looked over Susannah's portfolio approvingly, but asked why there weren't more new shots. Susannah was embarrassed. She was letting her work slip, focusing too much of her energy on Peter and not enough on her photography. She resolved to remedy that.

Tears came to Susannah's eyes when she had to say goodbye to Bibi. Her friend hugged her and made her swear she would visit Los Angeles. Susannah could see the old fears and vulnerabilities in Bibi's eyes.

"It might be a while," Susannah reassured her, as the cabby loaded Bibi's luggage into the taxi, "but I'll definitely come out. And we'll still talk on the telephone all the time."

Bibi gave a small sigh. Then the moment passed. "Love you, babe, let's do lunch," she said laughingly, getting into the cab with a wave.

Susannah grinned as she waved back from the curb. But her grin faded as the cab turned the corner. As happy as she was with Peter, Susannah sorely missed Bibi's companionship. Glum, she took a walk, relieved that Peter would be coming home that night from his trip. When she got back to the apartment, she was delighted to find him already there, unpacking his bag.

"Hey, I thought you weren't due back for another couple of hours." She hugged and kissed him.

He smiled at her. "Slight change in plans, so here I am."

She rubbed her cheek against his. "I'm so glad to see you, honey. Bibi just left, and I miss her already."

He rubbed the back of her neck soothingly. "I've got just the answer. We'll have a quiet night together. I'll make dinner."

"You will?" Susannah said, startled. Peter had never cooked for her before.

"Sure." He laughed. "You've never experienced my fried eggs, have you? You're in for a rare treat."

Quickly changing from his suit into a pair of slacks and a tennis shirt, Peter poured them each a glass of wine and sat her down in a chair in the kitchen. The two of them talked as he prepared the eggs and English muffins, Susannah chattering on about her visit with Bibi. They ate by candlelight. Later that night, they made love. As always, Peter prolonged her pleasure before letting go to climax himself. Afterward, snuggling against him, half asleep, Susannah marveled again at her good fortune.

It was the middle of May when Peter suggested they take advantage of the warm night air and go for a horse-drawn carriage ride around Central Park.

"I know it's a corny thing to do," he told her, "but you've got to experience it at least once in your life."

"I think that's a great idea," Susannah said enthusiastically. "It's something I've always wanted to do."

They took a cab to Central Park South, where the carriages were lined up waiting for customers. Peter helped Susannah into one and jumped up next to her, telling the driver to take his time, they wanted the longest ride he was willing to give. It was when they were deep inside the park, the clicking of the horses' hooves rhythmic and soothing, that he took Susannah's hand, and turned to face her.

"For what I'm about to say, I wanted just the right setting," he said.

"This is the right setting for just about anything," Susannah replied, enjoying the passing scenery.

He paused for a moment. Susannah looked directly at him, realizing he was going to say something important.

"Susannah, will you marry me?"

She caught her breath. "What?"

"I want us to get married." His eyes searched hers. "What do you say?"

"I say —" she threw both arms around his neck — "yes, absolutely yes."

The first person Susannah called with the news the next morning was Bibi, who screamed with delight. Susannah felt that her entire life was finally falling into place. She and Peter im-

mediately began shopping for china and silver, Peter standing back
in amusement as she debated aloud the various merits of different
patterns. Maybe it was silly, she admitted, but she was overwhelmed at the idea of having a home and a family, and she wanted
everything to be just right.

They opened a joint checking account, to which each of them
contributed five thousand dollars. Susannah was pleased she had
been able to put aside that much money in the years since she'd
come to New York, but she knew that part of the reason was that
she'd been devoting so much time to Peter instead of her own
work; guiltily, she realized she should have been spending money
on new equipment, on photography courses, on going for job
interviews. Well, it would be used for a good cause now, to start
their life together. When the checks for their new account arrived
from the bank, she looked in amazement at the words Peter and
Susannah Manzoni written across the top. She could hardly believe it. In a few more months, they would be married and the
names would be real. It was actually going to happen.

Finally, she would be part of a regular, normal family. They
would have lots of children and fill their home with the love and
security she had thought she could never have. Sometimes, late
at night, she would creep softly out of bed so as not to disturb
Peter's sleep, and sit by the window, looking out at the view she
knew so well, thinking about her incredible good luck.

If Peter couldn't meet Bibi, Susannah was glad she would at
least have an opportunity to introduce him to Jamie. Bibi's cousin
came often to stay in her apartment — Bibi was glad to have someone house-sitting — and he called Susannah to tell her he would
be there for a month in June. He'd given up his job as a tour
guide at Universal, and was trying to decide what his next step
should be. Susannah immediately made a date for the three of
them to get together when Jamie arrived.

Over their dinner at a neighborhood Italian restaurant a few
days after Jamie arrived in New York, Peter was charming, but
Susannah sensed that Jamie didn't like him as much as she hoped
he would. Then, she was unpleasantly surprised when, as soon as
they finished their cappuccino, Peter announced that he had a late

meeting and had to excuse himself. Maybe he could sense Jamie's disapproval, she thought, but that didn't justify picking himself up and leaving. Frowning slightly at him, she nonetheless kept quiet, accepting the kiss he planted on her cheek and nodding when he said he would see her later. Turning back to Jamie, she restrained herself from asking him what he thought of Peter. Next time it would go better.

"Jamie," she said, taking his hand affectionately. "Tell me how you're doing. It's been a long time since we've really talked."

"I'm not bad, actually," he answered, flashing his boyish smile. "I don't know what to do when I grow up, but that's nothing new. And I've just come off a rotten love affair, but I'll spare you the details. Suffice it to say you've never seen such ugliness."

Susannah looked sympathetic. "Oh, I'm sorry."

"Don't be. He was the former lover of Don Edmund, by the way, in case you're interested."

"Don Edmund, the senator? The one who's supposed to be such a ladies' man?"

"The very same." He smiled mischievously.

"You're dangerous, really and truly," Susannah said with a laugh. "You've got the dirt on everybody."

"And don't you forget it," Jamie answered. He suddenly seemed to remember something. "Oh, by the way, I wanted to mention this to you. A photography thing. You've probably heard about it, but if not, you should be interested."

Jamie knew all about Susannah's efforts to break into photography. He genuinely seemed to like her work, and was always trying to come up with ways for her to make the right contact at a gallery, or get some job he'd heard about through his own remarkably efficient grapevine. But he was constantly urging Susannah to do whatever it took to get people to pay attention, suggesting tactics that she found shameless. Susannah invariably ignored his advice; it just wasn't her style.

He signaled to the waitress to bring two more cappuccinos. "I had lunch yesterday with a friend who works at the company that's sponsoring it. He happened to say something about it, so of course I immediately thought of you, and I pumped him for information. It's a very big deal, called the International Forum on Children, I think, and photography is a big part of it. Stop me if you already know about it."

Susannah thought ruefully of all the photography magazines piled unread in her bedroom; no doubt this would have been publicized in the trade journals. She'd really fallen behind.

As if reading her mind, Jamie gave her a disapproving look. "They're going to pick three photographers to go on a worldwide shoot, to take pictures of children of all nations or something. It's going to be a major thing — can you see the great PR angles — big corporation sponsoring all this cute stuff?" He took another sip of his cappuccino. "A publisher has signed to do a book of the photos. There'll also be a traveling museum show of the pictures touring the country."

"My God, what an opportunity for those photographers. All that would make your career," Susannah said.

"What do you mean '*those* photographers'? What about you?"

"Oh, come on, Jamie, how could I enter?" Susannah took a spoon and skimmed some of the frothy milk off her cappuccino, enjoying its sweetness. "I barely have a portfolio to show."

"Susannah," Jamie warned, "you've got to stop thinking like that."

She sighed. "You're right, I know."

"Okay, then," he went on, "now listen to the rest of it. My friend told me they're going to let the photographers spend as much time as they want in each place as long as they cover all their ground within a year. Nice, right? And, last but not least, each winner gets seventy-five grand."

"Like a dream come true, isn't it?" she said wistfully.

"Oh, get real, honey," Jamie retorted. "Nothing comes true if you just sit around dreaming about it. I told you this for a reason. Tomorrow, I want you to call and find out about entering. Are you still doing pictures of lovable little tykes doing adorable things?"

She nodded. "I still shoot children."

"I've met a few I'd like to shoot myself," Jamie answered. They both laughed. "Now, promise you'll call."

"Okay, okay, I'll call. It can't hurt, but nothing will come of it. You know that as well as I do. Imagine the kind of people who must be competing."

"*That's* the attitude," Jamie answered sarcastically. "What a can-do kind of gal you are."

Susannah smiled as they stood to leave, both of them reaching for their wallets. Quickly, Susannah picked up the check. "Please, Jamie, I insist. Dinner's on me. Now, what's the name of this company I'm supposed to call tomorrow?"

"Little Angel Baby Food," Jamie said, putting on his jacket. "Their headquarters is on Fifth Avenue in the Fifties."

"Little Angel," Susannah echoed as they turned to go. "Got it."

Chapter 17

At nine o'clock the next morning, Susannah sat at her desk at Paradise Photos, sipping a cup of coffee as she checked the number for Little Angel Baby Food Company in the telephone book. It was always quiet in the office until about ten, when the phones began to ring steadily.

As she ran her finger down the page of L's, Susannah wondered briefly why Jack hadn't mentioned anything to her about this International Forum. He was invariably tuned in to whatever new and important was going on in the business, and he would have known this was exactly the sort of thing she would be interested in. It had to be because of the unpleasantness with Claudia over Peter. The two women hadn't talked since Claudia had warned Susannah about Peter's reputation. For a couple of months Susannah had been angry, but now she saw how foolish it was. Claudia was entitled to her opinion, and she would no doubt be glad for Susannah, seeing that it all worked out. Susannah decided she would make an effort to patch things up as soon as the Traldis returned from vacation next week.

Maybe the four of them could go out to dinner one night. Her thoughts turned to Peter, and she frowned. He had been acting so jumpy lately. Tonight she would fix him steak au poivre, his favorite, then they would relax together.

She dialed the number for Little Angel's headquarters, and was put through to the firm's public relations office.

"Mrs. West." The woman who picked up the telephone spoke in a clipped, slightly annoyed voice.

"Good morning," Susannah said politely. "I'm a photographer, and I wondered if I might enter your photo competition. Are you the person I should talk to?"

Mrs. West answered without interest. "I'm in charge of all the submissions, yes. The deadline was last Friday."

"Ohhh," Susannah exhaled disappointedly. "Well, if it was only last week, is there any way I could still enter? I know I'm late, but —"

"No." The answer came back flatly. "The deadline has passed, and no exceptions will be made. Thank you for calling."

There was a loud click in Susannah's ear. Sighing, she dialed Jamie in Bibi's apartment and told him what happened.

"Last Friday? You missed it by three days? Come on, there's definitely some way around it."

"Jamie, the lovely woman I spoke with said no exceptions. And she didn't seem to be kidding."

He thought for a minute.

"We're not done yet. There's no reason you shouldn't be in that contest. We'll find a way in."

"Thank you, I really appreciate that you want to help me." Susannah took another sip of her coffee, now icy cold. "But I don't see what we could possibly do."

"Let me get back to you," Jamie said, and hung up.

Susannah shook her head. God knows what Jamie might

dream up, some nonsense about her portfolio being stolen, or lent
out to the British Museum, some extravagant excuse to get Little
Angel to extend the deadline for her. As always, she would listen
to him and say it was a great idea, and do nothing about it.

She reached across the table for her appointment book and
flipped it open. It was time for her to get cracking. There was no
excuse for having missed a major event like this, even though she
knew she wouldn't win. It was critical to keep circulating, get her
work out there. You could never tell who might see a shot you
did and like it enough to pursue you for some other job. There
was that print she'd sold to the Minar Corporation nearly a month
before for eight hundred dollars, a photograph of a ten-year-old
girl dribbling a basketball, all alone in a schoolyard. Making the
sale had been practically the biggest thrill of her life, and they
were even going to display it in their lobby, along with other
pictures of children engaged in sports. But they hadn't paid her
for it yet, and a month was a long time to be resting on her laurels.
She'd better start drumming up new work, or she was never going
to get anywhere.

Her eye fell on a note she had made to herself the previous
day to call Ruth Mitchell. She'd been so busy with Peter that she
hadn't spoken to Ruth in months. How could she have let so much
time slip by without being in touch, she admonished herself, picking up the phone again. The last time she'd seen Ruth had been
the day before New Year's, before the Traldis' New Year's Eve
party. Until then, they'd spoken on the phone often, but once
Peter came along, Susannah never seemed to have time even for
that. As a matter of fact, she now realized, she'd never even told
Ruth about Peter. That meant she hadn't spoken to her since the
new year began. Briefly, she wondered why Ruth hadn't called
her, either, but that didn't help much to assuage her guilt.

"Hello."

Susannah recognized the male voice on the other end. "Hello,
Timmy, it's Susannah."

"Sooze? Hi."

She smiled. "How are you?"

"Okay, fine, I guess."

"Is everybody okay? Sam and Lily? All the children?"

"They're great, thanks."

"I'm so glad to hear it. I haven't spoken with Ruth in a while, so I thought I'd just check in and say hello."

There was a pause. "She's not here. She's in the hospital."

Susannah caught her breath. "Nothing serious, right?"

"Well," Timmy said slowly, "yes, it is serious."

As she closed her eyes, a feeling of dread swept through Susannah. Please don't let anything happen to Ruth, she prayed silently.

"She has cancer. And it's not going to get any better. She hadn't been feeling well for a while, but we just found out what's going on."

So that was why she hadn't heard from her. Susannah covered her eyes with her hand.

"Is it really bad?"

He hesitated. "They say eight months to a year. Lily and I have been meaning to call you, but we just haven't had the heart."

Susannah's stomach tightened into a knot. Oh, God.

"Can I see her?"

"If you want to. But she's not in good shape. It might be upsetting for you."

"Have the doctors done everything?"

"Everything. There's nothing left to try. Now we wait. The worst part is that she's not going to be able to come home."

She grabbed a pencil and wrote down the name and address of the hospital, just outside Harrisburg. They spoke for a few minutes more before saying good-bye. As soon as they'd hung up, Susannah called for bus information for the following day. She couldn't wait for the hours to pass; the day seemed endless. Back at home, she told Peter the story. He knew who Ruth Mitchell was, but Susannah hadn't told him just how important Ruth was to her. Now, she tried to explain.

Peter nodded understandingly. "Don't worry," he said. "I'll take care of things while you're gone. Take as long as you need."

It was after five o'clock the next day when Susannah arrived at the hospital in Pennsylvania. She stopped at the front desk to ask for Ruth's room number, looking around at the filthy reception area and unmopped floors. The lobby smelled of urine. What kind of place was this? It took a full ten minutes until one of the old, creaky elevators arrived in the lobby to take her to the seventh floor.

Heading toward Ruth's room, she began to feel sick to her stomach. Elderly patients were lying in the hallway, either on gurneys or in wheelchairs, unkempt and uncared for, some stained with their own feces, muttering or singing to themselves. One woman kept up a constant wail, rocking back and forth in her chair. Glancing into a few of the rooms as she passed, she saw old, broken-down beds and chairs, everything seemingly one step away from falling apart. It was the dirt that upset her the most, nothing washed, everything smelling so foul. What was Ruth doing here?

She found Room 719 and knocked on the door. Pushing it open, she saw four beds and looked from face to face at the women occupying them. Ruth, her eyes shut, was in the bed over by the window.

Seeing her, Susannah tried not to appear shocked. She strode across the room, ignoring the stale smell, the stained tiled floor, and struggled to maintain her composure as she gazed into the sleeping face of the woman who meant more to her than anyone else. Ruth's illness had aged her thirty years. Once red-cheeked and robust, she was skinny and ashen, her thick brown hair reduced to straggly wisps. Susannah brushed away the tears that immediately formed in her eyes, and resolved not to let Ruth see her cry. She pulled a chair up next to the bed and sat down, gently taking Ruth's hand in hers, noting how frail it was, how thin and dry the skin appeared.

Ruth opened her eyes. Her pleasure at seeing Susannah was immediate. Weakly, she smiled.

"Hello, sweetheart," she whispered.

"Hiya," Susannah answered softly with a big smile. "You still refuse to get an answering machine, so I had to come in person to get through to you."

Talking was obviously an effort for Ruth. "So happy . . . you came."

"Is there anything I can do for you, anything at all?" Susannah leaned forward anxiously.

"No, baby." Ruth closed her eyes again. "But thank you."

Susannah was afraid she might break down. She couldn't do that to Ruth. She was momentarily diverted when a nurse came into the room, turning off the call light above the head of a patient who was moaning.

"What is it, Mrs. Herlihy?" the nurse asked in a loud, irritated voice. "I've told you already, there's no more pain medication."

"But it hurts so much. Please . . ." The woman in the bed began to weep.

The nurse spoke sternly. "You stop it now. When it's time, we'll tell you." Spinning on her heel, she was gone.

Shocked, Susannah turned back to Ruth. She knew what she could do for her. She could get her out of this terrible place, find somewhere she could die with dignity. None of the Mitchells could afford any kind of private hospital. Lily, Mal, and Timmy were all assembly-line workers, while Sam had married a Canadian woman and was farming up in New Brunswick; Ruth's sister had died last spring and her husband had moved to Florida soon afterward. Peter and she didn't have much, but there must be something they could do. She was going to talk to him about it the second she got home.

Susannah sat with Ruth until the nurses made her leave when visiting hours were over. In fits and starts, her voice barely audible, Ruth tried to talk with Susannah, and managed to tell her that Timmy had gone away with his wife for a christening, and would be gone for the next two days. Sam had come down from Canada three weeks earlier. Lily was usually around, Ruth whispered, but this week one of her sons was home with the measles, so she couldn't get to the hospital. Susannah was glad she was there so Ruth wouldn't have to be alone.

When she left that night, she telephoned Lily, who insisted she come over to the house right away. As they shared a pot of coffee, Lily confirmed what Susannah suspected: they all hated the hospital, but didn't have the money to move Ruth anyplace else. They had applied for every type of financial assistance Ruth was eligible for, but there weren't that many places that would care for terminally ill patients, and the good ones were much too expensive.

Susannah checked into a motel a few miles away, where she spent most of the night tossing in bed, wondering what she could do. By nine o'clock the next morning she was back at Ruth's bedside, keeping a constant stream of cheerful conversation going when she thought the older woman was up to it, and sitting quietly, just stroking her hand, when she thought Ruth needed to rest. She consulted with the doctor, and during the afternoon, slipped out to call the small hospice Lily had mentioned. It was only an hour away, and had an excellent reputation. Susannah decided to extend her visit for another day so she could check it out. She called her number in New York and left Peter a message on the answering machine, telling him she would be staying, and asking him to let Jack know she'd need another day off. The next morning, she drove out to see the hospice. In minutes, she knew it was the right place, clean, pleasant, and well run, with modern facilities. The only problem was that it cost a thousand dollars a week.

When it was time for her to catch her bus back to New York, Susannah promised Ruth she would come again as soon as she could. Ruth tried to squeeze her hand and whispered a thank you. Susannah barely made it out into the hallway before the tears began streaming down her face. Somehow, she had to find a way to help Ruth.

As the taxi pulled up in front of her apartment, Susannah thought how much she would enjoy a long, hot bath. It would be so good to see Peter. She was just going to crawl into his arms and be thankful they were both healthy and together. Then, he would help her come up with a solution to the problem, maybe a way to borrow the money for the hospice. He would know what to do.

Turning the key in the lock, Susannah pushed open the door as she set her overnight bag down. Immediately, she sensed something was wrong.

They'd been robbed. Closet doors were open, and things had been pushed out of place. The small television and portable CD player, which she had saved up so long to buy, were gone. Cautiously, she stopped and listened. It was silent. She doubted anyone was still here; it could have happened at any point over the weekend. But where was Peter? She'd left her motel number. Why hadn't he called to tell her? She went into the bedroom, afraid of what she might find, but breathed a sigh of relief when she saw he wasn't there. Thank God, nothing had happened to him.

But her files, the files containing all her photos and negatives, were a mess. The cabinet drawers were pulled open, and someone had scrambled through them, tossing aside whatever wasn't wanted, leaving shots scattered everywhere. Had they stolen anything? It would take weeks to sort it all out.

She sat down on the edge of the bed, overwhelmed. From where she was, she gazed directly into the closet she and Peter shared. All his clothes were gone. In fact, she noticed, all his belongings, which were normally spread out on the dresser and night table, were gone. Yet, oddly, it seemed as if none of *her* clothes were missing. She opened her jewelry box. Everything was there. Walking back into the living room, she stood in the middle of the floor and stared, trying to figure out exactly what had been taken. Just the small TV and CD player. Nothing else. Nothing big, just what could be carried out quickly and inconspicuously.

She didn't know what made her do it, but she went over to the desk where they kept their joint account checkbook, and opened the top drawer. The checkbook, the one with the checks that said Peter and Susannah Manzoni on them, wasn't there. Her hand trembling, trying not to think, she called the telephone number on the bank form they had gotten after opening the account. Giving the account number, she asked for her balance. Zero, the woman on the telephone told her. All the money had been drawn out of the account and it had been closed on Tuesday.

Hanging up, Susannah sank down onto the couch. Peter had done it all himself. He had left, and taken with him her television, her CD player, maybe some of her pictures, and all the money she had in the world. Just like that. He didn't clean out her apartment, just took the couple of things he really liked. And of course he wouldn't have had any trouble at the bank: it was a joint account, so he had every right to withdraw all the money.

Maybe she was crazy. Maybe Peter was just away, and some thief was responsible for all this. She almost laughed, realizing how unlikely the whole scenario was, how impossible it would be for Peter to do such a thing. Jack Traldi, she would call Jack. He might be able to help her find Peter so she could straighten this out right away. Relieved, she dialed the office. Left on hold for nearly five minutes, she was getting nervous by the time he finally picked up.

"Hello, Susannah." His voice sounded stiff and formal.

"Jack, hi," she said, her words rushing out. "Can you tell me where Peter is? We've had a robbery and I need to talk to him."

"A robbery?" Jack was taken aback.

"Yes. I just got home from Pennsylvania and found out. A lot of Peter's stuff is missing, along with some other things."

"Oh. Peter's stuff." His tone flat, it seemed as if Jack suddenly knew what she was talking about.

"Jack, what's going on?" Anxiety was creeping into Susannah's voice.

"Look, I'm really sorry this happened. I thought you guys were doing great together."

She felt a sharp pang in her chest. "Sorry *what* happened?"

"Jesus, you don't even know, do you?" Jack sounded pained. "Susannah, Peter's got someone else. His things are gone, I guess, because he's living with her now."

"What are you saying?" Susannah barely got the words out.

"I thought it was a mutual thing, you two breaking up, but I see now that wasn't it. I feel bad about this, but there it is. He's got someone else."

Susannah shut her eyes and tried to stay calm. "Where is he, Jack? What's his number?"

She heard his hesitation. "Gee, I don't know, Susannah. I don't have an address or a number for him."

Susannah didn't tell Jack she knew he was lying. "Thank you for explaining this to me. I appreciate it. I'll see you in the office tomorrow morning."

There was a momentary silence. "Well, you know . . ." Jack paused. "Look, you're a great gal, but Peter and I go back to childhood. I just don't think, given what's going on, that it would be so smart for you to keep working here. It could get awkward."

Susannah's eyes flew open. "Are you firing me?"

"Come on, it's not like that," he said plaintively. "I just don't think it would be a good idea for you to come back. You can see yourself how difficult it could get, and I'd sort of be in the middle."

Susannah was speechless. Jack didn't want to have to look at her anymore. It would make him uncomfortable to have her around, one of the girls his buddy had jilted.

"Listen, if there's anything Claudia or I can do for you, just name it and we'll be there."

She didn't bother to reply before hanging up. Claudia had warned her about Peter, and Susannah had virtually cut off their friendship because of it. Now she wasn't in a position to talk to Claudia about it at all. She dialed Bibi's number in Los Angeles, but no one answered.

She made several more calls, to Peter's friends, trying to locate him. No one knew where he was — or they were unwilling to tell her. With each call, she felt her chest constricting more tightly. It was as if the ground had opened up beneath her feet, and she was falling straight down into the pitch black. This couldn't be happening. He loved her, she *knew* he did. And she adored him. For a moment, she thought of what it would be like without him, all alone again. The pain of it hit her like a blow.

Finally, she went back into the bedroom, took off all her clothes, and got under the covers. It was warm in the room, but she began to shiver uncontrollably. Peter was gone, and he had taken every dime. She had no job. The one person who had ever been truly giving to her, who had loved her all her life, lay dying in a hospital, needing the help Susannah would never be able to come up with now. She couldn't think about it all, she just couldn't. Shutting her eyes, she fell into a deep sleep.

When she woke up, it was dark. Disoriented and groggy, she looked at the clock radio. Ten-thirty. Why was she in bed? Suddenly, it came flooding back to her, everything that had happened. Peter had left her for someone else. He hadn't loved her at all, probably never had. He'd been seeing someone behind her back and sneaked away without a word. Not even a note. And he'd robbed her, there was no other way to put it. How was it possible, her darling Peter had actually stolen her money? She thought about how little she had really known him. In a million years, she would never have dreamed he would do such a thing.

Her mind traveled back. Now that she thought about it, there was something erratic about the way he spent money frivolously, then suddenly wanted to stay at home for nights on end. It was all a lot of talk, then, his real estate deals, his big-time connections. He must have had some sort of business transactions going, because he did have money sporadically. But he obviously wasn't the entrepreneur he portrayed himself to be.

It was so painfully clear now. Something had been wrong all along. How quickly he had moved into her apartment, telling her he loved her after such a short time. The constant togetherness from the beginning. If she hadn't been so crazy about him, she would have seen that things were moving much too fast. And now she knew why she'd never been taken to the fabulous apartment where his renovations were always in progress; she wondered if he even *had* an apartment anywhere, let alone the palace he described.

Peter Manzoni was nothing more than a con artist. Gorgeous, traveling in the right circles, manipulating his way into the appearance of luxury and success. God, what a smooth operator. And what a perfect little victim she'd been, how easily she'd been sucked into his game. She had broken her own rule, her determination never to be dependent on anyone again. He hadn't just taken control of her life — she'd practically forced it on him.

The heartlessness, the cold-blooded way he used her, then abandoned her without a word. She was engulfed by a wave of conflicting emotions. Anger, grief, humiliation, sadness — she couldn't sort them out. I almost *married* him, she thought, frightened at how she could have gotten so caught up with a man like that. But of course, she *hadn't* almost married him; he never had any intention of going through with it. She thought of him laying the trap to get her money, ordering the checks with their names on them. He had been such an expert lover, so caring, he'd made her feel so desirable and needed. But now she understood why he never seemed to lose himself in their lovemaking as she did, why he always held himself back somehow, staying in control. All that effort on his part, the months invested in their relationship, for so little money; he had been willing to destroy her, to break her heart, for a few thousand dollars.

It was a long night. Susannah slept only fitfully, and when the morning came, she was exhausted. She lay in bed staring at the ceiling. At around eleven, she forced herself to get up, and threw on some jeans. At the small deli a couple of blocks away, she bought a pint of coffee ice cream, a box of Oreos, a half dozen doughnuts, and a pile of magazines. Upstairs again, she pulled off her clothes and got right back into bed. Fluffing up her pillows, she ate the ice cream and read two of the magazines from cover to cover. When she'd finished, she tossed them on the floor. She wondered if she would ever get up again. What was the point? She had no place to go, no one who cared about her, no career.

Her career. What a joke. She should have stayed in business school. Who did I think I was? she asked herself. As if I, stupid little Susannah Holland, could have become a photographer. At least with an MBA I could have gotten a decent job, a real job. I'd have some kind of a life.

And she was going to *be* someone. What a laugh. She would never be anyone.

She punched her pillow and turned onto her side. All of that paled next to the anguish she felt at the thought of Ruth Mitchell. Now she was useless — just when Ruth needed her most. If she'd stayed in graduate school, she would be able to help, instead of being this unsuccessful free-lancer who didn't even really work. She was consumed with regret. If I hadn't been so selfish, I could have paid for that damned hospice. It's my own fault.

The day passed slowly. Susannah spent it dozing, eating and reading, occasionally watching the grainy picture on the small television she pulled out from the back of her closet. When the mail came, she saw she'd finally been paid the eight hundred dollars from the Minar Corporation for her photograph. She regarded the check ruefully. This would have been extra money to spend on new things for her home with Peter. Now, she realized, it was what she would be living on.

It was another interminable night. She was sleeping when the doorbell rang early the next morning. She ignored it. It rang again.

"Go away," she yelled out. There was no one she wanted to see.

"Who do you think you're talking to?" Jamie's indignation was easily audible through the thick wood.

Jamie. She wouldn't mind seeing him. Throwing off the covers, she put on a robe and went to let him in. When he saw her, he raised an eyebrow.

"Jeez, you look like something the cat wouldn't even bother dragging in."

"Thanks, Jamie," Susannah said dully. She turned and headed back to her bed, not waiting to see if he followed her.

"Hey, wait a second, I didn't mean it. What's wrong?" His voice rose in concern. He ran after her, standing in the doorway to her bedroom as she settled herself back under the covers.

"Peter left me and he took all my money. Jack fired me. My foster mother is sick and dying." Susannah looked up at him. "That's just today. Tomorrow we may have even better news."

"Oh, honey." Jamie sat down on the edge of the bed and took Susannah in his arms, cradling her, stroking her head. "I'm so sorry. What can I do?"

Susannah began to cry. As Jamie rocked her, the sobs came, shaking her body. The two of them stayed that way for a long time, until well after she quieted down.

"What am I going to do?" she asked finally. "I loved him, and he was such a bastard. I feel like a stupid fool. And my life, look at what a mess I've made of it."

Jamie took her hand. "You've got to pull yourself together. Nobody's worth going to pieces over like this. I know it's terrible, but, come on, stop beating yourself over the head."

"If only I could." Susannah raised her tear-stained face to him. "Thank you for being so nice."

"Oh, stop it. I'm not nice." He perked up a bit. "And to prove how not nice I really am, wait till you hear what I came to tell you."

"What *are* you doing here so early?" Susannah asked, suddenly realizing that Jamie wasn't usually up until ten. "What time is it?"

"Seven-thirty. But there's someone on the *Today* show I want you to see, so I came up to tell you. We'll watch together. This will take your mind off Peter."

He went over to the small television and positioned it on the bureau so they could both see it. Adjusting it, he saw that whoever he was looking for wasn't on yet. With the volume lowered, he faced Susannah.

"I've figured out how you're going to get into that Little Angel Forum thing," he announced.

"Oh, Jamie." Susannah's shoulders sagged. "I don't care about that anymore."

"Well, you should care. You need something to do, some way to get back on track."

Susannah shook her head.

"Just listen to me. It took me days to come up with it and I had to do lots of homework, so I hope you'll appreciate my brilliance, not to mention the devotion to your cause."

Sighing, Susannah said, "Go ahead. The floor is all yours."

"Okay." Jamie drew himself up, enjoying his little show. "The guy who owns Little Angel, Cameron Hawkes, was a notorious womanizer. A long time ago, he used to hang out with starlets and the like. Just before he married his first wife, he had an affair with an actress named Dorrie Gordon. I'd always known that."

"Of course you would. You know everything about everybody," Susannah interjected mildly.

"True," Jamie said, looking pleased. "Anyway, I'm a big fan of hers, so I know a lot about her life. And, get this, she killed herself not that long after their affair ended, back in 1967. Her suicide was big news at the time."

Susannah smiled for the first time in days. "God, Jamie, what useless information you keep circulating in your brain."

"On the contrary, my dear. Hardly useless at all. She died in 1967, out in California, the same state where you come from. Get it?"

Susannah looked at him blankly. "Get what?"

"You're going to pass yourself off as Cameron Hawkes's long-lost illegitimate daughter, the poor orphaned child of Dorrie Gordon. It's the right year, the right place. In the time it takes for Hawkes to check out your story, you can manage to get into the competition."

For a moment, Susannah just stared at him. Finally, she spoke. "You're completely out of your mind. You shouldn't be giving tours for the studios, you should be writing screenplays."

"No, no, it can work," Jamie said insistently. "It really makes sense."

"Jamie." Susannah spoke slowly, as if to a child. "It's impossible. A long-lost daughter turning up after nearly twenty-five years from out of the blue. That makes no sense. Besides, I would never do a thing like that. It isn't right. It's fraud."

"All right, all right," Jamie said dismissively, clearly not listening to her. He turned back to the television set. "Look, he's on."

"Who?"

"Cameron Hawkes. That's what I've been trying to tell you. He's on the *Today* show talking about some new product line. I want you to see him." Jamie turned up the volume, then sat down on the bed next to Susannah.

She watched the man on the screen. Cameron Hawkes was tall and slender, with thick, silver-white hair. He was very attractive, and she could guess how charismatic he would be in person. Charming and comfortable on the air, he still projected an aura of excitement around him, a kind of tension. It came through even in the few minutes she listened to him talk to the interviewer.

"See, your looks are kind of similar," Jamie pointed out. "You could easily be his daughter."

"Yes, naturally," Susannah said sarcastically. "And where have I been hiding? Why have I chosen this moment to appear?"

Jamie looked a bit sheepish. "Well, okay, I haven't gotten it all figured out yet. But I will." He stood up. "It could work, just a few bugs to be sorted out."

"Thank you for cheering me up," Susannah said with a smile. "You sure got my mind off things. But you're truly over the edge."

"We'll see." With a wave, he left.

She was sorry to see him go. Sooner or later, she thought, she was going to have to get up and do something. But she couldn't face it, not yet.

The following evening, Jamie returned, waving a piece of paper.

"I've got it all figured out," he cried excitedly. "It's simple, a piece of cake."

"Don't tell me you're still at it." Susannah was wearing her robe, but this time she curled up on the couch in the living room instead of retreating back to her bed. "You can't still be thinking about this nonsense."

"It's not nonsense, it's a great challenge," Jamie said indignantly. "This letter I hold in my hand is from Dorrie Gordon's lawyer, Patrick Sutherland."

"It is? Why do you have it?"

"Come on, Susannah, get with the program. It's not really from him, I'm making this up."

"Oh, sorry. Go on," she said with a smile.

"Sutherland was a big-name lawyer, represented zillions of celebrities, a flamboyant kind of guy. He died a couple of months ago. That much is true. In our story, this letter from him states that you're Dorrie's daughter. That Cameron Hawkes was your daddy, and Dorrie killed herself because Cameron jilted her. Dorrie was pregnant when Cameron gave her the heave-ho, and she never told him she was going to have his child."

"Wait a second." Susannah put her hand up. "According to you, the woman got pregnant by Hawkes and never told him?"

"Right. He gave her the kiss-off before she *could* tell him. And she had her pride, you know. So she had the kid and then killed herself. There's no way Hawkes could ever prove she *wasn't* pregnant, or that she *didn't* have a child."

"What a morbid story."

"No, it's not, it's great," Jamie said. "And the supposed kid was dumped in an orphanage — guess which one."

Susannah answered like a fourth-grader reciting the Pledge of Allegiance. "The Franklin Orphanage in Hampton, California."

"Exactamento," Jamie answered triumphantly. "It fits. Same year you were born, same general region."

"There must be loopholes."

"Don't worry," Jamie said, "I've worked it out, got it all covered."

Susannah shook her head, amazed at his ingenuity. "You're brilliant, no doubt about it. But let me tell you for the record: this is out of the question. Completely."

"Oh, come on." Jamie's voice was wheedling, like a child who was being denied candy. "I spent so much time dreaming this up, and it's so clever."

"*Jamie,*" Susannah said sternly, "this is not a joke. I could go to jail for something like that."

"No, you just want to get into the competition. Once the winners are picked, we'll have an escape hatch. We'll come up with some other evidence, showing you're not his daughter, but you didn't know it, or something like that. Maybe we could act like it was all a hoax on Dorrie's part, to get back at Hawkes for leaving her."

Susannah stood up. "Thanks for the entertainment. But enough is enough. Forget it."

"No nerve." Jamie shook his head. "And I've got all the rest of the details worked out. It can't fail."

"Good-bye, Jamie." Susannah pointed to the door. "Go."

"Chicken." Jamie made a face and left. For a few minutes, Susannah forgot how depressed she was, marveling at the intricacy of his plan. But the silence in the apartment grew heavy again and she went back to bed, feeling worse than ever.

The next day, Susannah showered and went out to buy milk and orange juice, more cookies, a box of cereal. Was she just going to spend the rest of her life in the house, she wondered. Maybe. Her cash wouldn't last forever, and she had no idea what she would do then. But she couldn't seem to make herself care. Back upstairs, she lay back down on the bed, her hands behind her head, staring at the ceiling. Her own problems were one thing, but Ruth was sick and in pain, and she wasn't doing anything about it.

Bibi. She would ask Bibi to lend her the money.

Of course, Susannah thought, grabbing the telephone, she should have thought of it right away. Excited, she dialed Bibi's number in LA.

"Hello?" She heard the familiar lilt of Bibi's voice.

"Hi, Bibi, it's Susannah."

"How dare you call me!" There was fury in her voice. "You sonofabitch, you sold me out without a backward glance."

What on earth was Bibi talking about? "Bibi, it's Sus—"

Bibi was shouting. "I trusted you and you did *this*? You *know* how I feel about appearing naked in anything, that I would never even consider doing a nude scene. But you thought it would be just fine to expose me in *People* magazine as long as you made a buck out of it."

Susannah broke in frantically. "No, no, what are you saying?"

"You betrayed me. I trusted you, and you exploited our

friendship." Bibi was almost hysterical. *"People's* not bad enough, but *Playboy! How could you do this to me?"*

She didn't wait for an answer, slamming down the phone before Susannah could say another word.

Susannah bolted out of the apartment and raced down the stairs, not stopping to wait for the elevator. She ran to the newsstand on the corner, grabbing an issue of *People* from a tall stack on display. Frantically flipping through it, she stopped suddenly, holding her breath. The headline over the story read BIBI FROST-BITTEN IN THE NUDE. There were discreet portions of photographs of Bibi, cropped to keep them from showing too much. But Susannah knew exactly what the entire shots looked like. They were her photographs, the ones she had taken that night back in Bibi's apartment. Her heart pounding, she scanned the article. It explained that nude photos of the sizzling hot new star had been sold to *Playboy* by an unnamed source for two hundred thousand dollars.

Now Susannah knew why her photos were a wreck when she'd come back that day. This was what Peter had taken from her files, what he had really been after. She remembered that she'd once mentioned the photos to Peter casually. So that was what was worth his time and effort. But as cruelly as he had betrayed her, Bibi must have felt Susannah's betrayal just as strongly. What was she going to do?

As fast as she could, she ran back to her apartment and called Bibi's number, relieved when her friend picked up.

"Bibi, please listen, let me explain —"

Bibi had already hung up.

Susannah dialed again. This time no one answered.

Defeated, Susannah sat down on the bed. She would try a letter, explain the whole thing that way. But would Bibi even believe her? Her best friend, the only real friend she'd ever had, hated her now, and with good reason. It would kill Bibi when the *Playboy* issue came out, staring at her from every newsstand. There was no way Susannah could ever make it up to her.

The only person left who really loved her was Ruth. And Ruth really needed her now. But what good was Susannah to her? If she could just find a way to get that money for the hospice.

Of course there *was* a way. The International Forum for Children. Winners got seventy-five thousand each — it would pay for Ruth's care for at least a year. She could use Jamie's crazy plan to enter the competition.

Unthinkable. And there was no guarantee she could win. In fact, she wondered why she thought she even had a chance. But it was the only place she could possibly lay her hands on so much money. No, it was wrong. There was no way to justify a scam like that. That wasn't who she was, going around impersonating someone else.

But who was she? No one at all. She had nothing. She'd destroyed every opportunity that had come her way. What else could she do? I'm going completely insane, she said to herself. I'm actually thinking about going through with it. Just the idea of that frightened her. She could never do such a thing. She was a straight arrow, a good person.

And where had being a Goody Two-shoes gotten her? Why shouldn't she take a chance, use a little imagination just to bypass a deadline that she'd hardly missed, after all.

But it wasn't about her, really. It was about Ruth. She had always said she would do anything for Ruth. Well, this was what it was going to take. And what did she have to lose? She'd already lost everything that mattered to her.

For a few minutes Susannah sat there quietly. Then she reached out for the telephone and dialed Jamie. He answered on the second ring.

"Jamie," she said, her voice even, "could you come upstairs? We need to go over your plan again." She took a deep breath. "I'm going to do it."

Chapter 18

"*P*lus ça change . . ."* Henri
Stern didn't stop muttering, even as the stewardess
was retrieving the dinner trays. All through the
flight to Bangkok, he had been complaining about
the situation in the refugee camps. Since Henri
was the person who introduced Jean-Paul to the
plight of the Cambodian refugees, his monologue
was especially discouraging. "It looks exactly as
it did eleven years ago, but now everything is
eleven years older. The tents, the temporary huts,
the temporary wooden shacks, the temporary food
lines. Temporary. Hah!"

Jean-Paul listened in dismay as Henri went
on. Food and medical supplies provided by relief
organizations were erratic at best, and outside the
camps constant violence erupted among the various Cambodian resistance groups. At every step,
villagers found themselves at the mercy of gunfire

between the Khmer Rouge just a few miles north and roaming bands of soldiers loyal to Hun Sen, the current leader of Cambodia. Only one road was passable; every other thoroughfare had been packed with land mines by the Khmer Rouge. And shelling between resistance groups made even the one "safe" road unusable much of the time.

Throughout the trip, Henri had bombarded Jean-Paul with stories of torment: of the relief team that got stuck in the "fire pit," the deep ravines dug specifically so tanks would get caught and could be firebombed without any means of escape; of the men who had been taken from the camps and forced into the Khmer army; of the thousands dying of disease and vitamin A deficiencies for lack of simple medical supplies.

"So little has changed for the better, no matter how much we try to do. Suicides, gang wars within the camp — I'm beginning to feel it's a losing battle."

Jean-Paul nodded gravely. If Henri Stern could sound so depressed, the situation must have gotten much worse in the two years since he'd been there. Last year, he just couldn't get himself to go. He had claimed that he wasn't able to leave the hospital so soon after its inception, and none of his colleagues from Médecins sans Frontières questioned his absence. But they should have, he admitted to himself. He could have left. It wasn't leaving the hospital that was impossible; it was the rage he felt at the thought of seeing Kailey again.

But two years of separation were enough. He was over her, he was sure of it. After all, how long had he really known her? One month? Two at the most. She was just a woman, and the work among the refugees was more important than a romantic betrayal. Everything in Paris could practically run itself by now. Besides, presiding over a hospital could never replace the joy of hands-on medicine. And these were *his* people, these were the ones who needed him.

Henri's face lost its animation, with only sadness left. "You know, Jean-Paul, a hundred thousand babies have been born in these camps. They'll grow up thinking that random violence and barbed wire are what life is about."

Jean-Paul sighed. "Henri, everything you say is true, but we have to go on doing whatever we can do."

"Well, you're right, of course. I'm glad you're with me this year." A slight smile lit Henri's face as he leaned back in his seat. "You know, there was one tiny sign of hope, that American friend of yours. I tell you, some of the Cambodians believe she's a saint."

Jean-Paul said nothing. Of course, Henri meant Kailey. But he had no way of knowing what their relationship had been.

Henri warmed to his subject. "She's amazing, that woman. Because of her, when the UN food supplies come in, they get distributed fairly. And she's finally getting some attention from the foreign media. In the last couple of years, her letter-writing campaigns have produced more articles in the *Washington Post* and *The New York Times* than anyone else managed in the ten years before she got here."

Jean-Paul wasn't surprised. For the last two years, he'd been receiving letters from friends in UNICEF and Oxfam exclaiming over everything Kailey was doing. And each time he saw her name, he felt the same anger.

How could she have left him like that, changed her mind so suddenly? For months after she'd left, he felt uncontrollable fury, attempting to cover it with twelve- and fifteen-hour days at the hospital. But as he sat back in his uncomfortable airplane seat trying to get a few hours' sleep on the long flight, he admitted to himself that his efforts had been a failure. He was proud of his hospital, but he felt curiously detached, like an onlooker just going through the motions. He was missing something, and he was afraid he knew exactly what it was.

"Everything should be here by Thursday afternoon, so if we could all meet at three-thirty, that should give us plenty of time to get organized." Kailey looked around the room to see if there were any questions. Seeing no hands up, she adjourned the meeting.

The three other workers ambled out of the makeshift administration headquarters slowly, the humid, hot air making quicker action impossible. Kailey worried as she watched them leave.

Could so few people oversee what was supposed to be an unusually large food distribution? She was probably lucky to have rounded up even this many, she thought as she gathered her notes together.

Smoothing the distribution process hadn't been easy. She'd had to fight her way through red tape all the way from Thai officials to the Cambodian refugees themselves. But she'd been fairly successful. At least, the people in the camp got *something*. Kailey looked at her watch. Eleven already. Time for that meeting with the French WPF group. She walked out and started upstairs to the second floor. Even here, thousands of miles from Rome, she was still using her skills as an interpreter. See, Ben, I'm not wasting my education, she said to herself, smiling at the thought.

Ben and Risa both had argued strenuously against her moving to Thailand permanently. "You'll be alone," they'd said, "you'll be throwing away your contacts, your professional credentials."

Well, the refugee camp needed her more than the American diplomats and Italian businessmen, who'd probably replaced her within minutes. It would have been impossible to stay in Rome after leaving Jean-Paul. To translate at large, elegant parties in swanky homes and offices, to go home alone at night with nothing to do but think about all the mistakes she'd made — she couldn't have stood it. Here in Thailand, at least she could accomplish something.

She heard the hum of conversation as she walked upstairs. Rounding the corner at the top of the stairwell, she saw a group of people dressed more formally than any camp worker would be: women in skirts and dresses, men in sports jackets and slacks. Kailey scanned the group, wondering if any of them would be familiar from her WPF work in Rome. Yes, there was Gianni D'Adamo; and who was that woman next to him?

She felt his presence before she even saw him, recoiling as if she had received a physical blow. Just twenty feet or so ahead of her stood Jean-Paul, deep in conversation with the camp's chief administrator. His back was to her, but she recognized him immediately. Even from this distance, he looked impressive, tan and attractive in chinos and a blue cotton shirt, the familiarity of his slender, muscular back and thick brown hair coming as a shock.

Quickly, she stepped back. She wasn't ready to see him today. She didn't know if she'd ever be ready.

She knew Jean-Paul's routine had been to work in the camp one month every year. When he hadn't shown up the year before, she thought perhaps he would never come again. Had she been relieved, had she been unhappy? Both, she admitted to herself. But as she stared at him, she found it impossible to deal with the fact of him right now. She'd tried so hard to put him out of her mind, hiding her feelings from him, from herself.

Only one thought consumed her as she walked down the steps and out of the building. For the next month, she would keep as far from the medical facility as she possibly could.

The walk back from the Khmer Rouge encampment was over two miles. It must be ninety-five degrees, Kailey thought, mopping her forehead with a handkerchief. No matter how comfortable she had come to feel in Thailand, she could never get used to the constant, oppressive humidity. When the monsoon season started, sheeting rain went on for weeks, forcing the residents of the camps to huddle in their inadequate huts. The lucky ones were housed in battered wooden buildings, erected on tall stilts to keep the rains from washing them away. By now, most of the wooden stilts tilted at odd angles, making the camp look like a child's toy village.

Once every couple of months Kailey forced herself to go just a mile outside the Khmer-controlled camp, where she would meet with two brothers who were part of the Khmer inner circle. The Li brothers had cousins living in her UN-supervised facility, and could be sympathetic to her requests — at the right price. Often she would bring cartons of food as an inducement, cigarettes, boxes of tissues, anything that might make the Khmers less likely to plant more land mines right near her camp, where a child might lose a leg or an arm if he ventured even a few feet from the entrance. Once she had succeeded in talking a Khmer leader they'd brought with them into calling off a planned foray into her camp. Succeeded, that is, at the cost of fifty pounds of grain and several thousand dollars' worth of antibiotics. Humanity, charm, concern for their fellow Cambodians — these were not inducements for the Khmer Rouge. But every now and then a delivery of consumer goods would work, at least for a short time.

The quiet was broken by the familiar sound of gunfire. Terrified, Kailey moved quickly behind a patch of trees. She sat silently on the soft, wet earth, hugging the tree for support as she tried to block out the frightening noise of the guns. She knew there were small groups of Hun Sen supporters in this area. Probably some of the Khmer fighters had come upon the rival faction. This was the way so many of the refugees she worked with had lost their lives, caught between the factions of Pol Pot and Hun Sen, innocent victims of the civil war that wouldn't end. She waited for the sounds of gunfire to stop. Looking around, she realized she was only a hundred yards or so from the camp.

Kailey concentrated on watching the sun quickly setting over the horizon, breathing deeply to calm herself. These visits near the Khmer installations always provoked an almost overwhelming anxiety. She told herself she would get back safely tonight. She was too close to home not to.

There was quiet again. Tensely, she began to move toward the camp. Ninety yards, she thought, eighty, seventy. Suddenly she saw a sight that was all too familiar. Lying just a few feet in front of her was a man she knew, blood pouring out of his arm, his entire torso soaking in red. Softly she called out his name, and hearing her voice, he began to whimper. Kailey kneeled down, urging him to tell her exactly where he'd been hit. He clutched his arm, moaning as Kailey helped him to his feet, and walked him along toward home. Fifty yards, forty, thirty. Kailey could have wept with joy when she saw Henri Stern in conversation with one of the guards.

"Henri," she screamed, waving her arms over her head as she saw him make her out in the distance and begin to run to her. Henri knelt next to the wounded man, first feeling for his pulse, then asking hurried questions about exactly where the pain was. They carried him inside the camp to medical headquarters and placed him on one of the tattered cots.

"The only place actually hit by the bullets is his arm. That's what all this blood is from," Henri told Kailey. "You must have reached him right after he was hit."

Kailey stood by quietly as Henri cleaned the wound, searching for the bullets and all the time comforting his patient. She didn't see Jean-Paul, wasn't aware of the color rushing to his face as he entered the room and realized she was standing there.

Only when a pregnant young woman burst in, bleeding profusely and screaming in pain, did Kailey turn around. As Jean-Paul ran toward the woman, Kailey saw him. She watched in silence as he engaged in rapid-fire questioning of the injured woman, all the while gently settling her on one of the examining tables. Finally, Jean-Paul looked at Kailey.

"I need some help here. I have to do a C-section."

"I have no training, no idea what to do," Kailey said breathlessly.

"This woman may not be alive ten minutes from now." His voice was harsh. He waited a few seconds, then went on in a calmer tone. "Henri can't help right now, and you're the only other person here. So just do what I tell you. Bring some towels, and please, do it fast."

"What happened?" she asked, hurrying to obey Jean-Paul's commands.

"A land mine," Jean-Paul answered in disgust as he began to administer anesthesia. "She was one of the scouts for the Khmer Rouge a few miles inside Cambodia, one of the women they use to locate the mines."

Kailey shuddered. She had heard stories of these women, virtual human sacrifices who were forced to walk thirty or forty feet in front of the rebel armies, stepping on land mines and being blown up in the process. Often these women were widowed by the Khmer terrorists just before they were forced into these suicide missions. Rarely did any of them escape. This woman must have been very strong; she had made it all the way to the Thai border.

"Imagine," he said, "she got here alive, just to step on the goddamned mine as she reached the camp."

Suddenly, the woman moaned, and Jean-Paul tensed.

"Kailey, she's about to die. I have to get the baby out right now. Hurry, stand on the other side of her."

They were both covered in blood as they worked together frantically. Kailey tried to soothe the woman, but soon gave up; she wasn't even conscious.

Within seconds, Jean-Paul made the incision. Just as he pulled a baby boy from her, she let out a long gasp and lay completely still.

Cutting the umbilical cord, Jean-Paul handed the baby to Kailey, then turned back, trying to revive the mother. Kailey sponged the baby off, fascinated by the squirming infant. How amazing, she thought, that this beautiful baby could have come through this ordeal, so perfect, so exquisite.

Wrapping the infant in a clean, threadbare towel, she held him tightly against her chest, quieting the cries that had begun while she was wiping him off. She looked over at Jean-Paul. He was standing still now. The woman was dead.

Wearily, Kailey rocked the baby. He was so sweet, his crying silenced by her touch. It was such a magical feeling, holding a baby, easing its pain, making it feel safe in a cold, new place. For the moment, she let her mind wander back in time, not trying to stem the flood of emotion that swept over her, remembering, remembering. Her Bonnie, over twenty years ago, her own little girl. She had helped thousands of children over the last two years, but never had she come so close to unlocking her heart as right now.

Kailey glanced over at Jean-Paul. "Does the baby have a father?"

"No. She said they finished her husband off before they sent her to her wonderful work." His voice was bitter.

Kailey held the baby slightly away from her as she supported his neck. She saw the soft curve of his cheeks, the tiny ears, such miniature perfection. It had been years since she had really allowed herself to love a child. This baby had no one. Perhaps the time had come.

"I want to adopt him, Jean-Paul. Do you think there would be any problems?"

"No, Kailey." His voice betrayed nothing of what he was thinking. "I'm sure there will be no problem."

Inhaling the baby scent as she once again held the infant close, she turned to go. "From now on, it's just you and me," she whispered as she began to walk away. I'll name him Daniel, she thought, after my father.

Jean-Paul watched until she reached the doorway.

"Kailey." He had worked so hard not to care, but seeing her like this, he couldn't let her walk away. He wanted the truth. "Kailey, I have to know. What happened?"

She stood still, not looking at him. He could barely hear her words. "It's . . . it's hard to explain."

Jean-Paul walked to where she stood, forcing her to turn back and look at him. His hand stayed on her shoulder as if he thought she would run away. "It's *hard to explain* why you ripped my life to shreds, why you lied to me, why you broke my goddamn heart."

"You don't understand," Kailey said, trying to wrest herself from his grip and wrapping her arms more tightly around the infant, as if that would hold her together. "I left for both of us. You have to believe me."

He withdrew his hand and turned away from her, disgusted. "You left because you didn't care," he said bitterly as he began to walk away.

"I loved you."

The words stopped him. For two long years, he had battled the pain of losing her, forced himself to think of her as icy cold, a woman who wasn't capable of love. But seeing her today, watching her with this baby, he realized he'd been lying to himself. "If you loved me, why did you walk out?" he asked, his tone softening slightly.

Kailey tried to contain her emotion. Seeing Jean-Paul again, hearing his voice, she wanted him so much. She'd imagined the touch of him, the taste of him every day for two years. But nothing had changed. There was still danger in loving him.

"I had to go." Only four syllables, but she couldn't keep her voice from shaking.

Jean-Paul was suddenly furious. "You *had* to go!" He screamed the words back to her. Without warning, he grabbed the back of her head and pulled her forward, kissing her hard, claiming her, daring her not to respond. Finally he drew away. "That is what you *have* to do," he said as his breathing became even, carefully placing his hand under hers so they were cradling the baby together.

Kailey was incapable of stopping the tears that were flooding her cheeks.

"Jean-Paul, you don't understand how dangerous this is."

"Darling, Khmer Rouge terrorists are dangerous, land mines are dangerous. Love, passion, these aren't dangerous."

Kailey pushed away from him, just far enough to see the whole of him, his strength, his kindness. Cameron and his threats seemed a million miles away. Jean-Paul was right. Nothing could be as dangerous as losing him again.

His voice remained urgent. "We'll raise the baby together."

It sounded magical. She had been sure she'd never see him again, certain she had ruined her chances for happiness forever. How many times had she questioned her actions that terrible night she'd refused to marry him, wondered if she should have told him the truth, let him decide what risks he was willing to face. Now she was getting a second chance. No, two, she realized as she held the baby a little closer. A chance to love Jean-Paul and a chance to raise this little boy. It was time to tell him everything.

"There's so much I was afraid of, Jean-Paul, so many things you can't possibly understand." She looked at him sadly. "I was so afraid for you, for your hospital."

Taking his hand, she led him to his small room in back and sat beside him on the bed.

"My husband was a man named Cameron Hawkes," she began reluctantly. "We had a daughter named Bonnie."

It took barely half an hour to say all the words she'd been afraid to speak — such a brief time to describe the events that had destroyed twenty years of her life. As she finished, Jean-Paul took the baby gently from her. He pulled her close to him with one arm as he held the baby in the other.

"Cameron Hawkes means nothing to us now. He's no part of our world. All that was thousands of miles away, and so many years ago. You and I and this baby, we're here, right now, and that's the only thing that matters."

Lovingly, he stroked her shoulder, her neck, her hair. "None of it matters anymore, Kailey. We have each other, whatever comes. And I'll never let anyone hurt you, I swear it."

Chapter 19

"**I** firmly believe we should go with the premixed fruit and cereal, Mr. Hawkes." Randy Lake spoke earnestly.

Cameron leaned back in his chair. "Yes, you've made that clear, Randy." He gestured toward the third man in the meeting. "But Malcolm has a point too. Organic baby food is coming into its own, and we don't want to be left behind. We can't launch both at the same time."

Malcolm Billings beamed. Cameron was aware that his two top executives were fierce competitors, and saw each new business situation as an opportunity to defeat the other man. That was exactly the way Cameron liked it.

"I'll have to think this over," he went on. "You've both made excellent presentations. Let me study the figures, and I'll get back to you."

That ought to keep them on their toes, he

thought as the two left his office. He was willing to bet that neither one would get any sleep that night. Whoever won this little battle would score a significant victory, and would be heading up a major new venture. Not that Cameron cared about their petty power struggles. He was concerned only with what was best for the Hawkes Corporation. But it amused him to watch the two parry.

Marianne buzzed him on the intercom. "Philippe Briault's office is on the line, sir. They say his schedule has changed. He won't have time to be one of our judges."

"*What?*" Cameron exploded. "He can't do that."

"They said to tell you he's sorry, but he has to withdraw."

Philippe Briault was one of the most important art critics in the country. Getting him to be a judge for the International Forum for Children's photo competition had been a personal coup for Cameron. It would have helped position the competition as a serious one, which would in turn have strengthened the company's image. And that was critical to Cameron. Over the last few years he'd realized that, with a few smart moves, he and his company could be seen as a major cultural force. He'd already given a fortune to charities over the years, not to mention five million dollars in one fell swoop for that hospital in Paris. But none of that carried the same kind of status as being known as a patron of the arts. Why should corporations like IBM and the Chubb Group grab all the glory? He wanted to be one of the big players, one of the corporate chairmen wooed by museums and symphonies, opera and ballet companies. This photo competition was the linchpin of his efforts. Losing Briault could be a serious blow to its prestige.

Quickly recovering his temper, Cameron thought for a minute, while his secretary waited patiently on the other end of the intercom.

"Try Forrest Taylor," he said finally. "He owns the Taylor Gallery on Madison Avenue. Get Sylvia in PR to talk to him. And tell her not to give up until she gets a yes."

Forrest Taylor had plenty of clout. He wasn't Briault, but he was close enough. Satisfied, Cameron picked up a printout with next month's projections for sales of the Little Angel clothing line. The company had expanded into childrenswear only two years before, so Cameron was paying strict attention to every nuance of the clothing line's performance. Attached to the printout were minutes from last week's marketing meeting for the birth-to-six-months' division. Cameron scanned the pages. Apparently, his executives had spent most of their time debating how to manufacture socks that would stay on babies' feet; market research indicated that mothers complained about their infants' continually kicking off their socks. Cameron didn't have the interest or patience to contemplate such minutiae, but he'd make sure his people found a way to solve this problem. The way he saw it, once you were smart enough or lucky enough to identify an open hole in the market, you were a fool if you didn't leap to fill it. For the moment, he had to smile, thinking what a far cry selling baby socks was from the old days of selling heroin.

His intercom buzzed again.

"What is it?" he asked, annoyed at yet another interruption.

"There's a young woman here, sir. A Susannah Holland. She has no appointment but insists on seeing you."

He didn't recognize the name. "Tell her to wait."

When he had completed going over the projections almost forty minutes later, he told Marianne to send the woman in. The door opened to a tall, very attractive brunette in a taupe dress. Mid-twenties, he guessed, thinking there was something quite appealing about her, aside from her obvious good looks. Maybe it was in the eyes, the intelligent light there. What could she want? A journalist, probably, hoping to do a piece on him, thinking she was being cagey by not telling his secretary what publication she was with. He stood to greet her, offering his hand and flashing a broad smile. It always paid to be nice to the press.

Susannah felt her heart beating way too fast, and breathing was suddenly next to impossible. She couldn't imagine how she had sat on that chair in the outer office all this time, how she had gotten up and walked into this room when his secretary summoned her. Here she was, right in front of the man upon whom she was about to perpetrate the wildest fraud imaginable. She wondered if it were possible to pass out from fright. As she approached his desk, she saw he was even more handsome in person than he had appeared on television. His smile was friendly and inviting.

Finding herself face to face with him, feeling the cool strength of his handshake, it dawned on her that somehow she had never believed she would actually get this far. She was about to tell her story to someone who might not follow the imaginary script she conjured up in her head. Think of it as acting, she said to herself. Act as if.

"Nice to meet you, Miss — ?" Cameron paused.

"Holland," she managed to say, relieved her voice came out at all. "Susannah Holland."

He sat, and indicated the chair on the opposite side of his desk. She lowered herself into it gingerly. The room was comfortably air-conditioned, but she could feel the perspiration on her back.

"What brings you here?" he asked mildly. "I don't believe we've ever met before."

"No, no, we haven't." Susannah wanted to run. God, what a mistake this was. Think of Ruth, dying in that horrible place. This will work, Jamie had sworn it. Think of Ruth. Ruth.

She smiled and went on. "I have some news that will be a surprise to you, Mr. Hawkes. It certainly was to me."

"I'm listening."

He was polite and receptive, Susannah thought, relieved. So far so good. Jamie's research had told her he was an avid tennis and golf player, an owner and rider of expensive horses, and something of an expert on world affairs. But she had no idea what sort of man he was beneath all that.

She took a deep breath. "I've been presented with evidence indicating that you're my father, Mr. Hawkes."

There was the barest flicker of something in his eyes, but no expression crossed his face. "I'm not sure I understand" was all he said.

"You see, Dorrie Gordon was my mother. You remember her, the actress?"

"She was fairly famous." Cameron's answer revealed nothing.

Knowing that this man had actually had an affair with Dorrie Gordon, Susannah forgot her own nervousness for a moment, admiring his ability to react so coolly. She went on. "It seems that she became pregnant by you, but before she could tell you, you broke off the relationship. After she had the baby — me, that is — she committed suicide."

There, she'd said it. Cameron Hawkes gazed steadily at her without saying anything for what seemed like an eternity. Susannah thought she would die of fright. Finally, he spoke.

"May I ask what brings you here now with this story?"

"I just discovered it myself. You see, I was brought up as an orphan and never knew who my real parents were. But Dorrie Gordon gave her lawyer a letter. . . ." Here Susannah faltered for a moment. "She hoped that I would get this letter when I was still a little girl. For some reason, her request wasn't carried out. The lawyer himself died recently, and the letter surfaced. His estate tracked me down."

Cameron's gaze was more piercing now. "I imagine you have this letter with you."

"Yes, yes, of course." Susannah prayed he couldn't see her hands trembling as she reached into her purse. She pulled out the letter, so painstakingly prepared by Jamie, and slid it across the desk to him. As he was reading it, she took out a heart-shaped locket on a chain and a bracelet of multicolored stones, also courtesy of Jamie. A few extra touches to make it more realistic, he'd said. Cameron glanced up at the objects, then back down at the piece of paper he held.

"Those must be what she refers to here as the 'trinkets for my poor baby daughter,' " he said, only the faintest trace of irony in his voice.

"Yes," Susannah replied softly.

Cameron put the letter down and got up from his chair, walking to the window and looking out, his back to Susannah. He said nothing. Susannah wanted to jump up and shout that she was sorry, it was all a joke, she would never do something like this again if he would just let her go away. Calm down, she said to herself. This was for the best cause in the world, and Jamie had said over and over that she really *did* have a chance to win the competition; he believed she had the talent to do it, and she had to try. He kept insisting the story was perfect. Dorrie Gordon committed suicide in California the same year that Susannah was born. Susannah actually *was* brought up in an orphanage and foster homes in California. The real facts of her life fit right in with this tale. And Cameron wouldn't be able to find out anything about Susannah's real parents, since she was left at the orphanage with nothing but a note. The trail would die for him just as it had for her.

Besides, she reminded herself, this scam had a beginning, a middle, and an end. As soon as she either won the competition or was eliminated, she would tell Cameron Hawkes it had been a terrible mistake. She would "discover" additional evidence that she wasn't Cameron Hawkes' daughter, that the letter had been a setup on Dorrie's part to extort money from Cameron all those years before. That Dorrie had never played out the setup, and had killed herself instead.

As Susannah sat quietly behind him, Cameron stared unseeing at the busy Manhattan streets below, his mind racing. Christ, this couldn't happen at a worse time, he thought angrily. He certainly didn't believe the woman's story; her real motive would become clear in time. But he wasn't in a convenient position to throw her out. The situation could cause havoc.

For the past two months, Cameron had been engineering a friendly takeover of Awareness Industries, the educational toy company started by Lionel Shea and his brother Thaddeus back in the sixties. Awareness had become far more successful than they ever dreamed possible, but they were still hippies at heart. They sincerely believed that business should be for the good of the people. They both loved children, loved creating something of value for them. But the fun had been in doing it together. After Thaddeus's death the previous year, Lionel had lost the heart for running the company alone and wanted to sell it off. Cameron had been working on Lionel, trying to convince him that the Hawkes Corporation would continue to run the same-quality operation Awareness had always been. Moreover, he knew Lionel would sell only to someone who cared about children as much as he did. It was boring and tiresome, playing up to Lionel's do-gooder sensibilities. But the bottom line of Awareness's sales made it well worth Cameron's efforts, and he believed he was very close to convincing Shea that he was the right choice.

Still, anything could happen. These transactions were extremely fragile, and Susannah Holland could ruin it for him. For a moment, he wondered if she actually was whom she claimed to be. He remembered Dorrie Gordon. She had been very beautiful and very neurotic. Now that he thought about it, he recalled how overly dramatic she was, a self-obsessed actress who needed everything to be larger than life. He wouldn't put it past her to have pulled a stunt like this, delivering his illegitimate child, then deciding to kill herself, leaving that note so he would be hounded by their child for the rest of his life. What a bitch.

Chances were none of that had happened. Whoever this Holland woman was, she was undoubtedly lying. Still, if she should tell the press that Cameron had treated her unfairly or cruelly, it could look very bad for him indeed. He was enough of a public figure that the media would pay attention to the story. It certainly had quite a human-interest angle. How could a man whose entire business was based on children be unkind to a woman who might be his own long-lost daughter? Lionel Shea would never speak to him again, much less sell him Awareness Industries. If this story hit the papers, reporters would probably start digging up ancient history about his numerous other love affairs as well, which could only hurt his image further. If they dug back far enough, they might accidentally turn up a few things that would be disastrous for him.

On the other hand, this could be played as a heartwarming tale of parent and child reunited, which might have tremendous advantages for him. Without giving her anything, he could handle it in such a way that Lionel would consider him a loving, caring man with a big heart. That was the kind of crap Shea really responded to. As soon as he had the Awareness deal nailed down, he could throw her out.

He'd made his decision. Cameron turned back to face Susannah.

"Well, Miss Holland, you can imagine that this comes as quite a shock," he said to her in a low voice. "I cared very much for Dorrie, and this has brought back a lot of feelings."

Susannah was taken aback. She hadn't considered that her story might stir up strong emotions in him. There was nothing that said powerful men couldn't be loving or sentimental, she supposed.

"I'm sure you're sincere, but you can understand that some-one in my position has to be very careful in a matter like this."

"Of course, Mr. Hawkes." Susannah knew what was coming. He would want to check her out.

He smiled warmly. "Call me Cameron, please. After all, there might have been a time when you would have called me Dad."

Susannah was thrown off balance. Maybe he really *was* a nice man.

He walked around his desk to stand before her. "This is truly an incredible tale. I already have one daughter whom I love very much. It would certainly be something to learn I have another one."

"I was as amazed as you are," Susannah answered, equally relieved by his response and shocked at her own audacity.

They shook hands again and Cameron escorted her to the door.

"We'll talk again no doubt, Susannah," he said to her as he ushered her out.

Returning to his desk, he opened the top drawer and removed a small black lacquered box, opening it and flipping through the stack of business cards inside. These were the people he called without his secretary's knowledge or involvement. When he came to the name he wanted, he stopped and reached for the telephone. Jack Milford was a private detective who had done some work for him in the past. He would have Milford find out who the hell Susannah Holland really was. No doubt the young woman would be exposed as a fraud within a day or two. If it somehow went longer than that, he would find a way to turn it to his advantage with Shea.

What a story, Cameron thought. But you had to hand it to her, trying to get away with that one. He found himself laughing out loud, admiring her nerve. When he was a younger man, it was exactly the kind of thing he himself might have tried to pull off. The girl had guts. He liked that.

Chapter 20

―――――――

Tish Hawkes sat on the living-room sofa, sipping a glass of vodka and flipping idly through the pages of *Town & Country*. She figured lunch would take about an hour and then she could retreat to her bedroom for a nap before having to get dressed to go out that night. She thought of her bed longingly, the lacy pillows and cool sheets. That was just about the only place she wanted to be these days, lying down, her Valium and her vodka within reach on the bedside table as she dozed on and off. But she'd kept up her side of the bargain, no one could deny that: whenever Cameron told her they had plans, she was sober, presentable, and ready to go out with him by seven. As long as she could still pull herself together, she could spend the rest of her time as she wished.

Putting aside the magazine, she sighed heavily. God only knew what Cameron had in mind for this afternoon. Tish couldn't imagine what the whole situation was about, some young woman appearing out of nowhere, claiming to be Cameron's daughter. It was probably true. No doubt her husband had left plenty of women pregnant in his day. Maybe he was still leaving them pregnant. As long as he didn't bother her anymore, his extracurricular activities were of no interest to her. Still, she wondered why he had invited the girl to Bedford. She knew he wouldn't ordinarily respond pleasantly to a stranger turning up and making such a claim. If this girl didn't turn out to be the real thing, he would make her pay heavily, one way or another.

But it wasn't Tish's problem. She no longer cared what went on around her, with the exception of her own children. Unfortunately, they were grown and there was virtually nothing she could do for them. Olivia was busy with her job at Hawkes, and Evan was always off somewhere, traveling with the baseball team. It was wonderful having him in the house this summer, a real treat for her. At least she had made the right choice for them, ensuring financial security throughout their childhood, getting Olivia through Brearley and Evan through Yale. She had done that much with her life, if nothing else.

Cameron walked into the living room, pulling on a navy blazer. He wore freshly pressed khaki pants and a white shirt. As usual her husband looked as neat as a pin.

"Where's my briefcase?" he asked in annoyance. "I had it in here when I got back last night, then I took it to my study."

Tish didn't respond.

He looked between the sofa and a nearby armchair. "Did someone move the damn thing?"

She ignored his question. "This Holland woman is coming any minute, isn't she? You said one o'clock."

Cameron glanced at her. "That's right. Don't worry, you'll only have to prop yourself up for a brief period. Then you can go back to bed and drink yourself into a stupor."

"Good," she said mildly.

Olivia appeared in the wide entryway to the living room, a large piece of posterboard under one arm, a folder in her hand.

Tish frowned, thinking again how sorry she was that Olivia had cut her long blond hair the previous month. Perhaps it was quicker to dry, but it was as short as a boy's. She probably thought it would look better for her in business.

When Olivia saw her father, she stepped inside.

"Dad, I've been looking for you." She came toward him, extending the folder. "I've got the latest productivity figures from the day-care centers."

"I'm busy now, Olivia," Cameron replied, turning to leave.

"Please, just take a quick look," she begged. "They're really terrific. And I want to show you this, too." She put the posterboard on the sofa next to Tish, positioning it so both her parents could see the picture on the front. It was a full-color drawing of a group of children playing in a sunny, toy-filled room. Beneath it were the words "We're taking good care of *your* Little Angels. The Hawkes Day-care Centers."

Olivia spoke excitedly. "Isn't that great? One of our advertising guys drew it for us. It's to encourage the employees who don't use it to bring in their children."

Cameron took the file as he glanced over at the picture. "Fine." He looked hurriedly through the papers.

Tish watched her daughter anxiously awaiting her father's pronouncement. It broke Tish's heart. At nineteen, Olivia was still like a puppy dog, doing tricks to get a smile from her father. Tish had fought with Olivia about her decision to go to work for the Hawkes Corporation right after high school instead of going to college. But the girl had been adamant. Cameron had assigned her the meaningless title of Marketing Coordinator in the Little Angel division, and after that it was clear to Tish that he never gave her involvement with the company another thought. Yet Olivia had run with the job, developing two day-care centers for Hawkes employees. Over the last year, she'd told her mother, they had resulted in lower absenteeism and higher productivity. Tish had been so proud of her daughter, but it was Cameron's words of encouragement the girl needed, his approval she craved.

Tish was sickened by Cameron's response to his daughter's ingenuity. He had given her the go-ahead to start up the centers, but displayed little interest in them. He never gave Olivia either public or private credit for her accomplishments. Since Olivia had gone to work for the Hawkes Corporation, Tish had often come upon her daughter hard at work at one or two in the morning, poring over research, developing new ideas. Tish wanted to tell her that she was wasting her time trying to get something her father would never be willing to give. But there was no point, Tish knew that. Her daughter didn't want to hear what she had to say about Cameron. Olivia would have to learn what kind of a man her father was for herself.

Cameron handed the folder back to Olivia. "Looks okay," he said distractedly, crossing to leave the room. He stopped and turned back to the two women. "At lunch today, I expect you both to be pleasant and polite."

"Yes, Dad." Olivia smiled agreeably.

Tish picked up another magazine. She didn't have to be told what her job was. She knew it all too well.

Susannah nervously approached the front door of the Hawkes's estate. She wished she could turn around, jump into the taxi that had left her in the driveway, and take the train straight home to her apartment. If only she could forget the whole thing, pretend she had never started all this. The ride from Grand Central had been agonizing. Two days before, she'd been amazed to get a telephone call inviting her to lunch at Cameron Hawkes's country home. Only a week had passed since their initial meeting; surely he hadn't made up his mind about her, nor could there have been enough time to check out her story. And she'd never anticipated being asked to his home. Well, in any case, she'd been summoned and she knew she had to show up. She only hoped he wasn't planning to use this lunch to expose her as a fraud in front of an audience.

The house was enormous, its grandeur making her lie seem even more outrageous. If you give up now, she reminded herself, it means going home and sitting there alone, wondering what to do about Ruth. This is your only chance to get the money for her.

Torn by indecision, raising, then lowering her hand from the doorbell, she was startled when a tall, blond-haired man in blue jeans suddenly opened the door from inside. He held a set of car keys in one hand, a tennis ball in the other. Standing there in the doorway, chewing gum, he casually tossed the ball up in the air a few times, blocking her entrance as he looked her over. Susannah took a step back, wishing she could escape the intensity of his green eyes. This had to be Evan Gardiner, Tish Hawkes's son from her previous marriage. Jamie had come across his name in researching the family for Susannah. He'd told her that Cameron's stepson was the same Evan Gardiner who played first base for the Pittsburgh Pirates. She'd recognized his name, but had never seen him play. Jamie had also mentioned that he'd gone through his share of women; the ladies take to him in a big way, that was how Jamie laughingly put it. Seeing how handsome he was, Susannah could understand why.

Finally, he spoke. "You must be the long-lost daughter," he said, his skepticism unhidden.

Susannah couldn't think of a response that didn't sound disingenuous or downright silly. She stood there, unable to walk past him.

"You'd best improve your delivery before you hit the big time," he went on after a moment, moving aside at last and ushering her in with a grand sweeping motion. "I was going out for a while, but I think I'll stay and watch. This should be much more entertaining."

Suddenly energized by his rudeness, Susannah responded to the challenge in his tone. "If you want a show, I recommend Broadway," she retorted, stepping past him. "It's about fifty minutes by car."

His eyebrows shot up. "Well, well, so that's how it's going to be. This certainly promises to be fun."

"I hope you have a wonderful time," she snapped back. She had come this far, and she wasn't going to let this arrogant man get the best of her. Still, she was relieved to see a maid coming toward them.

"Miss Holland?" queried the maid. "Please follow me."

"Thank you," Susannah answered, grateful for the rescue.

She glanced back at Evan. "Lovely to meet you," she said dryly.

"I suspect we'll be seeing more of each other," he called out as she started to walk away. "I'm definitely staying for lunch."

Susannah flinched as she heard the deliberately loud crack of his gum and the popping of a bubble behind her.

Evan watched her walk down the hall. He was surprised by his response. She was obviously a fake, and fun to tease, but he still felt a bit sorry for her. She's in way over her head, he said to himself, thinking just how ruthless his stepfather could be when faced with anything that threatened him. Then he shrugged. She must be better at this game than she looks, he decided. Here she had him wasting his sympathy when she was attempting to pick his family's pocket. Not that his stepfather's money meant anything to him; he had refused to take a dime from Cameron from the moment he finished college, and had repaid him the cost of Yale's tuition as soon as he was able to. His only concern was protecting his mother. On the other hand, he couldn't deny that the girl was attractive. Feeling like a fool, he vowed to be no help whatsoever through what would undoubtedly be a very long afternoon for Susannah Holland.

Evan put his car keys back in his pocket. What would Cameron do to her once he established that she was lying? Maybe he knew it already. Cameron played his cards very close to the vest. In fact he got a perverse pleasure out of toying with people, giving them enough rope to hang themselves. Perhaps he just wanted to watch this girl squirm as a Saturday afternoon amusement. It would be like him.

That was one area in which Cameron never disappointed: he could always be counted on to act like a bastard. Evan had mistrusted him from the first — and rightly so, it had turned out. His childhood instinct that Cameron would do everything in his power to keep his new stepson out of the way had proved correct. Sure enough, Cameron had packed him off to prep school immediately after his marriage to Tish. When Evan was home he would watch his stepfather take constant advantage of his mother, playing up to her important friends, criticizing her if she didn't do things exactly as he thought they should be done.

Evan had been thrilled when his mother left all those years ago to go into business for herself. His anger at Cameron only grew when he saw her go crawling back. These days, Evan had no doubt that Cameron was responsible for his mother's constant drinking. It drove him wild to watch his stepfather continually hold up his first wife, Kailey, as a shining example of the perfect woman. All these years and he was still pulling that crap. Evan was disgusted every time he heard it.

Maybe this Susannah Holland had a few cards of her own to play today. If Cameron hadn't yet established that she was lying, it would be intriguing to watch. He headed toward the back of the house, wincing at the pain in his knee as he walked. Lying down might relieve it a little; at least the knee was better than last week.

He tried not to think about it. Being sidelined for most of the season with an injury had always been his worst nightmare. The career of a professional baseball player was short enough to begin with. At thirty years old, he could ill afford to lose this much time. His mother had begged him to nurse his injury here in Bedford with her, where she could take care of him. Knowing how rarely his mother was sober these days, Evan translated that to mean where the maids could take care of him. But he knew her intentions were good and he didn't want to disappoint her. Still, the main reason he had agreed to stay here was so he could make one last attempt at getting her away from Cameron and into some kind of treatment. He had tried so many times, but it always proved fruitless. Maybe by spending a couple of months at home, he had a better chance of getting through to her.

He opened the French doors leading out to the garden and saw the kitchen maid setting the table under the shade of a large tree. It was a breezy June day, just a few clouds in the azure sky. The heavy silverware and cut crystal glasses gleamed, set off by two small but colorful floral arrangements. Quite a setting for this little drama, he thought, like something straight out of a painting. The artifice of Cameron Hawkes. He smiled ruefully as he made his way to the large net hammock hanging between two enormous weeping willow trees.

As she was led through an ornate foyer, Susannah asked the maid where she could freshen up. She was directed to a large guest bathroom at the end of a hallway. Her meeting with Evan had thrown her completely. She stood at the sink, splashing water on her face as all her fears, all her guilt threatened to overwhelm her. I can't get away with this, I *shouldn't* get away with this. She was almost nauseated at the thought of meeting the rest of the family and carrying through her deception.

I'm leaving, she decided. I just can't do it. She reached for one of the small monogrammed towels hanging next to the sink, and dried her face, relieved that she wouldn't have to go on with this charade. The towel smelled pleasantly of lavender. As she inhaled its fragrance, she suddenly recalled the foul odor of the hospital where Ruth was. She thought of what it was like for Ruth to lie in that dirty, dingy place day after day.

Slowly, she put the towel back on the rack. Then she went back into the hall and nodded to the waiting maid.

Susannah was ushered into the living room. Two women were already seated next to each other on a large sofa. She didn't have to be told who they were. The older one, Tish Hawkes, appeared to be about fifty, but her age was hard to guess; despite her welcoming smile, her face looked puffy and tired, her skin pale. She wore tailored white pants and a lightweight striped sweater, with large gold earrings, her clothes and accessories all muted but obviously expensive. As she rose to greet her, Susannah could see that she had once been quite beautiful. The younger one would be her daughter, Olivia Hawkes. Dressed in black pants and a pale green silk blouse, she had her mother's blond hair, cut very short, and a delicate face — a nice-looking girl, though not as stunning as her mother had undoubtedly been at that age. She too came over to shake Susannah's hand and introduce herself. Susannah was pleasantly surprised by their friendliness.

Tish asked if she would like something to drink. Susannah declined, casting about for something interesting to say. Her eye fell on the poster propped up on the couch.

"Hawkes Day-care Centers? I know about Little Angel Baby Food, like everybody else, but I didn't know the company ran day-care centers," she said.

"We don't, actually," Olivia replied. "It's just for the employees, so they can have a place to leave their children."

Relieved to have started a conversation, Susannah was impressed that Cameron Hawkes was so forward-thinking. Clearly, he cared about his people and their children. "That's terrific," she responded sincerely. "Your father is very progressive."

"Thank you." Olivia fingered the short strand of pearls she was wearing, but said nothing else.

"You work at the company, don't you?" Susannah asked. Thank God, Jamie had prepped her with a few facts.

The girl looked surprised that Susannah knew this much about her. "Yes, I do. As a matter of fact, I'm in charge of the day-care project."

"I'd love to hear more about that," Susannah said.

Olivia looked dubious, but before Susannah had a chance to say anything else, the maid returned to announce that lunch was being served. Mrs. Hawkes rose and led the way. Relieved, Susannah decided she had gotten through the introductions better than she might have hoped.

Cameron Hawkes was already outside. He came to greet Susannah as the three emerged into the sunlight.

"How are you this afternoon?" he asked warmly, bringing her over to the round wrought-iron table and holding out a chair for her.

"I'm very well, thank you. It was so kind of you to invite me to lunch."

Cameron smiled. "I thought my family should meet you. You say you're one of us, so they should have the opportunity to know you, don't you think?"

Susannah smiled back, although she knew she had lost control of the situation and lunch hadn't even begun. With dismay, she noted Evan Gardiner approaching, limping slightly. Damn, he really was joining them. She took a deep breath. You can handle this, she reassured herself once more.

"Hello, again," he said to her, a smile on his face. He walked around to where his mother sat, leaning down to kiss her on the cheek. "I haven't seen you this morning," he said. "How do you feel?"

"Fine, darling, thank you for asking." Speaking to her son, Tish Hawkes grew more animated. Her love for him was obvious. "Are you joining us for lunch? I thought you were going out for the afternoon."

"A change of plans seemed called for." Evan looked over at Susannah, a glint in his eye.

Susannah was horrified to find herself thinking again about how handsome Tish Hawkes's son was. Go down that path, she thought, and you'll give yourself away in no time flat. She would make sure to stay far away from him.

"Wonderful," Tish said. She gestured to Susannah. "Have you met Miss Holland?"

"I've had the pleasure." Evan took his seat.

"Glad you could stay." Cameron's words to Evan sounded affectionate. He held up a hand, signaling the maid to bring the first course. "And, Olivia, darling, if I can free up my schedule, let's spend some time together after lunch. I might want you to add another day-care area out at the plant."

Olivia's eyes lit up. "Great. I have lots of ideas for a new one. We've learned quite a bit from the first two."

Susannah felt a pang as she watched Olivia and her father talking. Wouldn't it be wonderful if she really *were* a member of this family? To have a mother who adored her, to have a father to work with and learn from. It would be so nice, she thought wistfully.

As one maid poured ice water into all their glasses, another brought out a tray with five plates of smoked trout. Cameron continued to speak as she moved silently among them, setting the plates down.

"Tish, while I'm thinking of it — let's take along that book for Marge tonight, the one she was asking for."

His wife spoke sweetly. "Of course. It's so thoughtful of you to remember."

Cameron smiled at her. He knew their guest wouldn't pick up on the sarcasm hidden beneath her words. Now he had done just enough to establish that his was a tightly knit family, to show this girl how kind and loving he was with them. He'd had to — especially since she would be around a bit longer than he'd anticipated. He'd been amazed when, a couple of days earlier, his detective confirmed Susannah's story, at least as far back as the orphanage.

"I'm sure she's a fake, Mr. Hawkes," Jack Milford had said, "but it's going to take some time for me to prove it, to figure out how she got to that orphanage." Clearly the detective himself had been surprised that so much of her tale was true.

Cameron had to be careful now. This situation had developed the potential to drag on for weeks, even months, and he was more convinced than ever that it could jeopardize his takeover of Awareness. He wasn't about to let one young woman get in the way of this deal, but he was certain that Lionel Shea wouldn't take kindly to his being anything less than welcoming to his newly found daughter. Keep your friends close and your enemies closer, Cameron believed.

"So, Susannah," he said finally, "tell us something about yourself. Not about your past, for the moment." He laughed. "About you now."

She smiled. "It's pretty simple, really. I came to New York right after graduating from Berkeley, and I've been in the city ever since."

"Are you married?" Evan asked.

She looked over at him. His face was impassive. "No," she replied. "I've never been married."

"Do you work?" Cameron asked politely.

"I'm a photographer." Susannah and Jamie had agreed that she might as well be up front about this as soon as the subject came up.

Cameron stiffened. "I don't suppose you happened to hear that my company is sponsoring a major photo competition." He couldn't keep the sarcasm out of his voice.

Susannah put down her fork. She had to watch her step here, though she had rehearsed her answer to this many times.

"Yes, of course I've heard of it," she said carefully. "In fact, I thought of applying. But I know the deadline has passed, and what I'm here about doesn't have anything to do with that." She picked up her fork and resumed eating.

Cameron leaned back in his chair. If she wasn't after his money, then surely this was it, she was after the Forum competition. He sat back, amused. He liked this girl, no question about it. How many people would try a stunt like this to advance their careers?

Tish indicated to the maid that they were ready for the next course. As the woman bent over to take her plate, Tish whispered something in her ear.

"So, you're a photographer. What kind of pictures do you take?" Cameron was enjoying himself thoroughly.

"Actually," Susannah replied, "the main reason I wanted to be considered for the Forum is that my specialty is photographing children."

The maid reappeared, holding a large pitcher.

"Bloody Marys, anyone?" Tish asked brightly. The maid filled the glass in front of Tish, then waited for further instructions. The rest of them declined, so she set the pitcher down on the table before leaving.

"You know, I'm very interested in the day-care centers at Hawkes," Susannah went on, "and I was hoping Olivia would tell me more about them."

Olivia looked up, in the middle of breaking off a piece of French bread from the loaf in a basket next to her. Her father had asked her to be pleasant to this girl, so she had to try. But she was having a hard time hiding her true feelings. How ridiculous, a daughter from over twenty years ago. If this girl tried to pull anything on her father, Olivia would be right there to fight. In the meantime, she would be as sweet as sugar, if that was what Cameron wanted.

"I'd be glad to answer whatever questions you have," she finally said.

Susannah was struck by an idea. It was the perfect opening for Cameron to see her work.

"Perhaps," she said to him, "I could follow Olivia around the day-care centers." She looked back to Olivia. "Just snap you doing whatever it is you normally do with the other people who work there."

"What?" Olivia stared at her.

Susannah went on. "You could use the photos for the company."

"I don't think that's a good idea." It was clear Olivia's words didn't express just how negative her reaction really was to the suggestion.

But Cameron was amused by Susannah's nerve. It wasn't something he would have gone out of his way to arrange, but now that he thought about it, it would be good for his image — giving Olivia her little moment of glory, the doting father helping his daughter build a career. And, as far as the Holland woman went, he didn't see any potential harm in it. In fact, he would maneuver Shea into meeting Susannah while she was there. They would all pose together. He liked the idea more and more.

"Well, why not?" he said expansively. "Olivia, have my secretary give you a couple of dates when I can make it, and I'll even drop by to have my picture taken with you."

His daughter was unable to hide her unhappy surprise, but all she said was "Fine, Dad."

Cameron changed the subject, and the rest of lunch passed quickly, the conversation shallow and polite. He and Susannah discussed an upcoming art exhibition at the Metropolitan Museum, and he offered to take her to the black-tie opening party, although it was an offer he had no intention of carrying out. He continued to be impressed by her poise and the smooth way she handled herself, watching her compliment Tish on the garden, then drawing Olivia out with her interest in the work going on at the day-care centers. Then Evan and Tish began talking about one of his recent ball games. Evan included Susannah in the conversation, and they quickly got sidelined into a discussion of sports photography.

Cameron watched Susannah listening, her eyes alert, taking in everything that was being said. Maybe Dorrie Gordon really *had* been pregnant, he thought. God knows, it was possible. What she'd lacked in brains, she'd made up in sexual skill, and they had spent most of their time together in bed. So there'd been plenty of opportunities. Perhaps Susannah truly was his daughter. Cameron laughed to himself. Well, whether she was or wasn't, she was one cool customer.

When lunch was over, he escorted Susannah to the limousine he had waiting out front to drive her to the train station.

"Thank you so much for lunch," she said, thinking that in an odd way it had turned out to be a very nice afternoon.

"We'll speak soon," Cameron said, shaking her hand. He liked this girl. She had a lot of potential, he could see that.

He returned to the house, coming upon Evan in the hallway.

"It must warm your heart to be reunited with your little girl," Evan said archly as his stepfather passed.

Cameron bristled, but wasn't about to explain himself to Evan. "I suppose you'll never grow out of discussing things you know nothing about," he said over his shoulder, not breaking his stride.

"She's got you nervous, hasn't she?"

Cameron stopped and turned to look at Evan, the anger clear in his eyes. Then, abruptly, he walked off.

It pleased Evan to get a rise out of Cameron. After all, he'd been watching Cameron make people squirm his whole life. Maybe this girl had turned the tables on the old man, even if it was only for a short time. Whistling, he went out the front door and headed toward his car. He'd planned on doing a few errands before meeting up with Dennis Coe, his roommate from Yale, but staying home for lunch meant he wouldn't have time. He was looking forward to seeing Dennis again; if nothing else, at least his knee injury gave him some free time to keep up with old friends during the summer. Maybe later he would call that woman he'd met at a post-game party at the beginning of the season. As he got into his car, he wondered where he put the napkin with her phone number on it.

Leaving Evan, Cameron continued on his way, but instead of going to his study, where he had been headed originally, he went back out to the garden, where Tish was still seated at the table, finishing the last of the Bloody Marys.

"So," she said, as she saw him approach, "that was quite a scene. Your missing child. What a loving welcome." She took another sip from her glass. "I don't imagine we'll be seeing her around again, though, will we? You have a way of making these little problems disappear."

"On the contrary, my darling," Cameron said sweetly. "I want you to instruct Evan to escort Miss Holland to our party on Saturday night."

Tish looked at him in surprise. Each June, they hosted a large party for Cameron's business associates. It was exhausting for Tish, and she couldn't wait for it to be over. But it was critical to Cameron, who spent a small fortune making the black-tie event one that people would talk about for weeks afterward. She couldn't imagine why he would want that girl to attend. "You want her at the party? What for? And Evan won't do it, anyway."

"He will if you ask him to." Cameron reached over to pluck a strawberry from the bowl in the center of the table, and popped it into his mouth, chewing with great enjoyment. "He won't refuse his dear mother."

"But I won't ask him." Tish was defiant.

Cameron fixed his gaze on her. His words were low and even. "You *will* ask him. In fact, you will *tell* him to. Like I'm telling you now."

Tish looked away. When Cameron told her to do something in that tone of voice it was a given that she would obey. Having found out the hard way, she knew the consequences of refusing him. He would make her life a complete misery. Well, she supposed Evan's escorting Susannah made no difference one way or the other. Evan dated plenty of women, and this would be just one more evening for him. She even seemed to be fairly nice. Tish closed her eyes, sickeningly ashamed of her own weakness.

Evan was back at the house by seven o'clock, when he'd

promised to drive his mother into Manhattan. She and Cameron were attending a benefit at the Waldorf, but Cameron had gone on ahead in the limousine to his office, wanting to put in a couple of hours' work. As they drove, Tish forced herself to raise the subject of Evan's bringing Susannah to the party. Just as Cameron had predicted, he was reluctant, but willing to do as his mother asked.

"The whole thing is pretty strange," he said, keeping his eyes on the traffic as they turned onto Fifth Avenue.

"I realize that," Tish sighed. She knew better than to tell him this was actually Cameron's request. He would never do it then, no matter how much she begged. "But we need to see what she's all about. Having her there should be helpful."

Evan cast a sideways glance at her, but said nothing. As they approached Cameron's office, he pulled the car into a garage. They took the long elevator ride up, walking through the silent halls, past the secretaries' empty desks. Cameron was sitting in his office, dictating letters into a tape recorder for his secretary to type Monday morning.

As Evan set down the small suitcase his mother needed for the evening, Tish suddenly remembered that she wanted to check a florist's phone number on Marianne's Rolodex for an upcoming company cocktail party. She asked Evan to wait for her.

As soon as Tish left the room, Cameron shut off the tape recorder and came over to talk to Evan.

He spoke with a smile. "You know, Evan, it's no secret that we don't get along all that well," he began.

Evan only laughed.

"But that doesn't mean we can't do some business together." Cameron went on. "Hawkes is launching a new line of children's sportswear. You're pretty well known as a ball player, and you'd be a good candidate to endorse the clothes."

"What?" Evan stared at him in disbelief.

"You'd be a celebrity spokesman for us," Cameron said. "We'd set you up for television and print ads, some promotion on talk shows, that sort of thing."

Evan shook his head. "You must be kidding."

"Think about it. It would be good for you, good for me, good for your mother and the family."

"Since when did you care about the family?" Evan snapped.

Cameron was placid. "I don't know why you'd say that."

Evan's annoyance grew. "Boy, you are some piece of work."

Pointing a finger at him, Cameron spoke sharply. "Don't forget that I paid to raise you, and put you through plenty of years of expensive schools. Because of me, you've had it easy."

"Right, it was all a breeze," Evan said bitterly. "But just because you used my mother doesn't mean I'll let you use me."

"Look, this is a damned good offer I'm making." Cameron was getting angry. "Face it, you're thirty. You don't have that many years left to play—or to market your name. Hell, you're not even playing this summer. As a matter of fact, we're taking something of a risk with you, given that knee injury."

Evan could barely contain his fury. "Do you really think I'll say yes? That you would have me gratefully signing a contract? You must be out of your mind."

Cameron sat down on the couch, quickly regaining his composure. "Business is business," he said calmly, crossing his legs as he leaned back comfortably.

Evan went to the door. "I'd starve before I'd work for you. Is that answer clear enough?"

Cameron reached out to pick up a glass paperweight on the side table, turning it over in one hand and examining it, appearing to be barely listening. "Fine. You may be sorry later, but of course the offer won't be there."

Evan struggled to control his temper. "Just tell my mother I couldn't wait for her."

Damn Cameron, he thought as he slammed the door behind him. It wasn't enough that he knew what your weaknesses were. He was always ready to exploit them. No wonder his mother had fallen to pieces. He *had* to find a way to get her out of there, away from that son of a bitch.

Chapter 21

Susannah shaded her eyes from the summer sun as she looked around, anxiously searching for Bibi. It was a hot day but comfortably breezy, and nearly all the tables in the outdoor café at Rockefeller Center were filled. She was glad she'd arrived early so she could be seated and ready when Bibi got there. She didn't want anything to go wrong; this meeting was too important to her.

Thank God for Jamie, she thought, rearranging her camera equipment on the ground beside her. Although she had wanted desperately to explain to Bibi how the nude photographs of her wound up in *People,* Susannah's dozens of phone calls and all of her letters had gone unanswered. Finally, Jamie interceded. He called Bibi and told her that it had been Peter Manzoni who had stolen and sold the negatives. And although Bibi sounded

wary, she'd taken Susannah's phone call the next day. When Bibi
mentioned that she was coming to New York to audition for a
Broadway play, Susannah asked if they could get together. Hesitantly, Bibi had agreed.

There she was, wearing a bright yellow minidress and sandals.
Susannah was flooded with relief as she watched her approach.
Bibi's eyes were hidden behind oversized sunglasses, but her red
hair, fiery in the noonday sun, gave her away at once. As she
made her way through the tables, several people stopped her to
ask for an autograph.

The dark sunglasses made it impossible for Susannah to read
her expression as they came face to face.

"Well, hello there." Bibi spoke slowly. Susannah had never
heard that reserve in her voice before.

Susannah couldn't contain her emotion. "Oh, I'm so glad
you're here." She leaned forward and was relieved to find that
Bibi permitted a kiss on her cheek. "Please, please don't be
angry with me," she blurted out. "I can't stand it."

Bibi sat down, putting her shoulder bag on the ground, pushing her sunglasses up on her head. "Susannah," she said ruefully.
"What the hell happened?"

"I swear to you I had no idea what Peter was up to, I really
didn't," Susannah exclaimed. "My God, I was ready to *marry* him.
And he stole my money, took the negatives, and disappeared in
a puff of smoke."

Bibi pursed her lips. "You didn't see it coming?"

Susannah smiled sadly. "I suppose I should have. And I
should have had those negatives locked in a bank vault. That was
a stupid mistake and I'll never forgive myself. But you have to
understand that I wouldn't have sold them to anyone for all the
money in the world. *Never.*"

"No, I suppose you wouldn't." Bibi's tone softened. "I guess
if you pose for nudes you have to consider something like that
might happen, no matter whose fault it turns out to be."

"I feel so rotten about it." Susannah looked at her friend. "I
know there's no way I can make it up to you."

"Hey, you don't have to grovel." The old warmth was creeping back into Bibi's voice. "Well . . . maybe a little groveling is in order. But now that you've done it we can get on with our lives, don't you think?"

Susannah sighed with relief. "Oh, yes."

"Besides," Bibi went on, "I've missed you a lot. It's so hard to make real friends out there."

"It's amazing — only a couple of movies, but your picture seems to be everywhere. Every magazine I see has something on you. What's it like?" Susannah asked.

Bibi answered thoughtfully. "It's hard to grasp and harder to deal with. I like being successful, I do. But on the other hand, the isolation that comes with being famous is a shock. On the third hand, how can you complain when this is what you asked for? And I've made some mistakes already, big ones. Like investing most of my money in some crummy deal that went under."

She put her hand out to cover Susannah's. "I could use an old friend to stick close when things get tough. It's pretty scary, so many people tugging at me from all directions."

"I'm here whenever you need me," Susannah said, smiling.

"Good."

The two women locked eyes, the trouble between them past.

"Now, guess what," Bibi said animatedly, moving on to another subject.

"What? Don't make me guess, tell me."

Bibi paused for dramatic effect.

"Kurt and I are getting married."

Susannah let out a small scream of delight. "Oh, that's incredible. When?"

"The end of August, in New York. We're making a big wedding, doing the whole number. Will you come?"

"Are you kidding? Of course!"

The waiter came over to their table.

"We're not ready just yet. Would you give us another minute?" Bibi asked.

"Yes, Miss Frost," he answered respectfully. "Allow me to say that I love your movies."

"Thank you so much." Bibi fixed a warm gaze on him. "You're very kind."

As he walked away, Susannah grinned. "I can relax now. We'll be getting the best service of any table here."

Bibi shrugged helplessly. "What can I do? Besides, it won't last forever. I could be history in the flash of an eye."

"Well, enjoy it while it does last," Susannah answered. "You earned it. I for one am going to sit here and bask in your reflected glory."

They both laughed and went back to Bibi's wedding plans, their talk soon drifting to other things. When Susannah happened to glance at her watch she was dismayed to see that two hours had passed.

"Damn, I didn't realize how late it was," she said, trying to get the waiter's attention so she could ask for their check. "I've got to go."

"Do you have to run right now?" Bibi said wistfully.

Susannah looked at her fondly. "I don't want to, but I have to shoot some pictures."

"Of what?" Bibi was interested.

Susannah hesitated. She knew Jamie hadn't told his cousin about what she was doing to get into the Forum competition. But it would be such a relief to be able to discuss this with Bibi.

"Do you remember my telling you about my first foster mother, how good she was to me?" she began.

"Of course." Bibi nodded.

"Well, she's very sick now. Dying of cancer."

"Oh, I'm so sorry," Bibi said sympathetically.

"She's in the most terrible hospital you can imagine, Bibi, an awful place. There's a hospice she could go to, but it costs a fortune, and none of her children have the money for it. I don't have it either."

"Isn't there some way . . . ?"

Susannah shook her head. "I didn't know what to do." She paused. "It was Jamie who came up with a suggestion."

Bibi was surprised. "My cousin Jamie?"

Susannah nodded. "You see, there's this competition for photographers, and the winners each get seventy-five thousand dollars — enough to pay for the hospice. I was too late to enter, but then Jamie dreamed up this idea. I thought it was ridiculous at first, but after a while . . ."

She unfolded the rest of the story, about how she was pretending to be Cameron Hawkes's daughter. Bibi's eyes grew wider and wider as Susannah laid out the details of the hoax. When she described having lunch at the Hawkes's Bedford home two Saturdays before, how pleasant it had turned out to be, Bibi shook her head in total disbelief.

"Now I'm on my way to see their daughter, Olivia," Susannah finished up, "to take some pictures of her at work. It's a great opportunity to get Cameron Hawkes to look at my stuff, maybe even take a special interest in it."

When Susannah was done, she sat back and waited. There was a brief silence.

"This is the craziest thing I've ever heard," Bibi finally said. "It doesn't surprise me that Jamie would come up with an insane idea like this. But *you,* actually going along with it. *Doing* it. I realize it's for a good cause, but I can't believe the Susannah Holland I know would even consider it."

"Hey, didn't you tell me to get out and make things happen?" Susannah asked, smiling.

"I didn't mean like *this*!"

"You know, it's been quite an experience. The Hawkes family is very nice. I'm sure they're a little distrustful right now on some level. But that's logical, given the circumstances. I think they'll get to like me."

Bibi exploded. "What the hell are you talking about? Are you going to try to get away with this *permanently*?"

Susannah shrank back. "No, no. I only meant that as long as this goes on, we can have a good relationship. They'll have me as a sister, and I'll have them."

Bibi regarded her in amazement. She spoke quietly but forcefully. "You can't just fabricate a family because you want it."

Susannah spoke defensively. "I'm not. I'm only saying they're nice people."

"Oh, come on." Bibi's voice rose. "How can you believe they would all really be welcoming to you, some nobody from nowhere claiming to be related to them and all their money? And the way you describe them, everyone sickeningly sweet to everyone else, everything so perfect." She shook her head. "Something tells me there's a lot of wishful thinking going on."

"That's not so," Susannah protested. "They happen to be open-minded about this situation. And I'm not going to take advantage of any of them — I just want a shot at the Forum. It's not so terrible if I like them and they like me."

"This isn't a game," Bibi said sharply. "You're acting like you're all going to love each other, like they won't even mind your lying about something this serious." Her tone became more gentle. "You're getting emotionally involved in something that's not real."

"That's not so," Susannah insisted.

Bibi regarded her for a moment. "You know, if it hadn't been for that damn deal that went bad, I could have helped you. But I could get about five thousand dollars together if you need it. Would that do any good?"

Susannah smiled gratefully. "That's very nice of you, but it wouldn't pay for even a month in the hospice. It's just not enough. I've got to give this my best shot."

Bibi sighed. "Okay, Susannah, but please try to stay out of trouble. I hope you win that contest and get the money for Ruth. But I also hope you know what you're doing."

"I do," Susannah said stubbornly.

Bibi laughed, trying to lighten the mood. "And do me a favor, please — from now on, don't ever do anything my cousin Jamie tells you to do."

Susannah smiled back at her. "Okay, I promise. And don't worry. It'll turn out all right."

They hugged as they left each other on Fifth Avenue. "I'll call you tomorrow," Bibi said.

Susannah walked over to the Hawkes Corporation headquarters a few blocks away, pushing Bibi out of her thoughts to concentrate on what lay ahead.

Olivia's office was on a different floor from her father's, the reception area far less grand and imposing. A receptionist dialed Olivia's number and announced that Susannah was there, but nearly twenty-five minutes passed before Olivia came out to the reception area to greet her.

"I'm so sorry to keep you waiting," she said, smiling as she shook Susannah's hand briskly. "It's been a hectic day, but I'm all yours now."

Olivia didn't know whether Susannah would guess that the delay had been intentional. She was damned if she was going to jump through hoops because this fake had decided to interrupt her work. What was wrong with her father, she wondered, that he had agreed to this?

Susannah noted that Olivia's clothes resembled the ones she herself had adopted back when she was in business school. She wore a conservative black suit, beige silk blouse, and low heels. Following her back into the elevator to go down to the day-care center, Susannah noticed her small gold earrings, the fine gold chain around her neck. Just the way I used to dress, she thought with a smile, looking down at her own outfit: khaki pants and a white shirt with the sleeves rolled up, a print scarf woven around her belt for color, her tan leather satchel and the camera equipment strung around her neck all banging against each other as she walked. So Olivia was struggling to find her identity too, to make it in the corporate world, Susannah thought, feeling a rush of empathy.

The day-care center was at the end of the hall. As they walked, Olivia filled Susannah in on the details, explaining how she had come up with the idea after studying worker absenteeism and lateness. So often, she said, people were delayed or kept at home because of problems with their children, suddenly finding that their arrangements for child care had fallen through. This way, their problems were permanently solved. Susannah was intrigued, genuinely impressed that Olivia had recognized this need and done something about it. So the day care was really her work, not Cameron's.

"Here we are," Olivia said, opening a bright blue door. "We broke through several offices to make this space."

They entered the vast room, an open, airy environment painted in different primary colors and decorated with children's drawings, collages, and cutouts. At a glance, Susannah estimated that there were about thirty children, ranging in age from one to four, playing in small groups.

"The parents can leave them and pick them up anytime between eight in the morning and six at night," Olivia said, as they headed to a corner.

Several of the children looked over at Olivia, as the adults supervising them acknowledged her presence with a smile and a nod. She smiled back. Listening to the babble of the children, Susannah began asking questions about them. The two women found themselves in an animated discussion about how inadequate child care was across the country. Finally, Susannah reached for her camera.

"I guess we should get started, if that's all right with you," she said, removing the lens cap. "Just try to ignore me."

Olivia suddenly looked shy. "What do you want me to do?"

For the next half hour, Susannah took pictures, catching every combination of Olivia with the staff members and the children. She tried to capture the spirit of the place, the lively, easygoing atmosphere. At the same time, she wanted to show Olivia in a variety of moods, from the efficient, young corporate woman she appeared when she had first come out to greet Susannah that afternoon, to the soft, laughing nineteen-year-old that emerged as she played with the children.

When Susannah was satisfied, the two women left the center together.

"Do you think you'll stay in this part of the company?" Susannah asked as they walked down the hall.

"Maybe I'm fooling myself, but I believe this has meant something to the parents who work at Hawkes," Olivia said. "They give me great feedback, which is a tremendous reward."

Susannah nodded.

"And now," Olivia went on, "I'm trying to establish another center, at a medical research center the Hawkes Corporation endowed several years ago. I want to spread the idea around. This new location is perfect. It's a separate company, not just a Hawkes division, but we're closely connected. That way, I hope we won't be seen as intruders."

"That's great," Susannah said admiringly.

Olivia blushed slightly. "Thanks." She suddenly remembered something. "Oh, my father mentioned joining us to have his picture taken, but it didn't work out. He's always so busy. But he told me to pass on his regards to you and to say he looks forward to seeing you on Saturday."

"Saturday?"

The elevator arrived and they both stepped in, Olivia pressing the button marked *L*.

"The party in Bedford. Didn't Evan ask you? My father said he was inviting you to our big soiree over the weekend. It's a black-tie buffet dinner—we have it every year."

Susannah couldn't hide her surprise. Going to a formal dinner at the Hawkes home with Evan Gardiner. What a mess this could be, she thought. It had been such an interesting hour with Olivia, she had actually forgotten to be frightened. Now her fear returned in full force.

"Well, if you decide to come, I guess I'll see you then." Olivia had adopted a more formal tone as the elevator reached the lobby. They stepped out, and Olivia paused. "I trust you got what you needed today."

"Thanks so much," Susannah said sincerely. "I hope I have something here you'll like. You've done such a wonderful job— your father must be very proud of you."

With a wave, Susannah left. Olivia watched her go. Susannah Holland wasn't really that bad after all. That didn't mean she was telling the truth, but she was an awfully nice person, the kind of person Olivia wouldn't mind having as a friend. She'd been so busy with her work, she hadn't devoted much time to keeping up with her old high school friends or making any new ones. That was a mistake, she realized. But Susannah might actually be her half sister. She wondered what it would be like to have a sister, someone to talk over all your problems with, to share the fun times, too. Her mother had retreated into alcohol so long ago,

Olivia couldn't remember ever talking about anything important with her. It wasn't worth the effort, since Tish was just as likely to forget what had been said by the next day. No, a sister would be something special.

Olivia shook her head. She shouldn't be thinking like this. Susannah Holland wasn't her sister. She was some impostor who wanted something from Cameron. Ringing for the elevator to take her back upstairs, she sighed.

"Jamie, I can't do it. Do you know what could happen?" Susannah was frantic. "It'll be a disaster!"

Jamie's voice came over the phone line soothingly. "Don't worry. If Cameron Hawkes was going to expose you as a liar, he wouldn't do it tonight. Why would he ruin his own party with a scene like that?"

Susannah ignored him. "And going with Evan — he's already decided I'm lying, that's obvious. The whole night with him will be torture."

"You can handle him," Jamie said reassuringly. "He's just a dumb jock."

"That's easy for you to say, safely tucked away in California." She groaned. "Oh, this is so awful."

"Come on, you can't give up now."

Susannah exhaled slowly. "Okay, okay. I'll let you know what calamity occurs tonight."

"Good girl," Jamie replied cheerfully. "Go get 'em."

After sending her love to Bibi, Susannah hung up and went over to her closet, unhappily surveying the clothes inside. The day after she had photographed Olivia, an engraved invitation to the Hawkes party had arrived by messenger, followed that evening by a telephone call from Evan asking if he could pick her up and drive her out to Bedford for the occasion. The two of them had been polite but cautious with each other on the telephone, which resulted in a conversation so stilted she was sure he was as relieved as she was when it was over. Still, she couldn't imagine why he'd bothered to ask her to go as his date. She supposed it was to help his stepfather out.

But what should she wear? Nothing too revealing, but something that showed she was confident. It took several changes, but she eventually decided on a black crepe dress with a plain round neck and a low-cut back; it was simple but elegant, a wildly expensive present she had splurged on for herself six months before when it was on sale at Barney's. She put on sheer black stockings and black pumps, and clipped on her best gold earrings in the shape of bows. That was fine, she thought, observing herself in the mirror as she brushed her long hair. The back was a little daring, while the rest was properly conservative.

She was ready well before eight o'clock, when Evan was due to pick her up. Her nervousness mounted as she sat stiffly on the couch, trying not to wrinkle her dress, and distractedly checked the contents of her evening bag. Would any of the guests there know who she was — or, rather, who she was supposed to be? How could she manage to spend an entire evening with Evan?

She jumped at the sound of the doorbell.

"Mademoiselle." Dressed in a tuxedo, Evan bowed deeply as Susannah opened the door. Not overly friendly, he was nonetheless making an effort. As he stood up again, he smiled, revealing dimples. "The festivities await."

She smiled back with relief. If he was going to torment her about her claim to be a Hawkes, at least he was going to use humor to do it.

"Thank you for bringing the chariot," she said, grabbing a black evening wrap and her bag, along with a manila envelope containing the pictures she had taken of Olivia.

As she passed Evan, she could feel his eyes on her bare back. A chill went up her spine. Again, she felt that mixture of attraction and fear, both of which she knew would prove dangerous if she was going to accomplish what she had set out to do.

Down on the street, Evan opened the door to his Volvo for her. Settling herself on the seat, Susannah wondered about the car, which was obviously an old one; she would have expected a rich baseball player from a wealthy family to drive something flashier. She observed him as he sharply pulled away from the curb. He appeared engrossed in his driving, almost oblivious to her presence.

"You were lucky to get a parking spot here," she said to break the silence.

He glanced at her. "I'm a lucky guy, no doubt about it."

She would have bristled if it weren't for the self-deprecating smile that accompanied his words.

"Well, you are pretty lucky, aren't you?" she responded. "You play professional baseball, and that must be a good life."

He looked at her more squarely before turning back to the road. "Of course, you're right. I was injured recently and it looks like I'm sidelined for the rest of the season. I suppose I'm feeling a bit sorry for myself."

"Is it your leg?"

Evan looked startled. "My knee. How did you know?"

So that was why he'd been limping, Susannah thought. Apparently he didn't realize how evident it was.

"Just a guess" was all she said aloud.

"I tore a ligament sliding into second."

From the annoyed look on his face, Susannah could tell he was replaying the moment in his mind. "I'm sorry. Will it take long to heal?"

"I've had surgery on it, so after a few months of physical therapy, it should be fine. My knee is the reason I'm staying at Bedford, actually."

"Then I take it you don't usually live with your family?"

There was a short burst of laughter. "No, not usually," he said. "I keep an apartment in Pittsburgh, but I live in New York during the off-season." He set his mouth. "I'm never at the Bedford house."

Susannah wondered what he meant, but saw that he didn't want her to pursue it. As he pulled the car onto the highway, the traffic cleared, and he stepped on the gas. Susannah noted that he was going seventy-five miles an hour, but she didn't comment. They were both silent for a minute.

"I spent some time with Olivia the other day," she said at last. "We were at the day-care center." She indicated the envelope in her lap. "As a matter of fact, I have my photos of her right here."

"Olivia's done a great job there." Evan was visibly proud of his sister. "I wish she got more recognition for it. She really cares about finding solutions for working parents. I think she's going to do some important things — if she can get the backing she needs."

Susannah was slightly taken aback by his adamancy. Hardly the sort of thing a jock, single and on the loose, would be expected to have on his mind. "Are you interested in child care?" she asked.

"I do charity work in my spare time — a lot of the players do. And Olivia and I are cooking up a few ideas on something we can do together."

They continued to discuss Olivia's work, and Susannah was pleasantly surprised to find that, far from being dumb, as Jamie had predicted, Evan was very bright. He knew far more about the politics of child care than she would have expected. Their talk turned to Susannah's past in California.

"Would you ever want to go back West?" Evan asked.

"I have some good memories connected with California," Susannah told him, "but some bad associations, too. I like it in the East, and I don't see any reason to go back out there."

He nodded, and Susannah checked herself, falling silent. She had grown comfortable talking with him, but she needed to be more careful. He had every reason to want to trick her into revealing the truth about herself. She bit her lip, her conscience bothering her. Under other circumstances . . . well, there was no point in thinking about that.

"What's it like to be a ball player?" she asked him. "How did you get into it?"

"I always loved to play, and I worked hard at it, but it was just for fun," Evan said, his eyes still on the road. "I got on the team at Yale, and I was recruited there."

"Yale seems like an odd place to recruit baseball players," Susannah commented.

"It's not the first place they look, I suppose," Evan smiled. "That's how I got my nickname, of course."

"Your nickname?"

"They call me Professor."

Susannah laughed.

"But how did you get on the team to begin with?" she asked.

"When I was a junior, one of my friends brought his father to a game. The guy had played third base for Houston. Anyway, he spoke to someone who spoke to someone else, and one thing led to another. In the second half of my junior year, the scouts started showing up, making offers. I'd actually planned to become an architect, so I had a lot of doubts at first. But in the end, I signed on."

"You went right to Pittsburgh?"

"Oh, no," Evan corrected her. "First I did three years on the San Diego Padres' farm team before I was even tapped to play in the majors. I joined the Pirates three years ago."

"Are you glad about the way things worked out?" she asked curiously.

His expression was deadpan. "Endless hours of practice, a million hours spent on the road, sore everything. Of course I'm glad."

She smiled. "I don't believe it's that bad."

"Of course not." He returned the smile. "It's an incredible life. I get to play baseball, see the country, travel with a bunch of great guys — most of them, anyway."

Susannah listened as he went on, describing the thrill of tagging a runner out, or being down two strikes and hitting a home run. He talked about the competition and camaraderie among the players. His dedication to the sport and his joy at being part of it were obvious.

Susannah was so absorbed she didn't notice that they were approaching the Bedford house. Evan pulled into the circular driveway and turned off the motor. Strains of music and laughter reached the car, and the two of them fell silent, realizing they should be getting out and joining the others. Suddenly, Evan restarted the car and drove off.

"Aren't we going in?" Susannah asked.

"We will," he responded. "But first, I have something to do."

He drove until they reached the center of town, then parked the car and got out. When he returned, he was carrying two dozen roses.

"Something to remember the evening by," he said, offering them to her.

Again, he had surprised her. Susannah took the fragrant flowers, admiring their beauty as she wondered what he was up to, given how skeptical he'd been. Without another word, he drove them back to the party. As they entered, his hand gently rested against the small of her back.

Inside, the house had been transformed. Susannah remembered it as being so formal, so imposing. Tonight, every room was warmly aglow with candlelight, the vibrant colors of summer flowers everywhere. As Evan dropped off her wrap and the envelope with her photos at the cloak room, Susannah glanced into the study and saw a chamber quartet playing, their melodies providing a gentle background to the sounds of clinking glasses and cocktail party chatter. It was very crowded, and Susannah observed the other guests, as waiters served tall stem glasses of champagne from silver trays. Women in magnificent full-length gowns, their jewels glittering, were set off against the black of the tuxedos worn by their escorts. Tish Hawkes stood off in one corner, talking with a tall, sun-tanned couple and looking regal in a long gown of pale yellow chiffon, her blond hair swept up in her signature chignon.

This was a gathering of the rich and powerful that people like Susannah rarely got to see. Several men and women called out hellos to Evan as they passed, and he nodded in return. Trying to hide her nervousness, she didn't know whether to be glad that the front of her dress was modest or that the back of it dared to be different.

Pointing out various people as they went, Evan led her out to the garden. It was the perfect weather for an outdoor party, the summer evening cool and comfortable. A huge blue-and-white striped tent had been erected near the spot where lunch had been served two weeks before. Torches, strings of white lights on the trees, and garlands of white flowers strung around blue columns lent an air of magic to the night. Through the tent's open entrance, she saw an eight-piece orchestra playing for elegantly dressed couples gliding to the music on a wooden floor constructed for the evening.

"How beautiful," Susannah breathed, taking it all in.

"I suppose," Evan said with a small smile. "Not my idea of an intimate evening, but it serves its purpose."

Susannah looked at him. "What purpose is that?"

"It's just business, you know. Business, pleasure, friends, associates — it's all the same thing for some people."

Before Susannah could comment, Cameron Hawkes appeared before them, as if out of nowhere. His silver hair shone in the garden lighting, and Susannah thought fleetingly that he was still an exceedingly handsome man.

"Susannah, my dear," he said, taking her hand and smiling. "I was very angry to learn that your invitation was nearly overlooked. But I'm so glad you could join us."

"Thank you very much," Susannah replied. She couldn't get over how kind Cameron Hawkes was being. And she'd been right about the magnetism of his personality; he had the ability to make her feel as if she were the only person there, at least the only one who mattered. "You were so thoughtful to include me."

"Nonsense." Cameron dismissed her gratitude lightly, as he waved to someone in the crowd. "Lionel, can you join us?" he called out. "There's someone here I want you to meet."

A balding man with smiling eyes came over, a drink in one hand. His tuxedo jacket pulled slightly at his paunch, and his bow tie was crooked, but somehow it seemed to Susannah as if that was just how he should look. He had a gentleness in his face, she decided. She liked him instantly.

Cameron spoke with a broad smile. "Lionel Shea, I want you to meet Susannah Holland."

"Well, young lady, Cameron here has been telling me about you." The man stuck out a hand and vigorously shook Susannah's.

"Quite a story, and so wonderful you could get together after all these years."

How many people had Cameron told? Susannah wondered. She would have guessed he wouldn't court that kind of outside interest until he felt more certain about her. Maybe he was convinced already. The idea encouraged her as she smiled at the man.

"Thank you, Mr. Shea, it's a pleasure to meet you."

"Call me Lionel, please." He beamed. "It's the damnedest thing, your finding out about Cameron here so late in life. But I love a happy ending, and this sure qualifies."

"You're very kind." Oh, if you only knew, Susannah groaned inwardly.

"And this is my stepson, Evan," Cameron said. The two men shook hands.

"A thrill to meet you, Evan. I'm a baseball nut, so naturally I'm a fan of yours."

"Thank you, Mr. Shea."

"I'll spare you my insights on the game right now, but if you ever want to hear them, just let me know." His voice revealed that he was teasing. "My advice will doubtless do wonders for your team."

Evan laughed. "Okay, thanks."

Lionel turned back to Susannah. "Cameron and I are considering a little deal, so we've seen a lot of each other the past few months. He's told me so much about you."

"Lionel and his brother were the founders of Awareness Industries, the toy manufacturer," Cameron interjected. Susannah and Evan nodded; they both had heard of the famous company. The story of its humanist founders and their offbeat personalities was a bit of corporate lore that numerous magazines had written up over the years. "My company is thinking about acquiring it. In a friendly way, of course."

"Of course," Evan echoed, with a trace of sarcasm. Only he noticed the sharp look Cameron threw his way.

Lionel spoke directly to Susannah. "I understand from Cameron that you photograph children."

"That's right."

He smiled. "I'd like to see some of your pictures sometime. I'm probably going to retire soon, but I have some ideas about what I'm going to do later. I do some work with a children's charity now, and you might be just the person I should be talking to."

"I'd love that, Mr. Shea," Susannah answered enthusiastically.

"Okay, we'll make a date for later then," he said. "Why don't you enjoy the party now." He turned to Evan. "Hope you're back on the field soon."

"Thank you," Evan said. "A pleasure to meet you."

They watched Cameron and Lionel walk off, the two of them disappearing into the crowd.

"What a sweet man," Susannah said.

"Yes." Evan's next words were barely audible. "And no doubt about to be suckered by Cameron."

Susannah hadn't heard him. "Excuse me?"

"Nothing." He smiled at her. "Let's get something to eat."

He ushered Susannah into a large room she hadn't seen when she'd last been at the house. Long tables lined the perimeter of the room, laden with magnificent arrangements of fruits, meats, cheeses, and an assortment of more hot and cold hors d'oeuvres. Two bartenders manned their posts at opposite ends of the room. Guests roamed in and out, heaping their plates with food, replenishing their drinks, as a violinist circled the room, his playing unobtrusive but exquisite.

Evan was filling a plate for Susannah. "Would you like some veal?" he asked, stopping before a platter.

"Sounds delicious." Susannah smiled and glanced up, her gaze distracted from Evan's face for a moment by a noise off to one side.

Then she saw him. He was all the way across the room, downing a drink and standing with a tall, reed-thin, blond woman. He'd put on a few pounds and his face was flushed from the alcohol. But it was Peter Manzoni, no mistake about it. Her Peter.

Standing there, enjoying himself — at the expense of her broken heart. Quickly, she looked down at the floor. She was suddenly humiliated all over again, reliving the agony of those weeks after he had left her. Her face flushed. Did everyone here know what he had done to her?

She realized she was being completely irrational. As she looked up, rage swept through her, anger so intense she thought she might burst. She struggled to get control of herself.

"Susannah?" Evan was regarding her with concern. "Are you all right?"

She turned back to him, trying to hide her feelings, taking a deep breath. "Yes, of course," she said as lightly as she could.

He nodded. "Okay, if you say so. You just looked a little odd."

She managed a smile. "No, I'm fine. What do you say to a glass of champagne?"

"Of course." He set down the plate. "I'll be right back."

"Yes." She wasn't really listening. Evan walked off and she craned her neck so she could get a better view of Peter. The bastard, right out in the open here. But what did I expect? she asked herself. That he would be in hiding? She watched him lean over and say something to his date. He didn't look particularly happy. Good.

The couple left the room, and without thinking, Susannah followed them. They hadn't gone far down the hall when Peter happened to turn and glimpse Susannah. His face turned white, but he composed himself quickly.

She had no idea what she was going to do or say, but she wasn't going to let him just walk away without a word.

He beat her to the punch. "Susannah," he said jovially. "What a surprise!"

So that was how he was going to play it. She didn't reply as the blond woman with him eyed her curiously. Peter saw he had no choice but to make the introduction.

"Susannah Holland, this is my friend Leslie Thayer," he said quickly.

"Your fiancée, you mean," she corrected him, slipping her arm through his playfully. She turned to Susannah. "Hi there. Are you a friend of the Hawkes family?"

"Sort of," Susannah replied. It dawned on her that Peter would be shocked if she told him she was related to the Hawkes. He would eat his heart out thinking he had passed up a chance at swindling her out of some of their money as well. It was irresistible. Besides, she was in this deep, she might as well take advantage of the situation. "Actually, Cameron is my father."

"Your *father*?" Peter clearly couldn't believe his ears. "I thought you didn't have a family."

Susannah smiled sweetly. "Isn't it incredible? It turned out . . . otherwise."

He was shaking his head in confusion, when Leslie jumped back into the conversation. "Well, isn't that something! My father has been a business associate of Cameron's for a hundred years at least. I always come to his parties."

Peter cut her off. "Come on, Susannah. How could he be your father?"

Just listen to the tone of his voice, she said to herself, anger boiling again. As if he has a right to even talk to me, much less demand that I explain myself.

Leslie saw someone she knew, and removed her arm from Peter's. "Would you excuse me one tiny second? I must say hello to Delia over there."

Susannah and Peter were alone. She began walking away. Peter hurried behind, trying to hold her.

"Wait a second, honey," he pleaded. "Let's talk. I'm really happy to see you."

Susannah didn't respond. She saw a small room ahead, the door partially open. It appeared to be empty and she headed toward it.

"This fiancée thing isn't exactly the way Leslie made it sound." Peter went on, his voice more urgent. "In fact, we've been talking about breaking up. The truth is, I can't get you out of my head. I've wanted to call you a hundred times, but I've been afraid."

He followed her into the empty room. She shut the door.

Fighting the urge to scream, she forced herself to keep her voice down practically to a whisper. "You're a cruel and sick man, and the most despicable person I've ever had the bad fortune to meet."

Peter moved closer. "No, no, honey, you're wrong about me." He smiled intimately. "Seeing you tonight—I realize I've made a terrible mistake."

He took another step forward and put out a hand. Susannah slapped it away.

"*Don't touch me,*" she hissed.

Peter's face took on a placating look. "I realize you're upset, but we can work it out. I miss you."

Susannah practically spat out the words. "You lying bastard."

"I'm not lying. I really care about you." His eyes were filled with longing.

"The negatives, you son of a bitch." Susannah's voice rose. "*How could you steal my negatives!*"

He looked her straight in the eye. "I needed the money," he said unapologetically.

"*You needed the money?*" Susannah echoed him in fury. "Do you know what that did to Bibi? What that did to *me*? Those pictures were private. She posed as a special favor, and you sold them—as if you were trading coffee beans in some marketplace. As long as you made money, what difference did it make if they weren't your property?" She clenched her fists. "You stole from me. Even the little bit of savings I had. You made me fall in love with you and then you twisted it all into something so ugly and horrible—" She couldn't go on.

"Oh, honey, let me make it all up to you." Peter put his arms out, intending to enfold her. "I'm sorry about the pictures. I guess that was wrong. But that's in the past."

As she watched him standing there, all Susannah's shame and hurt fell away. The only thing she felt was gratitude at being rid of him.

"You disgust me," she said to him. "This conversation is over."

She opened the door and stepped outside, slamming it shut. With a start, she saw Evan casually leaning against the wall nearby, holding two glasses. Had he heard?

He straightened up and came toward her, his face impassive. "I've brought you champagne."

She gave him a small smile. "Thank you. I'm sorry I wandered off."

His dimples showed again in his grin. "You're forgiven. Now how about a dance?"

They went back outside. Olivia passed by in a blue taffeta dress, talking with an older man. She caught sight of Evan and Susannah, and waved to them.

"Olivia looks lovely," Susannah said, admiring her dress.

Evan shook his head. "She's talking to some banker friend of Cameron's who does deals for the company. I'd rather see her with a young guy, having some fun."

Lucky Olivia, Susannah thought with a twinge of envy, to have such a caring brother. She watched as Olivia and the older man approached Cameron. The two men immediately began to converse as the young girl stood there, clearly wanting to be part of the dialogue but unable to break in.

They had reached the tent, but instead of going inside, Evan led Susannah around it to a small open space near the neatly clipped shrubs. The area was deserted, but the moon cast a soft glow and the music drifted out to them. He took Susannah's hand in his, putting his other arm smoothly around her waist and gently bringing her closer to him. He was slender, but as she brought her arm up to rest on his shoulder, she felt how muscular he was beneath the confines of his tuxedo.

He looked down at her. "I hate dancing in crowds," he said with a slight smile. "Do you mind?"

She saw a twinkle in his eyes, but there was kindness there too. How kind would he be if he found out the truth about her? Look out, she warned herself, look out. This was the last man on earth she should be dancing with in the moonlight.

Evan was turning out to be so different, so much nicer than her initial impression of him. For the moment, she just wanted to be herself again, to forget how complicated everything had become. She put her head down on Evan's broad shoulder, and they danced silently, just moving to the strains of Cole Porter's music.

When they finally went inside, three men came over to Evan, strangers to him but firmly insistent on talking baseball.

"That game in Montreal last August," one of them began indignantly, "the one when you hit the ball deep into right — that umpire was crazy. We were sitting right there. It wasn't foul, no way. It was good for two."

The Pirates did so much traveling, Evan barely remembered being in Montreal the previous summer, let alone being robbed of a double. Politely, he tried to extricate himself from the men and return to Susannah.

"I guess umpires are as human as the rest of us," he said lightly, turning pointedly toward his date.

But the tallest of the three men wasn't about to give up.

"That guy had it in for you, I swear. You lost that game by one run. If that lousy ruling hadn't come down, it would have gone into extra innings."

Evan began to recall the game. It had been the ninth inning of a tight game, and this guy was right. That umpire had infuriated him. "You know, it was —"

As Evan got caught up in the conversation, two other men passed by, one nudging the other as they recognized him. They stopped, waiting for the chance to talk to him next.

In the middle of a sentence, Evan suddenly remembered Susannah and looked at her, guilt on his face. She laughed and, not wanting to make him feel rushed, gestured that she would be down the hall. She walked through the living room, quietly watching the party going on around her. After a few minutes, she strolled over to a door on the opposite side of the room that led to another hallway.

It was so quiet here that she wondered if this area was off limits to the guests. Spotting a half-open door down the hall, she could hear Cameron's voice coming from inside the room.

"Fine. Let's meet on it next Thursday."

There was silence; Cameron was talking on the telephone. Suddenly, Susannah had an idea. Hurrying back to the cloak room, she retrieved the envelope with her photographs. This might be the perfect moment to catch Cameron and have him all to herself for a few minutes, probably her only chance for the rest of the night.

Hearing him hang up the telephone, she knocked gently on the door and was rewarded with a deep "Come in."

"Good evening." She stepped inside, clutching the envelope. The room appeared to be his study or perhaps a family library.

Cameron came over and took her hand.

"This is an unexpected pleasure, meeting up with you here," he said. "Come join me in a brandy."

Susannah sat down as he picked up a decanter and poured the amber fluid inside into two snifters. Handing her one, he swirled the liquid in the other, bringing his nose close to the glass to inhale the aroma.

She put her glass down. "Mr. Hawkes — I mean, Cameron," she began. "Here . . . I . . ." Pausing, she took a breath. This was not the time to be stumbling over words like a fool. "Cameron, I thought you might like to see the photographs I took of Olivia the other day."

He regarded her over the rim of his glass as he sipped the brandy.

"I certainly would."

She handed him the envelope and barely dared to breathe as he flipped through the two dozen large prints: Olivia pointing as she made an observation to one of the staff members; Olivia down on her knees, laughing broadly as a little girl threw both arms around her neck; Olivia in a circle of children, bending over to ask them a question, a delighted expression on her face.

Susannah waited nervously. Were they good enough? She thought she had captured something special. But would he? Finally, Cameron spoke, still looking at the prints in his hand.

"These are excellent. Olivia will certainly be pleased, and I think we can get some mileage from them." His gaze came up to meet Susannah's. "Thank you. They're really good."

Relieved, Susannah decided it was time to take the big step, the one she'd been dreading. She mustered up all her courage. "Are they good enough to get me into the International Forum for Children?"

Cameron stared at her, then burst out laughing. She could feel herself reddening, but sat still.

"I tell you what," he said with a broad grin, "I'll send them along to the judges and let them decide."

"I might have some others that would be suitable as well." Susannah could barely believe her own nerve.

Cameron's eyes showed his vast amusement. "You're pushing your luck, my dear. But all right, send them to my office in the morning."

"Thank you," Susannah said. "It means a lot to me. I appreciate your doing this."

"It's no problem." Cameron refilled his glass after noting that hers was still full. "Now, in return, you can answer a question for me. Do you know Peter Manzoni? I saw the two of you talking earlier."

Susannah stiffened. Why would he be interested in Peter?

"Are you a friend of his?" she asked tentatively.

"No, not at all. But I have other reasons for asking."

What should she say? Turning it over rapidly in her mind, she decided there wasn't any reason not to tell him the truth. If he was involved with Peter somehow, the least she could do was warn him.

"Well, since you asked, the fact is I used to date Peter. I was in love with him, and he treated me very badly."

"In what way?" Cameron leaned forward, interested.

Susannah felt a bit odd, telling these intimate details to Cameron Hawkes. "He stole from me. What he took was valuable, but it also caused me a great deal of pain. I take it he's engaged to the woman he was with tonight, Leslie — I forget her last name." She paused. "He's not a particularly trustworthy man, so please be careful if you have any dealings with him."

"I appreciate your warning me," Cameron replied. "And I'll keep this in confidence."

"Thank you," Susannah said, standing to leave. "And really — I'm very grateful for your sending my pictures in."

"Don't mention it. You understand that all I'll do is give them to the judges. After that, you're on your own." Cameron ushered her out. "Enjoy the rest of the party."

As he went back to his chair, Cameron chuckled. The surprise was that her photographs really *were* good. They were outstanding, in fact. Otherwise he would never have agreed to enter them in the Forum competition, no matter how entertaining her little games might be.

And she had inadvertently done him a service. Looking through a leather address book, he found the number he was seeking, then picked up the telephone and dialed. Leslie Thayer's father was a longtime business associate and golfing partner of Cameron's. The only reason Ansel Thayer hadn't come to the party was because he was in Florida on a business deal. But just last Sunday, he'd mentioned that Leslie had been dating this Manzoni fellow. Ansel had said he didn't know much about the young man, that he had his doubts. Still, it might be no more than a passing fling. It looked to Cameron as if things were a lot further along than Ansel realized.

"Ansel, it's Cameron Hawkes."

"Cameron, old man, how are you?" Ansel's voice boomed back. "Hey, it's good to hear from you as always, but aren't you in the middle of hosting a party?"

"I've got something to tell you. It's not good news, but I wouldn't be able to sleep if I kept it from you."

The other man's voice was concerned. "What is it? Are you all right?"

"Oh, yes, yes, it's not about me." Cameron paused for effect. "Unfortunately, it's about the fellow your Leslie is dating, Peter Manzoni. I'm afraid I have some bad news about him."

"Yes?" The concern was evident in Ansel Thayer's voice.

"He's a thief, Ansel. Swindled a past girlfriend."

Cameron could hear the fury behind his casual answer.

"Thanks for letting me know, old friend. I'll take it from here."

"Right. Talk to you when you get back to New York."

As he hung up, Cameron sat back, satisfied. Ansel Thayer was an extremely influential man, and Cameron had just done him an extremely large favor. Now Thayer owed him. That was exactly the position in which Cameron liked to be.

Evan stared out his window at the garden below. It was five-thirty in the morning and the party was long over. The crew hired for the event had left the grounds in perfect condition, dismantling the tent and cleaning up so thoroughly it looked as if nothing at all had taken place that night. Day was breaking, and the trees and flowers below were sharply outlined in the crisp morning light. It was a beautiful garden, the place where, as a teenager, he had always retreated to find peace, hiding up in the trees.

The house was silent. Up until an hour or so ago, Evan could hear his mother moving about in her room. He was accustomed to her restless wanderings, though it saddened him to know that she still hadn't found a way to sleep through the night. He had tried to ignore her pacing, and the clinking of glass as she poured herself another vodka. If only he could find a way to get through to her.

But tonight he had other things on his mind as well. He was wondering about his own future. It had been a shock to discover from Susannah Holland that his injury was so noticeable. He thought he was doing a masterful job of hiding it, but a near stranger could see he was hurt. If he couldn't do better at disguising his pain, he would have a hard time convincing the team manager he was ready to play again. Just this morning, he'd begun hoping he might beat the odds and make it back for part of the season; if he could just ignore the pain, he could slip past the doctors. But it didn't look as if that was going to happen.

It was just as well Susannah had told him, he decided. Better than making a fool of himself in front of the other guys, having his knee go out from under him, blowing a play — and if he wanted to be truthful — maybe doing some permanent damage.

Susannah. What a tangle that was turning out to be. There

was no point in denying that he was attracted to her. She'd looked so beautiful in that black dress, her hair flowing, her eyes that sparkling blue. And she'd turned out to be a great date, fun, interesting, intelligent. Here he was, a grown man, old and smart enough to know better, getting caught up with a woman who was involved in the damnedest scam he'd ever come across. It was so strange. Even if she was lying — which she certainly was — there was something about her that was so honest, so sincere. In his career, Evan had met a lot of people, and by now he felt he could get a handle on someone's character fairly quickly. This woman just didn't seem the type to pull something like this for a fast buck.

The whole thing was very odd. He would have sworn she enjoyed the evening with him, but she was quiet on the ride back to her apartment in Manhattan. Then, when he had taken her upstairs to the door and reached for her to give her a kiss good night, she had backed up nervously, politely but quickly retreating behind her door.

One thing that concerned him was the glowing way she spoke of Cameron Hawkes. Before they left, she'd told Evan how much she liked Cameron, how she appreciated all he had done for her. She clearly didn't have any idea whom she was dealing with. And, though Evan hadn't mentioned it, he'd overheard part of her conversation with that man at the party. She'd obviously been through something terrible with him. He'd felt a rush of sympathy for her, listening to the way the guy tried to snow her, understanding from what she said that he'd done something far worse than just break off a romance. It had impressed him to hear Susannah tell the guy off. Good for her, he'd thought. But how had she gotten caught up with him in the first place? Evan couldn't get a fix on what she was all about. Innocence and calculation all mixed together. What he did know was that he wanted to see her again, and he didn't give a damn if she was Cameron's daughter or not.

Damn Cameron. It was he who'd started Evan's mind going on the future. The son of a bitch was right. Evan wouldn't be able to play baseball forever — or even for that much longer. The night he'd blown his stack at Cameron had left him shaken, no matter how little he'd felt like agreeing with his stepfather. It was time to look ahead, much as he'd always dreaded it, wanting to believe his career would go on forever.

Evan had given up on sleep for the night. Again and again, he went over that play in the game, the one where he'd injured his knee. If only he could have another chance at it, come into the base just a bit to the left, slid a little differently. Of course, he knew why it happened: he'd violated the ritual. Like a lot of ball players, he was superstitious, and long ago, he had established that he had to sit on the steps leading down to the dugout while his team was at bat. Other guys might not shave for three weeks if they were on a hot streak, or always insist on arriving at the ballpark at exactly the same time before a game. Whatever brought them good luck, or simply staved off bad luck. Evan knew that he had to be in his spot, watching home plate from the far end of the dugout's top step, or he could be in big trouble when he came up to bat. Stupidly, he had gotten caught up in a conversation in the dugout during the bottom of the second inning, and wound up sitting on the bench until they went back on the field. The next time he came up to hit, it was all over for him.

Damn, almost an entire season blown, and everyone feeling sorry for him, the media sympathizing as they speculated what effect it would have on his game. That was the last thing he or any other player needed, people wondering if they would be the same when they got off the disabled list. He could just hear the commentators the next time he got tagged out. *Gee, folks, it looks like Evan Gardiner may have lost a step since that injury.* He'd figured he had some great years left, but who knew what would happen now? He cursed aloud, his stomach in knots as he envisioned the team management trading him for someone better or releasing him once his contract was over, the unofficial word out that he was finished.

Finally, he calmed down. The future might not be as terrible as he feared. After all, he'd been invited to do color commentary for a game the summer before when he was out briefly with a sprained wrist. The networks loved having actual players in the booth talking about what was going on out in the field and possibly in the players' minds, providing all the chatter besides the statistics and play-by-play announcing that made listening to the games even more interesting. He'd declined then, but he'd gotten the impression the guy at WOR was interested in him long term. A lot of the players went into broadcasting; it could be a great second career.

He sat down in an armchair and put his throbbing leg up on the ottoman. Being on it all night had taken a lot out of him; the doctor had told him to stay off it as much as possible, not that he had any intention of listening to that advice. But he was glad to sit down and close his eyes, here where no one could see him. Tomorrow he would call WOR. What was that guy's name? Frank something. And he would make another call, a call to Susannah. He didn't know what she was up to, but maybe he could find out. Oh, hell, the truth was he just wanted to see her again.

His eyes still closed, Evan smiled. The sun was coming up, its bright rays warm on his face.

Chapter 22

———

Susannah licked the envelope and sealed it, then affixed a stamp. It was so frustrating, not being able to talk to Ruth, having to make do with writing letters. But there wasn't any other choice. Ruth didn't have a telephone in her hospital room, and she was almost too weak to talk on one anyway. Susannah spoke regularly with Lily just to be sure Ruth was all right, and mailed a card or letter directly to the hospital at least once a week.

She hated thinking of Ruth in that hellish place all this time. But it was even worse to contemplate the future if she didn't win the competition. And the way she was feeling about Evan wasn't helping matters any. Not that she would hear from him again; after her silence on the ride home from the party last week, and the way she'd avoided him when they'd said good night, she imagined he wouldn't turn up again. She'd had a wonderful time, but reality had sunk in as they started the drive back to Manhattan. It was crazy to encourage him, to expose herself even further with this family. Besides, a famous athlete, especially one who looked like Evan, wouldn't have any trouble finding dozens of girls to fill his nights.

She went downstairs to mail her letter. As she was letting herself back into the apartment, the telephone began to ring. Hurriedly, she got the door unlocked and rushed over to pick up the receiver.

"Susannah. This is Evan Gardiner."

She tried to keep the surprise out of her voice. "Hello, Evan."

"I hope I'm not calling at a bad time. Listen, I was wondering if you were free on Saturday. Assuming this good weather holds up, I'm thinking of taking a drive in the country, maybe go up Route 7 in Connecticut. If you come with me, we could pack lunch and make a day of it."

Say no, she told herself sternly. Say no.

"That sounds great. What time?"

Susannah reached for the neatly folded navy plaid blanket in the Volvo's trunk as Evan pulled out a large wicker picnic basket. They'd gotten an early start that morning and had been enjoying the balmy day, driving along country roads, stopping to browse in antique shops along the way and to admire the scenery. It was nearly one-thirty before they both realized they were starving, and it took another fifteen minutes to find a grassy spot where they could park the car and eat their lunch.

"Boy, this weighs a ton," Evan said as he set the basket down. He came over to help Susannah spread out the blanket. "Where are we? Did you catch what town this is?"

"It's Kent," Susannah said. "I don't know how we got this far north already."

They smiled at each other, neither of them wanting to voice what they were both thinking: they had been enjoying each other's company so much, the miles had flown by without their noticing.

Evan busied himself opening the leather buckles on the picnic basket. Looking inside, he groaned.

"What's wrong?" Susannah asked, kneeling next to him to help unpack it.

"Nothing really, but I sense my mother's hand in this. No wonder it was so heavy. I asked Alice to pack a few sandwiches, something simple."

He began taking out the basket's contents. "Paté, three kinds of cheese, French bread, grapes. Two bottles of wine." He glanced at the labels. "Fancy wine at that. Caviar and chopped egg to go with it. And little cakes with pink frosting." He sighed. "Not that I don't like the food, but all this fussiness . . . Real china plates. How did she even know where I was going? She must have heard the word 'picnic' from Alice, and that was all she needed."

Susannah laughed. "It'll be sheer torture to eat all those awful things."

He grinned sheepishly. "I sound like an ingrate, don't I? I'm sorry. If I'd been at my own apartment, I would have packed the food myself, but I'm barely allowed in the kitchen at Bedford." He held up a container marked EGGPLANT SALAD. "I guess a big hero sandwich and potato chips are more my style for a fun outdoor lunch."

Susannah smiled. "Mine, too. But let's try to make do."

They filled their plates and started eating.

"So tell me," Evan said, leaning forward to tear off a hunk of the bread. "How did you get started in photography?"

Susannah stopped, knife poised in midair above some Brie. God, she was so tired of censoring herself. She would give anything to stop worrying about tripping up somehow. But, her mind racing ahead, she couldn't see anything wrong in answering his question.

She finished slicing the Brie and lay back, propping herself up on one elbow. "I was in business school. The photography was just a hobby." A mosquito buzzed near her ear and she swatted it away. "It was really my friend Bibi who gave me the courage to take it seriously."

"Who's Bibi?" Evan passed the grapes over to her.

"Thanks," she said, taking a small bunch. "Her name's Bibi Frost. We got friendly when she was my neighbor."

"Bibi Frost, the actress?"

"You've heard of her?"

"Everyone has, I guess. She came out of nowhere and now she's the hottest actress in Hollywood."

"I didn't know you sports types kept up with show biz," Susannah said teasingly. "I thought all you cared about were RBI's and shutouts. And then there are the ladies, of course, all your fans."

"Hey, we do see a movie, have a normal conversation, even read a newspaper or two once in a decade," Evan laughed. "As for the ladies, well, that's not a subject a gentleman discusses."

"I'll bet," Susannah said wryly.

Evan looked hurt. "That's not fair."

She smiled. "You're a grown man. What you do is your own business."

He regarded her seriously. "Maybe some of it might become your business."

The smile froze on Susannah's face. She looked down at her plate.

"Right." Evan jumped up and brushed the crumbs off his jeans. "I guess we'd better start back."

They started gathering up the dirty dishes and containers. As Evan bent down next to Susannah, his forearm, exposed beneath his short-sleeved tennis shirt, brushed against hers. She quickly pulled back, hoping he didn't notice how nervous it made her. Her eyes went to his arm, and she saw how soft the fine blond hair on it was, how well-defined the muscles. She wished she could touch him. She wished she didn't want to.

Susannah hurriedly straightened up. How had the living room gotten quite so messy? It was nearly four o'clock. Evan would be there any minute. What had happened to the days when she was so incredibly neat, everything in its place? That girl was gone, the one who spent hours ironing her clothes for school so she would look just so, who stayed up late at night to be sure the dishes were washed and dried. And good riddance, she thought, grinning as she picked up two photography books from the coffee table and put them back on the bookcase. She liked things better this way.

Still, she wanted the apartment to be presentable. Over the past few weeks, Evan had continued calling and she'd been unable to resist saying yes. A few days after their picnic in Connecticut, they had lunch in SoHo, then wandered through the art galleries and shops. The following week, he took her to dinner and the theater. Teasingly, he reminded her of the first time they met, when she had recommended he make a trip to Broadway. Now here she was doing it with him. They went sailing off Long Island one day, and to the beach at Amagansett the next weekend. They talked and laughed, but he did nothing more intimate than hold Susannah's hand, and she tried not to encourage him any further.

She also tried to ignore the fact that just holding his hand made her feel ridiculously happy. Though she never initiated it, when he reached for her as they walked or sat across from each other at a restaurant table, she was inwardly thrilled to feel the cool strength of his touch. It took every ounce of restraint she could summon up to keep from kissing him. Instead, she looked into his intelligent blue eyes and silently prayed he wouldn't find out the truth about her.

She stooped down to pick up a pair of sneakers. However successful she was in hiding the way she felt, it was silly to pretend to herself. She was falling in love with him. She had to admit that she'd found him attractive as soon as he'd opened the door to the Hawkes' house that day. But it was during these last weeks that she had discovered how smart he was, how easy to talk to. He had a great sense of humor and was fun to be with. At the same time, it was hard to forget how easily she'd been taken in by Peter Manzoni. She kept reminding herself that she could be making another terrible mistake. But in her heart she knew better. Evan was completely different, genuine and caring. It was there in the way he looked at her, the tone of his voice, the way he reached to steady her when the water suddenly got rough that day on the boat, or insisted she take his jacket when they were out walking and the night air grew cool.

She remembered how he'd treated those little boys that afternoon in SoHo. She and Evan had been walking along Prince Street when the two kids, maybe seven or eight years old, had recognized him and come running up to them.

"Oh, wow, you're Evan Gardiner, right?" the taller one had exclaimed, unable to believe his good fortune. "I see you on TV all the time, and my dad took me to see you play in person once. You're great."

"Hey, there, hi." Evan smiled.

The other boy had stood there, just staring in awe.

"Wait, wait, I've got my baseball cards here." The first boy dug into the knapsack he had slung over his shoulder and pulled out a two-inch-thick stack of cards held together by a rubber band. He hurriedly began sorting through them. "Please, you gotta sign your card. Oh, it would be so cool."

While they waited for him to find the right card, Evan pulled a pen from his jacket pocket and turned to the other boy, still standing there in silence. "What's your name?" he asked.

Shocked at having a famous baseball player speak directly to him, the boy looked down at the ground. His voice was barely audible. "Jason."

"Oh, Jason's shy," the first boy explained, still rifling furiously through his cards. "But he likes you too."

Evan knelt. "Would you like to have an autograph, Jason?"

The boy looked up with a smile, but it faded almost instantly. "I don't have my cards with me."

"Maybe I can help." Susannah dug around in her purse for a piece of paper. All she came up with was an envelope, but she tore off the back.

"Here it is!" The first boy had located Evan's baseball card. "Oh, wow," he breathed as Evan scrawled his signature across it.

Evan handed it back, then put the pen to the paper Susannah had given him. She watched what he wrote: *To my pal, Jason. Best regards. Your buddy, Evan Gardiner.*

"Here you go, sport," he said to Jason, giving him the paper. "Keep the pen, too."

He waved good-bye and they walked off. Susannah turned around. She saw Jason's head bowed as he read what Evan had written. He quickly looked up, staring after them, shock on his face. The other boy snatched the paper out of his hand and read it. "Oh, wow!" Susannah heard him say. She smiled.

The problem was that every time she saw Evan, she knew she was increasing the risk of his finding out what a fraud she was. But every time he left, she couldn't wait to see him again. She wanted to spend all her time with him.

Of course, it didn't matter what she wanted. When he found out the truth—and she didn't doubt that he would—he would hate her, and that would be the end of it. She couldn't bear to think about it. If only they could go on this way forever, in this sort of limbo. She'd made no effort to contact Cameron beyond sending him some more of her photographs, as they'd discussed; if she were smart and crafty the way Jamie wanted her to be, she would be concentrating on Cameron, spending as much time as she could with him. But she only wanted to be with Evan. By avoiding Cameron, she could almost pretend that her relationship with Evan was normal.

Susannah shook her head as if to clear it. "You are really far gone," she said aloud, walking into the bathroom and picking up a hairbrush. She contemplated her face in the mirror above the sink. "Enjoy him while it lasts, because this is all there's going to be."

Just as she finished brushing her hair, Evan arrived, wearing gray slacks, a navy blazer, and a tie.

"Hi. All ready?" he asked as she opened the door for him.

"Absolutely. I wouldn't want to make you late." Susannah picked up her purse. "You look great."

"Do you think so?" He glanced down at his striped tie, lifting the ends to inspect it. "You don't think this is too boring?"

So Evan was nervous. Usually he seemed completely in control, and easygoing about everything. Susannah wanted to smile, but she was afraid he might be embarrassed if he caught her. He certainly had good reason to be nervous. Being an announcer at a nationally televised baseball game was a big deal, even if he had sounded casual about it when he asked her to go along.

As usual, Evan drove fast, but Susannah could see that his tension was growing as they approached Shea Stadium. This was a huge opportunity for him. He had told her that WOR-TV was delighted by the prospect of the Pittsburgh Pirates' first baseman doing color commentary on a game between his team and the New York Mets. And his contact at WOR had gone one step further. If he did a good job, this could be the stepping stone to much more, possibly a second career when the time came. Of course, if he blew it, he could forget about broadcasting; it was hard to imagine he'd ever get another chance as good as this one.

She wished she could find just the right thing to say.

"I know you'll be wonderful," she said finally, feeling at a loss for words. "It'll probably be like falling off a log, talking about your own team."

He grimaced. "If only it was just a matter of getting up there and saying whatever came into your head. Good work requires preparation, and there just wasn't enough time."

"It's not your fault they sprang this on you yesterday," Susannah protested.

"Hey, I'm fortunate to have been asked at all. You can't pick and choose your lucky breaks." Evan turned the car off Northern Boulevard. "I just better be good, that's all."

Susannah wanted to reach over and stroke his hair, to reassure him that he would be more than good. It was a new experience, seeing Evan so vulnerable.

They drove past the main stadium parking, back to an area set aside for the press and other guests. A policeman with a clipboard approached the car and asked Evan for his name, consulting a list and then waving them in. They stopped to pick up the ticket and press pass that had been left in Evan's name, then, entering through a turnstile, walked through the long, gloomy hallways beneath the stadium. Having played against the Mets in the past, Evan already knew his way around, and he quickly led Susannah up to the level where her seat was located; he would be spending the game in the booth with the other broadcasters. An usher took her ticket, and they followed him to her seat, just three rows behind home plate. Evan had been asked to get there an hour and a half before the game began, so most of the other stadium seats were still empty. They both sat down.

"This is so close," Susannah said to Evan. "What an incredible view of the field."

"You know, it's funny, but I rarely see a stadium from this perspective. I'm always in the locker room or the dugout, and then on the field. I don't spend time in the stands." He turned to her. "I wish you could come to the booth with me."

"Don't be silly, I'm fine here. You have other things to worry about besides entertaining me. And these are great seats."

"This is set aside for the players' wives and VIP's." He pointed to his right. "There's also an ambulance crew and a doctor here — for accidents, brawls, stuff like that."

Susannah could see that he was distracted, rattling on without paying much attention to what he was saying. She glanced at her watch. It was early, but she suspected he could use some time alone to collect his thoughts.

"Hey, the hour approaches," she said. "Why don't you go ahead? There's no reason for you to stay here with me."

He looked at her gratefully. "You'll be all right?"

She laughed. "Of course." She pointed to her large leather shoulder bag. "I've even got a good book with me. You should be getting ready."

He got up and stepped back out into the aisle. "I'll come back here to get you later. I hope it won't be too long after the game's over. You'll be okay?"

Susannah looked at him standing there, so anxious about what he was leaving to do, yet still concerned for her. She wanted so badly to kiss him. She knew her feelings for him were written all over her face, but she couldn't help it. "Good luck, Evan."

He didn't say anything, but she saw in his eyes that he knew what she was feeling. Then he turned and was gone.

Slowly, the stadium began filling up. Susannah got herself a hot dog and soda, and watched the fans coming in. A lot of the people in her section seemed to know one another. She amused herself by trying to guess their relation to the different players: somebody's wife or girlfriend, the in-laws, a rowdy younger brother. Finally, the game got under way.

Evan and Susannah had agreed that he would set the VCR at his Manhattan apartment to videotape the broadcast. That way the two of them could watch it later and critique his performance. Sitting in the stadium itself, Susannah had no way of hearing what the announcers said, and she tried not to worry about how Evan was doing. She wanted to follow the game as closely as she could so she would be able to discuss it with him, and she quickly got caught up in the action. It was a close game, tied at 3-3 in the ninth inning. In the end the Pirates won with a home run, and Susannah found herself on her feet, cheering along with the rest of the Pittsburgh fans as all around them Mets fans glared.

The stadium emptied out rapidly. From her seat, Susannah gazed up at the blackness of the night sky beyond the brilliant illumination of the stadium's lights. Only minutes before, there had been thousands of people yelling and clapping. Now they had all but vanished. It was oddly peaceful, the feeling of being only one of a few people left in this vast arena.

She heard a noise and craned her neck to see Evan hurrying toward her. He was grinning, his excitement evident.

"Hi, how'd it go?" She stood up and came into the aisle to greet him.

He put his hands around her waist. "I don't know, but I think it went well. Better than well, even."

Her grin matched his. "I knew you'd be great."

Without thinking, she threw her arms around his neck and hugged him. Their faces touched and then, suddenly, they were kissing. After waiting so long, she was finally tasting his lips, his tongue, the sweet pressure of his mouth upon hers. She felt his desire for her in the way his arms quickly came around her, bringing her to him. Finally, finally, she was allowed to run her hands along his broad shoulders, to hold him close. She never wanted to let go. But with a supreme effort, she pulled back.

Evan's arms fell to his sides. Shaken, she looked away, then retrieved her purse and hurried up the stadium steps.

As he drove along the Grand Central Parkway for the ride back toward Manhattan, Susannah was quiet. But Evan was still charged up with adrenaline from the game, exuberant with the release of its being over. She was soon caught up once again in his enthusiasm.

"There's so much going on at once, so many things you might say. But you only have a second to decide which point to make and how to make it." He was talking so fast his words tumbled out one on top of the other. "It took me a while to get going — I missed the chance to talk about the speed of a ball on Astroturf versus grass on that play in the top of the second — but there's a rhythm." He looked at her. "You know?"

Susannah laughed. "Not exactly, but I can imagine. It sounds as if you were a big success."

Evan's face looked boyish. "I don't want to jinx anything, but everybody seemed pretty satisfied at the end. And Walter Markham, the lead announcer, shook my hand and told me I did — and I quote — an outstanding job for a first-timer."

"Evan, that's sensational!" She turned in her seat to grin at him.

He looked bashful suddenly. "Don't let me brag. They probably flatter every player who goes into that booth."

"Maybe," Susannah said. "But I'll bet you really were great. I can't wait to see the tape. Let's watch it right away when we get back."

Twenty minutes later, Evan pulled the car into a garage near his apartment. He had told Susannah about the apartment on West Eighty-ninth Street, but she'd never seen it. They approached a large, prewar building. The lobby inside was dimly lit, outfitted with inviting armchairs. A welcoming, unpretentious building, she thought, just the kind of place she would expect him to live.

The living room in his apartment was modest but comfortable, with an Oriental rug, two plush sofas, and a deep armchair and floor-to-ceiling bookcases near the windows. She saw a doorway leading to a study. Inside was a large desk and a leather armchair. There were more books, lining nearly every inch of the room's walls.

Evan pulled off his jacket and threw it over a chair in the foyer as he loosened his tie. "Are you sure you want to watch this? You really don't have to."

"Are you nuts?" Susannah kicked off her shoes, settling herself on the couch. "I can't wait."

"Okay. You asked for it." He headed toward the kitchen. "Want something to drink before we watch?"

"No, thanks."

He disappeared for a moment, reemerging with a bag of popcorn and a big bowl.

"Can't watch a ball game without this," he said, setting it down on the coffee table in front of her. He rewound the videotape, turned the television on, then came to join her on the couch, holding the remote control.

"Before we start," he said to her, "I want to ask you to be honest about how I did. But not too honest."

She laughed. "No problem."

The picture filled the screen and the announcer's voice rang out over the image of the players on the field warming up, throwing the ball around the bases.

". . . someone special here today. As you know, Evan Gardiner, first baseman for the Pirates, has been out with a knee injury since June. He's here to give us his perspective on the game. Delighted you could make it, Evan."

Evan's voice was strong, betraying none of the nervousness Susannah knew he'd been feeling.

"I couldn't be more pleased to be here. If you can't play, at least you can point out what a great job you _would_ have done if you _were_ playing."

There was laughter in the booth.

Susannah smiled at him. "Off to a terrific start. You got a laugh with your very first line."

"That helped, I have to admit."

For the second time that day, Susannah watched the game get under way. But this time, she had the benefit of the announcers' explanations. Evan had clearly held his own with the other two, speculating on what was coming or how a play could have been handled differently, giving concise explanations of what the pitcher might be thinking, or how the batter was likely to react. The other two men asked him a lot of questions about the first basemen on both teams. Evan's analysis of their strategies and difficulties was straightforward and interesting. Susannah found herself intrigued by the game all over again. Evan repeatedly told her they had seen enough, that she didn't have to watch it all, but she insisted she wanted to see the whole thing. It was the first time she had really understood all the intricacies of a baseball game. She was surprised to discover that it was fascinating.

"Tell us how you got your start, Evan," one of the announcers asked as the fourth inning was getting under way.

Evan's voice recounted his days of playing ball at prep school and Yale. "In my Little League days, I didn't know what position I wanted to play," he added. "My first coach steered me to first base, of course, because I'm left-handed."

Susannah turned to Evan on the couch beside her. "What does being left-handed have to do with it?"

Evan took some more popcorn from the bowl. "Well, whether you're right- or left-handed, you catch with your *other* hand, the less dominant one. So I catch with my right hand. When you're standing with one foot on the base and your right hand is extended, you're facing the infield. That gives you a lot of advantages."

"*That's* how you decide to become a first baseman?" Susannah was surprised. "I would have thought it was based on some special skill or something."

Evan laughed. "It can mean the difference between winning or losing a game. First basemen are almost always left-handed."

When the last hitter had thrown down his bat in disgust at being struck out, Evan got up to turn off the television.

"God, it's two in the morning," he said, glancing at a clock on the bookcase. "How could you have sat through it all twice?"

"It was easy." She smiled.

Evan turned to face her, neither one of them saying anything. Then he came toward the couch. As he moved closer, Susannah held her breath. It was happening, what she had longed for, she saw it in his eyes. She should stop him, get up and leave right away. But she couldn't move. He sat down beside her and gently ran his finger along her lips, then slowly brought his face closer to hers. He paused for a moment before covering her mouth with his. Encircling her with his arms, he drew back slightly. "Susannah," he whispered, then kissed her again, more deeply now, more intense.

She sighed with pleasure. Her hands went up to his chest, his cheek, stroking his hair and the back of his neck. His caresses were igniting every nerve inside her, a white heat spreading through her body. She wanted to feel him, to touch him everywhere.

Evan stood, and pulled her up along with him, pressing her to him urgently, kissing her face.

"Susannah," he whispered hoarsely, "let me make love to you."

Kissing him in response, she wrapped her arms around him again, knowing now that he had been as hungry for her as she'd been for him. He reached behind her and effortlessly lifted her off the ground, her legs coming around him as she clung to him. Still kissing her, he carried her into the bedroom, and they sank down onto the bed together. Susannah felt as if she were slipping into a dark pool, losing herself in the power of her longing, in the sensations of his lips and hands.

He unbuttoned her blouse and she shivered with pleasure, burying her head in his neck, inhaling his masculine scent. They both fumbled with the rest of their clothes, impatient to have nothing between them. Stretching out along the bed, she felt Evan, so lean and hard, his athlete's body full of controlled energy. She molded herself against him. His hands moved more slowly now, arousing her all over again. His touch was gentle, tender.

"You're so beautiful," he whispered, his eyes traveling the length of her body, bringing his mouth to kiss her neck, her breasts, her stomach.

She drank him in, the feel of his naked shoulders and chest, the velvety hardness of his penis. "Evan . . ."

"Susannah, oh, God, I want you so much."

She gasped as his hand found her center, the intensity of her pent-up passion shocking her. Moments later, she was guiding him inside her, their breathing labored as they moved together, holding on tightly to each other, their mouths everywhere at once. Susannah felt herself losing control, and she gave herself over to it, crying out. Hearing her, Evan stopped holding back, and his body arched as he called out her name.

When it was over, they lay still on the bed, their arms and legs intertwined. Susannah buried her face in his chest, trying to sort out a flood of thoughts and feelings. It had been so different with him, sex and warmth and loving all combined. He had shown her tenderness through his kisses, through the way he caressed her, wanting to feel every inch of her, not to miss anything. It was a shock, surrendering to the rush of sexual desire and feeling cherished at the same time.

She gazed up at him, and he smiled lovingly in return. Then his expression grew serious. He raised himself up on one elbow.

"Susannah," he said quietly. "Who are you?"

She stared at him. "I . . ." She didn't know what she was going to say.

"No, wait." He shook his head. "Never mind." He lay back against the pillows and put his arm around her. "I don't want to know."

In the morning, she awoke to find Evan gone from the bed. It was just seven-thirty. She slipped on her slacks and blouse, and padded barefoot out toward the kitchen. Evan, already showered and dressed in jeans and a tennis shirt, stood at the stove, sipping a cup of coffee as he scrambled a large panful of eggs. She could smell bread toasting. He didn't hear her, and she stood just beyond the doorway observing him. How handsome he is, she thought, watching him brush his still-damp blond hair back from his forehead.

He turned and caught sight of her. Putting down his coffee

mug and the wooden spoon he was holding, he came over to take
her in his arms.

"Good morning." He gave her a long kiss.

"What are you doing up?"

"I've got to get back to Bedford. I scheduled an appointment
with some guy about an endorsement and he's meeting me up
there." Susannah nodded as he held up a cup to ask if she wanted
some coffee. "Milk and sugar?"

"Just milk, please." Susannah took the steaming cup from
him and inhaled the strong aroma. He got a container of milk
from the refrigerator and poured some into her coffee. "Thanks.
So you have to get moving."

"Not until we have some breakfast. And, then, I was going
to ask you if you'd like to come with me. The meeting shouldn't
take too long, and afterward we can do something."

She tried not to show how happy she was that he wasn't
sending her home. She couldn't stand the idea of being apart from
him. "Could we stop at my place so I can get changed and cleaned
up before we go?"

"Sure." Evan dished the scrambled eggs out onto two plates
just as four pieces of toast popped up from the toaster.

Susannah abruptly stood up straighter. Where was her brain?
Going to Bedford meant she might encounter Cameron and the
rest of the family again. Did it make any difference? She couldn't
think clearly. All she wanted was to be with him. She sighed.
"Anything wrong?" He turned to her, concerned.

"No, nothing," Susannah replied.

He smiled and turned back to the stove. A combination of
love and pain swept over her. When he found out what she was
up to, he would hate her. And there was no way out now. She
couldn't stand to think about it. Coming up behind him, she gently
kissed the back of his neck.

"No, everything is perfect," she whispered.

"More coffee, Mr. Hawkes?"

"No, thank you, Mary."

Cameron couldn't remember what the woman's name was, but Mary would do; he didn't want Lionel thinking he didn't know the names of his own household staff. But who the hell could keep track of them, coming and going as frequently as they did?

"Perhaps Mr. Shea will have another cup. Lionel?"

Lionel Shea held up his hand. "No, thanks, I'm stuffed. Wonderful breakfast, Cameron. My cholesterol will skyrocket, but it was worth it. Best eggs Benedict I've had in years. *Only* eggs Benedict I've had in years, as a matter of fact."

Cameron laughed at the remark. You should have them more often, he told Lionel silently. Maybe you'd drop dead and I could get your damn company without all this sucking up.

Lionel stood up and pushed his chair back into place under the dining-room table. "It's a shame your wife isn't feeling well. I wish she could have joined us."

"Yes. I think I'll check on her before we leave." Cameron's expression was serious as they walked to the door. "It worries me when Tish stays in bed; it's so unlike her."

"Why don't I get the racquets and meet you out front," Lionel said. "Please give her my regards."

"I will," Cameron replied, heading off.

He had no intention of going to see Tish. She wasn't sick, merely upstairs in bed with her vodka, as she usually was in the early part of the day. It was Cameron who had told her not to come downstairs while Lionel was there. Tish could pull herself together by the evenings, but he didn't want anyone important seeing what she looked like in the mornings. Certainly not Lionel, and especially not at this critical juncture in their deal. Cameron went into his study and grabbed two good cigars from a box in his desk. Lionel would enjoy having them after their game. Cameron frowned. Playing tennis with Shea was like hitting to a hippopotamus. The man couldn't play at all and was completely out of shape, but he said he liked the game, and that meant Cameron would play it with him.

When he emerged from the house a few minutes later, he was startled to see Lionel deep in conversation with Susannah

Holland. Evan was standing nearby, leaning against the hood of his Volvo.

"Hello, there," Cameron said jovially to Susannah. "What brings you to Bedford this fine morning?"

"Charming girl you've got here," Lionel interjected. "Quite a head on her. She's got some valuable things to say."

Susannah smiled. "Cameron, it's nice to see you again. I'm just here with Evan for a little while." She turned and exchanged glances with his stepson.

So they've slept together, Cameron said to himself, observing them. Probably for the first time last night. He wanted to laugh. Their mutual attraction had been no secret to him; it was obvious that night at the party. They may have been lukewarm at her first visit to the house, but something had definitely ignited after that. He'd had his detective keep tabs on Susannah, and he knew she was spending a great deal of time with Evan. His initial response had been to separate them immediately. But upon further reflection, he decided there was no reason to intervene in their little budding romance. If Evan was stupid enough to fall for her, he would be devastated when she was exposed as a fraud. If he wanted to invite that kind of humiliation upon himself, so be it. Cameron was vastly amused by the idea of felling them both with one blow.

"You must stay for dinner, Susannah," Cameron said to her. "Evan has to share you with the rest of us."

"I don't think we'll be around." Evan folded his arms across his chest, but his tone was neutral. "I have an appointment and then I want to see Mother. After that, we're leaving."

Cameron looked regretful. "What a shame. Well, your mother's not feeling well. So unusual for her, isn't it?"

Susannah thought she saw something pass between Cameron and Evan, but it was so fleeting she wondered if she'd imagined it.

"Yes, it is. I'll go see her now." Evan turned to Lionel. "Hope to see you again. Be sure to beat Cameron at tennis."

Lionel laughed. "Not much chance of that, I'm afraid."

Good-byes were said all around.

"Your stepfather is certainly an impressive man," Susannah said to Evan as they entered the house.

"Jesus, look a little closer, Susannah," Evan began, following her into the foyer. "He's a bastard, can't you see that?"

"What are you talking about?" Susannah had never heard Evan sound like this before.

Evan realized that he had surprised her, but it was hard to keep the meanness out of his voice. "My stepfather's a very dangerous man. He's —"

"Evan, darling, you're home. How lovely."

Tish Hawkes was coming down the stairs. She was wearing a pink silk robe, and her hair was unkempt. Yet she had makeup on, overdone and inappropriate for ten o'clock in the morning. Susannah was stunned. This couldn't possibly be the elegant woman she'd seen at lunch and then at their formal party. She watched, transfixed, as the older woman nearly missed a step on the staircase.

Evan hurried forward to help her.

Grabbing the stair rail with one hand, she held up the other to stop him. "Don't worry about me, I'm fine. Just *ducky*, in fact." She looked around and whispered conspiratorially. "Are they gone?"

Dear God, Susannah thought, she's dead drunk.

Evan looked at Susannah, pain in his eyes at the knowledge that she was seeing his mother this way. He turned away.

"Mother, let's go back upstairs. You should lie down and take a little rest."

"I don't need a rest," Tish said belligerently. "I'll rest when I'm dead." She continued down the steps, muttering half audibly. "Which I'll probably be soon anyway. Just as well."

Evan rushed to meet her halfway up the stairs and put an arm around her. "You know, Mom, I'm not feeling all that well myself. Maybe you could walk me to my bedroom and help me get my leg up. I'd really appreciate it."

Tish was instantly all sympathy. "Sweetheart, of course, let me help you. My poor baby."

She allowed Evan to lead her back upstairs. "Don't worry,

I'll make the hurt go away," she was saying as they reached the landing.

Susannah remained where she was, too shocked to move. She'd had absolutely no idea. Her heart went out to both Evan and his mother. They so obviously loved each other, Evan trying to preserve his mother's dignity, and she responding immediately when she thought he needed her.

Susannah heard a door shut. Evan appeared at the top of the stairs, lost in thought. She watched him descend slowly. He's so wonderful, she thought. And he cares for me. She had felt it in every touch and every kiss last night. She didn't deserve him, not when what she was doing was so wrong.

An overwhelming sadness swept through her. She needn't spend time worrying about losing him. It was a foregone conclusion that she would.

Chapter 23

Kailey still couldn't get over the cool, dry air. As she combed her hair in the bathroom mirror, she luxuriated in her surroundings. Electric lights, air conditioning, sophisticated plumbing—these were comforts she wasn't used to anymore. Pulling a tube of lipstick from her purse, she laughed at how long it had been since she'd bothered to apply makeup. How long it had been since she'd thought about herself at all. The past few days in Djakarta had been all business. But here in Bangkok, alone in the elegant hotel with Jean-Paul for two days of relaxation before returning to the camp, she felt like a princess.

No, she thought, I feel like a happy woman. A princess is exactly what I used to be. She remembered the eighteen-year-old girl who first danced with Cameron Hawkes at Radost: protected, spoiled, tortured by self-consciousness, too insecure even to have a friend. The memories might have been of another lifetime.

She would never stop hating Cameron, never forget the loss of her baby girl. But she had come to realize that the tragedies in her life had forced her to grow. She'd been on her own, built a career in Rome, then come to the refugee camp. Now she had Daniel, and she and Jean-Paul were building a life together.

"Darling, we don't want to miss the kites," Jean-Paul called to her from the bedroom.

"I'll be with you in a minute." Kailey wished they could stay inside tonight, but Jean-Paul was so eager for her to see the event that took place every year. Bangkok had been a fascinating city to walk through all afternoon, but she was exhausted now, anxious to have uninterrupted hours with him; it was their first time alone since she had adopted Daniel three months before. The baby was back at the camp, and though Kailey missed him terribly, she wanted to enjoy these precious moments.

"Okay, darling, let's go fly a kite." Kailey smiled at Jean-Paul as she stepped into the bedroom, spinning in her almost backless white silk dress in a way that sent the full skirt whirling around her.

Jean-Paul looked at her from head to toe, admiring her long, slender body, her shapely legs shown to advantage in high-heeled pumps, then whistled. "So, why don't you dress this way for me back home?"

Both of them began to laugh, imagining how ridiculous her outfit would look in the refugee camp. She hadn't put on a dress or even a skirt since she'd been there. Tonight's costume was special. Silly, she'd said to herself when she packed it, but special.

The meeting in Djakarta had been difficult, just as they knew it would be, and Kailey felt that Jean-Paul deserved some days that were out of the ordinary. She couldn't re-create Paris for him, but she could at least provide an oasis of romance. The long talks involving the three resistance groups fighting to regain control of Cambodia plus the government spokesman for Hun Sen were bound to be acrimonious, and in the end it had been a fruitless exercise. There, ready to talk, were representatives of all three resistance parties, the Khmer Rouge, the Khmer People's National Liberation Front, and Prince Norodom Sihanouk's faction, which had finally achieved some kind of reconciliation with its old enemy, Pol Pot. All had agreed at least to discuss the possibility of United Nations participation in a coalition Cambodian government, one that would allow a cease-fire and enable the hundreds of thousands of refugees to return to a peaceful homeland.

To Jean-Paul's great embarrassment, the French foreign minister arrived a full day late, forcing the talks to begin well after they were supposed to, then remained in Djakarta for under a day. Why sponsor a conference and then doom it to failure, Jean-Paul had complained to Kailey as the minister left the meeting room barely twelve hours after his arrival.

The meeting had been a disappointment for both of them, but Kailey vowed she would make their two days in Bangkok special. And for hours that afternoon, they had walked the streets of the city, shielding their faces from the excessive pollution caught in the hot, narrow streets always filled with car exhaust, admiring the perfect Buddhist temples that they came upon in the midst of poverty and squalor, even buying some perfume and a handbag from one of the thousands of black-market vendors who were everywhere.

Now taking Jean-Paul's hand as they walked, she looked up at him and smiled.

"What's that for?" he asked.

"I don't know," she began, uncertain how to put her thoughts into words. "Just that I love you, and I love Daniel."

Jean-Paul pulled her closer.

She continued, wanting him to understand everything that was in her heart. "I love it here . . . I don't mean just Bangkok," she added quickly. "Despite the tragedy of it all, the uncertainty, the poverty, I feel as if we're at least *trying* to do something. And I love that we're doing it together."

"Even without hotel plumbing?" Jean-Paul asked mischievously.

Kailey was about to respond when the path they were on

turned toward the park across from the hotel, revealing hundreds of kites flying in the breeze. Kailey gasped in delight as Jean-Paul enjoyed her obvious pleasure at the homemade paper contraptions, one more imaginative than the next. It seemed as if the entire city's population turned into children during those rare breezy periods when the hot muggy air finally dissipated, making life outdoors tolerable, enjoyable even.

"Like Venice, Bangkok is built on many canals," the oarswoman told them the next day as she pushed the boat's one oar slowly through the still waters on a leisurely sightseeing tour. "All comes from Chao Phraya River. Used to be swampland."

Kailey listened politely, but she found herself unable to take in much, simply enjoying the sensation of gliding through the city with no more to do than lean against Jean-Paul and listen to the sounds from the small houses along the banks of the *klongs*. She was exhausted from walking the Bangkok streets from early morning on. Now, with dusk just beginning, she enjoyed the peaceful time with Jean-Paul, their privacy invaded only occasionally by brief comments from the elderly oarswoman.

Mosquitoes began to circle around them, the high-pitched whine warning of their approach in the half light. The oarswoman turned just as Jean-Paul waved at one of the insects coming to land on Kailey's shoulder.

"You must cover yourselves," she said impatiently as she turned back to her task.

Looking around, Jean-Paul couldn't figure out what they could possibly cover themselves with. It had been hot and humid all day, and neither of them had thought to bring a sweater or a coat.

"Do you want to go back to the hotel?" he asked Kailey, waving off yet another mosquito.

She shifted her body, sitting up straight on the wooden seat, and sighed. "It's so beautiful, I hate to go back. But I guess we have to."

Jean-Paul looked around once more, his eyes coming to rest on the shopping bags they had carelessly thrown in the canoe's flat bottom. He reached down into a large white bag, pulling out a bolt of brightly colored cotton cloth Kailey had bought earlier that day.

Unrolling the fabric, he saw there was no way to cover both of them.

"How adventurous do you feel?" he asked, grinning like a small boy.

"What do you mean?"

Holding the cloth, Jean-Paul eased himself to the floor of the boat, which was longer and flatter than a regular canoe, but just about as narrow. "Come on down here," he said, his back against the join of the canoe, indicating a space for her between his knees.

Kailey slid off her seat, joining him on the bottom and relaxing against his chest. As she made a place for herself, he drew the large piece of cloth over both of them, bringing it just under Kailey's chin, then tucking it carefully around their sides so the insects could find no entry.

Their actions caused the canoe to tip perilously, and the oarswoman turned to look at them and shook her head, murmuring a word that was indecipherable, but clearly conveyed disdain.

Jean-Paul began to laugh, Kailey joining him, as they realized how ridiculous they looked to the woman. Jean-Paul inched forward a little, making each of them more comfortable. Seeing the driver's back turned to them, Jean-Paul placed his arms around Kailey, caressing her breasts through the soft colorful fabric, then going underneath the cloth and starting to unbutton her blouse.

Kailey began to giggle at his unexpected touch, then stopped when her laughter caused the old woman to turn around. Both she and Jean-Paul sat, motionless, until the driver went back to her rowing. After a quick look at the oarswoman, Jean-Paul unhooked Kailey's bra and, under the cover of the cloth, enclosed the firm flesh of her breasts, exciting her nipples with his supple fingers.

Kailey didn't make a sound, but Jean-Paul could feel her reaction. Slowly he moved his hands farther down, over her short, pleated skirt, under the hem, up the insides of her thighs. His fingers snaked under the leg of her underpants, moving toward her moist center. He felt her stiffen, as she hugged back into his chest, and opened her legs slightly, inviting him to go farther. Slowly, he eased into her, his fingers going deeper now. Kailey couldn't help moving in rhythm with his touch, making the small vessel rock again. Once again, the oarswoman turned to them questioningly, and Jean-Paul stopped. When she went back to her work, his fingers moved once more, even deeper and more slowly.

Mischievously, he penetrated even farther, almost daring Kailey not to cry out. Only the barking of a dog from a small, white house along the canal saved them from discovery as Kailey peaked, her breathless spasms signaling to Jean-Paul, who held her fast.

"I love you," she whispered as her body relaxed.

Jean-Paul bent his head and kissed the back of her neck. She was a precious gift, one he had almost lost. He raised his eyes and gazed at the darkening sky.

And until they returned to the camp, the image of the kites, their relaxed walks through the city streets, their adolescent behavior on the canal stayed with them, making the situation in Thailand somehow seem hopeful. Even the long editorial in the *International Herald Tribune* describing the Djakarta conference as "lackluster" didn't dampen their mood. On the four-hour drive back, she felt happy and content, looking forward to holding Daniel in her arms.

It was only the next morning, when Jean-Paul returned from a briefing with the camp supervisor, that she found out how bad things had become in the brief two weeks since they left for Djakarta. She could see when he entered the room that something terrible must have happened.

She looked at him questioningly.

"The Khmers have refused to let four thousand people move from Borai to Site K." Jean-Paul sat down dejectedly.

Kailey felt heartsick. Site K was a UN-administered camp; the move had been agreed to. But now the Khmers would be keeping them under their own control.

"Of course, that means a good number will be sent into the

hidden camps inside Cambodia," he said glumly. "But that's not the worst of it."

Kailey looked at him with alarm.

"About fifteen of our boys decided to go along with them."

"With the Khmers!" Kailey was incredulous. How could any youngster under UN protection leave voluntarily, after all the damage of the Pol Pot years, all the horror stories that circulated in the camps.

"These kids are fourteen, fifteen years old, nowhere near old enough to remember mass evacuations and forced marches. All they knew was what the Khmers said, Cambodia run by Cambodians. They make it sound so patriotic, so exciting. I guess it shouldn't be that much of a surprise."

As Jean-Paul ran down the list of names, Kailey's heart sank. She understood that for Jean-Paul, it was even worse. He had treated these youngsters, had known some of them practically since birth. For Jean-Paul, this was more than bad news; it felt like a personal failure.

"What can we do?" she asked.

"Darling, right now there's nothing. Not one damn thing."

Kailey looked at him carefully. The hollows in his cheeks seemed deeper, the dark rings under his eyes more pronounced. The effects of their two-day holiday had disappeared, replaced by the signs of complete exhaustion. She sensed that he needed some time alone.

"Some of the mothers of the boys should be working in the nursery this afternoon. Why don't I run over and see how they're holding up? You take a nap. I'll bring Daniel with me."

Jean-Paul kissed her gratefully. Kailey picked up the baby and walked outside. The heat and humidity seemed to hover above the tents and huts. It was just a short walk to the nursery, where babies and young children were cared for by volunteer Cambodian women who lived in the camp. She spotted the mother of one of the boys who had chosen to leave in earnest conversation with two other women, but she hesitated to interrupt them.

Daniel shifted in her arms and began to cry. He's probably hungry, she realized, heading for the kitchen behind the central playroom. Opening one of the cupboards, she found a container of formula, and began to mix it with water from a nearby container.

It's sad to feed him this, she thought, remembering her long hours of breast-feeding Bonnie, making that intimate connection that still left her lonely for her daughter even all these years later. But she had no choice with Daniel; she hadn't given birth to him so she had no breast milk to offer. Formula would just have to do. She consoled herself with the fact that, except for their trip to Djakarta, she was almost never away from him, and she found it hard to imagine she could love a baby she'd borne more.

She felt so frustrated with some of the new mothers in the camp, who used formula instead of breast milk. Many times she had tried to explain to the Cambodian women that their own milk was healthier, that by nursing they provided their babies with antibodies and escaped the danger of feeding them polluted water. But a number of manufacturers had found there was a fortune to be made in third-world markets, promoting their formulas as the best choice for nutrition. And a number of young women were more impressed with corporate claims than they were with their own bodies. Kailey looked absently at the box of formula as she began to mix it. The price was still on the package. Much too high, she thought, struggling to remember how much she paid for the brand that friends had been sending them from Paris. So the formula in the nursery here was both less healthy and badly overpriced.

She looked more closely at the label. Butterfly, the company was called. Her eyes dropping down to the address, she shuddered as the familiar street address leapt out at her. It was the Hawkes Corporation. They must have assumed a different name for exports. So Cameron had started exporting baby formula at inflated prices, and mostly to people who shouldn't even be using it. Yet another disgusting way to make money. But this time it was legal. Perfect. He must be raking in millions. Kailey dumped the contents of Daniel's bottle out. She had to use formula, but she didn't have to use Cameron's formula.

No. She refused to let him get away with it any longer. There were thousands of women in the camp, mothers who would be outraged when they understood what was being done to them. Already, the basics of a peaceful assault were forming in her mind. A mail campaign. Press attention. None of the letters had to bear her name, of course, but she could organize things.

Let's just see how long you go on stealing from us, Cameron Hawkes, she said to herself as she walked purposefully out the door.

Chapter 24

—————

"I like these, that's the bottom line." Forrest Taylor relaxed in his chair, sliding a sheaf of photographs back into an envelope and tossing it into the center of the table. "This guy has my vote."

Calvin Giles scowled at him. "Come on, Forrest. They're too pretentious. Give him another five years to work it out of his system and he may be something. For now, I have to vote no."

"I'm with Cal." Judith Lacy tapped her pencil on the table. "Close but no cigar."

The three of them looked up at the sound of the conference room door opening. Cameron Hawkes entered the room, smiling. He was pleased to note the platters of thick sandwiches, fresh fruit, and pastry from Bonté, juices and bottled water, and a few fifths of liquor discreetly placed off to one side, plus an ample supply of pads and pencils. His secretary had been instructed to assign someone to the specific task of making the judges comfortable; he wanted word to get out that being a judge for the Hawkes Corporation's International Forum for Children was not only prestigious but loaded with perks that made it both lucrative and enjoyable. Along with a generous honorarium, the other bonuses included limousines for the three judges to and from lavish meals at Chanterelle, Bernardin, and Le Cirque.

"I see you're hard at work," he said. "Please don't let me interrupt." He pulled one of the empty chairs at the conference table closer to Judith Lacy and sat down. "I just wanted to sit in for a few minutes. That is, if you don't mind, of course." And even if you do mind, he thought, since I'm footing the bill.

"Fine. Let's move on." Barely acknowledging Cameron's presence, Cal Giles picked up another envelope from a stack and pulled out the pictures inside, consulting some notes on the pad before him.

These art people were so damned self-important, Cameron thought. They could barely take a second from their earth-shattering work to greet the man who was sponsoring this event. Giles was the worst. Just because he was a critic, he believed he was a king among men, divinely blessed to pass judgment on everything in and out of the art field. Cameron couldn't stand him, but Giles was a powerful figure and gave the Forum competition added stature. Taylor wasn't as bad; the gallery owner's primary interest was in making money, although he too was perfectly happy to flex his ego when an opportunity presented itself. Judith Lacy was no prize either. As dean of the city's best school for photography, she was also used to getting her own way, having people jump at her every command. The cast of characters was new to Cameron, but if these people were any indication, the art world was like any other business, a web of politics and deals, money and power.

Giles was talking about the photographs he held in his hand. "I had trouble making up my mind, but I vote to eliminate. Something static here. Good composition, he's got all the elements right, but there's a lifelessness that troubles me."

This time, Lacy disagreed with him. "Not at all. They're terrific, each one better than the last." She held up a photograph of a child standing in the rain, his arms outstretched, his tongue out to catch raindrops. "The spontaneity is there, he caught the moment just right. I don't know what you're talking about, Cal."

Forrest Taylor tilted his head. "I was undecided, and I still don't know what to say, but I'm leaning in favor."

They argued for a few minutes more before deciding to put the envelope in a pile set aside for further review. Today they were choosing ten semifinalists from the two hundred–plus entries. All the entries had been put into envelopes, the entrant's name written in red marker across the front. The judges had taken them home to review, twenty or so submissions at a time. They had been given ample opportunity to digest them and make notes. Two weeks ago, they'd gotten together over lunch at the Russian Tea Room to talk about the overall quality of the photographs before deciding on their final recommendations. Cameron had been delighted to learn that, aside from a few dozen amateurish entries, they felt the quality was fairly high.

Sitting quietly, he listened to their debate as they rejected the next candidate; that envelope went into a pile over to the right. But they were unanimous in choosing the next person as one of the ten semifinalists; that pile was to the left. He leaned over to examine it and counted six envelopes. Pulling them closer, he flipped through to see the names.

Well, I'll be damned, he thought, extracting the third one and removing its contents. Susannah Holland had made it to the final ten. There were her shots of Olivia in the day-care center, plus the other ones Susannah had had delivered to his office the Monday after the party. He'd thought they were pretty good, but he had no idea how they would do against the rest of the entries.

He glanced through them again now with a newly appreciative eye. They were all in black and white. A small child knelt on the sidewalk, deep in concentration as he played with a rusty can of Budweiser. Two stern-looking nannies in starched white uniforms wheeled enormous carriages side by side through a tree-lined walk in the park. A dark-haired boy and a blond girl fought over a pair of roller skates in the middle of a busy playground, both of them tugging at the skates, anger contorting their faces. A girl of about four stood alone in a grassy field happily clutching a doll in her arms, her eyes shut tight with the energy of the hug, as storm clouds gathered above her head. Very nice indeed, he thought as he looked over the rest before putting them away.

For a brief moment, Cameron reflected that it might be interesting to have a daughter with such talent. Finding out Susannah Holland was really his wouldn't be such a bad thing. She was smart, gifted, attractive — the kind of girl he would be glad to introduce as his daughter. Of course, he *had* a daughter, he reminded himself, but Olivia was so insecure, so needy; her constant plays for his attention irritated him beyond endurance. Maybe Susannah was telling the truth. Imagine that.

"Oh, please, these are greeting cards." Forrest Taylor spoke disgustedly about the batch of photographs in his hand.

Giles bristled. "You don't know what you're talking about."

"Stop it, Cal," Lacy interjected in annoyance. "They're garbage. How could you have put this guy on your list?"

Cameron didn't wait to hear the rest. With a brief wave, he got up. The three judges took little notice as he shut the door behind him. So Susannah had made it this far, and all on her own. Things were getting interesting now.

"Good evening, miss."

Susannah stepped inside. "Good evening."

The maid closed the door behind her, then turned to attend to another guest. Susannah stood there, uncertain what to do next. Her heart was beating wildly. The New York apartment wasn't as big as the Hawkes's house in Bedford, but even here in the foyer, something about its grand scale frightened her. With the family spending most of their time at the country house this summer, she'd never had occasion to visit their city residence. Until now. She wished desperately that Evan were here, that he hadn't had to go to Pittsburgh to do color commentary for another game. Of course, she was glad for him, but she could have used his support tonight.

She squared her shoulders. Tonight wasn't the night to be thinking about Evan. This dinner for the ten semifinalists was her big chance. After the meal each photographer would have a private interview with the three judges. She had to be at her best.

Walking down a long hallway, Susannah noted the magnificent paintings on the walls. She was able to recognize a Renoir and Degas as she passed. In the living room she found about two dozen people, drinking and talking quietly.

Stay calm, she ordered herself. You can do it. And when you're done, you can kill Jamie. If he hadn't gotten her into this, she wouldn't be standing here scared out of her wits. Susannah had been astounded to find out she was a semifinalist. Even after rereading the letter several times, it had taken hours before the fact had actually sunk in. Of course it was incredible news, wonderful news, exactly what she'd hoped for. She might really have a shot at the unthinkable, being named one of the winners and getting the money for Ruth. But it also meant that she had to maintain the facade of being Cameron's daughter. The tension was wearing her down. How much longer could she get away with this?

She went over to the bar set up in one corner of the room and asked for a glass of white wine. Just like the living room in Bedford, this room spoke of money, everything in it understated but expensive. She took in the deep sofas and armchairs, the intricately carved end tables upon which antiques were displayed in a casual but no doubt calculated arrangement. The effect suddenly struck her as cold and overdone, the work of a decorator paid to make the room look lived in. The truth was there was nothing personal anywhere, just high-priced and correct bric-a-brac. Bedford was the same way, now that she thought about it. That house, too, was tasteful and gracious, but it could have belonged to anyone — that is, anyone with enough money to pay for the best.

She moved away from the bar, noticing only one other woman

in the room. That would be Judith Lacy, one of the judges, wearing a plain print dress and a bored expression as she sipped from a highball glass, the young man talking animatedly next to her on the couch oblivious to her lack of interest. The two other judges were easy to pick out; Calvin Giles's and Forrest Taylor's names were well known to her, and she had seen their pictures in photography and art magazines. She also spotted Lionel Shea near the window. And over by the bookcase was Cameron, tan and handsome in a navy blue suit. The other guests were quite an assortment; most had on suits, but a few wore sports jackets and one was in jeans and a work shirt. There were more than nine other people — the rest of the semifinalists — so she supposed some of the others must have been Hawkes employees. She decided her raw silk suit had been a good choice, and she was glad she had also kept her jewelry conservative, just large pearl earrings and a long, heavy gold chain.

"Wishing you were someplace else?"

Susannah turned, startled. Cal Giles had come up behind her.

"Not at all. This is the most important place for any photographer in the country tonight." As soon as the words were out she regretted them, annoyed with herself for sounding so obsequious.

"True." Giles looked pleased by her comment. "But only a few others were lucky enough to have been invited. I like your work, Miss Holland."

"That's very kind. Thank you." She smiled.

Giles moved a step closer. "And you are very lovely as well. It reinforces my faith in my own judgment. I picked you without even knowing how beautiful you are."

She tried not to show her annoyance. Her instinct was to tell him curtly that she couldn't imagine what her appearance had to do with her photography, but before she could respond, a butler appeared in the doorway, announcing that dinner was served. As the crowd began filing out of the room, Cameron came over to Susannah. He took her arm as they walked, leaning in to speak to her quietly.

"Well, congratulations are in order. Our judges were quite impressed with your pictures."

"Thank you for letting me enter," Susannah said. "I'm very grateful. And delighted, of course, at the outcome."

"You haven't won yet." Cameron held up a finger, admonishing her. "And isn't that what matters?"

Susannah's answer was entirely truthful. "I'd like to win, but it means a lot to me to have been among these ten. It's quite a thrill."

He looked at her appraisingly. "Let me give you some advice, Susannah. Never settle for anything less than the big prize. Nothing else counts."

A male voice called out. "Cameron, could you join us for a second?"

Cameron glanced over to see who was calling him. "It's Lionel," he said to Susannah. "He wanted to meet all the photographers tonight. Please excuse me."

Susannah nodded and watched him walk off, wondering why he'd given her that bit of advice. She thought how wonderful it would have been to have grown up with a father who taught her things, who helped and guided her. She wished so badly she really *was* one of the Hawkes. Maybe she could even have done something for Tish if they were mother and daughter, stopped her from drinking that way. And she would have loved to have Olivia as a younger sister. But there was no use wishing.

When she reached the large dining room, the rest of the guests were already there, settling into their seats once they had found their place cards. Susannah saw her name and moved to pull out the chair.

"Allow me." Lionel Shea extended a hand. His voice dropped to a whisper. "I've been a terrible guest and done the forbidden: switched the place cards so I could sit next to you. I hope you don't mind."

She laughed. "Not at all."

They sat down together as waiters moved smoothly around the table. Lionel immediately began asking Susannah about her photographic technique, listening intently as she explained how she went about determining what she wanted to shoot, asking her question after question.

"It sounds to me as if you enjoy the subject," Susannah observed as a waiter placed a bowl of vichyssoise in front of her. "What do you like to shoot?"

Lionel looked abashed. "No, I don't do anything like that. I can barely work my Instamatic. I'm just interested."

"Well, why don't you try it yourself? You'd probably have a good time."

"Oh, I can't face all that equipment." He picked up a soup spoon. "I'd have to learn from the beginning, and I don't have an eye for that sort of thing anyway."

"From what I know about you, that doesn't seem like your usual attitude. Besides, it's for fun. You don't have to become an expert."

"I guess it intimidates me. It's so technical."

"But you design and manufacture toys!" Susannah's voice rose in surprise. "That requires a tremendous amount of technical knowledge."

He laughed. "That's different. It's easy for me."

"This could be too," she insisted. "I'd be glad to show you how to use a camera. There are cameras out now that do practically everything for you. It's a breeze."

"Come on, you don't want to waste your time with an old geezer like me." Lionel chuckled. "You're a young girl with better things to do."

"It would be a pleasure." Susannah meant it. "If you can find the free time, it's a date."

Lionel didn't say anything, but she could see he was pleased. He really was a sweet man, she thought, as the waiter removed their soup bowls. If he and Cameron stayed friendly after their business was done, it would be like having an uncle around. She froze. *What's wrong with me? Cameron's not my father and I'm not part of the family.*

When the meal was over, the contestants retired to the living room for brandy while the interviews were being conducted in a study down the hall. Susannah's stomach began to flutter again, and she noted that the rest of the semifinalists appeared equally ill at ease. Cameron had disappeared, and Lionel had left before dessert, explaining that he had to go on to a charity benefit. He took her telephone number and reminded her of her promise to teach him something about photography. Susannah genuinely looked forward to their spending an afternoon taking pictures together. Maybe she would take him to the park for starters.

"Ms. Holland."

It was her turn. Opening the door to the study, she saw the three judges seated behind a table. They gazed at her stonily as she took the seat facing them across the table and folded her hands in her lap.

Cal Giles spoke first, his words forceful and direct. "Why should we trust you to travel around the world on behalf of the Forum? How can we be sure you'll deliver pictures — the right pictures?"

So it was going to be that kind of interview. She took a deep breath.

". . . till death do you part."

"I do."

Susannah glanced out at the throng of people watching the ceremony. They were transfixed by the sight before them, Kurt so handsome in his tuxedo, Bibi a vision in white tulle. Her friend had never looked more beautiful, so absolutely serene. Standing right beside Bibi as the maid of honor, wearing the dove gray silk dress Bibi had had custom-made for her, Susannah turned her attention back to them. She could see the love radiating in the bride's gaze as she slipped a gold band on Kurt's finger.

Flashbulbs went off in rapid succession as the few photographers who had been allowed into the ceremony scrambled to capture the moment. Bibi had worried that her wedding might become a free-for-all, what with her fame and Kurt's recent high profile as the star in a new dramatic series on television. But her publicity people had done a superb job of keeping the date and location secret from all but the invited guests and a small group of journalists and photographers Bibi and Kurt had approved. Susannah shifted her weight slightly. By now, every tabloid must know the ceremony was in progress. Getting from the church to the reception would doubtless prove to be an adventure.

She looked out again at the crowd of guests. Several famous faces stood out, actors and actresses she recognized from movies and the theater, new friends of Bibi's from Los Angeles, she supposed. Jamie sat in the front row alongside Bibi's parents. It was the first time Susannah had seen him in nearly three months, since they'd started the scam back in June. He had carried on like a jubilant madman when she'd phoned him a few weeks ago with the news about being selected as a semifinalist, as thrilled with her victory as if he had won it himself. He would no doubt be crowing with delight again when they met up later. She only hoped he would be discreet around Evan.

She turned to search out Evan's face. He was sitting five rows back and when she caught his eye, he smiled. Maybe she had been crazy to ask him here as her date, knowing Jamie would be present as well. But she was relishing every minute she had with him, painfully aware it wouldn't last much longer. The judges would announce the winners soon. Then she would have to use the escape hatch, tell the Hawkes that it was all a mistake and she wasn't really Cameron's daughter. She glanced down at the bouquet of white roses she held in her hands. It would all be over. The family would be gone from her forever. But Evan would be angry, realizing she'd been lying all along. It would be impossible to look him in the eye and tell him another lie, try to get him to believe that it had been an innocent misunderstanding on her part.

Cheers and applause broke out. Startled, Susannah realized the ceremony was over and the bride and groom were kissing. She grinned and applauded with everyone else as Bibi and Kurt refused to release each other from their embrace, finally turning their heads to look out, still clutching each other. Their friends whooped with delight. Bibi gathered up her billowing white skirt in one hand and they walked arm in arm down the steps from the altar to hurry back up the aisle. Kurt's younger brother, Jonathan, was the best man, and he stepped forward next, extending an arm for Susannah, leading her down the steps behind the bride and groom. Out in the vestibule, Jonathan slapped Kurt on the back and congratulated him. Bibi turned to Susannah, hugging her tightly. The two friends gazed at each other.

"I'm so thrilled for you," Susannah exclaimed. "You two deserve a wonderful life together."

"Thanks, sweetie." Bibi gave Susannah another quick squeeze. "It's time you had all the happiness *you* deserve."

A woman's voice rang out. "Bibi, darling!"

The doors to the chapel were propped open as the guests began to pour out, everyone trying to get to Bibi and Kurt. Susannah watched as the couple was whisked out a side door to a waiting limousine, an attempt to avoid the crowd of photographers waiting by the front entrance. She saw Evan approaching.

"Hey, there. You were great, a top-flight maid of honor," he said, putting an arm around her and drawing her close.

"Why, thanks," she replied, batting her eyes exaggeratedly. "I took lessons."

He laughed. "It *was* a nice ceremony. And now comes the fun part. Ready to brave the reporters?"

"I don't know. But, I guess you know how to do this sort of thing. You have to deal with these guys all the time."

"You flatter me." Evan grinned. "Not all the time." He took her hand. "Just stick with me, kid."

They emerged into the bright light of the late August day. Susannah was stunned to see how many photographers had assembled on the street outside. There must have been more than fifty of them, pressing forward, anxious to capture the famous faces attending the wedding even if they weren't lucky enough to get the bride and groom. She heard the whirring of television equipment and blinked at the still cameras clicking in their faces. Evan held on to her tightly, moving quickly through the crowd.

"Hey, is that Evan Gardiner? Evan, what are you doing here?" a voice yelled.

He paused long enough to wave. "I'm a great admirer of the bride's."

"Who's your date, Evan?"

He smiled down at her. "Susannah Holland." He looked again in the direction of the reporter who'd called out to him. "With two *L*'s."

Cameras went off furiously as the reporters began yelling questions at her.

"Aren't you the Cameron Hawkes girl — the one who says she's his daughter?"

"Why haven't you come forward until now?"

"Can you prove who you are?"

They hurried into one of the limousines set aside for the wedding party.

Evan could see Susannah was shaken. "I'm sorry about that," he said to her as they settled into their seats.

"No, no, it's fine." Susannah kept her voice light. But she averted her face from Evan as they sat back to wait for Jonathan and his wife to join them.

Susannah stared out at the dark street below, and took another sip of coffee. It was nearly three in the morning, but she knew she wouldn't be able to go to sleep. The wedding had been magnificent, the party afterward beautiful and happy. She and Evan had danced most of the night, drunk champagne, toasted the bride and groom — they'd enjoyed every second. For those hours, at least, she had put the whole business of her lie out of her mind. But when he'd dropped her off afterward, it had all come rushing back.

Those reporters outside the church had frightened her. Until that moment, she hadn't realized that the press was so interested in her story. She'd seen how vulnerable she was to being found out, how quickly the whole thing could come unraveled. Her picture would be in the paper. Reporters were digging up information about her. Cameron hadn't found out the truth, but maybe one of those journalists would come up with something that could expose her.

It makes no difference, she told herself. I swore I'd put an end to this whole thing when the competition judging is over. It's not that much longer anyway.

But she couldn't stand the thought of it all coming to an end, because that meant losing Evan. She was so in love with him by now, she knew she would never get over losing him. How could she sit around, waiting for the boom to drop when someone uncovered her lie, or when the winners of the contest were announced. She couldn't tell which emotion was more overwhelming, her fear of discovery or her guilt at success.

But there wasn't any way out that she could see, no way around the mess she'd created. Evan was slipping away, and there was nothing she could do to stop it.

She had to do something, get away from him somehow and prepare herself for the terrible truth that was coming. For the moment when Evan would despise her.

It had been a long day. Evan entered his bedroom, exhausted and ready for a shower. He was sick and tired of those sessions with the physical therapist, but he knew he didn't have much choice if he wanted his knee to improve. And driving all the way back out from the city to Bedford at rush hour was a pain in the neck. He wouldn't have minded if he thought he was doing something for his mother, getting through to her in some way. But she was oblivious to his gentler hints and suggestions, and downright angry when he tried to approach the subject of her drinking directly. He was getting nowhere. On top of everything, it looked like the Pirates might be headed for the play-offs. Without any help from him.

Frustrated, he threw his car keys down on the dresser. He'd had a separate telephone line installed in this room when he'd come at the beginning of the summer, and he saw the light on his answering machine blinking. Yanking his T-shirt off over his head, he hit the play button.

Evan, it's Susannah. Her voice on the tape was hesitant. *I'm going away for a little while. I need some time alone. Please don't call me. I'll talk to you when I get back.*

What the hell? Evan rewound the tape and played the message again. He had just been with Susannah at Bibi's wedding and she'd never mentioned a thing about going away, much less needing some time alone. He had no idea what brought this on, and racked his brain to see if he had said or done anything that might have upset her, driven her away.

He dialed her number. No answer. Evan sat down on the edge of the bed. She'd said not to call her, that she would call him when she got back. In his experience, when a lover said that, it meant good-bye for good. Had she left him?

I should have told her I love her, he thought. Maybe she has doubts about me, thinks I'm not serious. Maybe if she realized . . . He ran a hand through his hair. Susannah was a mystery in so many ways. He still didn't know if she were telling the truth or not about being related to Cameron, and he never mentioned it when they were together. The fact was he doubted her story, but he had long ago stopped caring if it was true or not. He only knew he was in love with her. All the rest didn't matter. But she had some reservations about *him*, it seemed. He thought of Bibi —maybe Susannah had gone to see her in LA, or at least Bibi would have some ideas about where she might be. He reached for the phone. No, Bibi and Kurt were in Europe on their honeymoon.

"Damn. *Damn.*"

He lay down on the bed, crossing his arms behind his head. There had been a lot of women over the years. But this was the one he'd been waiting for, the one he wanted. And now he was finding out she didn't want him.

Chapter 25

"That's unacceptable." Cameron's tone as he spoke on the telephone was quietly furious. "You have to prove her story one way or the other."

"I'm sorry, Mr. Hawkes," Jack Milford said. "I did my best, but I can't make the connection. The damnedest thing is, I thought I had it locked up there for a minute in California — with a nun, of all people. But that turned out to be a blind alley too."

Cameron had no patience for the detective's excuses. "What other leads do you have?" he asked curtly.

"That's just it, sir." Milford's voice had the resignation of a man who knew he was about to lose one of his best clients. "There aren't any. Susannah Holland may be Dorrie Gordon's daughter. And she may not be. I can't get beyond that orphanage."

Cameron hung up the phone. Christ, this was incredible. What was he supposed to do, go on forever wondering if the girl was telling the truth? Half the time he was certain she was lying, the other half he thought the story was too outrageous for her to have fabricated it. And she'd asked for nothing besides being allowed to enter the photo competition. Was she so ambitious, so interested in advancing her career, that she would have gone to this much trouble just to get her name known?

"Damn it." He brought his fist down on the desk. It made him look like an idiot, not knowing the truth, allowing himself to be manipulated.

The intercom near his elbow buzzed and he heard Marianne's voice. "Your meeting's in five minutes."

Well, any kind of decision about Susannah would have to wait. The meeting was to discuss a new Little Angel logo, which had remained unchanged since he started the company back in the late sixties. He'd told his marketing people to put together some prototypes for him to consider by this afternoon at two. It was a sensitive matter, not to mention expensive, and he needed a clear head.

Nodding briefly to his secretary as he passed, he strode purposefully toward the elevators. He was unpleasantly surprised to see Olivia approaching from the opposite direction, obviously on her way to his office.

"Just the man I wanted to see," she said. "Got a second, Dad?"

"What is it, Olivia?" Cameron made no effort to hide his annoyance, wondering irritably why she always expected to waltz in without an appointment. Just because she was his daughter didn't mean she could get his ear anytime she felt like it. Olivia and Susannah, damn both of them. "I'm in a hurry."

She fell in step beside him. "I've been talking with some of our employees. It seems to me we should distribute more information on infant nutrition. A lot of mothers could use it, and we could get it out in the communities as a gesture of good will."

"We've already got an 800 number for that kind of thing," Cameron said dismissively.

"But poorer people aren't calling, they don't know anything about it. I'd like us to bring the information to them, through community groups and churches." She pressed on. "Maybe include some formula samples, tell them about problems to watch for, how to keep themselves healthy if they're breast-feeding."

"Olivia, we print an enormous amount of literature on these kinds of things. We advertise in magazines for new mothers, distribute materials in hospitals and so on." Cameron glanced at his watch. He despised being late for meetings, and insisted his employees be punctual as well. It was now five past two.

"But I want to give things out where it's needed, bring it to the streets," she said, her voice rising in excitement. "Do some real good out there."

"We already donate millions to charitable causes," Cameron said as they reached the elevators. He pressed the button. "Just look at the International Forum — that will bring global attention to children around the world."

"Not hungry children," Olivia protested. "It's not about that. Come on, Dad, the Forum is really for the benefit of the company's image."

"All right, that's enough," Cameron said curtly. "I tried to explain to you on an adult level, but you can't grasp it. So here's my answer. No." A bell rang faintly and one of the elevators opened. Cameron stepped inside and pressed his floor, his mind already on other things, the conversation clearly terminated.

Olivia watched the door close. She wondered how many ideas she had brought to him that he had dismissed in exactly the same angry fashion. Other than the day-care centers, he'd never acknowledged a single proposal of hers as even being worthy of discussion. Before she could stop herself, she thought about how enthusiastic he was whenever Susannah Holland was around, how eagerly he listened to what she had to say. He didn't even know if she was his real daughter or just some gold digger, but he gave her more respect and attention than he gave his own flesh and blood.

A surge of jealousy jolted Olivia. She was surprised by the intensity of the feeling, since she had actually started to grow fond of Susannah, especially when she saw how much Evan liked her. If her brother thought Susannah worth dating, there must be something genuine there. Olivia had begun to wonder if maybe Susannah's story were true. A part of her fervently wished it were. It would be such a relief to find out they really were related, to build the kind of friendship sisters had. But another part of her wished just as powerfully that Susannah would disappear off the face of the earth. She had won Evan's affection and Cameron's as well. Olivia didn't care if her stepbrother preferred Susannah to her. But her own father — she didn't think she could stand that.

Ashamed and embarrassed, she walked back down the hall.

Chapter 26

After smoothing the blankets on Ruth's bed, Susannah poured herself a glass of water from the pitcher on the night table, then sat back down on the hard wooden chair nearby. Ruth had been dozing off and on since Susannah had arrived at the hospital that morning, and she was asleep again now. She was getting a lot of medication, which made it difficult for her to talk for more than a few seconds at a time before drifting off.

Ruth's breathing was raspy but regular. Susannah watched her. She couldn't permit herself to feel anything; it would be too painful to bear. Finishing her water, she sat back and closed her eyes, rubbing her forehead tiredly.

This had been a chance to see Ruth again, and she had hoped to get away from the entire hoax, forget about the Hawkes family for a while.

But just the opposite had happened: when she wasn't with Ruth, she'd been unable to think about anything but Evan.

It had now been a full ten days since she'd last seen Evan. She gazed out the small, grimy window at the parking lot below, envisioning his face. It felt like a year since they'd been together. From the moment she'd come, she'd been torn, unable to figure out which was worse, staying in New York and falling even more deeply in love, or hiding out in Harrisburg and giving up the last days she would have with him. As glad as Lily and Timmy Mitchell were to have her, she knew even they were surprised she was staying so long. She couldn't stay here forever. After ten days, she realized she was more an imposition than a help. She would just have to make sense of it back in New York.

For the first few days after she arrived home, Susannah didn't allow herself to call Evan. She was both relieved and hurt that he wasn't trying to reach her. Surely he would give her apartment a call every so often to see if she'd come back to town. Maybe he didn't care that she'd left. It was becoming impossible to sleep at night, his face before her whenever she closed her eyes, her body longing for the feeling of his again.

At the end of the week, Susannah was sitting on the edge of her bed, carefully cleaning her camera, when the telephone rang and Bibi announced that she and Kurt had just gotten in from London, and were downstairs in her old apartment. She demanded that Susannah come down right away.

"I'll be there in a second," Susannah said with a laugh.

Kurt opened the door, a towel around his waist, his hair still wet from the shower.

"Come on in." He reached into the hall, lifting Susannah off the floor in a bear hug and depositing her on his side of the doorjamb.

Bibi came out in her flowered kimono, the same one she'd worn the first day she'd invited Susannah down to her apartment for coffee and croissants. Susannah smiled at the sight of it.

"Remember this robe?" Bibi grinned. "I never wear it anymore, but I forgot my other one in LA."

"Truthfully, I always liked this one, Bibi," Susannah said. "It's so . . . *you*."

Bibi puckered her lips and struck a pose. "But now I'm a fabulous movie star and can only wear the finest of silk and satin."

Susannah shook her head, laughing. "Indeed."

"God help us," Kurt added with a grin. He headed toward the bedroom. "I'm going to finish getting dressed. Then what do you say the three of us grab a bite of dinner?"

"Sounds good," Susannah said.

The two women watched him depart.

"He's sensational. And you look great, Bibi, as always."

"I feel great," Bibi said simply. "Getting married was good for both of us."

"How was Europe?"

Bibi sighed happily. "The best. I'll tell you all about it over dinner, in excruciating detail."

"I can't wait to hear it."

Susannah hesitated. Maybe this was the time to bring it up, to broach the idea that had been brewing in her head for weeks. She'd been reluctant to ask Bibi, but the more she'd thought about it, the more she felt it was worth taking the chance.

"Would you sit down for a minute?" she said finally. "I want to talk to you about something."

"Mrs. Hawkes is in the study, but she doesn't wish to be disturbed."

Susannah nodded at the maid who had just returned with Tish Hawkes's rejection.

"Please tell her I apologize for barging in like this, but I have someone here I'd like her to meet."

The maid went off once more.

Bibi was skeptical. "You can't do it like this if she's not ready, Susannah."

"I know, but all I ask is that we give it a shot."

A few minutes later, Tish Hawkes appeared before them wearing neatly pressed peach pants and a matching blouse, a glass of clear liquid in her hand. Her eyes were bloodshot, and she regarded Susannah with annoyance. When she spoke, her words were slurred.

"My husband is quite taken with you, I know. But I have no involvement in this affair. Frankly, I'm not up to these little games in the middle of the afternoon."

The words stung Susannah. "I realize it's an imposition, having me intrude this way."

Tish suddenly appeared tired, as if she had lost interest in the conversation.

"What is it you want?"

Susannah gestured to Bibi. "I wanted you to meet a friend of mine, Bibi Frost."

Tish stared at the red-haired woman beside Susannah, showing no recognition of either her name or her famous face.

"I don't want to meet anyone," Tish responded irritably. Her gaze then drifted to some point beyond the two women, as if she'd forgotten they were there. When she looked back, she seemed surprised to see them. Observing her, Susannah realized that Tish must be getting worse. It was only one o'clock and she was not only drunk but disoriented.

Susannah hesitated, unsure how to proceed. She had wanted so badly to help Evan with his mother, to work some kind of miracle. But she could see she had overstepped her boundaries here. This was none of her business.

Bibi stepped forward. "There's no reason at all you should want to meet me, Tish. Still, I'm here, so why don't we sit down in the study and have a cup of coffee together?"

Tish looked confused as Bibi led her back to the room from which she had emerged. "We're going to get to know each other a little bit, that's all," Bibi was saying as they disappeared behind the study door.

Susannah sank down onto a bench in the foyer. She'd been crazy to think she could help Tish. Even Bibi couldn't pull off a miracle like that, although she was obviously going to give it her best try. It was selfish to drag her friend here, to waste so much of her time.

The front door opened. With a shock, Susannah saw Evan pull his key out of the door and come inside, his attention still focused on some papers in his hand. She had assumed he would be out in the middle of a weekday. Too startled to move, she held her breath as he came closer. Her heart was pounding. She wanted to run to him, to throw her arms around him.

When he saw her, he seemed disconcerted, but quickly regained his composure.

"Well, well, this is . . . odd." His tone was mildly sarcastic.

"I'm, I'm sorry," she stammered. "Bibi and I . . ." She stopped. It didn't matter that he had told her he wanted to do something for his mother; she had no right to interfere. Especially after running off like that. "I'm sorry," she repeated, feeling like a fool.

Evan put his papers down on a table and looked at her. "Let's cut to the chase. A telephone message. No word in weeks. What's up, Susannah?"

They stared at each other. The deep hurt on his face belied his tough words. Oh, God, I love him so much, she thought.

Her voice came out in a whisper. "I don't know."

"If you wanted to call it quits all you had to do was say so," he said quietly. "I'm not some schoolboy, I can take it. Just say the words and you never have to see me again."

Never see him again. The thought of being without him suddenly became real to her in a way it somehow hadn't been in these past weeks. She wouldn't feel him against her as they slept, his arm curled around her protectively, or watch him shudder as he took his first sip of coffee in the morning, exaggerating the jolt of the caffeine. He wouldn't give her that long kiss whenever he came along to meet her, or reach for her hand in the movies. She'd never make love with him again.

She jumped up. Maybe she had only a few weeks or even days with him. But she'd already wasted too much time. She would take what time she could get and be grateful for it.

"Evan, no, no, you're wrong." She went to him, not stopping to think what he might do, just bringing her arms around his neck and holding on tight. "I want to stay with you. For as long as I can."

He was taken aback, but his expression softened and a smile creased his face. He leaned down to kiss her softly.

"That's what I wanted to hear," he said.

They kissed again, more passionately this time. Susannah ran her hands along his cheeks, his arms, his broad back. She pushed aside her fear of what would happen, and gave herself over to the thrill of being close to him again, her eyes shut as his hand stroked her long hair.

They pulled apart and looked at each other.

"Swear to me you'll never run off like that again," Evan said. "Swear you won't leave me."

It didn't matter what she said. He would be the one to leave soon enough.

"I swear."

They heard a door down the hall open and turned to see Bibi and Tish emerge.

"Hello," Bibi said to a startled Evan. "Nice to see you again. But we'll have to talk later. Tish and I are on our way out."

Evan looked at his mother, confused. She was fiddling with a pendant around her neck, apparently reluctant to return her son's gaze.

"Susannah, we need the car," Bibi went on. "Can you get back to the city some other way?"

Susannah nodded, secretly delighted. Bibi had succeeded. She had said on the drive out to Bedford that the best possible outcome would be if Tish allowed Bibi to take her to an AA meeting right away, without putting it off. If they were leaving together, Bibi had somehow managed to get Tish to agree to go.

"Mother, are you all right?" Evan asked.

Tish glanced at him briefly. "Please, dear, everything's fine. Don't worry."

"We'll be back in a few hours." Bibi waved as she ushered Tish out the front door. "See you."

Evan turned to Susannah. "What the hell was that about?"

Susannah was both relieved that things had worked out this well and embarrassed to admit her part in it. "Bibi's taking your mother to Alcoholics Anonymous," she said quietly.

Evan stared at her. "You're joking. My mother would never go to AA. She doesn't even admit she has a drinking problem."

"Bibi did it. I can't claim any credit. It was my pigheaded idea to bring her up here today, which I probably shouldn't have done and for which I apologize. But Bibi was the one who got her to go."

Evan was amazed. "How did she do it? I've been trying for so long. What did she say?"

Vastly relieved that he wasn't angry with her for interfering, Susannah gave him a small smile. "Bibi's a recovering alcoholic herself."

Evan shook his head reflectively. Then he smiled. "You're right, you know. You were way out of line." He put his arms around her. "But I love you for doing it. Thank you."

It was nearly ten o'clock that night when Evan and Susannah pulled up in front of her building. They kissed in his car, unwilling to let the day end. Evan was doing color commentary on another ball game the next day, and Susannah insisted he go home for a good night's rest.

He leaned over to nibble her neck as she reached for the car door handle. "Come on, let me stay with you tonight."

Susannah struggled not to give in to her own desire to have him come upstairs. "No, tomorrow's important for you. We won't get any sleep at all."

He grinned. "And why is that?"

She pushed him away. "The rock band upstairs, of course. They practice all night. No other reason."

"Ah, I see." He nodded gravely, then suddenly grabbed her, kissing her face all over, making loud smooching sounds.

Laughing, Susannah managed to get the door open and slip out of the car. Quickly, she shut the door, leaning down to talk to him through the open window.

"Will you come by after the game? I'll make a late dinner."

"You're on." Evan straightened up again in the driver's seat, saluted smartly, and turned on the engine.

She smiled at him. "Good night, Evan."

He looked directly into her eyes. "Good night, sweetheart. I love you, you know."

The car pulled away and Susannah stood on the curb, staring after it. When it turned the corner, she headed into her building, replaying the day they had spent together. It had been perfect, she thought, absolutely perfect. But, of course, it was just being with Evan that had made it that way. Humming, she went to her mailbox.

There it was. A registered letter from the Hawkes Corporation. The judges' final decision on the International Forum winners.

Susannah stood there. Then, with a rapid movement, she tore the envelope open and yanked out the heavy sheet of paper inside.

Dear Ms. Holland:

The panel of judges for the International Forum for Children is delighted to inform you . . .

Quickly, she scanned the lines, her heart doing somersaults in her chest. Dear God, she had won. She had actually won.

Chapter 27

————

Frustrated, Susannah pulled the rental car onto the side of the road to consult the map. She should have already reached the street she wanted and now that she was almost there, any further delay seemed unendurable. She'd driven there before; how had she missed it? Hurriedly, she unfolded the map. Damn, she'd made a wrong turn nearly a mile back.

She eased the car back onto the road, looking for a place to turn around. In the two weeks since she had learned that she was to be one of the Forum's three photographers, so much had been happening she'd barely had a chance to think straight. The day after she got the news, she had drinks with the other two winners. Jim Driscoll would be starting his work in Argentina the following week, while Eric Rothenberg was slated to begin in Paris on the first of the month. The

Hawkes Corporation hadn't wasted any time making plans for her trip to the Far East, either, drawing up an itinerary, instructing her on everything from international protocol to what medicines she should pack. In between meetings with various Hawkes representatives, she had been on the phone with Sam, Timmy, and Lily Mitchell, making the arrangements for Ruth.

At last, Susannah saw the hospital ahead. Relieved, she sped up, more anxious than ever to get to Ruth. Before she could see her, though, she would have to deal with the hospital administration, filling out forms to arrange for Ruth's transfer to the hospice next week.

It was nearly two hours later when Susannah finally reached the door to Ruth's room. She stepped inside, unhappily recognizing the sights and smells of the unwashed room. Thank God, Ruth would be getting out of here. As she walked slowly to the bedside, she steeled herself for what she might find.

Ruth looked worse than she had on Susannah's last visit, even thinner and chalky white. An oxygen tube was in her nose, strapped across her face to keep it in place. She appeared to be sleeping, but she must have sensed someone's presence because her eyes fluttered, as if she were almost too weak to open them. At last, she was able to focus more fully, and Susannah saw a momentary spark as Ruth realized who her visitor was.

"Hi, there," Susannah said gently. She took Ruth's hand. "I'm so happy to see you."

She was rewarded with a faint smile. Ruth struggled to say something, then gave up.

Susannah swallowed. This was going to be even harder than she'd imagined. She pulled a chair up right beside the bed and sat down.

"I'm going away for a while," she said, looking into Ruth's eyes. "I've been chosen in this competition, and I'll be traveling around the world for a year, taking pictures of children."

Susannah felt her hand being squeezed gently, Ruth's eyes crinkling with pleasure at the good news. With great effort, the older woman managed to speak.

"Always knew you'd do great things."

Tears filled Susannah's eyes and she looked away. She didn't know if she could go on. Taking a deep breath, she spoke as brightly as she could. "You're going to be moved to a much nicer place in a few days. You won't have to stay here anymore."

Ruth's eyes were questioning, and Susannah could barely hear her. "Can't afford . . ."

"Don't you worry, it's all taken care of." Susannah leaned forward, bringing Ruth's hand close to her heart. "I want you to rest and get well. When I come home, we'll spend lots of time together."

She stood, knowing if she didn't leave she would break down completely.

Ruth summoned all her strength to speak once more. "Have a good trip, darling. See you when you get back."

The two women gazed at each other. They both knew they would never see each other again.

"Good-bye, Ruth," Susannah said, a sob catching in her throat. She moved to go, but felt a faint tug at her hand and turned back.

"Thank you," Ruth whispered. "I love you."

"Olivia, I have had all I can take of your opinions." Cameron's tone was biting.

Olivia flushed, but forced herself to stand up a bit straighter and go on.

"You're wrong, I'm sorry. It's a problem and you need to recognize that."

Cameron waved his hand disgustedly. "A few feminist groups whining to you, a few letters."

"Whining? They're furious. And they came to me because they believe I'll see the logic in what they're saying. Which I do. This could be real trouble for Hawkes."

"You have no idea what real trouble in business looks like," Cameron said sharply. "This isn't it."

"It's terrible publicity for the company." Olivia searched for a way to make him understand. "Dad, you can't keep shipping that formula to Thailand. This is going to escalate into a scandal."

"That's enough." Cameron's voice grew louder. "It's not that big an issue."

Olivia exploded in frustration. "How can you say that when there's some kind of organized letter-writing campaign waiting to hit every major paper with the news that we're exploiting poor women?"

"They don't have to use our formula. No one's forcing them," Cameron snapped.

She knew she was risking her father's wrath, but Olivia couldn't stop now. "They trust what we tell them, that the formula is better. I can't believe you're making that claim when you know the only water they have access to may be contaminated." She banged her fist on his desk. "It's *wrong*. We don't need to trade on the misery of these people to make a dollar."

Cameron stood up. His patience was at an end. "I'm sick of your pious lectures. Become a missionary if you care so much about the poor. Work in the streets, give up your nice job and clothes and everything I struggled to provide you with. See how you like it. Maybe then you'll know why I make the decisions I do."

Olivia stood there, her face turning red.

"You know nothing about this," Cameron finished angrily. "Keep your high and mighty philosophizing to yourself."

There was nothing else to say. Olivia went to the door, but before she could leave, it opened. Lionel Shea stood in front of her. From the shocked expression on his face, Olivia guessed he must have heard some of her argument with Cameron. She glanced at her father. He had turned pale. She supposed that Cameron's biting tirade at his own daughter wouldn't sit well with the avuncular owner of Awareness Industries. Angry at the position her father had taken on the Thailand problem and humiliated by the way he had treated her, for the first time Olivia felt a twinge of pleasure that something had gone wrong for him.

She nodded at Lionel Shea as she passed. "Good afternoon."

"Lionel, come in. I didn't realize it was time for our appointment. What can we get you to drink?"

She recognized the forced joviality in her father's words as she walked out the door.

Susannah stepped into the elevator and pressed the button for Cameron's floor. She was far more nervous than the first time she had come here, claiming to be his long-lost daughter. But she couldn't stand it anymore. For the past few nights she had been consumed with guilt. The whole thing had gone much too far. She argued with herself that she had been selected for the Forum on her own merit, but it was no use. The only reason she'd been able to enter the competition was because of this elaborate lie. She just couldn't go off on a year-long trip with so many people thinking she was Cameron's illegitimate child.

It would have been so much easier if she hadn't become so involved with Cameron's family. Even if they had their doubts about her story, they had all — especially Cameron and Olivia — been kind to her. Tish's difficulties had drawn her in even further. Then, of course, there was Evan.

She remembered the day she telephoned Jamie in Los Angeles to let him know she had actually won. She had dreaded making the call, knowing he would gloat over how well his scheme had worked. But of course she had to tell him. When she reached him, she blurted out the news, hurriedly explaining that the winners had drawn itineraries out of a hat and she had picked Australia and all of Asia. He assumed she was joking and yelled at her for putting him on. It was only when she tersely told him she was already packing her bags for Japan, the first country on her list, that he started believing her. As she had predicted, his glee only made her feel worse.

Finally, she had come to the decision she knew was inevitable. She had to go to Cameron and tell him the truth. If they disqualified her, she would just have to come up with the money for Ruth some other way. She didn't dare think about how impossible that would be.

Cameron sat with Lionel, only half listening to what he was saying. This was a disaster, having him come in at the tail end of his fight with Olivia. Lionel had given no indication that anything out of the ordinary had occurred, but his estimation of Cameron must have plummeted. He handled it just as I would have, Cameron thought. Maybe Lionel was a bit shrewder than he'd originally figured. But what could be done about repairing the damage? Because of that damned Olivia, this whole deal could be blown right out of the water. And he was so close.

The door to his office was slightly ajar, and both men heard the sound of Susannah Holland's voice. "Do you think he could spare a few minutes?" they heard her ask Marianne.

Lionel immediately twisted around in his chair. "Susannah," he boomed. She stuck her head in the door.

"My dear, join us. What a pleasant surprise," Lionel said with evident fondness. "I never did take you up on that offer to learn photography, and now it's too late. You're a top photographer off on an international adventure. Congratulations."

"Hello, Lionel," she nodded, giving him a small smile.

More interference, Cameron thought. "Yes, Susannah, what can we do for you? All ready to go?"

He saw that she was hesitating. "I have something pretty awful to tell you. Maybe I should wait until you're alone."

"What's the matter, dear?" Lionel's sympathy came before Cameron could even respond.

Cameron felt annoyed, but didn't dare show it. The incident with Olivia was quite enough for one day. "There's nothing we can't talk about in front of Lionel," he said soothingly. "Please go ahead."

It seemed to take an act of will for her to look Cameron in the eye. When she spoke again, her words came out in a rush.

"I have no right to make excuses, so I'm just going to tell you. You were right to suspect me. I'm not your daughter. It was just a story I made up so I could get into the Forum."

There was a shocked silence in the room.

"I knew it!" Cameron's eyes blazed.

Lionel tilted his head, contemplating Susannah. "Just a minute. Is your name really Susannah Holland?"

Susannah turned to him. "Oh, yes, of course. That's true. And I did start out in an orphanage in California. But Dorrie Gordon wasn't my mother. I don't know who my mother or father were."

"My dear girl," Lionel asked, "what could possibly have made you invent such a story?"

Susannah's voice was small. "I wanted to be considered for the competition and I had missed the deadline."

Cameron exploded. "And you thought you would get away with this?"

Lionel's voice was amused. "Cameron, she already has. She won the damn thing." He leaned forward and addressed Susannah. "You did all this just to win?"

"Well . . ." She was uncertain if she should continue. "I did it for the money. There's a woman I love very much, my foster mother a long time ago. She's dying and I needed the money for her."

Cameron was seething inside as he listened. This little tramp had made a complete fool out of him. He'd always suspected her, but after his detective's reports he was beginning to think the story might actually be true. Now she was making matters even worse by revealing everything on her own, making it look as if he was too stupid to figure it out himself. At least she should have been smart enough to keep her mouth shut and go on the lousy trip. He'd have her arrested immediately. Putting a finger on his intercom button to have his secretary call Security, he glanced at Lionel and noticed that the other man was still chuckling in amusement. Something made him take his hand away from the intercom.

"Susannah," Lionel was saying gently, "there are other ways to get money."

Susannah looked miserable. "I was desperate. It was wrong and of course I'll return the money. I'll never bother any of you again." She reached into her purse, pulling out an envelope that she placed on Cameron's desk. "Here's my plane ticket for Japan."

Lionel leaned back in his chair and slapped his leg. "I'll be goddamned." He looked at Cameron. "But she really won the contest fair and square, didn't she?"

Cameron's instincts told him to move slowly here. Lionel liked Susannah. Maybe Cameron could even find a way to take advantage of this situation to make Lionel forget that scene with Olivia. After all, Susannah Holland and her little charade were unimportant compared to the scope of the deal for Awareness. If letting this girl get away with her scam for the moment could put him back in Lionel's good graces, it was well worth it. He could deal with her properly — later.

Cameron put his fingertips together as if considering the matter. "You've got nerve all right, I'll give you that," he said to Susannah. "I'm not going to pretend I'm happy you lied to me. You know I have every right to have you arrested."

Seeing Lionel's sharp look at that comment, Cameron was gratified to note he had read the other man correctly. He went on. "But the fact is, you *did* win the contest, and I imagine anyone with the determination and guts to do what you did probably has what it takes to get some great pictures out there."

Susannah's amazement was plain. "You mean you still want me to go on the trip?"

"Yes, I do." Cameron nodded. "The truth is out now, and we can all live with it — no harm's been done. Send me back good work, and we'll call it even."

The delighted look on Lionel's face at this benevolent approach assured Cameron he had made the right move. It was a small price to pay to save a multimillion-dollar deal. He smiled with satisfaction.

Chapter 28

Susannah unzipped her black suitcase. Every time she had to repack, she said a mental thank you to the travel agent back at Hawkes who had urged her to take only one bag. It hadn't been easy selecting clothes to suffice for an entire year, but having decided she could buy some things along the way, she was grateful she had kept her luggage to a bare minimum.

She rolled up a T-shirt and slipped it inside the bag. That was something she had learned from an American woman she'd met in Shanghai; if you rolled the clothes instead of folding them, they had fewer wrinkles when you took them out. She smiled. When she had imagined winning the Forum competition, she had only considered getting the award money for Ruth; she'd never looked far enough down the road to envision what a thrill it would be to travel this way, free to come and go as she liked, exploring different countries.

She slipped the rolls of film she'd shot here in Hong Kong into a pre-addressed envelope and sealed it, idly wondering how many rolls the other photographers were taking in each country. On her first stop in Tokyo, she had gone through far too many, worrying that she might miss the perfect shot, knowing she was being insecure but unable to calm her nerves. Then, on her fourth night there, she had gone to the home of a Japanese couple to have dinner. They were friends of one of the Hawkes executives back in New York, who had arranged the meeting for her. The couple had four daughters, ranging from two to seven years old. The little girls didn't speak English, but they had instantly charmed Susannah, quietly studying her and returning her smile with shy smiles of their own. She brought out her camera. The children came closer, pointing and giggling as they touched her hair, passed her sunglasses around, and examined the contents of her purse. After dinner, she asked their parents' permission to photograph the four of them. As they sat in a row, holding one another's hands and fidgeting, she forgot her nervousness and let her instincts take over. By the end of the evening, she had two rolls of pictures that she knew captured their beauty and innocence. Her confidence returned. Since then, she had let her instincts lead her, and she was certain it was proving to be a wiser course. Even though she couldn't see her pictures developed — by pre-arrangement, the rolls of film were sent back to the Hawkes Corporation in New York in small batches — she could sense that these were the best she'd shot so far.

It was funny, she thought, zipping her suitcase closed and looking around to see if she'd forgotten anything. Instinct was something she had fought for so long. She'd always tried to control things, to act rationally, listening only to her head. But everything she did lately had to do with instincts, with following her heart instead. Her entire life had changed, and she had changed with it. Or was it the other way around? Entering the Forum competition the way she had was hardly the act of a logical person, she reflected wryly. Nor was getting involved with Evan.

As quickly as she thought of him, she pushed the thought away. The pain of losing him was too great. She remembered the flight over to Japan, how she had sat there imagining his getting her letter. It would have reached him a day or two after she'd left. She envisioned him opening it, reading the lines that told him she had lied about who she was. He would be shocked, remembering how passionately they had made love that last night together and how close they had felt, how tenderly they said good-bye in the morning. Even as she had written the letter, apologizing for having deceived him and his family, she knew how woefully inadequate it would sound. She had betrayed his trust, and he would hate her for it. She had spent most of the flight in tears. When she'd first found out she'd won, he'd talked about meeting her in Tokyo or Beijing. Now that would never happen.

She took a deep breath. Evan. She saw his face, his sad smile as he held her at the door in their last moments together. She couldn't think about him. Pursing her lips, she slung her bag over one shoulder and left the room, forcing herself to concentrate on her next destination. The night before, she had decided on the spur of the moment to leave Hong Kong four days early and go on to the next stop on her itinerary instead of waiting until Friday, as she had originally planned. She had gotten what she needed here. Thailand promised to be both fascinating and emotionally grueling, and she suspected she would want to spend some extra time shooting there.

She headed toward the hotel's front desk to check out.

Cameron's secretary stood in his doorway.

"Still no answer at her hotel room, Mr. Hawkes," she said.

"Christ, don't we have any better way of communicating with these photographers," Cameron snapped. "We pay to send them trotting around the globe and then can't get a simple message through."

"I'm sorry," Marianne replied evenly. "I don't think that hotel has a fax machine, but perhaps we could send a telegram."

"Will it get to her in time?" Cameron glanced over at his

calendar. Dammit, he thought, how the hell was he supposed to know this baby formula thing was going to get worse? He'd have bet money that the whole business would have blown over by now. But instead, the mail campaign was escalating and there'd been a number of demonstrations outside his office. Right now, the last thing he needed was someone associated with his company walking into the middle of this mess.

"It should get to her," his secretary answered. "Today's only Tuesday. Ms. Holland's not scheduled to leave for Thailand until Friday."

"All right." Cameron made no effort to hide his annoyance. "Get it out right away. Just make sure you stop her."

"That's right, pussycat, Mommy will be here soon."

Susannah smiled as the baby wrapped his arms around her neck. For three days, she had been only an observer in the refugee camp nursery, watching the action, taking pictures. But today, Daniel's mother was fifteen minutes late, and the worker assigned to him was frantic; her children were with her sister, and she was rushing to pick them up.

Susannah had offered to help out of politeness, but now that she was holding the baby, she was amazed at how wonderful it felt. Daniel started to whimper slightly, and Susannah walked around the room, rocking him gently, imitating what she'd seen other women doing. What do you know, she thought as he quieted down. It works.

As soon as she was certain he was asleep, she sat down and lay the baby on her lap. What a beautiful little boy, she thought, unable to keep herself from touching his soft skin and perfect tiny fingers. She was curious about this baby, and about his parents. When she'd first arrived in Thailand, it seemed as if everyone she spoke to mentioned Daniel's mother. Do you know each other, several people asked, as if all Americans would have met back home. The women in the nursery raved about Kailey Davids, telling Susannah about the baby food letter-writing campaign that was causing such a stir in the English-language newspapers. Yet

Kailey herself rarely seemed to be in the nursery. Once or twice, she had stopped in quickly, but at the sight of Susannah and her camera, had left immediately. It would be nice to talk to Kailey, Susannah reflected, fun to hear her own language and get an American's perspective on the refugee situation.

Susannah stared at the baby's face, struck by the fact that he looked completely Asian; there was none of the mix of features that most Amerasian children displayed. As she watched him sleep, she thought about his mother. Kailey Davids was the kind of woman Susannah had always dreamed of being: strong, effective, dedicated. Not a person who'd lie to the man she loved, or pretend to be something she wasn't in order to win a competition.

Susannah suffered a pang of guilt as she thought about Kailey's virtues. It had been clear to her from the first time Kailey had shown up in the nursery that she was camera shy. Yet Susannah had taken a quick shot of her later in the day without the other woman even being aware of it. Kailey had run into a handsome Eurasian man in front of the nursery, and as they hugged, her face showed such joy that Susannah couldn't stop herself from snapping the picture. She had sworn to herself she'd never sneak a picture again, but at that moment the woman looked so radiant, her large green eyes glowing, her face absent of makeup but beautiful in the afternoon light. Now Susannah knew that the man was Jean-Paul Lassier, the man Kailey lived with.

Soon after that, Susannah had learned about Kailey's campaign against the Hawkes brand baby formula. From what Susannah could tell, it seemed the campaign was wreaking havoc.

Well, that wasn't what she was here to cover, although it was an interesting counterpoint to the charitable side of the Hawkes Corporation from which she herself was benefiting. Cameron had been very nice to her, yet the literature lying around the nursery indicated that his business practices left something to be desired.

Daniel sighed in his sleep. He was so adorable it made all her other thoughts seem boring. Susannah couldn't take her eyes off him as he stirred, moving his lips in and out, then opening and closing his eyes quickly. She began to hum, although lullabies eluded her. Instead she softly launched into a medley of Rodgers and Hammerstein, beginning with *Oklahoma!* and segueing neatly into *Carousel.* She knew how silly it was, singing about ranchers and clambakes to a baby, but he seemed to like it, even smiling slightly as he once again edged into sleep.

Kailey was breathless as she peered into the nursery. She knew she was late, but she never expected to find Susannah Holland holding Daniel. It was disconcerting, watching the lovely young woman singing to her baby. All this time she'd been avoiding her, wishing to be as far as possible from Susannah's ever-present camera. The fact that Susannah came directly from the Hawkes Corporation made Kailey shy away from her all the more. Yet here the girl was, patient and serene, treating Daniel as sweetly as she might a child of her own.

Well, I can't stand here all day, Kailey realized, finally entering the small building.

"Thank you for looking after my son, Miss Holland. I hope he hasn't been too much trouble," Kailey said as she gathered the baby into her arms and began to walk away.

Susannah wasn't about to let her leave. Here they were, finally alone. At least she could try to draw out the reticent Kailey. "Actually, I loved every minute of it. He's an enchanting baby."

"Thank you."

Kailey smiled at the compliment and moved off once more. To her consternation, Susannah started walking alongside her, out of the nursery toward the medical headquarters.

Susannah took a deep breath. "Daniel doesn't look much like you," she offered, immediately realizing how stupid it must have sounded.

But Kailey didn't seem offended. "Actually, I adopted him. Both his parents died at the hands of the Khmer Rouge."

"How awful," Susannah said, horrified. She was embarrassed by how little she knew about the political upheavals of the people she was photographing. "I'm sorry to be so ignorant, but I didn't have much of a chance to study the countries I'm visiting before I left on the tour."

Kailey saw real interest in the young woman's eyes, and quickly offered a brief explanation of how so many Cambodians ended up refugees in Thailand. But as she came to present-day issues, she couldn't keep her bitterness out of her voice. Angrily, she described the formula price gouging and false promotion campaign promulgated by the Hawkes Corporation.

Susannah was stunned. This was much worse than what she had gleaned from skimming through the literature the day before.

"Does Cameron Hawkes himself really know about this? He didn't seem like the kind of person who'd let it happen."

Kailey was careful to contain her emotion. "Oh, he knows all right. He's been sent about ten thousand letters addressed to him personally, not to mention at least a score of articles on the subject in the last month or so."

Susannah felt outraged. What kind of man was Cameron Hawkes, anyway? Sickened, she remembered Evan's muttered comments about Cameron, the look of disgust on his face whenever he encountered his stepfather. She recalled Evan's warning her about him. So Evan had been right after all. What an idiot I am, she chided herself, so busy with the competition I didn't even see what was right smack in front of me!

Kailey realized from the expression on Susannah's face that the girl had known nothing of the real Cameron Hawkes. She felt protective somehow, as if Susannah needed to be armed, and as soon as possible. She tried to say it gently.

"Listen, Miss Holland . . ."

"Susannah, please."

"Okay, Susannah. Cameron Hawkes was very nice to you, I'm sure, but you have to be careful around him. He's a very dangerous man. Please believe me. People around him are apt to get hurt in ways they never imagined."

I wonder how she knows so much about him, Susannah thought as she listened closely. Yet she didn't doubt the truth of Kailey's perception; it was too close to the portrait painted by Evan. Assuming what she says is true, Susannah mused, I ought to take advantage of being here and record what's going on. There was one thing she could do right away: earmark those rolls of film for Olivia. This was the kind of thing the girl would want to do something about.

Kailey couldn't believe she was being so open about Cameron. But she couldn't help it. This girl was bright and lovely. Kailey couldn't bear to think of her hurt. I'm being crazy, she thought, saying all this. For so many years I've hidden the truth from everyone, and now I'm practically spilling my guts — and to a photojournalist, Cameron's employee, of all people.

"Susannah." She knew she was acting against her better judgment, but she couldn't stop herself. "Come and have dinner with Jean-Paul and me. He'll have a lot to tell you about the situation here. In fact, he'll have a lot of information on all the stops you'll be making."

Susannah beamed. "I'd love to. I'll watch Daniel while you cook. You know, I've never even *held* a baby so little before." Susannah's eyes sparkled as she chattered on.

Kailey felt oddly touched. There was something about this girl. Something that reminded her of . . . well, she wasn't exactly sure what it reminded her of.

"The photo lab asked me to drop these off, Ms. Hawkes."

"Thanks, Ricky."

Olivia picked up the interoffice envelope the mailboy had just placed on her desk. She was curious to discover what Susannah Holland would be sending to her in a package marked "Confidential." Usually, Olivia knew, the Forum photographers mailed their film back. But two Hawkes publicity people had gone over to Thailand, and met up with Susannah, so she had given her most recent rolls of film directly to them, asking that four of the rolls go straight to Olivia. As soon as she'd received them, Olivia had immediately sent them to the art department to be developed.

Hurriedly, she pulled out the prints. Susannah was shooting in and around a camp of Cambodian refugees run by the United Nations. The photographs showed mothers and their children, malnourished, diseased, misery in their eyes. Some of the mothers were feeding their children from bottles — no doubt filled with

Hawkes formula sold under the Butterfly label and mixed with
the impure local water. Several of the women held up their children, pathetically thin, their skin marred by scabs. The photos
were heartbreaking. There was one picture that seemed oddly out
of place, a shot of a pretty American woman embracing a tall,
dark-haired man whose back was to the camera. The look on her
face, the way the two people fit together, made their love for each
other clear. But the rest of the photos documented all too painfully
the unrelenting suffering of the camp's inhabitants. Going from
one to the next, Olivia could practically smell the stench of sickness
and death.

She didn't waste any time. Pictures in hand, she hurried to
her father's office, insisting to Marianne that she had to see Cameron at once. He was alone, reading some papers. He looked up,
displeased at the interruption. Olivia didn't bother to apologize.

"Just look at these, Dad." She set the pictures down in front
of him, flipping through them quickly before he could refuse her
request. "These are from Susannah, pictures of the Thai camps.
Our formula is making these children sick. Just *look*."

"Dear God, Olivia," Cameron began in exasperation, giving
an unwilling glance at the photos on his desk, "if I have to listen
to one more — "

Olivia was startled when he stopped in mid-sentence. She
turned to look at him, but he was staring down at the photographs,
his face ashen. Well, good, she thought. Finally, something had
reached him.

"We've got to stop," she urged him.

Her father seemed to be struggling. For a second, Olivia
thought he might be ill, maybe having a heart attack.

"Dad, are you all right?" she asked anxiously, putting a hand
on his shoulder.

His voice was quiet. "I'm fine."

"Oh, I was worried." Olivia paused, surprised at how upset
he seemed.

Cameron appeared to regain control, drawing himself up in
his chair. "I will not entertain another word about this matter

from you. Leave these with me — I can't imagine how you got them in the first place."

Olivia was confused by the sudden change in his mood. "They came — " she began.

Her father interrupted. "This entire thing is none of your damn business. The subject is closed."

Olivia stared at him. For a moment, she believed that he was moved by the plight of these people. But it didn't matter to him at all.

"I don't understand you," she shouted. "You don't care what you do or who you hurt. It's wrong for the company, it's wrong for these people. None of it seems to make any difference to you."

"The day I need advice from you, I'll ask for it," Cameron informed her coldly.

"You *do* need my advice. You're affecting people's lives. It's not as if you need the money. There's a lot more at stake here."

"Olivia, you're wasting my time." Cameron regarded her with distaste. "If you could apply your mind to something really interesting, perhaps you could make some friends your own age and stop chasing after me." He returned his attention back to the work on his desk without another word.

Olivia paled, astounded by his cruelty. But her father didn't even notice, once again completely absorbed in what he was doing.

She walked to the door, standing there as he continued to ignore her. It all felt so familiar. Not just the way he treated her at work. It was how he'd acted all her life. She felt a flush of embarrassment as she remembered waiting for him when she was little, standing by the front door of the Bedford house for hours late Friday afternoons. When he finally got home, he would sweep past her, barely noticing she was there.

It was no different when Cameron deigned to approach her. She thought of that awful night her mother was too sick to accompany him to the huge banquet at the Plaza. There she was, sixteen years old, alone in the center of the dais, while he methodically worked the room. When he finally spoke to her, it was to tell her the car was waiting. She recalled only too well apologizing as they were driven back to the apartment. *Daddy, I'm sorry. I just couldn't think of anything to say to those people.* She could still see him perfectly, looking out the car window. *It doesn't matter,* he'd responded without even turning his head. She'd thought he was being sympathetic, but now she understood so clearly: it really *hadn't* mattered. He was genuinely indifferent to her. Why hadn't she ever grasped that?

She walked out of the room, and back to her office. Sinking into her chair, she looked around at the photos on her wall of the original day-care center. It was so simple really. She was wasting her time. He had never been the father she needed, and he never would be. She should have been living her own life, the life any other nineteen-year-old would live. She would look for another job; surely some company would appreciate her. Maybe she would even think about going to college. And she would move out, get a place of her own.

She felt relieved at her decisions, but she wished there was someone around to talk to about all this. Perhaps her mother was home. She reached for the phone, lifting the receiver, then putting it down. Tish had every right to be furious with her. Here her mother was, sober, alone, making her way without Cameron, and where had her daughter been all this time?

It made Olivia cringe to think about all those times she had secretly sided with her father as he criticized his wife. What a fool I am, she thought. I'm going to make it up to her. And I'm going to make a few things up to myself.

Chapter 29

Cameron took a sip of Scotch and set the heavy crystal glass back down on the table beside him. It was nearly two in the morning, and the apartment was quiet, empty except for one of the maids asleep in her room. Seated in an armchair, his legs up on an ottoman, Cameron held Susannah's photographs in his lap. Slowly, he picked them up and leafed through them until he came to the one of her.

Kailey. There was no question about it. When Olivia had initially shown him the pictures that morning, he'd recognized her immediately. Then he'd decided he was mistaken; it was impossible. But as soon as Olivia had left his office, he'd grabbed them, hastily searching for the one he'd seen. When he'd found it, he sat there, immobilized. His first reaction had been correct. The woman in the picture was unquestionably his first wife, still alive. Just then, his secretary had buzzed him about a meeting, and he'd tossed the pictures in his briefcase to look at later. At home.

Finally, he was alone, with no one to disturb him. He examined the shot of her carefully. Incredible, there she was after all these years. She looked a little older, he saw, but not very much. Her dark hair was full and shining, her face still beautiful — maybe even more so. Maturity had actually improved her looks, he saw. He detected a self-confidence that had never been there in their time together.

Susannah had taken this picture, although Kailey obviously didn't realize she was being photographed. But Kailey had to have been aware an American photographer was right nearby. Did they know each other? Had they spoken?

Cameron's mind raced. Could Susannah know that Kailey had been his wife? And, worse, had Kailey told her anything about him, about what he'd done years before? What if there was some connection between Susannah and Kailey? Maybe Susannah really *was* Dorrie Gordon's daughter, and had lied about *not* being related to him because she was in cahoots with Kailey somehow. Jesus, this was an impossible tangle. His face flushed with anger, he reached for his Scotch.

What a mistake to let Susannah go on that trip. It was a miscalculation, a hasty decision made to impress Lionel Shea. If it hadn't been for that, he would have thrown Susannah out and that would have been the end of it. He cursed, unable to see how the pieces of this puzzle fit together.

Cameron got up and restlessly roamed the silent apartment, his agitation growing. This protest in Thailand was becoming far worse than he'd estimated. It was going to affect his takeover of Awareness Industries, he knew that. The problem was already having an impact on the public perception of him, which would probably lead to Lionel's calling off the deal. He had already questioned Cameron about the situation, and gone away with a sour expression on his face as Cameron tried to find a graceful way to explain. He'd stopped the formula shipments to Bangkok, but it was too late to contain the damage that had already been done.

On top of everything, his first wife was in Thailand, right in the midst of it all. Suddenly, he stopped, so angry he had to grip the edge of a table for a moment. She had to be the one who'd started the whole campaign against the formula. Of course. She'd been waiting all these years for the right opening to take revenge. By ruining his public image, she would bring him to his knees. Undoubtedly, her next move would be to expose him as the man responsible for the death of an infant by LSD poisoning years before. That was her trump card. She was just waiting for the right time to play it.

And did he have anyone here to help him, to support him when he needed it, when he was under siege? After all he'd done for them, his entire family had deserted him. Tish, the ungrateful drunken bitch, was long gone without a word. Only a saint would have put up with her the way he did. And Olivia had told him she was leaving as well; tonight she was sleeping out at Bedford, but she would come by the Manhattan apartment tomorrow to get her things. That was it. No gratitude from either one. Hell, he had a stepson, too, and some men could have expected a little support from that corner. But not from Evan. He'd never appreciated that it was Cameron's sweat that paid for his upbringing and fancy Ivy League education; he'd been a thankless brat as a child, and he'd never changed. There was no one, not a soul there when it was time to pay him back for his hard work and effort on their behalf.

Cameron went back to the living-room bar and poured himself another hefty Scotch.

"Screw them all," he muttered, lifting the glass.

Despite everything, Sister Marie Frances was enjoying the taxi ride from Kennedy Airport into Manhattan. It had been so many years since she'd been back East—she couldn't even remember when the last time was—and there were so many changes in the

Manhattan skyline. Her eyesight wasn't what it used to be, either, and she squinted as she gazed out the dirty taxi window, not wanting to miss anything. Still, even as she marveled at the sights before her, the memory of why she had come pricked at her conscience. She shouldn't forget that under happier circumstances, she wouldn't be here.

It wasn't right for her to lie to that detective, she knew that. But it had been so frightening, having that man appear out of the blue at her church, questioning her about the little baby that Sister Marie had given to the orphanage twenty-five years before. The detective seemed to have some inkling that she was connected, and she wondered how he found that out. But he couldn't have known much, because when she told him there must be some mistake, he accepted her word and that was the end of it.

It wasn't the end of it for Sister Marie. She couldn't sleep, thinking about the conversation she and the detective had had. He told her he was trying to locate the girl — now a woman — for her father, a man named Cameron Hawkes, who had never given up loving her and looking for her. His description of this father had been of someone caring and kind, desperate to find his child. How different from the way the baby's mother had described her husband on that day years before. Sister Marie wondered whether the mother had been lying. Maybe the father had changed. Perhaps there was another explanation altogether. But if the father was in fact a good, kind man, then she had made a terrible mistake in depriving the little girl of her parent. There wasn't anything she could do to take back the past, but she could try to set things right now. That was why she had come to New York, to find the father and tell him the truth face to face.

The taxi pulled up in front of a tall building. A doorman in a uniform with gold braiding hurried out to the curb to open the car door for her. Sister Marie got out, noting the opulence of the neighborhood, momentarily intimidated by the wealth surrounding her. Then she steeled herself and addressed the doorman.

"In which apartment would I find a Mr. Cameron Hawkes, please?"

Upstairs, as the maid showed her into the study, Sister Marie tried to hide her awe at the magnificent home of this Mr. Hawkes. She was horrified at the thought that she had relegated a child to the brutal life of an orphan who might have had both a loving father and all the opportunities this wealth could have afforded her. She wondered how she could ever be forgiven for such an error, for altering a life when she had no right to interfere. She sat down heavily in a chair, her agitation growing.

Cameron Hawkes entered the room a moment later. Sister Marie saw he was a handsome man, although he looked tired, dark rings beneath his eyes.

"Oh, Mr. Hawkes," Sister Marie burst out. "I'm so sorry, so very sorry."

He looked at her questioningly. "I don't understand. My maid told me you wanted to talk to me about something. Are you collecting for a charity?"

Sister Marie fell silent. For all his wealth, she had made this man poor, depriving him of the love of a daughter. Haltingly, she began to speak. Then the words came faster, and the story poured out, how the lovely young woman had come to her church and asked her to watch the baby for just a short time, how she had heard on the radio about the car accident, how she had taken it as a sign from God that the baby had been left in her care.

There was silence in the room after she finished. She waited, knowing he would need some time to digest all this. But then he had simply nodded and smiled graciously.

"I want to thank you for coming here in person and explaining all this to me," he said.

Sister Marie was vastly relieved by his reaction, but surprised at the same time. She had expected shock, anger, maybe tears. "I can't even begin to say how terrible I feel about this," she said.

His tone was reassuring. "You did what you thought was best. I don't blame you."

"Will this information help you to find your daughter?"

He smiled again. "You can't imagine how valuable it is. Now, don't let me keep you. I'll have the maid call downstairs to get you a cab."

Startled, Sister Marie realized that she was being dismissed.

She gazed at Cameron Hawkes, uncertain what to make of this man. It had been wrong to hide the truth from him for so long. But now she wasn't sure that it had been any wiser to tell him after all.

The door closed behind the nun. It was incredible, Cameron thought. Susannah had said she didn't know anything about her past prior to being left at that orphanage. That meant she didn't know that the reason she ended up there was because this nun had kept her from being killed when Kailey's car went over the cliff.

And she didn't know that she was actually his daughter. Bonnie. She had survived. And so had Kailey.

But someone had died in the car. He combed his brain, wondering who it could have been. It had been so many years ago. Then he dimly remembered getting a letter from Norway inquiring about that au pair, the one whom he had caught stealing. He had had a secretary reply that he had fired her and had no idea where she was. Of course — it made perfect sense. Kailey had taken her along when she left the house that day. She must have been the one in the car. Amazing. Susannah had tried to con him into thinking she was his illegitimate child, when she really was his daughter. The girl didn't begin to know what she had on him.

He rubbed his eyes tiredly. He hadn't been sleeping at night, furious over a situation he saw spinning out of his control, wondering how he could save himself. Now it was even worse. Kailey and his daughter were alive and together in Thailand.

His anger rose. Suddenly, Cameron was filled with new resolve. He wouldn't just sit there and wait for the boom to be lowered on him. Hell, he hadn't gotten where he was that way. He would seize control again, not just lie back and let them destroy him. But there was no one he could trust to handle this. He would have to go to Thailand and deal with it himself.

Chapter 30

Tish wasn't surprised that the sound of the front door being opened brought the maid scurrying to see who was coming into the apartment.

"It's just me, Alice, don't worry," Tish said, reassuringly, as she put the key back in her purse and entered.

"Yes, Mrs. Hawkes," Alice said politely.

Tish could guess that the household staff in both Manhattan and Bedford were intrigued to know whether Mrs. Hawkes had really left her husband for good this time, especially considering the miserable failure of her first attempt years before. But she said nothing more to Alice, only smiling briefly as she walked off toward her bedroom. Even knowing that Cameron wasn't around couldn't keep her from feeling tense as she moved through the apartment. But this was the last time she would come here. Once she got the remainder of her personal papers today, she would be free of him forever. She quickened her pace. Funny, she thought. After spending so many years with him in this apartment, she could barely stand to be in the place for another minute.

It didn't matter, though. She was off to a new life. How lucky I am, she reflected, having so many people there for me. Bibi had been the catalyst, the one who had started her in the right direction. Tish would always be grateful to her. As busy as Bibi was, she called Tish nearly every day from the set of her new movie to see how she was doing and give her a few words of encouragement.

But it was her children, Evan and Olivia, who had come through for her in a way she never expected. Evan had helped her get settled in a new apartment, taking care of all the arrangements, assuming responsibility for the rent and depositing a generous sum of money into a bank account for her so she wouldn't have to worry about finances. Despite his own responsibilities, he still made time to visit nearly every other day, the two of them going out for walks, having lunch, taking in a movie. Now that she was sober, she was able to talk with him, really listen to what he had to say. There was no more hiding or pretending that things were all right; the two of them were finally opening up about the pain of the past. Just the day before they had gone for a stroll along Riverside Drive, and Evan told her just how awful her marriage to Cameron had been for him.

"I thought I was doing the right thing for you and your sister by staying with him," Tish said sadly. "Of course, now I understand how destructive it was for all three of us. But I wanted to keep you safe, and I couldn't provide for you alone. I tried and I failed."

Evan looked at his mother fondly. "You don't know how proud I was of you when you opened that tearoom."

"You were?" Tish was surprised. "I didn't think you gave it much thought. You were busy, off at college."

"Are you kidding? I rooted for you like crazy. Most people

wouldn't even have had the guts to try. I hated to see you go back to him, but you *weren't* a failure."

"Thank you for saying that," Tish said, touched.

"Besides," Evan went on, "by then, I was at school, out of his reach. It was when I was younger that he did the damage."

"After your father, that was quite a choice I made the second time, wasn't it?" Tish said regretfully.

Evan smiled. "I suppose you might have looked just a *little* bit further."

They both laughed.

Tish pulled open the drawer to her dressing table, reaching far into it to retrieve her passport. It was a blessing, having this time with Evan, finally facing the truth about things. But they had always had a special sort of bond. Olivia had surprised her even more. Having moved out of her father's house, she'd called Tish one day, asking if they could meet for lunch. Tish was so relieved to see the girl was ready to face the facts about Cameron, and get on with her life. But she and Olivia had drifted so far apart over the years. Now they would have to work hard to get acquainted all over again. Tish tried not to berate herself for having missed so much of Olivia's life, spending over a decade fogged in by alcohol and pills. The past couldn't be changed; what was important was the future between them. One day at a time. Tish was encouraging Olivia to speak up about the family, no matter how much it hurt Tish to listen. My poor children, she thought guiltily. God forgive me. Miraculously, the two of them seemed to have forgiven her.

Even so, Tish knew that she was far from done with the work she had to do on herself. Between Bibi and AA, she had hung on to her sobriety, but there were nights she didn't think she could make it another minute without a drink, or at least a pill to let her escape into sleep. She had discussed it with Bibi and her children, and they all agreed that she shouldn't risk her hard-won progress; tomorrow she was checking into a treatment center. It would be hard on her pride, but it was too late to worry about things like that anymore. Besides, she thought wryly, what could a woman who spent twenty years with Cameron Hawkes know about pride? She should thank her lucky stars, she reflected, that her children had such faith in her.

Actually, she mused, the truly incredible thing was that she really had Susannah Holland to thank for all this. Susannah was the one who had brought Bibi to her, who—for whatever reason—had cared enough to do something. Tish recalled with embarrassment her phony politeness toward Susannah during their early meetings, how downright rude she had been later on. Even if Susannah truly loved her son, she hadn't had to take on Tish's problems, too. As far as Tish was concerned, it didn't matter whether Susannah was who she claimed to be. Tish owed her a debt of thanks.

It took nearly half an hour to gather everything, but finally Tish was done. As she headed back out to leave, she saw Cameron's secretary leaning over the desk in his study.

"Mrs. Hawkes—hello, there, how nice to see you."

Tish couldn't imagine why Cameron would have sent her to his home.

"Hello, Marianne." She entered the room. "What are you doing here?"

The secretary smiled. "In the rush to leave, Mr. Hawkes left some files that we need at the office. He called from the airport to tell me to pick them up." She was suddenly embarrassed. "I hope you don't mind—I didn't mean to disturb you."

"No, not at all," Tish replied. "The rush to leave for where?"

Marianne looked surprised. "Thailand, of course. I certainly hope he can do something about what's going on over there."

Tish kept her face impassive. The secretary apparently was unaware that she and Cameron were no longer living together. "We didn't discuss it much. Can you fill me in a little?"

"There've been some demonstrations, something to do with our powdered formula. No violence yet, but I know everybody's concerned about that."

Tish smiled. "I'm certain Mr. Hawkes will take care of it. Now, if you'll excuse me. Nice to see you."

She hurried back to the bedroom and picked up the telephone, dialing Evan's number. Relieved to find him home, she quickly relayed to him what Marianne had said.

"It must be a lot worse than anybody knows if Cameron went there personally," Evan ventured.

"I'm also thinking of Susannah," Tish said. "When she was first selected, I remember your telling me some of the places she was going. Wasn't Thailand on her list? Has she called or written you about this?"

There was silence.

"Evan?" Tish prodded.

"We're not in touch," he said brusquely.

Tish was taken aback. "What? You never told me that."

"You've had enough on your mind."

"Honey, what happened?"

"She lied about being Cameron's daughter. It was just a hoax so she could get into the Forum."

Tish digested this for a moment. "But—all that to take pictures?"

"She said she needed the award money for a woman who was sick and dying." Evan paused. "Someone she loved."

Tish felt a sudden flash of identification with the woman, whoever she might be. She herself had been dying, slowly drowning in alcohol. And Susannah had helped her.

"I suppose I should be outraged," she said, "but the strange part is, I think that's a wonderful thing to do."

Evan's hurt was apparent behind his anger. "I really loved her—and I thought *I* was someone she loved too. I always suspected she'd made the story up, but she didn't trust me enough to tell me the truth. Then she goes off for a year and sends me a lousy letter to explain. I haven't heard another word from her."

"Have you tried to contact her?"

"Of course not."

"Maybe she's afraid to get in touch with you. Afraid you're angry at her."

Evan's voice rose to a shout. "Damn right I'm angry. Why shouldn't I be?"

Tish answered quietly. "Because you love her."

The hurt came back into her son's voice. "But it seems she doesn't feel the same."

"Yes, she does," Tish said. "She loves you very much. Even *I* could see how the two of you felt about each other — anyone could. And when two people have that, it's not something you let slip away so easily."

Evan was quiet.

"Your father and I were that way, Evan. No matter what happened, I never would have let Bill get away from me. I would have fought with everything I had to keep us together." Tish spoke sadly. "Death was the only thing I couldn't fight for him."

She paused, remembering. Then the resolve came back into her voice. "And you should fight for Susannah."

Evan was quiet for a moment, thinking about everything she had said.

"Jesus," he suddenly said in alarm, "if she's over in Thailand . . . She may not be related to Cameron, but she represents his company. If there's trouble, she'd be a perfect target."

"Is she there right now?" Tish asked.

"I don't know, but I'm going to call the Forum people and find out." Evan paused. "Thanks, Mom. Thank you very much."

Tish smiled. After so many years of leaning on her son, of depending on him to help her, had she finally done something to help him?

"Don't thank me, Evan. Just go after what you want."

Susannah slowly made her way along the path, the sun beating down on her back. There was no letup to the intense heat, and she had quickly discovered that hurrying only resulted in fatigue. Besides, she thought grimly, what was the rush; she had plenty of time to take pictures, because these people weren't going anywhere. They were trapped.

Shaking her head, she reflected how completely unprepared she had been for the overwhelming tragedy of the camps. And now that she understood she felt so useless, just standing around taking photographs. She wished she knew how to be of some genuine help. But Kailey and Jean-Paul had assured her that getting her photographs back to the States was the most important thing she could do. She only hoped those rolls of film had reached Olivia; Susannah was certain Olivia would be prompted to take some action on the formula. But even Kailey Davids couldn't come up with an answer to the bigger problems. Even she only struggled along, doing whatever she could to change things a little at a time.

Meeting Kailey had been the one bright light here amid so much darkness. Susannah admired her in so many ways, her selflessness, her warmth and devotion toward these people. Yet she was also down-to-earth, and when she and Jean-Paul invited Susannah for dinner, the three of them would stay up talking and laughing late into the small hours. Susannah loved those dinners. Kailey would cook exotic dishes with strange spices that Susannah had never tasted before. They would sit around a wooden table in the hut that served as their home, eating, drinking wine, finding a small escape from the terrible sadness that surrounded them during the day.

Susannah felt a powerful connection to Kailey; once the ice had been broken and they had begun to talk, it seemed as if they were old friends. She felt she could confide in Kailey, tell her anything. And Susannah loved to watch her with Daniel. She held the baby so tenderly, as if he were a gift, laughing with him and matching his joyful gurgles with so much love on her face. I hope I can be as good a mother as she is, Susannah thought as she observed them.

The only painful part was the hurt in Susannah's heart when she watched Kailey and Jean-Paul together. Their devotion to each other, the caring in every word they spoke made Susannah long so deeply for Evan. He had spoken to her that way, had stroked her hair the way Jean-Paul stroked Kailey's, put his arm around her with the same caring protectiveness Jean-Paul unconsciously displayed for Kailey. Susannah refused to let the pangs of jealousy at their happiness interfere with their friendship, but in bed at night she couldn't stop the pain from washing over her.

Her hair was tied up in a knot, the loose tendrils that had escaped hot and sticky against her neck. She felt as if she had dust in every pore of her body. Today, she had photographed a group of teenagers in the camp, and the few words of their stories that she managed to get translated into English had been unbearable — parents killed before their eyes, little sisters and brothers dead from malnutrition and disease.

Tiredly, she ran her hand across her forehead. She was approaching the simple wooden building that housed visitors, a structure meant to be temporary like everything else here. There were four rooms inside, each furnished with a cot and an old wooden cabinet. There was no electricity or indoor plumbing, and Susannah decided that if she could have anything in the world right now, she would undoubtedly choose a hot bath as the most luxurious treat imaginable. She was the only visitor at the camp, so the other rooms were unoccupied, her rented car the only one out front.

Today, however, she saw that she had company: a Jeep had been parked next to her car. She wondered whose it was, pleased by the prospect of having someone to talk with. Being so submerged in the situation here, she had no idea what was going on in the outside world. She would grab a washcloth and a basin of water to clean her face off, and when she was a bit more presentable, introduce herself to the other visitor.

Opening the door to her room, Susannah stopped, rooted to the spot.

"Oh, my God," she whispered.

Evan stood in the middle of the room facing her. Slowly, a smile spread across his face.

"I was in the neighborhood . . ."

"Oh, Evan." She started to laugh at the absurdity of what he had said, then stopped short. "But what are you doing here?"

"My mother told me about the trouble. I couldn't just sit around, doing nothing."

He had come to her, had traveled around the world to find her. "I thought you'd never want to speak to me again," she said quietly.

"Susannah," he said, shaking his head. "I don't understand.

Don't you know me at all by now? Why couldn't you tell me the truth in person?"

"I knew how angry you'd be when you found out I'd lied," she said slowly. "I just couldn't face it, seeing you hate me."

"Jesus," he exploded in frustration, "I assumed you were lying all along. I never really believed that story. But it didn't make any difference to me, couldn't you see that?"

Susannah stared at him, stunned.

He came closer. "I fell in love with *you*, not some made-up character you were pretending to be. I didn't give a damn about that."

"Oh, God, Evan, I'm so sorry for what I put you through. All of you."

"Susannah, sweetheart." In two long strides he was beside her, putting his arms around her to hold her close. "I love you."

She held tight to him. "I love you, too. More than anything on earth."

They stood there, locked in a silent embrace, reclaiming each other. Susannah buried her face in his neck. The worst had happened but he still wanted her. Raising her eyes to meet his, she whispered, "Thank you."

When they broke apart, Evan's tone suddenly grew serious. "We need to talk about the trouble here, about Cameron."

She nodded. "It shocked me at first, finding out he was behind all that."

Evan took a step back. "You don't know what Cameron's really like."

"Unfortunately, I'm beginning to find out," she replied. "I realize there were so many signs I missed."

"He's an expert at hiding the truth about himself. I'm surprised you picked up any of it."

"I wanted to believe you were one big, happy family, and he was the devoted father." She looked ashamed. "I guess I was too busy keeping up my own charade to see what was right in front of me."

Evan reached out to take her hand. "You know, you could

be in trouble here if the demonstrations turn violent. You're associated with Hawkes."

Susannah was startled. "I never thought of it that way. I haven't felt as if I was in any danger."

He smiled, love in his eyes. "Well, I'm going to make sure you stay that way. I'm not leaving until I see you safely to your next stop."

Susannah's eyes lit up. "Are you really staying with me for a while?" She kissed him again.

"And I may see you safely on your way to the *next* stop as well."

"Are you serious?" she asked happily.

"Would you mind, if I promise not to get in the way?"

"I work during the day, so we can have the evenings together." She hesitated. "I don't want to get greedy with my good fortune, but how long do you think you can stay with me?"

"I can't take too much time," he said. "But I'll hang around for as long as I can manage."

She put her hands on his shoulders and brought her face close to his. "Would you mind if I told you again how much I love you?"

"Susannah," Evan said, putting his arms around her, "I hope you'll be telling me that for the rest of your life."

Chapter 31

Kailey heard the sounds of the baby crying before she even entered the nursery. That's Daniel, she thought, surprised at the vehemence of the squeals. He was usually a quiet baby, happy to lie alone in his crib playing with his stuffed animals when she and Jean-Paul needed a few minutes to themselves. Here in the camp nursery, Eang Meas, the woman who usually looked after him, had often mentioned how little trouble he was to care for. It was too bad he'd picked today to change his stripes, she thought, feeling her fatigue. She'd spent a long day with Susannah Holland at another camp nearby.

As Kailey entered, she saw Eang Meas walking up and down, her head bent over the screaming infant she was trying to comfort.

"Looks like my son has big plans to keep us up tonight," Kailey said with a smile.

Eang Meas turned to her, confusion on her face. The baby she was holding wasn't her son at all. "But Kailey, your uncle picked up Daniel hours ago."

"My uncle?" Kailey echoed. "What do you mean?"

"You sent your uncle to pick up Daniel," Eang Meas said stubbornly.

Kailey stared at the other woman, a sense of uneasiness stealing over her. She couldn't imagine who the man might have been. Eang Meas would never have mistaken Jean-Paul for anyone else.

"What did he look like?" she asked.

Eang Meas could see something was wrong. She drew herself up and spoke sharply to cover her fears.

"He is your uncle, tall and handsome. He looks like you. He is your uncle."

Kailey didn't respond to the challenge in Eang Meas's tone. She was trying to make sense of the words. A man had taken Daniel. A tall Caucasian man had taken her son. Kailey began to shake. It was as if time had skipped back twenty-five years. To Bonnie. To Cameron.

"You gave Daniel to a strange man?" she cried. "How could you let him go?"

"I didn't let him go. Your uncle took him and brought him back to your house." The woman wouldn't give an inch.

"Did he say that, that he was going back to my house?"

What had he said? It had been so busy in the nursery this afternoon, Eang Meas couldn't even remember. " 'I'll see her later,' " she recalled slowly. " 'I'll see her at home.' Yes, that's what he said, 'I'll see her at home.' "

Realizing it was useless to ask any more questions, Kailey wheeled around and ran out the door. Daniel had to be at home. As she ran along the path to her house, the image of Nina came into her mind, a picture Kailey hadn't allowed herself to think about for many years. Stop it, she told herself. Stop it. Her panic escalating, she felt her heart in her throat by the time she reached home.

"Daniel," she screamed as she entered, as if the infant might somehow answer.

The hut was dark and quiet. There was no sign of anyone having been there, and apparently nothing had been touched in the small section they laughingly called the living room. Kailey quickly glanced into her bedroom, then walked more slowly to the baby's tiny room. At first she saw nothing out of the ordinary. Then she leaned over the crib. Right in the middle of the bunny print sheets lay a small white envelope, the words "Kailey Hawkes" written on the outside.

"Oh my God," she breathed. No one here knew her as "Hawkes." She picked the envelope up. It was his handwriting, of course, there was no mistaking it. Frantically, she tore open the envelope. The color drained from her face as she read the message inside.

Meet me. Enclosed was a UN map of the area, with a temple two miles east of Site 14 circled in red.

Kailey grabbed at the bars of the crib as the full significance of the message took hold. Somehow her husband had found her here. Despite all her efforts over the years, despite her belief that she had finally found a safe haven with Jean-Paul, Cameron had found her anyway. And he had taken Daniel. It was happening all over again.

She left her house immediately. Daniel, she had to find Daniel. That was her only thought as she ran toward her car. She knew the place Cameron had picked, a once-magnificent Buddhist temple that had been riddled with bullet holes since the Khmers entered the territory. Now it was abandoned. She drove as fast as she dared, too frightened to think. There was the white building edged in gold up ahead. Sharply, she pulled the car over and jumped out. Not again, please God, she whispered, starting to run. Suddenly, she came to a dead halt. She knew that the area around the temple had been seeded with land mines. She'd treated several people who'd been injured here, one of whom had lost both legs; two other people had been killed at this spot only last week. Without thinking she had run right into the middle of it, halfway to the temple's gate. It was incredible that she hadn't been blown up.

But her baby was inside that temple. She had to get to him.

She stood there, terrified. Her clothes were sticking to her in the heat of the day. It was so hot, she thought, so very hot. Just like that other day in California. For a minute, she shut her eyes tightly, the horror overwhelming her. When she opened them again, she took a deep breath. Daniel might still be alive. She scanned the ground before her, not knowing where to step next. There was no way to tell.

She took a step forward, holding her breath, waiting for the explosion. Silence.

"Okay," she murmured to reassure herself, her face set with determination. "Okay, Daniel, Mommy's coming."

Another tentative step. The only sound was a bird chirping nearby. "Right, here we come," she said firmly.

She continued to talk aloud to herself, fighting the terror as she slowly moved forward, one step at a time. Sweat ran into her eyes, but she didn't bother to wipe it away. As she got to within a few yards of the intricately carved gate, she could hold back no longer. She ran the rest of the way, gasping as she yanked open the gate and fell inside, panting with relief, amazed that she was still alive. Jumping up, she rushed up the broad steps to the heavy wooden door. Her footsteps echoed on the floor as she tore through the empty building calling out her child's name. There was no sign of Cameron or the baby. She stopped, and tears coursed down her face. I'm such a fool, she thought. Cameron had trapped her. She would never escape. It had been a miracle getting past the land mines on her way in; she could never be that lucky again.

So this is his final revenge, she thought, imagining how pleased Cameron would be by the success of his scheme. How had he even known about this place, she wondered. She allowed herself a small ray of hope. Might Daniel at least be left alive? It was probably too much to wish for, but Cameron could have lured her here, and left Daniel in some safer place. Fervently, she prayed that Cameron had kept the baby out of danger.

She returned to the front of the temple and opened the massive door. Perhaps she couldn't pull off a miracle twice, but for Daniel's sake she had to try. She felt weak as she imagined walking through the field of mines again. But she had no choice. As she tentatively placed her foot on the top step, she saw a car pull up.

The door opened. In the fading light of the day, she saw Cameron Hawkes, silver-haired now, get out of the driver's seat. Her worst nightmare had come true. He was here, right before her.

"Where's my son?" she screamed.

Not stopping to answer, he began to approach the temple. Kailey saw him put his hand in his pocket, as if he were reaching for a gun. So it had come to this. He would kill her himself, shoot her to silence her for good.

She had nothing left to lose anymore. She called out again. "I have a gun. I'll kill you."

Kailey could see the hatred on his face as he stopped at the edge of the road.

"I don't believe so." His tone was low and controlled. Hearing him speak again after so many years made Kailey shiver in fear.

"I'll kill you, I swear it." She hoped he wouldn't sense her terror.

"You can't kill me." Cameron smiled icily. "I'm the father of your child."

Her answer came in an agonized cry. *"The father of my child!* You murdered her twenty-five years ago, you bastard."

Cameron took another step.

"Susannah Holland is your child. *She's* Bonnie."

"Stop it." Kailey's voice was agonized, tears of rage and frustration stinging her eyes. "Bonnie's dead."

"But it's true, my dear." Cameron's tone was almost conversational. "You took that au pair, that girl who worked for us, to California, didn't you?"

Kailey stared out at him, frantically trying to guess what he was leading up to.

He continued without any response from her. "I had a visit from a nun a few days ago," he said pleasantly. "It turns out she was given a baby to watch by a young Norwegian girl in a red sports car, a Jaguar. The girl claimed her husband had hurt her, so after the red car went off the side of a cliff, the nun gave the baby over to an orphanage." He paused. "Surely Susannah's mentioned the Franklin Orphanage since the two of you became such close friends?"

Kailey took in the story piece by piece. She knew Cameron's talent at deception. Had he made this up to torture her further? she wondered, seeing the genuine satisfaction on his face. She thought about Susannah. Then, oddly, the image of her mother came into her mind. Susannah Holland looked so much like Sonia. Why hadn't she noticed that before? The generous mouth, the dark cascade of hair, the blue eyes. Cameron was telling the truth. Suddenly, she knew. But how could it be? Bonnie was Susannah, alive all this time and right here?

Cameron began to advance once again toward the perimeter around the church. Kailey gasped. Dear God, he didn't know about the land mines. But Cameron was the only one who could tell her where Daniel was. She couldn't let him die.

"Go back, Cameron, go back. There are land mines everywhere." She was on the verge of hysteria as he took another step forward.

"Cameron, listen to me," she begged. "Don't move. It's been mined."

He didn't believe her, moving forward with confidence. And she saw the beginning of surprise on his face as his foot hit a trip wire. The deafening blast of the explosion sent her reeling backward as fire and earth shot up toward the sky.

As he approached, Jean-Paul was startled to see that the house was dark. After his twelve-hour shift in the medical quarters, Kailey and Daniel were usually visible through the small windows, rich smells of dinner floating out to him as if in welcome.

"Kailey," he called as he walked toward the bedroom, already pulling his shirt over his head in anticipation of a cool shower. I wonder where they could be, he thought, taking a quick look into Daniel's room. He glanced at his watch. Seven-thirty. Late for her to have the baby out. He debated eating something before getting into the shower, then changed his mind.

Five minutes later, blessedly refreshed by the water, he wrapped a towel around his waist and let the warm air dry him as he combed his hair. This was his favorite part of the day; no more interruptions, no more emergencies, just Kailey and Daniel, the three of them over dinner, a family. He looked again at his watch. Almost eight o'clock now and growing dark outside. Kailey and Daniel were probably still at the nursery, although it was unusual for it to be open this late. He decided to walk over and pick them up.

Eang Meas was stirring some soup in a pot as Jean-Paul entered. As she recognized him, her face tightened in fright, which turned quickly to defiance.

"He went with Kailey's uncle," she said stubbornly before Jean-Paul had even said a word.

Jean-Paul spoke softly. "Could you start at the beginning, Eang Meas? Is there something I should know about Daniel or Kailey?"

"There is nothing to know." The woman stuck her chin out, then turned back to her cooking.

"Have you seen Kailey?" Jean-Paul began to worry. There were no children left in the nursery. What could have happened? His hand jingled the coins in his pocket nervously.

"Was Kailey here already? Did she go somewhere with Daniel?"

Eang Meas wasn't about to be chided by the doctor. She had done everything correctly. *Everything.*

"Kailey spent all day with the American girl, and Daniel went with her uncle. That's all." She turned her back on Jean-Paul again.

That's right, he thought. Kailey was spending the day with Susannah. She was bound to be in the girl's new quarters, the hut she'd been moved to the day before. Relieved, he walked out of the nursery without another word. The hike to Susannah's hut took only a few minutes. Knocking on the door, he could hear voices inside. Everything was fine.

"Hello, Jean-Paul." Susannah greeted him warmly when she saw him standing there. "How nice to get company."

He smiled at her. "I've come to collect my family."

Stepping inside, he looked around expectantly, but was puzzled when he saw only a handsome young man standing near the window.

"This is Evan." Susannah walked over and took his hand as she made the introduction. "Jean-Paul Lassier, Evan Gardiner. I'm glad the two of you are getting to meet."

"Where's Kailey?" Jean-Paul's relief had changed to dismay. "I assumed she was here."

"I haven't seen her in a couple of hours," Susannah explained. "We got home around seven and she went to pick up Daniel."

Susannah had seen Jean-Paul in more than one emergency since she'd arrived at the camp, and nothing had interfered with his even, competent air. Now he was clearly shaken.

"Jean-Paul, what's the matter?"

Jean-Paul tried to contain his fear, but as he described the empty house and Eang Meas's peculiar attitude, he became more and more upset.

"Who's Kailey's uncle?" Susannah asked.

"She has no uncle," Jean-Paul answered.

Evan watched the two with growing concern. Susannah had told him about Kailey's successful drive against the Hawkes baby formula. Could his stepfather actually be here to do Kailey harm? It seemed impossible, and yet . . . without thinking he said the name out loud.

"Cameron Hawkes."

Jean-Paul's attention shot to Evan. "What about Cameron Hawkes?" he asked sharply. "Do you know him?"

Evan was uncertain if he should go on. His instincts told him something was very wrong, and it just might involve Cameron.

"He's my stepfather. It's probably irrelevant, but he's also the owner of the company Kailey's been fighting against. And he's here in Thailand."

Jean-Paul stared at him. Kailey's husband was in Thailand.

How could he have caught up with her? It didn't matter. He had to do something quickly.

"Where is he staying?"

Evan looked apologetic. "I have no idea."

Susannah wasn't sure what was going on, but seeing Jean-Paul's horrified expression, she answered quickly. "The place where I was staying — you know, the visitors' housing. Maybe he's there."

Jean-Paul nodded. That made sense. He ran outside to the camp phone, hurriedly asked the operator to connect him with the VIP building. Susannah and Evan caught up with him as he waited for someone to pick up.

The call was answered on the second ring by the old man who kept the quarters clean for visitors. "Yes, Doctor Lassier. I've been waiting for your call. I was beginning to worry about the baby." The man's voice was querulous, but also frightened.

"You mean Daniel's there?" Jean-Paul asked breathlessly.

"Of course. The gentleman left him here when he went out before. I must go now. You must pick him up."

Jean-Paul breathed deeply in relief as he covered the phone and turned to Susannah and Evan. "Hawkes left Daniel there. He's safe." At least there was that. But Kailey. He had no idea what Cameron could be planning for her.

"Do you know where the man went?" Jean-Paul turned his attention back to the phone.

"No, he did not say."

"Did you see him leave? What direction did he go in?" Jean-Paul asked urgently.

"On the east road, toward the Khmers."

Jean-Paul hung up slowly. "Hawkes is going toward the Khmer camp. I wonder if he knows how dangerous that is."

"My Jeep is around back," said Evan.

Jean-Paul nodded thankfully. They were bound to find Hawkes. And where Hawkes was, Kailey would be. But the baby was alone. "Someone has to stay with Daniel," he said quickly.

If this was really as dangerous as Jean-Paul seemed to think,

Susannah knew that Evan could be of more help against Cameron Hawkes than she could.

"The two of you should go on ahead. I'll walk over and get Daniel. We'll wait for you there."

Jean-Paul embraced Susannah gratefully and Evan kissed her quickly. Then the two men ran toward the Jeep. With Jean-Paul at the wheel, they sped east. At first there was nothing, just the night's growing darkness and the hushed buzz of insects in the heavy shrubbery. Jean-Paul was approaching the unmarked cutoff to the old Buddhist temple when an explosion ripped through the trees, lighting the sky overhead in a deadly display of fireworks. Quickly he veered off the road, then turned the car once again toward the ancient building.

The acrid smell of charred leaves and burning wood filled the air around the stately Buddhist shrine, but whatever fire there had been was reduced to burning embers. Jean-Paul pulled over and turned off the motor. Leaping out, he ran toward the building.

Kailey, still steadying herself from the explosion, saw Jean-Paul approaching the deadly perimeter that had killed Cameron. "Stop, Jean-Paul, stop right now," she screamed hysterically. "The area's mined."

Jean-Paul stood still.

"Oh, God," Kailey sobbed, "don't move. Cameron's dead. Please don't move."

Jean-Paul peered in front of him, but all he could make out in the darkness were torn patches of earth. Then he saw the large mass off to one side. Cameron's body.

"I hear you, Kailey, darling," he called out to her. "Don't worry, we'll get you out of there."

He went back to the car where Evan waited. "Please, Evan, don't leave Kailey. I'll be back as soon as I can. I'll find some way to get her out of there. And don't move. There are land mines everywhere." Disgustedly, he looked back toward Hawkes' body. Jean-Paul was a doctor, a healer, yet he was glad Hawkes was dead.

"I love you, Kailey," he called into the darkness as he jumped in the Jeep and sped away.

Less than fifteen minutes later, Kailey and Evan were both shocked to see the sweeping beams of headlights in the sky and hear the sound of helicopter blades. Jean-Paul's voice came through a bullhorn from the helicopter, which was poised right above the temple.

"Kailey, grab the ladder when it reaches you."

From the road, Evan couldn't even see the ladder being lowered, but standing at the open door of the temple, Kailey could just make out the rope steps waving in front of her. She grabbed at it. Once, twice, three times she missed the waving staircase. Finally, on the fourth try, her fingers made contact with the lowest rung.

"I've got it," she yelled up toward the helicopter.

"Hold tight and we'll pull you up." Jean-Paul was frightened. He wasn't at all certain that she could hold on long enough to make it to safety. "Try to anchor your hands and feet in the rope as soon as you're off the ground."

Kailey felt the helicopter lift her. It moved slowly enough for her to pull at the higher rungs, and wrap her legs around the rope of the lower ones. Hold on, just hold on, she said to herself, swinging on the bottom of the rope ladder, branches scraping her legs as she was raised to the sky. She looked up, barely able to see Jean-Paul watching her from the cabin of the aircraft. I love you, she whispered, knowing that he couldn't possibly hear her.

Slowly, Kailey pushed open the door. Susannah was seated on the bed, gently rocking Daniel in her arms. Her face was bent low as she nuzzled the infant's cheek with her own, unaware that she was being observed.

Kailey stared at her. She could see the infant face she still remembered with perfect clarity, the bright, clear blue eyes, the rosebud mouth. Her baby had grown up into this lovely young woman. Kailey's knees were suddenly weak. She hadn't really grasped it until now. This girl was her own Bonnie. The baby she had lost, had wept for, longed for every day and night of her life. Kailey's eyes filled with tears. Her child had been alive, growing up in the world out there all the time without Kailey's knowing it.

"Is it you, is it really you?"

At the sound of her voice, Susannah looked up, relief on her face. She rose, turning so Kailey could immediately see Daniel.

"Daniel's fine, don't worry. He's sleeping." She smiled. "Thank God you're here. Are you okay? Where are Evan and Jean-Paul?"

The combination of sadness and joy almost overpowered Kailey. All those years lost. But now, suddenly, a miracle. She couldn't speak.

"Kailey?" Susannah was concerned. "Are you all right? My God, is it Evan?"

"Oh, my darling, Evan's just fine," Kailey whispered.

She crossed over to Susannah and wrapped her arms around her, the tears spilling over.

"I can't believe it. My little Bonnie."

She felt Susannah pull back slightly.

"Kailey, it's me, it's Susannah." She sounded alarmed. "Don't you know me?"

Kailey released her and turned away. She had frightened her, calling her Bonnie. She shouldn't have done that; this news was going to come as a shock.

Turning back, she took Daniel into her arms, giving him a long hug and rearranging the cotton blanket around him. When she'd finished, she looked up at Susannah reassuringly.

"I have some things to tell you."

Kailey set Daniel down on the bed, where he let out a small cry, then settled back into sleep.

"There's so much to explain, but it's hard to know where to begin." Kailey put out a hand, wanting to touch her, to connect, then pulled it back. "I knew Cameron Hawkes before he came here. We were married. And we had a child." She paused. "You."

Susannah's eyes grew wide and she started to rise. "Let me find Jean-Paul."

"Please, there's nothing wrong with me. Listen to me, darling," Kailey said urgently. "I was very young when I married him, and I didn't know what kind of man he was. But soon after you were born, I learned some things about him, and they were more terrible than you can imagine. It would have been dangerous for you if I'd stayed with him. So I took you and we ran away. Or we tried to . . ." Her voice trailed off.

Susannah was uncomprehending. "What on earth are you talking about?"

Kailey sat down on the bed next to Susannah and took both of her hands in her own, gazing intently into her eyes. She would have to tell her everything. She hoped Susannah was up to hearing it.

She started at the beginning, telling her daughter how she'd first met Cameron, how he'd swept her off her feet. Then she got to the bad times, the poisoning of that baby, her discovery of Cameron's connection to the murder. Susannah began to pace, listening but not saying a word.

Then came the hardest part, that day in California, that moment Kailey saw the burnt shell of her car at the water's edge.

"I thought you were lying dead in that car." Kailey took a deep breath. "It wasn't until tonight that I found out the truth. Cameron told me. The nun who brought you to the Franklin Orphanage went to see him last week, and he put the whole thing together. That's why he came here."

Susannah turned white at the mention of the orphanage's name.

Now she knows it's true, Kailey thought. Now she believes me.

"The Franklin Orphanage." Susannah repeated the name quietly.

"Darling," Kailey said gently, "Cameron was coming to that temple to kill me, but he didn't know there were land mines around it. He's dead."

Susannah stared at her. Kailey came over and put a hand on her shoulder. She was stunned as the girl began to scream.

"Get away from me! I don't know you, I don't want you near me."

"Susannah, honey . . . ," Kailey said pleadingly.

Susannah pushed her away. She had no idea why, but she was furious. *"Get out! Leave me alone!"*

Kailey stepped back. Their eyes locked, anguish on both their faces. Then, sadly, Kailey turned to Daniel. There was silence in the room as she picked him up and left.

Alone, Susannah sank down onto the bed and sobbed. She'd had a mother and a father all the time. All her fantasies, her imaginings. These were her parents, Cameron and Kailey.

Cameron. Her father was a murderer, an evil man she had tried to fool with her own amateurish games. She didn't know what to feel. He had liked her, she knew that, could tell from the almost affectionate way he sparred with her when they were together. And she had been so caught up with him, admiring him, thinking how nice it would have been to have him for a father. But he had actually tried to kill her when she was a baby, when he'd known her as his own child. Oh God, she'd been his real daughter all along.

She couldn't take it in. She really had parents. The parents she had longed for, dreamed of. She thought about the Rules, the grueling, lonely years of rigid discipline, keeping up her grades, performing the tedious jobs that had enabled her to get through college. The tears came again, tears for the life she'd never had, all the love she'd never gotten. And what had she done in the past few months when she pretended to be Cameron's daughter? Would any of that have happened if she'd had the life she was meant to? For twenty-five years she had maintained control. As the sobs racked her body, she felt it was lost for good.

Finally, the flood of tears began to subside. Exhausted, she sat quietly, remembering her conversations with Cameron, going over everything Kailey had just told her. She walked over to the window. Outside, a lantern illuminated the front of the house. She could see Jean-Paul holding Daniel, talking with Kailey and Evan. She moved to get a closer look. Pain was evident on all their faces, Evan looking toward the house as if expecting Susannah to appear, Kailey completely dejected.

She watched them for a while. All at once it seemed so simple.

These people were her family. Evan was the man she wanted to spend the rest of her life with.

And Kailey. Kailey was her mother. The mother who loved her. I found her, Susannah thought, the realization sinking in. I found her.

She ran to throw open the door. The three of them looked up at the sound. Kailey and Susannah stared at each other. Then, Susannah moved toward her. Kailey broke away from the two men, running to her daughter.

"My darling girl," Kailey whispered brokenly as they came together.

Susannah threw her arms around her mother as if she would never let go.